SWAMP THING

Below them lay a leprous swamp of rocks and scummy puddles, with scrub and tufty vegetation in lurid yellows and browns. Rain was falling, and wind ruffled the more open parts of the pools. Soupy mud bubbled in the tracks left by the wheeled vehicles at the end of the ramp, while right below the viewers was the largest growth of all, a lumpy thing that instantly squirted upward, extending into long white ropes to reach over the railing and wrap around Alya, scooping her up high and tearing her hand from Cedric's grip...

STRINGS

Dave Duncan

A Del Rey Book

BALLANTINE BOOKS • NEW YORK

A Del Rey Book
Published by Ballantine Books

Library of Congress Catalog Card Number: 89-91890

ISBN 0-345-36191-1

Manufactured in the United States of America

First Edition: February 1990

Cover Art by Neal McPheeters

WINDOWS

28 March to 12 April, 2050

(Life-bearing worlds only)

File name:	Nile	Orinoco	Po	Quinto	Rhine	Sask.	Tiber	Usk	
March 28	*	*		?					.
March 29			*			?			.
March 30			*						.
March 31		*	*		*				.
April 1	*		*	*					.
April 2			*				?		.
April 3		*	*	*		*			.
April 4			*						.
April 5	*		*				*	*	.
April 6		*	*						.
April 7			*	*					.
April 8			*		*	*	*		.
April 9	*	*	†						.
April 10				*				*	.
April 11							*		.
April 12		*							.

† No further investigation at these coordinates

ACKNOWLEDGMENT

I am grateful to Shelagh Hislop for reading the manuscript and vetting my biology. Any tangles in that particular string, though, are my fault and not hers.

1

Cainsville, April 6

THERE SEEMED TO be a window in the wall opposite the door, looking out at the landscape beyond the dome. From time to time Wilkins would pause in his restless pacing to stare at that view and shudder. There was no life out there, only gaunt gray granite, forged by ancient fires, clawed into hills by old ice sheets, and cauterized by deadly radiation. Even the misty rain blowing out there was poison. If the Institute's planetologists stumbled on a terrain like that anywhere else in the universe, they would slap a Class Four label on it without a second's hesitation and go off to find a more interesting world.

It was not a Class Four world, though, and had not always been quite so barren. The poison rain was a soup of industrial by-products, still falling from their long sojourn in the upper atmosphere. It was so murderously potent on those siliceous hills that even the little gunmetal lakes held no life anymore. The radiation was merely the normal ultraviolet of sunlight, because in these northerly latitudes the ozone layer was too thin to filter it out. And the window was not a window. In fact, Wilkins's cramped quarters were buried deep in the innards of Burton Dome, a long way from that stark exterior.

He was not quite sure why he had called up that view—possibly because it suited his evil mood, or possibly as a reminder that there was no escape overland from Cainsville. There would be no pursuit, and no rescue. A fugitive could safely be left alone to wander among those tangled crags until he froze, or starved. Certainly he would not live long enough to die of the carcinogenic sunlight.

There was no airport, either, only the lev station, which Security watched always, as a matter of course. If anything went wrong, he would be hopelessly trapped.

There were other ways out of Cainsville, but they led to places far, far worse than even that accursed rocky desert outside.

He had been pacing for a long time, much too long for a man who took no exercise. Wilkins J. S.—short and swarthy, born in 2027 and already going bald. Dr. Wilkins, employed by the Institute as a camera-repair technician. Wilkins Jules Smuts, potential traitor.

Without warning his legs began to tremble. He slumped into his chair and scowled at the seeming window. Well—why not? In truth, he had known for some time what his decision was going to be.

"Com mode!"

The comset became a sheet of blank plastic and said, "Proceed."

Damp-fingered, Wilkins pulled from his pocket a tiny scrap of paper, a secret he had been hoarding for almost two years. It had been slipped into his hand at a party, with a nod and a wink and a chunk of credit to establish goodwill, plus promises of much greater joy if he ever used it in a good cause. He cleared his throat and began to read.

"Code Caesar Columbus Dimanche Einfeuchten ..." Thirty-two words in all. His voice quavered by the end, for even to possess an illicit override code was a felony in Cainsville. To use one was worse than a crime—it was a blatant challenge to the deadliest security system on earth.

"Code acknowledged. Confirm activation."

It worked! Some small part of him had perhaps been hoping that it would not ... For a moment yet he hesitated, savoring a strange tingling seeping through him, a blend of fear and excitement. It reminded him of the real reason he was taking this risk—Wilkins Jules had a plugin habit, which was becoming very expensive. It had reached the point where his weekly pay transfer would barely cover both food and plugin. Soon he would have to choose between them, and his choice could never be food.

"Confirm activation," System repeated, impatient of human indecision.

"Activate." There—he had done it!

"Please wait." System began to play music at him, which he hated, and the gray plastic again became a window, now overlooking a somber view of water lilies floating on a tree-shadowed pool. To Wilkins Jules such a scene was irrelevant at best, and unattractive anyway. He fretted.

There was no reason why he should not make a call to the outside world—except that he almost never did. Everyone else did, often, but not him. Security called that "pattern breaking," and System watched for it. And if the override code itself had triggered alarms, then the call would certainly be either blocked or monitored. The illicit code and the record coin in his other pocket—either would make him a dead man. Nowhere in the world could a body be disposed of as easily as in Cainsville. *Nowhere in the world.*

One tune ended and another began. Why so long? He might very well have fallen into a trap. If this was all a fake, a loyalty test that he had now most certainly failed, then the goons were lining up outside the door already. The tingling had faded into an unpleasant full-bladder sensation. He always tended to sweat too much, and at the moment was dribbling like a marathon runner.

Dead man—or rich man?

He had never known a call to take this long. He must be getting through to someone very high up . . . high up in something.

Then he blinked at sudden brightness, seeing through the comset into a sunlit office. The desk was shiny and empty. If that were real wood, it had cost more money than he would earn in two years. The woman across from him was being masked. She wore an outfit of hard metallic blue, but that was all he could tell. Her face was an anonymous blur, although the rest of the room was as sharp as though he were sitting in it. Whoever her employers were, they could afford a first-class System.

"Report!" Probably her voice was disguised also.

He squirmed like a hooked worm. One-sided! He should have put a bag over his head or something. "You don't need to know my name . . ."

The woman drummed a hard fog of fingers on the wood. "I already know your name. I even know you have less than forty hectos left in the bank. Thirty-eight to be exact."

Wilkins's heart lurched. He had not expected the bargaining to start so soon.

"Now report," she repeated. "It had better be good."

He fumbled in his pocket and pulled out the coin. "I have evidence."

She seemed to shrug. "Evidence of what?" But he heard a trace more interest in that anonymous voice.

"They lost a team!"

"It happens. How many?"

"Three."

She waved a vague hand. "People get buttered over the tarmac outside this office all the time, and it's a poor week we don't drown a few million somewhere. Losing them on other worlds is a little more exotic, but not much. A hundred hectos."

She must know he would not have risked using the code unless he had more to offer than that. "One of them was an outsider—a mycologist from Moscow."

"Mycologist?"

"Expert in funguses. Fungi. They'd been overnighting—but this wasn't just a broken string. The skiv's back."

"Better," she admitted. "Two hundred. More if you've got some good damage pictures."

"No damage at all," Wilkins said, starting to enjoy himself at last. "The skiv's untouched. Two dead men, and the woman's missing."

That got her. He heard a hiss of breath. "Tell me about the woman."

"Name of Gill Adele. Staff ecologist."

"Age? Looks? Got pix of her?"

He shook his head. "Middle twenties. Said to be a looker."

"Pity. Any chance she's still alive?"

Wilkins laughed. "Not a chance in hell—and that's apt, for sure. Class Three world, code name 'Nile.' About two hundred Celsius and over half a bar of CO_2 . . . and she forgot to take her helmet."

The woman was silent for a minute, then admitted, "Okay! That's a story. She didn't just go fishin' on a Class Three. Tell me more."

"Lots of credit."

The blur nodded. "Lots of credit."

Wilkins shivered with deep-down joy. And she still had not heard the best of it! "It happened yesterday. They opened the window; got no response. So they brought the skiv back on remote control. There was a hell of a panic. The window was short, and they had no backup team standing by. Real incompetence, all shouting and no action. There's plenty of dirt here if you want to use it. Next window's not till the ninth."

The woman leaned forward. Even through the flickering, indistinct masking, her eagerness was showing. "How good's your clip?"

"Very good. One of the dome cameras malfunctioned. It got sent in for repairs right away. They thought it was the recording, but it was the playback. The recording was fine." He held up the coin again, to tantalize her a little.

"Any confirmation? I don't put it past the old hag to fake something like this."

Again Wilkins shivered, but this time for other reasons. He had wondered the same. This was so stupendously good—too good to be true, really, for a man with an expensive habit. "Not much . . . I think there's more tension about than usual. Nothing you can use. But I don't think even Hubbard would fake the rest of it."

"Such as?"

"The great Devlin shouting his head off? Almost having hysterics."

"Mmm. What'd the two men die of?"

"Head wounds." Let her suck on that!

"*Head wounds?* The woman killed them?"

Now came the moment he had been dreaming of. "Maybe. But there was a weapon, too."

"What sort of weapon?"

He played his ace, the trump he had been holding back. "A stone hand ax."

"No! I don't believe you!"

He held up the coin without a word.

"Sentience? After all this time?"

Wilkins's voice became shrill with excitement. He wanted to reach into the com and thump his fist on that opulent wooden desk. "Two men clubbed to death, a woman missing, the skiv intact, blood on the floor, and a stone ax—also with blood on it! Now, do I have a story?"

"Oh, do you have a story!" the woman said. "Oh, brother, do *I* have a story!" She sounded awed.

"First Contact!" Wilkins was gloating. "Men killed, woman abducted. Eyewitness record. Exclusive story . . . rich man?"

"You are a very rich man," she agreed.

Plugin! Lots of lovely plugin! Wilkins could feel his groin starting to glow already.

2

Banzarak, April 7

THE TROPICAL AFTERNOON was unbearably muggy. The air had died of heat prostration. The water in the bay was shiny-slick like polished lead, and the sky was a white pall, too bright to look at.

Alya had been walking the beach for hours, walking herself to exhaustion. Her sun block must have worn dangerously thin by now, and there were salt sores around the edges of her goggles. Her boots were slime-caked, stinking as bad as the fetid edges of the sea. They dragged like sacks of rocks as she plodded up the battered wooden steps to the Residence—steep stairs, shaded by trees and the aggressively impenetrable undergrowth. The old, old pictures showed this hillside as a formal garden. Not anymore.

Her body needed a long drink and then sleep, although it would probably agree to accept a shower and a snack somewhere after the drink. Her mind would refuse the sleep—it was churning with incoherent muddled demands like the angry mutterings of a crowd, incomprehensible mumblings, ancestral warnings. For two days these forebodings had been tormenting her. She wanted to scream and run, yet she also felt like crawling under a bed somewhere, or climbing a tree. Unable to concentrate on her studies or seek solace in company, she had gone out to walk by the sea.

She thought her pain must be like the pain of an addict deprived of his need. But what was her need except the need for the pain to stop? She knew what was happening, for she had felt it before, but never, never so strong. In a sense she had been waiting for it all her life, yet she had not expected this driving, twisting agony; and the cure, if she could find it, did not bear thinking about.

On the patio at the top of the steps she paused for a moment to catch her breath and wipe wrist across brow. Before her sprawled the Residence, her birthplace and her home; yet it had taken on a grotesque unfamiliarity. She had never thought of it as beautiful —it was a monstrosity of imperial Victorian vulgarity, all wide-eaved verandas and writhing sculptured woodwork, bijou windows and rambling halls—but in the past she had always found its awkward, ill proportions conveyed a wry friendship, like the easy-going, self-deprecating humor of a mongrel dog. Now, suddenly, she saw only a sinister and malevolent deformity which repelled her.

Even her home had been taken from her, then.

Overhead the scarlet flag of Banzarak hung limp in the damp heat, its folds hiding all of the emblem except for a glimpse of the cobra's head. She shivered and turned away, reluctant to enter the menacing shadows of the house, and yet, as she leaned on the rail and gazed out at the ash-gray bay, she was inexplicably seized with a sudden dread that she would never see all this again. The sun would still be there tomorrow, wouldn't it? Wouldn't she?

The water was a flat glare. She had never known it so calm, and she could feel the heat beating off it. Out to sea the line of the reef was barely visible, a subtle change in color and mood. Never since her childhood had she seen any real surf breaking out there. She could no longer bear to don scuba gear and visit that graveyard.

Landward was worse. The beach had gone completely, and more than half of the Old Town was underwater. On the opposite hill stood the palace, a rococo excrescence of pink and purple stucco. About a century earlier, when the British had left, her great-grandfather had given up most of his royal power and turned the palace over to the government. Now the government was billeted in the Grand Hotel, and the palace was full of refugees. The higher hills beyond were dotted with refugee camps. Banzarak was a very informal kingdom and a very small one— about a golf course and a half, her father had called it—but now many of its people had lost their homes and livelihood. Hundreds of thousands of others had flocked in from elsewhere. Food was a serious problem, and disease worse.

The hibiscuses were dying. Leaning on the half-rotted rail, staring back down the lush slope between the trunks of the higher trees, Alya wondered about the hibiscuses—why them? She would miss their beauty, joyful and transient . . .

Then footsteps sounded on the platform behind her. She wheeled and saw Kas, and instantly suppressed a frantic desire to rush at him. She turned away quickly.

He paced over to her side, tall and dark and solid as a stone pillar. Something unmoving in a shifting world was Kas, her much-older brother, deep-spoken Kas.

"Little sister?"

"Kas?"

"Is anything wrong?"

"No! I mean . . . I'm a little worried about the weather—the air's so dead. Just the weather. Worried about a typhoon."

"We never get typhoons here."

She forced her hands to release their death grip on the rail before he could notice. She was not a child, she reminded herself. She had lived on every continent, visited most of the great cities—had made her first trip around the world alone when she was only thirteen. *She was not a child!* She was not going to weep, and she did not need to be hugged by a big brother—that would be ridiculous. A lover, fine . . . but there was none handy at the moment.

"There was a typhoon here in 1717," she told the hillside. "It did a lot of damage. Think what one would do now, with no reef to stop it!" She did not look around.

"The forecast is good. Do you feel better on the shore than you do up here?"

Keeping her face as impassive as she could, Alya turned. "What do you mean, Kas?"

He smiled sadly. She noticed with surprise how much gray there was in his beard, how many wrinkles in the dusky face and how deep they were. Even in the tropics he was stupid to come outdoors without sun block and goggles.

"It started on the fifth, didn't it?" he said. "On Tuesday?"

Alya felt a mighty rush of relief. "You, too? You feel it, too?" She was not alone, not going mad.

"A little. Always I feel it a little. Not like you're doing."

So much for inscrutability! Then she did throw herself at Kas, and he squeezed her tight, crushing all the air out of her, and that was wonderful, just what she had needed. For a time she sniveled mutely against his shoulder. And Kas had the sense to say nothing at all.

"It's never been this bad," she said. "Never! It gets worse every time. When Omar went it was bad. Tal's time was worse yet—but not like this."

"This one is your call. Your kismet. That's why."

She had known that, really, but she wailed in horror when he put it into words. "No! No! I won't leave you. I won't go!"

He steadied her head with a big, strong hand. "Alya, dear Alya! They all said that at first, every one of them. You've been squirming like an eel for days. Don't fight it."

She mumbled stubborn refusals, but she could feel her resolution failing already.

"I've talked to Nauc," he said. "I called them on Tuesday."

"You—*Tuesday*?"

"I feel it, too, remember. You were smiling like an idiot, but you'd turned such a pretty shade of green—"

She pummeled him. "I did not!"

"Turquoise, actually."

"Swine!"

"Avocado in some lights. Anyway, they say yes."

"Yes what?" she demanded apprehensively, pulling back.

"They've got a whole basketful of candidates. They want your help to—"

"No!" She was aghast. "Suppose I make a mistake? Suppose I'm wrong?"

He shook his head in reproof. "Been bothered by snakebites lately?"

She twisted her face away from him.

"When?" she whispered.

"Alya . . . Little sister, why not go now?"

"Now? *Today?* But packing . . ."

"Leave right now," he said. "You won't sleep or eat until you start. Long farewells are sad farewells. You can just change and go."

Panic choked her, and she could only stare. He smiled cheerfully, but his eyes were glistening.

"Moala's finished your packing. The Air Force is standing by." That was a family joke, the government's only plane, an ancestral turbofan that had ferried tourists, back in the days when Banzarak had boasted one of the world's great beaches.

"By air across to Singapore," Kas said. "Then super to Nauc. You'll be there by dark—except it'll be early morning their time."

"Oh, you have been busy!" Alya said, struggling to match his counterfeit smile. Her heart was pounding insanely, and her knees wanted to liquefy. "I can't just rush off—"

"There may not be much time. You know that. Even one day might make much difference—for many people."

She felt drowned in a sudden flood. "The old man? Is it fair—"

Kas shook his head. "He's not going."

"Oh!" Alya bit her lip. All her life Dr. Piridinar Chan had been prime minister of Banzarak. She had no idea how old he was—she suspected she would be shocked to find out. A dear, gentle old man, Pirie had always headed up the Banzarak delegations to Cainsville.

"Dr. Jar Jathro," Kas said cautiously. "You know him?"

Alya pulled a face and nodded. "He just divorced his second wife, or was she his third?"

"He's a very acute politician, which is what matters. Piridinar took him along the last two or three times, so he knows how the negotiations are done. He'll have a couple of backups with him."

She nodded. If that was what Kas thought best, then she would not argue; but she wished that Jar Jathro did not always make her think of lizards.

When she said nothing, Kas added, "I didn't tell you because . . ."

Because he had not wanted to worry her? But it felt right. Oh, God! How right it felt!

No. She saw that Kas had been testing, making sure, watching her agony grow until there could be no doubt, because this was hellishly important. His eyes were anxious now that she might resent the testing. She grabbed her brother's beard in both hands and pulled his face down to kiss.

Hard and long.

"Allah and Krishna and Holy Etceteras!" he said afterward. "A sister is not supposed to kiss her brother like that!" But his eyes were gentled by relief that she was not mad at him. She tried to do it again, and he took hold of her wrists. "Wanton!" he said. "Pervert!"

"Why not? You enjoy it, don't you?"

"Certainly not! I keep wondering what the cabinet would say if they saw us. Besides, I have to keep my eyes open in case I forget who you are."

"An old family tradition," she said. Nauc tonight! Cainsville tomorrow, she supposed. What did she have to wear?

"Don't ever talk about that! You find a good strong pioneer type."

"Tall, dark, and handsome?" It only hurts when I laugh.

"Well, pick one of the above."

"Tall, then . . . Oh, Kas!" Her voice broke in remorse. "Oh Kas, come with me?"

He shook his head in silence. "Your kismet, Alya."

"Just come to help me choose. Not—" She felt a twist of nausea. "Not all the way. Just come and hold my hand."

He pulled a face. "And have to come away afterward?"

He was suffering much more than he had admitted, then. Alya squeezed him once more.

She was the last. Brothers, sisters, cousins—ten of them had gone, and now the *buddhi* was calling her, too. And then there would be only Kas, and Thalia. He was much more than a figurehead sultan, in spite of what the constitution said, but he would be the last of their generation.

Thalia was a cousin and had the *buddhi*, also. What of their children? Alya wondered. Kani was ten. Who would next feel a *satori*? Kas himself? Or would it start in on the youngsters? She shivered.

"I'll make my choice—and then come back here."

He smiled sadly. "That might not work. Others might accept it, but what of our own people? They won't go if you don't."

She shivered again, fear of the future looming very big. "How many?"

"As many as possible. You know that."

Cold, cold terror froze her bones. Thousands of lives! What if she chose wrong? What if they had all chosen wrong, all the others before her? Where could she find the courage to gamble so many human creatures?

"The *buddhi*," she whispered.

Again he smiled his sad smile. "You were certainly born with it."

That was another family joke: "You were certainly born with

it; you will certainly die with it; and you would certainly die sooner without it."

"I hate it!" she shouted. "The family curse."

"The family blessing," Kas insisted.

High above the royal residence a very faint breeze nudged the limp flag, the bloodred flag of Banzarak bearing the national emblem, a cobra entwined with a silken string.

3

How DID A caterpillar feel when it opened up in the butterfly business?

Small, Cedric thought.

Lonely.

The hotel room was cramped and dingy, stinking worse than the streets outside. Fungus flourished around the shower pad. The wallpaper looked like beans fried in blood. The single chair was hard and unsteady, and the bed would be too short for him.

For the third time he checked his credit. He had a clear choice: he could either call home to Madge at Meadowdale, or he could eat breakfast in the morning. That was not a hard decision. He pulled his chair closer to the com, but then he got distracted again by the action. God in Heaven! Were they going to . . . Yes, they were. Again! He squirmed with embarrassment. But he watched. Holo shows at Meadowdale had never been like this. And the quality of the image was so good! He could have sworn that he was looking through a window into the next room where a couple was—was doing certain things he had never seen done before. Doing, in fact, some things he had not known were possible. Great Heavens! At Meadowdale the images had been fuzzier, and there had been long periods of fog, on one channel or another, with nothing visible at all.

13

Everything was visible here.

Suddenly he became disgusted at his own reactions. He barked an order, switching to com mode. In two minutes Madge was standing on the other side of the window, smiling at him. Before she even spoke he knew he had erred. He had forgotten the time difference and caught her in the middle of putting youngsters to bed. But she did not complain; she merely smiled and sat down.

"I promised to call," he said.

"So you did. And you've survived your first day in the Big Wide World!" Rosy cheeks and white hair—no one could have looked more motherly than Madge. But when had she grown so small? She could hardly have shrunk since he had left that morning.

"I didn't buy Brooklyn Bridge, like Ben said I would."

"Ben didn't mean that!"

But Ben had meant the other things he had warned about. Cedric might think he owned nothing of value except the camera Gran had given him, Ben had said, but any healthy nineteen-year-old must look out for bodyshoppers, or he would soon discover he was a mindless zombie in one of the darker corners of the vice industry, with every prospect of eventual promotion to a freezerful of spare parts.

"I hired a percy," Cedric said. "Can you see it?" Madge leaned sideways and looked where he pointed. She said yes, she could. The big metal cylinder stood in a corner, dominating the room—a blank, blue, bullet-shaped pillar.

"I buzzed around all over the place like a native," Cedric said proudly. No one could get knocked off in a percy, which was why all city dwellers used them.

Percy: Personal Survival Aid.

"Doesn't look big enough," Madge said doubtfully.

"It's okay," Cedric insisted. "I was lucky. It's an XL, and they just happened to have it in stock."

In a percy, the occupant stayed upright, half sitting, half standing. It would have been quite comfortable, had his legs not been so damned long. His neck was still stiff.

"Did you see all the sights?" Madge asked.

He told her about his day, or most of it—his trip on the super, his sightseeing, and how he had tried to go to a ball game, but the new stadium was not complete yet and the old one had finally been abandoned after Hurricane Zelda last fall. He did not describe how he had gaped at the ads for surgical improvements to various body parts, nor did he detail the varieties of chemical and electronic stimulation he had declined, or the educational opportunities both erotic and exotic, some of them even promising real girls. He had not been tempted, and he had had no money anyway.

Nor did he mention that he had gone window shopping, because he had been choosing gifts he was going to give Madge herself, and Ben, and all the others. Of course, he had not been able actually to buy anything, but as soon as he started earning money he was going to send gifts to everyone at Meadowdale. Well, not truly everyone, but all the adults, certainly. Maybe some of the older kids, although all his own group had gone long since. He had been the oldest for almost a year now.

And then he asked if Gavin had used his fishing rod yet, and if Tess had had her pups, and stuff like that.

"Did you eat properly?" Madge asked, mother instincts roused.

"I had a pizza."

She pouted disapprovingly at the mention of pizza. "I'll get Ben. He took some of the small fry out to watch a calving."

But Cedric had just realized that his credit was about to die. The call would end without warning and Madge would guess why, and then she would worry. "I'd better go," he said. He sent his love to everyone and disconnected. He checked his credit and discovered that he had cut it very fine. He would not even be able to buy a Coke in the morning; but he had his ticket to HQ, and the percy was prepaid, so he was all right.

It was nice to know that Meadowdale was still there. It was the only home he had ever known.

He stayed where he was and watched the holo again for a while, seeming to jump from one bedroom to another—did the audiences never get tired of the same stuff? On an unfamiliar channel he found Dr. Eccles Pandora doing the news. Pandora had always been a Meadowdale favorite, being Garfield Glenda's cousin. And Glenda had certainly been a Cedric favorite.

Cedric abandoned the news halfway through the floodings— Neururb, now, and Thailand. That was after the food riots in Nipurb and before the usual update on the Mexican plague. He found an old Engels Brothers rerun and watched that instead.

Later he stared out for a long time at the shining towers of the city and the streets far below, still quite busy. He had never seen all this, except in the holo, and he had expected it to look more real than it did. Apparently streets full of racing percies seemed much the same whether one saw them directly or in three-dee image. These streets had more garbage lying around, that was all.

He set his watch alarm for 0800 and went to bed. The bed was not only too short, it was lumpy and it smelled wrong.

He had trouble sleeping, and that was another new experience. He wondered about Madge.

Madge had not wept when he said goodbye. And when he called on the com she had smiled. Madge always wept when someone left. Of course, he was older than the others had been. Of course, he had tried to leave on his own a few times in the past, but he did not think she resented those attempts. Strange that she had smiled and not cried. She had never hinted that she loved him any less than any of the others, so he could not help but be surprised that she had not cried, and surprised that he should care . . . and surprised that he should be surprised . . .

He slept.

When the lights came on he blinked at his watch; it registered 0316. Then he rolled over on his back and tried to focus on the gun lens at the end of his nose.

It had to be a gun, although it was as thick as his arm. He could not read the label, but it might very well be a Mitsubishi Hardwave, and one flash from a thing like that would vaporize him and his bed and the people downstairs.

He blinked a few times. He wanted to rub his eyes, but moving his hands might be risky. As his vision adjusted, he saw that the room was full of percies, at least five of them. His own was still standing in the corner—doing nothing, bloody nothing, two and a half meters of useless crysteel and whiskerfab.

So much for survival. First time off the farm, and he had crashed already.

On the safe end of the gun was a large, thick person, anonymous inside bulky combat gear that looked as if it were made of black leather. Just possibly it was a bull suit, in which case it would stop anything short of a fusion torch and the limbs would have full power assist. Or it might be only armor—not many could afford a real bull suit, and they took years of practice to manage. Its face was a shiny nothing, as noncommittal as the door of an icebox.

"Got you at last!" the intruder said in a voice like the San Andreas. It was male.

"M-M-Me?"

"Harper Peter Olsen!"

"No, sir! I'm Hubbard Cedric Dickson!"

"What kind of sap do you take me for?" the faceless helmet demanded. Actually it was not faceless—its shiny blackness bore a faint reflection of Cedric's own pale features, distorted into a wide-eyed omelet by the curve of the crysteel and by sheer witless terror. "Three years I've waited for this, Harper!"

"I'm not Harper!" Cedric shouted. "I'm Hubbard! Hubbard Cedric Dickson. Check my thumb." He had pulled his hand from under the covers before he remembered that sudden moves were supposed to be unwise.

The intruder did not seem worried—if anything, he was merely more contemptuous. "Thumbprints can be altered." The gun moved higher, blocking out Cedric's view of almost everything else. He saw his eyes reflected in the lens.

Cedric had rarely needed ID for anything, but on holo shows they used thumbs, or retinas. Or a sniffer. He had not known that thumbs could be changed in the real world. He had no other ID at all.

There was something completely unbelievable about all this.

If the intruder was a thief, then he was going to be sadly disappointed—and therefore, likely, irked. Cedric had the square root of fresh air left in his balance, but theft by enforced credit transfer was a crime for morons anyway. That left ransom, or possibly bodyshopping—and that brought up the curious question of why he had ever been allowed to wake up. But . . . his first day out in the world and he had spilled the whole bucket.

And yet, oddly, he felt no more scared than he had as a twelve-year-old when Greg and Dwayne had taken him behind the horse barns and explained what they were planning for him. That had been real terror, but although he had endured a nasty experience, he had suffered no real damage. Of course, this character was not in the same league as two muddled fifteen-year-olds.

"I've got nothing here worth taking, but help yourself," Cedric said, and was pleasantly surprised at how calm he sounded.

"I don't want your money, Harper. I want to watch you burn."

Breathe slow, he told himself. "Well I'm not Harper, whoever he is. So either shoot me in error, or go away and let me get back to sleep."

"Oh . . . big *brave* man!"

Cedric attempted to shrug. It was tricky while lying flat. "What else can I say, sir? I'm not Harper. Check my thumb."

The faceless intruder seemed to hesitate. "Thumbs get faked. I'll check your retinas, then."

Cedric felt relief in floods. "Go ahead."

The man barked an order, and one of the percies floated closer to the bed, while the others made way for it. He must have brought four of them with him. They looked very much the same as the one Cedric had hired at the station, and he could not tell if they were occupied. Bull Suit might be running them himself. The room was not large enough for all that equipment.

"Retina scanner," the man said, without moving his gun from the end of Cedric's nose. Something whirred faintly, a small hatch opened, and a binocular device dropped out, hanging on a helical cord. That was no standard percy.

Cedric had watched enough holodramas to know that he was supposed to put the gizmo to his eyes and focus on the center marks in the red glow, but he did not expect the sudden bright flash. Ouch!

"Well?" he said as he released the gadget. It whirred back out of sight again, and the percy floated away. "I'm not Harper." Green afterimages coated everything, and he felt sick. His throat hurt.

"Who?" the man asked.

"Harper—the guy you thought I was."

"Never heard of him. Appendectomy scar?" He whipped off the covers. Cedric yelped, but he was relieved to see that the gun was no longer pointing at him. "Yup," the man agreed. "Appendectomy scar."

"Then you know who I am?"

"Always did. Just like to confirm things." The stranger tipped back his helmet to reveal a completely bald head and a round, jowled face lacking both eyebrows and eyelashes.

"You mean all that crud about Harper. . ." Cedric's fear began to turn to anger, mostly anger at his own fear. He tried to sit up and was poked flat again by the cold tubular end of the gun. The safety catch was on, but it was a good club.

"Just relax, sonny. Yes, you're Hubbard Cedric. I checked out your pheromones before I opened the door."

"How did you open—"

"Quiet! You've got some explaining to do. Do you know where you are?"

An apology would be nice, Cedric thought. "North American Urban Complex."

The intruder's eyes narrowed.

The lack of hair, and the shiny, unnatural skin—the man's face had been regenerated with dermsym. That meant a major accident, or perhaps an illness or a bad cancer job. The gravelly voice might mean extensive work on his throat, too. Cedric could not even guess at his age. The man was reptilian—his scalp smooth and shiny and quite hairless, everything below his mouth concealed by the neck ring of his suit, as though his head had sunk into his shoulders, turtle fashion. His eyes were almost invisible, hooded by drooping flaps of skin below craggy overhanging brows. The slivers that did show were blue-gray as winter sky, and no more friendly.

"Nauc's a big place, sonny. Try to be a little more specific."

"The sixteenth floor of the President Lincoln Hotel." Cedric was resenting being exposed there like jam on bread, with only a few grams of cotton between him and total nudity. He groped for the covers, and the stranger flipped them out of reach with his gun.

"One more chance."

Damn you! "Well, with a name like that it must be somewhere between the Canadian border and the Mason-Dixon line."

The gun muzzle slammed into Cedric's solar plexus hard enough to double him up in a choking, gasping tangle of limbs. He had never been hit that hard before. He could not have guessed how bad it would feel. For a long age there was only pain and shock and lack of air. He heaved and strained, and there was no air in the world. Black fog and terror . . . then something seemed to snap, and he sucked in one long, shuddering breath, and the black fog began to clear. Agony! His assailant stood in patient silence, waiting as though the force of the impact had been calculated precisely, its effects guaranteed to wear off after an exactly predetermined interval.

Finally the man spoke. "Want some more, smartass?"

Speechless, Cedric shook his head.

"Right. You were credited first-class fare on the super and told to fly to HQ at Manchester on Thursday—that's today, now. You took peon class and flew to Norristown on Wednesday."

About to ask how the intruder knew all that, Cedric had an attack of discretion and stayed mute, still breathing through his mouth and fighting a shivering nausea.

"Why, Cedric?"

"I just wanted to see some of the world . . ." He had planned on adding "sir," and changed his mind.

The man's lip curled in a contemptuous snarl. "Anyone who

goes touristing in person is nuts. You can put credit in the holo and see it all at home."

Not the same—Cedric just shook his head.

"So what did you see, Cedric?"

"The White House. Capitol Hill. Independence Hall. Ply-mo—"

The man's expression stopped him. Cedric had been told that it was Plymouth Rock, but the original rock must be well out to sea now, and of course it would never have been so close to . . . He had been gulled. "I asked Ben where the best sightseeing was, and he said hereabouts."

The man raised dermsym where he should have had eyebrows.

"So I got taken?" Cedric muttered. "They're all fakes?"

"Replicas. Some of the originals got moved inland, but you didn't see any of those."

For a moment there was silence. Cedric's belly still throbbed, but now he was partly faking his panting, while he reviewed combat training. What would Gogarty suggest? That gun was being held much too close to him. Murder did not seem to be the intruder's intent, but what mattered was whether his outfit was a real bull suit or only armor. Cedric started to lever himself up on an elbow, and the man moved the gun to push him down again. Cedric slammed his free hand against the barrel and spun both legs around to impact the man at knee level and topple him backward.

The gun did not move one millimeter, and Cedric might as well have rammed his shins into a concrete post. Beyond a glare of pain, he heard the man chuckle. Then came the punishment— the gun was callously slammed into his gut again, and for a long while there was only the familiar black fog, and retching, choking agony.

Eventually—bruised, breathless, and half blinded by tears— Cedric was back where he had begun, flat out, staring up impotently at his tormentor with nothing to show for his feeble attempt at heroism except a throbbing monster of pain in his gut. Probably he would not even have a bruise there. The man was an expert.

"Who the hell are you?" Cedric rasped.

"Thought you'd never ask. Name's Bagshaw. I'm with the Institute."

That was much too good to be credible. "How'd you find me?"

Bagshaw snorted in derision. "You think it was hard? Still, that's the best defense you've got—if you were up to something, you'd never be so stupid. But I've heard it before."

"Me? Up to what?"

"That's what we want to find out. You came to meet someone. Who?"

"No one!" Cedric said, and hoped desperately that he had managed to sound convincing. "I've got no secrets to spill, nothing to sell. What—"

"Why did you come a day early?"

"I'm a free agent."

Bagshaw snorted. "You've never been a free agent in your life. You were livestock in an organage."

"Foster home! Not all of us are orphans. Wong Gavin's father's president of—"

The man looked so contemptuous that Cedric half expected him to spit. "All right, a maximum-security kindergarten. For rich kids—although by the look of you, fatso, someone hasn't been paying the food bills. Have you ever been out in the real world before?"

"Sure! Lots of times. I took first in the Pacurb junior skeet lasering two years ago. I didn't do that in Madge's kitchen. Cities—"

"Skeet lasering!" Bagshaw chuckled. "Who took you there?"

"Cheaver Ben."

"Have you ever been outside unsupervised?"

"Yes! I took younger kids on camping trips and—"

"And of course you couldn't abandon them when they were in your care?"

"Of course not."

Bagshaw's hairless head shook gently in massive contempt. "So? Ever been out in the real world by yourself? Ever once?"

"Yes."

"The times you went over the wall?" He smirked.

"If you know the answers, why ask?"

The gun's icy muzzle nudged his belly threateningly. "I'll ask what I like, sonny, and you'll answer. Why did you try to break out, anyway?"

Pride! "It was illegal incarceration." Cedric could still feel the old resentment. Keeping kids locked up might be permissible, but he had been eighteen by then. All the guys his age had been called back to their families, yet Gran had kept insisting that he must stay on at Meadowdale.

"Illegal bullshit," Bagshaw said. "You got picked up for vagrancy?"

Cedric nodded miserably. Three times he had skipped. Three times the cops had brought him back like a strayed puppy.

"And you never thought that you were in Meadowdale for a reason? You never thought about kidnapping and extortion?"

"Well . . . no."

The man shook his bull head pityingly. "So now you're on your way legally. Did the old bag say she had a job for you?"

Cedric hesitated again, and the pressure increased nauseatingly, as though he were about to be impaled. "Yes, sir."

Bagshaw's eyes slitted even more, and his face seemed to sink lower inside his suit. He was barely human, a mechanical construct fueled by anger. "So you got hired on by the Institute! Your academic standing must have been remarkable."

Cedric's father had been a ranger, his mother a medical doctor. They had died exploring a Class Two world for the Institute, so there was a fallen torch to be picked up. That argument would not likely carry much weight at the moment. Cedric said nothing.

"Most men would peel off their skins to land a job with the Institute, you know? They'd sell it in strips. I worked myself crazy to get mine—eighteen hours a day like a machine for a whole year. They took fifty of us, out of five thousand." Bagshaw's plasticized face was turning even redder, little nauseating jabs of the gun barrel emphasizing his words. "I came in forty-eighth—and I've had combat experience. I've got postdoc degrees in urban survival. But you get hired fresh out of the shell. Hot from the oven. Of course, your grandmother is director. Amazing coincidence, that. But then . . . Ah, but then do you do what you're told? No, you don't. You sneak out of the organage a day early and go to a part of Nauc that you've got no right to be in. Why, Cedric, why? This is what we need to know, Cedric."

Cedric's throat was very dry, and there was a sordid taste in his mouth. "I've told you, sir."

"No, you haven't. Just because you're the old broad's darling grandson doesn't mean you haven't been bought."

Nothing Cedric could say was going to make any difference. He might as well keep quiet and wait until he found out what this hoodlum really wanted. For a moment there was a staring match. The gun muzzle came up to his face again, and he just squinted past it defiantly. Then it vanished and began slithering icily down the center of his chest like a cold steel snail.

He grabbed it with both hands and totally failed to slow its progress at all—as well try to strongarm a truck. It scraped past his navel, mercifully jumped his shorts, and then poked between

his legs and stopped. Clutching it still, Cedric looked up to see
Bagshaw leering at him. The man pursed thick lips and scratched
an ear with one finger of his free gauntlet. There was no doubt
who had control, or whose health and happiness were at risk.

And then Bagshaw began to move the gun in the opposite
direction—slowly and irresistibly. "You can talk easy, sonny, or
you can talk hard. But now you're going to talk."

"I told you." Cedric was squeaking. Half sitting, straddling
that thick metal cylinder, gripping it hard to hold it away from
important things, he was being forced inexorably up the bed.

"No, you haven't. Who did you come to meet?"

"How do I know that you're from the Institute?"

"You'll tell me anyway."

Cedric set his teeth as the knobs on his backbone came into
contact with the headboard of the bed. For a moment the pressure
was checked—but the barrel was still between his thighs, and he
had nowhere left to go.

"You're sweating, Cedric. You'll sweat more soon. Lots
more."

Cedric made a discourteous suggestion, long on historical
precedent and short on anatomical plausibility.

"Now that is *really* stupid," Bagshaw said, shaking his polished head sadly. "In the sort of fix you're in, you do not say
things like that. You beg, you plead, you sing loud. You do not
say things like that. Well, get up." He stepped back and pulled.
Cedric, reluctant to let go of the gun, was almost hauled off the
bed.

"Up, sonny!"

Cedric dropped his feet to the floor and stood up, slowly and
painfully. It hurt to straighten, but pride insisted. Swaying, blink-
ing back tears, he gazed down at his tormentor. The ape was far
shorter than Cedric but about four times as thick, and just being
vertical did not help greatly. Contrary to first impressions, Bagshaw did have a neck; it just happened to be wider than his head.
Even on equal terms, unarmed, he could make coleslaw out of
Cedric, who was all reach and no weight.

And at the moment he could not quite stand straight and
breathe at the same time. Bagshaw looked at him with open
mockery in those curiously hooded eyes. "Want to play some
more?"

Cedric was an organage boy. He shrugged. "You decide. You
must be enjoying it."

He might have scored there. Bagshaw grunted softly, and

when he spoke it was in command mode. *"Com two: Relay message for Hubbard Cedric Dickson."* He nodded his head to indicate that Cedric should turn around.

It could be a trap—Cedric did not move until a familiar voice at his back made him whirl. Two people were standing behind him, and one of them was Gran. His first reaction was shame at being caught in his briefs, but comprehension came fast thereafter. It was a holo projection, of course, which was how she could be knee deep in his bed. The man beside her was this same Bagshaw character, wearing a standard business suit which amply confirmed his wrestler's build. He was a human barrel. But he could not be in two places at once, so it was not a live transmission, and in any case the figures had the fixed-eyed look of people dictating. It was certainly Gran—a slim, imperious woman with white hair and enough determination to break rocks. Hubbard Agnes.

". . . in every respect. *Com end*," Gran concluded, and the two images vanished.

"Huh?" Cedric said.

"You heard," Bagshaw said.

"No, I didn't. *Com two, repeat that transmission*."

Nothing happened.

Bagshaw sighed. "Not coded to your voice, sonny. All right, we'll try again; but I do wish you'd start behaving like a grownup." He repeated the command, and the two images flashed into existence again in the middle of the bed.

"Cedric, I am informed that you have departed from Meadowdale earlier than instructed. That was extremely foolish of you. I am very concerned for your safety. The man beside me is Dr. Bagshaw Barney, a personal security expert employed by the Institute. I have instructed him to locate you and bring you to HQ as soon as possible. You will obey his orders in every respect. *Com end*."

Cedric closed his mouth, which for some reason was hanging open. He turned back to face Bagshaw's contemptuous amusement.

"How do I know that was genuine?"

The contempt faded slightly. "You don't."

"You could have faked it."

"In about fifteen minutes, with the right equipment."

"Is that why you began by showing me I don't have any choice?"

For an instant Bagshaw seemed tempted to smile. "Naw, I just like hassling you. Which is it to be—force or cooperation?"

Cedric shrugged. "Cooperation, I guess. But I wish you'd explain . . ."

"You clean up, then, and I'll talk. Is this your month for shaving?"

Cedric squeezed between two of the percies and hobbled over to the basin. "I could call HQ and ask for confirmation that you're genuine."

Bagshaw made a scornful noise. "It happens to be five in the morning, and you have no priority codes. Security never answers questions, even about the weather. Those guys won't admit what day it is. You couldn't get through to Old Mother Hubbard in less than two hours at the best of times, and even then it would only be if you could prove your relationship."

"I've called Gran dozens of—well, often."

Bagshaw sighed dramatically. "From Meadowdale—priority call."

"But if she's really worried about me," Cedric said with a feeling of triumph, "she'll have told System to admit my calls!"

"I wouldn't let her."

"*You* wouldn't?"

"Breach of security. If she'd done that, then who knows who might have learned that we had a cannon loose? Pardon me— popgun loose. No, you can't call in. You can come willingly, or I take you by force. I don't care. You may, but I won't."

Still stroking his face with his shaver, Cedric peered around the percies. Bagshaw had seated himself in midair, as though there were an invisible chair under him. He looked quite relaxed and comfortable, so he must have locked his waldoes into position.

"How did you get into this room?"

"That's my job. I can get into a bank vault, given time. Hotel rooms? Took me half a minute, all three locks."

"And you knew I was in here?"

"Like I said, I tested for you with a gas detector—sucked some air from under the door and checked for human phero-mones. Another half minute. Your exhalations are on file. They matched. Of course, you might have had a friend in here with you, but I didn't give a damn about that, really."

He made it all sound infuriatingly easy. Cedric dropped shaver and shorts and stepped toward the shower pad.

"Water first!" Bagshaw snapped.

"Huh?"

"Turn on the water before you get under it. Always. Elementary precaution."

Growling, Cedric complied. "And what about my percy?"

Bagshaw snorted. "That junk? Those rental jobs are all right for two-bit lawyers or their wives coming into town for the day—mostly because no one cares about them except tin-pot muggers. Even them not much. No city resident would ever trust a rental; no one of any real importance."

So? Cedric was not of any real importance. He stepped under the shower, a fine, cold mist and a suffocating odor of chlorine. The rotting rug around it suggested the electronics were not working too well. He knew about percies from seeing holo commercials. Most people owned a percy. Anyone really important had half a dozen—one to ride in, the others to run interference.

Damn, but his gut hurt! He wondered about the four percies that Bagshaw had brought with him—were there watchers inside those, staying silent? Was Bagshaw genuine? If he was, then why so nasty? If not, then what use was all that extra equipment? None of that mattered much, Cedric decided. Having used up the last of his credit calling Madge, he had left himself with no options but to do as he was told.

"That rental abortion probably has more pitches and patches on it than you could believe," Bagshaw remarked. "I turned it off before I even opened the door. I could have taken it over and made it break your neck instead. Never, ever, trust anyone else's percy!"

Cedric gave up hope that the water would run hot, or the soap ever produce a lather. Perhaps such things were luxuries that only places like Meadowdale could provide. He turned off the water and reached for the dryer.

"Don't!" Bagshaw shouted. "Jeez, man! Those things are deadly!"

"I've used one hundreds of—"

"Easiest booby trap in the world!"

Cedric scowled back at the older man's glare. "All right, how do I dry myself?"

"With the bed sheets, dummy! You'll catch some bugs and funguses, of course, but we can treat most of those. You probably got them already, just sleeping there."

Not sure how much of that to believe, Cedric stalked across to the bed, feeling absurdly aware of his nudity as he did so. He hauled off a sheet. "Tell me about your friends," he said. He nodded at the percies.

Bagshaw had pivoted to watch him. "Those? Just some girls I know." He laughed meanly. "Naw, they're empty. Backup equipment."

"You run them?"

"Sure." Bagshaw frowned, making odd wrinkles in his synthetic skin. "My job. I'm a pro, sonny. Remember, percies are only robots. That means computers. Computers have limitations. They're not good enough for the real enchiladas, the nobs, the big bumps on the world's ass—*they* have personal guards as well, real human beings who go everywhere with them, who open the doors and taste the soup and defuse the bombs and step in front of the bullets . . . usually a team of two or three, taking shifts. They're known as bulls."

"Short for pit bulls," Cedric said, to show he knew such things. "You're telling me you're a bull? You guard Gran?"

"Naw. I'm not senior enough to be trusted with her. The Institute has five people who rank high enough for bulls—the old girl herself and the four horsemen . . . deputy directors."

"Five?" Cedric was impressed. "Five just in 4-I?"

"Don't call it that! It's the Institute. Yes, five—right up there with the Secretary General, and the chairman of IBM, and the Speaker of the Chamber."

Cedric threw his bag on the bed and rummaged for clothes. "So why are you telling me this?"

"Because from now on it's six. I'm your bull, buster."

Half into his pants, Cedric tried to turn around and almost fell over. "Me? You're crazy! I don't rank a bodyguard!"

Bagshaw rose from his invisible chair. He stretched and yawned. "Yes, you do. Two of us—me and Giles Ted. In future, one or the other of us will be breathing on your neck and stepping on your toes twenty-four hours a day. Like your grandmother said, you'll obey orders. Ted or me'll be calling the shots, and you will do *exactly* as we tell you. With a little luck, we'll keep you alive, healthy, and sane. That'll be nice, won't it?"

Cedric could only assume that the man was serious. He did not look as though he were joking. He might be crazy, of course. "But I—I'm nothing! You said yourself—fresh from a foster home, wet behind the ears. Green as grass."

"That's right, sonny. But you're grandson to the best hated woman in the world."

"Gran? Hated?"

"Get dressed!"

"But who—"

"Get dressed!" Bagshaw repeated. "I'll run you a list when we get back to HQ. It runs to ten or twelve pages: Earthfirsters and ecology freaks and pilgrim groups and half the cults on the globe; them that's scared the Institute will poison the planet, them that says it's doing too much, and them that says it ain't doing enough. People who want to disband it, and people who want to take it over. People who believe it really has discovered habitable worlds and is keeping them secret . . . every type of nut there is."

Cedric's head emerged through the top of his poncho. "But what has this to do with me?"

Bagshaw rolled his eyes. "Ever heard of the Trojan horse? How do I know you haven't already been rewired so's you'll strangle the old lady as soon as you meet her?"

"That's not possible!"

"No?" Bagshaw somehow conveyed a shrug. "Well, not without a small amount of cooperation, it isn't, I guess."

Cedric stood on one leg to pull on a sock. "So!"

"So? So, you say? How about the media, sonny? The media have more short-term power than anybody. Homogenize Old Mother Hubbard's grandson, and a thousand groups would try to claim credit. What you are is a bulletin standing by to interrupt normal programming."

Cedric found that his mouth was open again. He would have to watch that. "You are saying that . . . people . . . would kill me, just to spite Gran?"

"Spite? Score off? Coerce? Turn? It wouldn't matter much to you, would it? You'd be dead—or worse—in a week. I promise you. Why do you think she put you in Meadowdale in the first place?"

Shoving feet into sneakers, Cedric thought of Glenda, who was Eccles Pandora's cousin, and Gavin, whose father was president of ITT—and suddenly understood. "Neutral ground?"

"Hey! Maybe you're not quite as simple as you look. Of course, some of the real rabid groups wouldn't respect any sort of sanctuary—the Sierra Club, or such—but you were fairly safe there. Now you're in play, right? And the Institute has infinite money, so you're a potential kidnap, too. Ransom victims rarely earn pensions." Bagshaw was grinning grotesquely, enjoying Cedric's horror. "Your dear gran's got power, sonny, and anyone with power has enemies. She's got more than most. BEST for example."

"BEST?"

"Are you deaf? I thought you were just stupid. Hurry up and

let's get the hell out of here. Yes, BEST. She's fought it off for years, and almost no one else has ever won a single round against BEST. This area happens to be BEST's turf. You didn't know that? There are hundreds of little power centers scattered around Nauc—some just local gang barons, others more important; even a few of the old legit governments still survive in places. There's even a mob down Blue Ridge way calls itself the Congress of the United States. Has a good militia."

To save his life, Cedric could not have told how much truth there was in that tirade.

And Bagshaw knew that. "But BEST's HQ is less than ten miles from here, so of course it's staked out its own territory all around. Now do you see? Sweet little Cedric with his feathers still wet flies out of the nest and perches right on the cats' litter box. If BEST knew you were here, you'd be in surgery already. Apparently it doesn't."

Cedric grunted and began stuffing things into his bag. His gut still hurt.

"So just remember, sonny, that this ain't the Meadowdale Organage no more and—"

"Organage? What's that mean? That's the third time—"

Then the helmet that hung behind Bagshaw's head uttered a quiet *beep*. In an instant he had nodded the helmet into place, leaving Cedric to stare blankly at its shiny exterior. The inside would contain vid displays, of course, and speakers.

Bagshaw emerged again, grim-faced. All trace of banter had vanished and there was only business showing.

"We have company. Never mind all that stuff." He took two steps to one of the percies and opened it. "Have you got anything here that's valuable?"

"My camera."

"Forget it. Anything that can't be replaced—souvenirs, personal sentimental things?"

"Just my coins." Gran had given him that camera . . .

"Bring those, and leave the rest. They aren't worth running through decon. Don't leave any information, though. No letters, diaries?"

Feeling more bewildered than annoyed, Cedric shook his head. Clutching his small bag of personal recordings, he stepped backward into the percy. Bagshaw reached in and swiftly began making the adjustments for him—the saddle and the shin pads, the chest and head straps. He was making them tight, and he had a deft touch despite his massive gauntlets.

"Ouch!" Cedric muttered. His head felt as though it had just been set in concrete. The rental unit had not gripped nearly so hard. This one smelled much better—a clean, new, factory sort of smell. It was also larger.

"Pull your chin in!" Bagshaw snarled, nimbly crushing Cedric's aching belly with heavy padding. "This model's guaranteed to twenty-five meters. Know what that means?"

Cedric mumbled a negative as yet another strap immobilized his chin, wrenching his neck in the process.

"It means you can drop about eight stories in it. I've tested one at twelve. Now, I'll be running things, so you just relax and enjoy the ride. Keep your hands at your sides."

Cedric's hands were almost the only thing he could move at all below his eyelids. The curious half-sitting position was surprisingly comfortable, as he knew from the previous day's travels, and the new unit was a vastly better piece of machinery than the rental job that Bagshaw had scorned so much. It was even big enough for his freakish height. He had a good view through the front window, flanked by innumerable vids that he could see without moving his head, although few of their displays meant anything to him. He had a rear view through a mirror. A percy was a mobile coffin, a tomb with a view.

Eight stories? That was only halfway down. It was the second half that would hurt.

Bagshaw's voice spoke in his ear. "Hear me okay?"

"Fine."

The percies rose a few centimeters to lev position. They all tilted forward and began to move as a group for the door. Bagshaw was wearing only his bull suit, but his boots were off the floor also. He looked small and vulnerable between the five giant cylinders, as though he were a prisoner being escorted.

He had put the rental job in front. It reached out its claws to flip the locks. Then it threw open the door and floated out into the corridor. White-hot fire jetted in from one side, searing right through the rented percy, cutting it in half, causing it to explode in a shower of molten metal and flaming plasteel. The carpet burst into flames. Even inside his armored tube, Cedric heard the roar and felt the blast. The blaze was bright enough to overload his viewplate and turn the images momentarily violet and red.

"Well, damn!" Bagshaw's voice muttered in his ear. "Looks like they want to play rough."

4

ALYA AWOKE WHEN the seats were rotated to prepare for reentry. The cabin lights were still low. She had not been aware of dozing off, but the sudden return of her terror told her that it had been absent and therefore she must have been asleep. She had slept very little since the *buddhi* had begun tormenting her, two days before.

The last time she had looked up, the viewscreens had been showing heavens full of stars, the way heavens were supposed to be, while the cruder manmade glare of Pacurb glimmered far below like spilled milk trickling down out of the hills to puddle against the edge of the ocean. She had identified Baja California and the Salton Sea.

But then she must have dozed for a while. The world had grown closer and bigger, with a fiery sword slash of dawn showing dead ahead. The stars had fled, and even the myriad clotted lights of Nauc seemed faint. The super was pitching steeply downward, returning to Mother Earth.

Yes, she had slept a little. Of course, by her time it was evening; in Nauc it would be Thursday morning again. She should not have slept. Sleep had left her with a hollow, weightless feeling, and already some time-zone disorientation. And still the

31

wordless dread, that terrible *why me*? feeling. I do not wish to do this—let me go.

Thousands of people, men and women and—*Oh God, why me?*—children, of course. She wanted to crumble away like dust or shrivel into a husk that someone might throw in a waste bucket, so she would never be seen again. Why would they not all leave her alone? Why would *it* not leave her alone? Why had she been born with a curse upon her? And yet perhaps the biting was not quite as vicious as it had been. Just boarding the plane had helped a little.

Someone patted her hand, and she jumped. She had taken the seat next to the wall—the window seat, they called it still, although there were no windows on a super. Even in the twenty-first century a princess could pull rank once in a while, and she had established herself in a good defensive position between the wall and Moala, secure against unwelcome intruders. Obviously Moala had been removed while Alya slept. Jar Jathro was recognizable by his green *hajji* turban, although it seemed nearer black in the gloom. His greasy smile was not visible, but she could sense it. The lizard himself.

"You rested." He spoke Malay. "That is good. You are less troubled now?"

"Perhaps a little," she admitted.

"Your sister, the Princess Talach, and your honored brother, Prince Omar—both of these told me that the burden became less troublesome as they progressed toward . . . our destination."

Alya wondered if she dared ask for Moala back. But she must not insult this man, however sleazy she found him. He was a skilled politician. Kas said he might well succeed Piridinar as prime minister—and soon, for the old man's health was failing fast.

"Then I wish it were a little easier to get to."

"Ah!" he said, and some trick of the light caught his eyes in the dark. "But that was deliberate. Many people said it was too risky to build the transmensor anywhere on earth at all. Thinking of the power, you see; thinking of an explosion. I have studied this. When there was talk of using it also to explore other worlds, then of course the uproar was greater still. People said that monsters would escape! How foolish! But Labrador is a desert of bare rock, and safe. It was already connected to Nauc by powerlines. A most logical choice—distant but accessible."

"Thank you," Alya said softly, and at once wanted to rap herself on the knuckles.

"You are most welcome. The powerlines have been replaced now by satellite beams, of course." He fell silent, waiting politely for her to carry the conversation forward.

When she did not, he remarked, "You are the eleventh person in your family to make this pilgrimage."

"Yes." The eleventh victim.

"And you are also the youngest?"

Alya pondered. "I suppose so. It started before I was born; but yes, that's true."

"And all the other ladies were married."

She had not thought of that. Tal had been married, Omar not. Why should it matter that Alya was single and not matter about Omar? But, of course, Jathro was a Moslem. "Yes," she said.

"Your safety and comfort will always be nearest to my heart, Your Highness." He laid his hand on hers again and left it there. It was hot and sticky. There was a curious odor of cloves about Jathro. "Anything I can do—anything at all—you have only to ask."

Alya hoped he had not felt her flinch at his touch. Mentally she assembled a tirade of obscenities in several languages. But what she said was, "You are most kind."

"I am not without influence, of course." He leaned a little closer and peered at her. The lights were starting to brighten, but the cabin was still very dim. She could just make out the fringe of beard around a dark, narrow face. "My father was but a poor fisherman. The fisherfolk know me as one of their own."

"Their lot has been very hard. I have heard my brother speak of it many times." She wondered what all his talk was leading to. The man had had a spectacular career as a slum populist—forty years old and already running one of the three top ministries in the government. So Kas had said on the way to the airport.

"My people are aware of his concern," Jathro said. "They have great affection for all members of your noble family. They always cheer when I mention your brother. Two thousand years of devotion are not easily forgotten."

"Their love is dear to us." Alya toyed with the idea of removing the man's turban and garroting him with it—perhaps the exercise would revive her.

"The refugees, of course, do not have that same affection, although they are grateful to Banzarak for its help, and therefore they respect our national traditions."

Totally baffled, Alya crafted a smile. She did not enjoy being addressed like a public meeting. She wanted to be left alone with her misery.

"So you see, I am familiar with the poverty of Banzarak, but I have also seen even greater need among the unfortunates whom we have taken into our bosom."

Make one move at my bosom, man, and I'll break your neck.

"My brother spoke with wonder about your work in the camps," she said. A first-class demagogue, Kas had called him.

"I feel for them deeply. Director Hubbard is a hard woman, but fair. I shall insist that the refugees in Banzarak are afforded special status only marginally less favorable than that of our own nationals . . ."

Alya let him drone while she wandered away into her private desert. It was all very well to talk of negotiations, but what they all meant was haggling, and the goods on display were her. The precedents had been set before she was born. In a sense the dealing had begun centuries before—two thousand years, if one believed the legends. What am I offered? What price one princess of Banzarak, with guaranteed infallible *buddhi*? Start your bidding.

A hard woman? By all accounts, Director Hubbard was a human anvil. Few indeed were the governments who could hope to negotiate on anything near equal terms with the director of 4-I, for 4-I was also Stellar Power, Inc. The rumors said that Hubbard had more than once threatened to pull the plug on a continent.

And few indeed were the governments that could negotiate anything, for they had all been choked by their internal conflicts, the warring of special interest groups, loss of financial integrity . . . But Jathro would not appreciate a lecture on political science, not from a woman. For the son of an impoverished fisherman to negotiate with Old Mother Hubbard herself must be a delicious sensation. Jathro was going to be buying lives by the thousand, and his coin was Alya.

Suddenly her rambling mind stopped and peered back along its own tracks. That did not ring true! Why should a demagogue dispose of his own followers? Why ruin his own power base? And what in the name of all the gods was he getting at now?

". . . fortunes are linked. Our supporters would welcome evidence that our cooperation is a willing one. And will remain so."

The light was better now. He was leaning very close, squeezing her hand. Alya shied suddenly at the piercing intelligence in those jet eyes. She tried to pull her wits together—the man was dangerous—but she was too staggered by the implications. She had not realized! Even Kas had not guessed what Jathro must have in mind. Why be prime minister of a postage-stamp kingdom when one could hope for so very much more? The audacity of his ambition staggered her. And now this? He was twice her age and twice divorced. Oh, wonderful! Just what I need.

"Dr. Jar . . . this is a difficult time for me. You will pardon me if I reserve consideration of your words?"

Whatever all that meant, it seemed to satisfy him. He smiled, showing excellent teeth. The lights were up at last. The sky in the viewscreen was brightening. Reentry had started, and the passengers were sinking deeper into their seats.

"But of course. I will do everything to ease your burden. Rely on me totally."

"I appreciate that, Dr. Jar. You are very thoughtful."

What would Kas think, back in Banzarak, if she were to announce her engagement to Jar Jathro? It might even bring him running.

"For example, you may refer all questions to me. I speak good English. Questions about your predecessors, your relatives . . . I shall refuse such questions. I shall infer that it is impolite to ask about family matters."

Alya made noncommittal noises.

"If you do find yourself in conversation and I am not to hand, just keep these precepts in mind. I am visiting America on behalf of the World Refugee Authority. You are accompanying me as my—" He smiled brazenly. "But I just promised not to rush your decision, didn't I? Accompanying me to be shown a little of the world. Americans approve of women who know things, but keep the talk to babies and clothes if you can. That would be safest."

"I'd better write that down," Alya said, very quietly, hoping the rising clamor outside would drown the words.

"Oh, no, that will not be necessary. You'll remember. But just in case I am not around . . . keep in mind that there has never been a Class One world found. That is very important. Many Class Twos—those are worlds that look Earthlike, you understand? But detailed investigation has always turned up some flaw, a poison of one kind or another. Heavy metals, whatever they are, are mentioned a lot. A Class One world, one really safe for people— that would be an earth-shaking discovery."

"What's a Class Three world, then, Dr. Jar?" Alya felt sure that her fury must be showing—her cheeks felt hot enough to fry eggs—but that pompous little prick was probably interpreting it as something else. Lust, maybe? Everyone knew that women were unstable and prone to attacks of lust.

"You really don't need to worry about such things, but a Class Three is one with some sort of life on it, yet not like the Earth. Threes turn up all the time. Every week or so. Class Twos—the ones that look like our own world, remember?—only a few of those are discovered each year. Sometimes people even talk about Class Fours, which have no life at all. They are the most common. But stick to babies."

How could a successful politician be so blind? Perhaps he had never met an educated woman. He must truly believe that women should stick to babies. In the slums and the camps they had no choice. He could probably quote the Koran on the subject, too.

At last Jathro removed his sticky hand. He leaned back for a moment, yielding to the gee force, easing a back that must have grown stiff with leaning, looking pleased with himself. The roar of reentry rattled the cabin and every bone in it. The viewscreens showed hellfire glowing along leading edges.

Quickly the yammering softened, the force and noise began to wane. The pressure eased.

Jathro turned to her again, fumbling in his breast pocket. "I have something for you to look at, Highness."

A sudden prickling warned her. "Yes?"

He passed over a small scrap of paper, a leaf ripped from a spiral notebook. Eight words were written on it in pencil.

Nile
Orinoco
Po
Quinto
Rhine
Saskatchewan
Tiber
Usk

Oh God! *Satori!*

There it was!

For a moment Alya was incapable of speech. She feared she might vomit. She clutched her hands to her lap to hide their trembling.

"Rivers," she mumbled, unconsciously switching to English to match the spellings. "I don't know Quinto, and I'm not sure of Usk, but the others are all rivers."

The little turd had trapped her. Never had she felt so clear a *satori*, never had the *buddhi* shouted so loud—and Jathro was much too acute to have missed her reaction. His eyes burned like black lasers. "Yes, they're all rivers, Highness, but in fact they're code names. File names, if you prefer. These are rivers, but the name of cities get used, also. Or mountains, or poets. Fish, men, women, battles . . . eventually they start all over again. Any world of any interest is given a file name."

"Etna," she said, with sudden memories of Omar soaring in her mind like chords of funeral music. And Tal—Tal had drawn "Raven."

"Exactly," Jathro murmured. "I just wondered if any of the names on this list seemed . . . significant?"

She forced a swallow down a dry throat. "No," she murmured.

"Ah." He sounded disappointed. He looked unconvinced.

Alya returned the paper without a word. It quivered.

"None at all?" he persisted.

"No. They're just words."

"Ah. Just words?"

Seven names of rivers written in pencil, and one in letters of fire . . . How could he not see that one of the eight blazed as though scribed by the finger of God?

But she would not say. She must be sure. She must be absolutely certain, with no grain of doubt anywhere. Thousands of lives! Why her?

The captain completed his turn, shedding his sonic boom over the ocean. The super came wailing down the sky at subsonic speed, dropping rapidly, hunting for land like a storm-pressed gull. The screen showed a momentary image of stark city towers standing in the sea, waves running around their feet, and scavengers' barges floating in the debris-laden streets. Then it was gone and yellowish-green countryside drifted past below in a damp dawn light.

5

EVEN AS BAGSHAW'S armored gauntlet slammed the door, shutting out horrors of melted metal and burning carpet, all the percies sprang into motion. Cedric's leaped back so suddenly that he thought his eyeballs would fall out. Then it spun around and hurled itself across the room rear first, heading for the shower. He felt it flip up onto the pad; he saw the wall in his mirror, and then—*impact!*

The shock rang all the way to his teeth. Had he not been pinned like a pit in a plum, he would have been pulped. The wall shuddered and fractured. At once his percy hurtled forward toward the bed, passing one of the others, which had just attacked the wall on the far side of the room. The third had lifted the fourth in its claws and was pounding it into the ceiling. Tiles and dust and debris sprayed everywhere.

Cedric's percy twisted around so that it was again going backward as it slammed into the weakened wall by the bed. That reversed assault was probably designed to make things a little easier on him, he thought groggily, because he saw the second unit smash into the wall by the shower and it was still going face first. Nice of Bagshaw to be so considerate.

"Glee Club, this is Knuckles." Bagshaw's voice sounded close by Cedric's ear. He was speaking very quietly. Cedric could not

38

see where the man himself had gone, which was hardly surprising in the fog of dust and flying rubble. Again Cedric's robot and its opposing partner surged forward and flashed by each other. Again that lurch over the shower pad—and this time his percy burst right through the wall in an explosion of debris and broken pipes and jets of water. It tripped, tipping almost horizontal, and then straightened. Cedric's stomach stayed at floor level, and the percy was accelerating again even before it was upright.

"Knuckles, we read you." That must be Glee Club.

The room next door—where Cedric now found himself—was dark, but vision enhancement had clicked in for him. It gave false color images, so that the terrified face above the heap of bed-clothes was bright pink and the teeth in her mouth were red. He could not hear the woman's screams as his percy raced across the room toward her and impacted the wall beside the bed. He hoped she would have the sense to get out of the way quickly.

"Glee Club, I have picked up Sprout."

"Report Sprout's condition, Knuckles."

"Okay so far. *Virgo intacta*, I should think. But the natives are restless."

That was putting it mildly. Cedric's percy was backing up again, almost as far as his own room. It stopped just short of the aperture rimmed by twisted pipes squirting water and clouds of steam. Why could there not have been hot supplies like that when Cedric was having his shower? If things got much more exciting, he was going to need another shower very shortly. Fortunately, his brain did not seem to be accepting any of this as real.

Then he was being accelerated again for another attack on the wall by the bed. *My Life as the Human Hammer*, or *The School of Hard Knocks*. The pink-faced woman had dived for the floor on the far side and disappeared. How long would it be, Cedric wondered, before the attackers in the corridor came—*impact!*—came in through the doors?

"Angel, this is Glee Club. Do you read?"

"Glee Club, this is Angel. We have a fix on Knuckles. There's a swarm of hornets around, though."

Suddenly Cedric recalled Bagshaw's remark that these percies would survive a fall of twelve stories. No—the equipment would survive more than that. The *occupant* might survive twelve stories. How unfortunate that Cedric's room was on the sixteenth floor.

Impact! again . . .

Bagshaw's strategy was fairly obvious, although Cedric was

having trouble keeping his mind on logic. The enemy was out in
the corridor with a fusion cannon, and the good guys did not have
the armor to face that. So he had scattered his troops—Cedric
going one way, an empty percy in the opposite direction, and a
third straight up. It would take the baddies a few minutes to work
out which thimble hid the pea.

"Angel, give me an ETA."

A searing white flame filled the bedroom. Cedric saw the bed
sheets turn purple and burst into brown flames even before his
video overloaded and the percy was lifted by the blast and
rammed bodily into the wall it had been about to strike again.
The woman would have been charred instantly, he thought as the
wall collapsed, spilling him through into a third room and bury-
ing another bed in an avalanche of concrete. He could not see if
there had been anyone in it.

Please, God? People are dying here, God.

This was no holo drama. This was real, squalid murder. He
was rolling . . .

The vision enhancement had returned. The ceiling was a very
pretty green. He was lying on his back, and half the vids had
gone dark.

"Ced—Sprout? You okay?"

"Sprout fine," Cedric said weakly. He really did not believe
that all this was happening, but that had been Bagshaw's voice,
so somehow the bull had survived the explosion, too.

And so had Cedric's percy. The vids flickered on again—most
of them—and it swung up to a vertical position. He discovered a
curious salt taste in his mouth. That distracted him for a moment,
until the door of the room crashed down before him and he was
out in the bright lights again, hurtling along the corridor, swaying
mightily and gathering speed all the way. It was a very long
corridor. There were men behind him—at least three of them, all
wearing much the same sort of armored suit as Bagshaw—and
they were crouched over something that Cedric was certain was a
fusion cannon. Clearly they had just fired it into his original
room. At the moment they were turning it to point at him.

The carpet was still smoldering from the first blast. Burned
blotches scarred the walls at regular intervals, as though the
plasma had rippled from side to side. Doors were opening,
frightened guests coming out to see what was happening. All of
them managed to leap back to safety in time, before he ran them
down. The noise should have been shattering. There should have
been screaming and explosions and sirens, but he could hear

nothing at all from outside. Life seemed strangely peaceful around Cedric. Maybe his hearing had failed, or his brain.

The voices on the network were chattering, but he did not register what was being said. He was amazed at how time seemed to have slowed down, or his own thought processes speeded up, because years were going by while his percy raced along that corridor and the enemy did whatever they were doing to ready that gun.

And then the percy swerved, cannoned off a wall, and impacted another door, stumbling through into a stairwell. The corridor flamed white behind him, and half the vids winked off and then came on again. His ears popped. There was a strong smell of sweat, but so far only sweat. There had been people . . .

Oh, God! There had been people—doors open, people looking out.

He had thought that the percy would head downward; he had not even known that a percy could climb stairs, but this one could, jolting Cedric up and down like a maraca. One floor up it grabbed the doorhandle in its claw. Then it soared out into another bright corridor and headed back in the direction it had come.

A door just ahead of him burst open, erupting smoke and an armored man whose feet did not quite touch the floor. He raced along the corridor—not floating, but running like a skater, and gathering speed rapidly.

"Sprout, that's me ahead of you."

"Read you, Knuckles." Had that been his own voice? So calm? Cedric decided that he must be in shock. Shrieking hysterics would be the correct reaction.

The armored man was still accelerating. Cedric's percy seemed to be slowing, and he felt a sudden terror that it might have been damaged, that he would be left behind. Where was the enemy? Bagshaw had come up through the ceiling, of course. How had he kept control of so much equipment? How many innocent people had died?

"Sprout, we'll have to do something unorthodox here. Better keep your eyes closed for a while."

"Screw you," Cedric said—but quietly, and surprisingly matter-of-factly.

Bagshaw, far ahead now, reached the end of the corridor without breaking stride and then leaped upward. He threw out arms and legs to strike the window spread-eagled. Frame and glass and drapes and man vanished into darkness, leaving a rectangular black hole where there had not been one previously.

Seventeen floors, or somewhere between fifty and sixty meters—exact measurement did not matter much, did it?—Cedric wanted to scream. He opened his mouth to scream, but all he heard was his own voice dryly ordering his percy to stop. Vaguely he saw that armored figures had appeared in the distance behind him, visible in his mirror, and they had their cannon with them. His percy was losing speed, but he did not think it was obeying his commands, and the black rectangle was pouring itself straight at him, growing larger and larger, but more and more slowly. There was absolutely nothing more he could do. Bagshaw had the con—if Bagshaw was still alive—or else the machine was damaged and out of control. Cedric was immobilized in a traveling coffin, and the black space grew larger and larger, but slower and slower. He could not guess what the final result was going to be.

The pitch fell short. The percy reached the window just as it ran out of velocity and came to a complete stop. Relief! For a moment Cedric stared out at the lights of the city, a forest of towers still bright against a first faint light of morning. He breathed a deep sigh. He wondered how he went about surrendering. Surely the men behind him would see that he was trapped and helpless inside his percy? They would not fire at him now. Bagshaw had hinted at all sorts of horrors if he were to be captured, but those lay in the future. Cedric would much rather wait for them than be instantly fried by a fusion torch—or be jellied by falling seventeen stories out that window.

Then his percy tipped slowly and deliberately forward, and toppled over the sill.

He spent a little over three seconds falling to the street—he had System calculate it for him, much later. He thought that he was very young to die, but then he decided that he had aged many years in those three seconds. He never knew whether it was luck or Bagshaw's skill that had him flat on his back as he reached the ground, in the position where his fragile protoplasm could best take the stress, pressing back into restraining padding.

Bagshaw caught him.

IMPACT!

He was alive. The gray sky was still above him, there was rain on his viewplate, and he could hear his heart.

"Okay, Sprout?"

Cedric repeated the obscenity he had used earlier that evening and augmented it with every other one he could think of. Not very many, really. Not enough. A real man would know more bad words.

Bagshaw set him upright in the percy and flexed his arms as though they hurt. He bent over to view his feet. "Lookit that!" he said. "Cracked the sidewalk."

"I'd like to break it with your head." Cedric, tasting salt again, decided that he had bitten his tongue.

"Angel should be along shortly. Let's go meet him."

"And I'll have you know," Cedric said bitterly, "that I'm not *virgo intacta*."

Bagshaw drew in breath with a hiss. "Hot damn!" he said. "Tell me about it sometime."

Angel turned out to be a rackety Sikorsky of incredible antiquity. It set down right in a public square to pick up Cedric and Bagshaw, then took off again as calm as milk, woof...woof... woof into the dawn sky. It was only after they had cleared the tops of the nearby towers that someone opened fire. None of the occupants seemed very worried by that.

The interior was dark and empty and stank of oil. The pilot and his buddy jabbered into mikes and crouched over controls, with vague red lights flickering over their faces as though they were demons from the pit. Cedric's percy had been laid flat across the floor like a coffin, and Bagshaw helped him out of it. He was soaked, with his clothes clammy on his skin, but it was only sweat—his pants were no wetter than his poncho. He sat on a bench and leaned back against an icy window and tried not to shake. He felt sick.

Something went by at high speed, and the helicopter rocked in its wake. The pilot made a joke, but Cedric thought that the other two did not find it funny. Then other fast things roared by, and those were apparently goodies, and everyone relaxed.

He was still clutching his little bag of coins. It was all he had left. It held sanity. It held his childhood. It held all his memories—of Christmas parties with Victor playing Santa Claus, of camping trips and rafting and hikes, and himself lasering. He had recorded most of the coins himself, with his own camera, but he had traded with the others, too. There were lots of his favorite shows and dramas in there also, but the commercial stuff was not really important. It was the personal stuff, the junk that no one else would care about—that was what mattered. The images might be out of focus, or the world tilted, or everyone unrecognizable under masks and goggles in the outdoor shots. So what?

That was life. Now he had been pitched without warning into a madness of death and terror. Sanity and happiness and love had disappeared from the world, and all he had to hang on to—all he had to remember them by—was that little bag of coins.

Then he realized that he was grieving for Meadowdale, and he felt ashamed. He was a man now, out in the world at last. That was what he had wanted, was it not? He was going to be a ranger like his father. He just had not expected the world to get quite so rough quite so soon, that was all.

Bagshaw had stripped off his armor, down to his underwear. He was just as sweaty as Cedric, and he had pulled a blanket over his shoulders. From nowhere that Cedric could see, he produced two cans of beer.

Beer at that time of day? Cedric accepted one and drank greedily. The ranch hands had slipped him beer a few times, but he had never cared for the taste much. Until now. It went down good. How many people had died? The sky was still brightening slowly, and a fine rain was falling, smoking off the rotor edges. Towers and streets rolled by below.

"You said twelve stories." Cedric had not meant to talk, and he wondered why his mouth had spoken without warning him it was going to.

Bagshaw was not as sassy as he had been. He sat morosely on the bench, hunched under his blanket. He was immensely thick all over, like a weight lifter. Despite his globular belly, he probably carried more muscle than flab. The dermsym ended in a ragged edge at the top of his chest, yet as far as Cedric had been able to see, the man was completely hairless even where he had skin.

"I said twelve for that make of percy. Mine is a bull suit. They're better, but they do take practice." He drank, then wiped his lips. "I knew I could do forty-five meters in a bull suit. That wasn't much more than forty-five."

"The hell it wasn't."

Bagshaw shrugged. "The tricky part was catching you. There's no routine for that."

Cedric shuddered convulsively. "No routine . . . that was you?"

Thick lips parted in a leer. "Just me—my eye, my judgment. Glad I got it right? You'd not have been very interesting after the first bounce." He held out his arms, which were turning bruise colors. "I never caught anything going quite that fast, though." The waldoes had not shielded him totally.

"But you faked me!" Cedric said. "You slowed it down until I got to the window, and then you stopped it. I thought it wasn't going to happen. Then you went and did it to me anyway."

Bagshaw turned to study him for a moment. "I had to. First, I had to get ready. Second, a percy couldn't jump the ledge. If you'd hit the sill at speed, you'd have come out spinning, cartwheeling all over the sky."

Cedric grunted and looked away.

The flight continued. The sky grew paler yet, sick-looking. They were flying over patchy woodland and gullies, for Nauc was a conglomeration of many cities, not yet continuous. Here and there Cedric noticed buildings being thrown up in haste. Despite the falling population, the whole world was in a building frenzy.

"You never went over a hundred," Bagshaw said softly.

"Huh?"

"You've got a real slow heartbeat at the best of times, but even coming down the sky, it never went over one hundred. A guy could brag about that a little, I guess."

Cedric shivered in early morning chill and reaction.

"How many deaths?" he asked. "How many died?"

"I don't know. We didn't start it."

"Just to kill me? Just to spite Gran and get on the evening news?"

Bagshaw shrugged. "Maybe. Maybe not. Maybe they didn't even know who you were. Just knew there was a big force on their turf, thought they could scare us into surrendering. Then they'd have taken us apart and decided who we were and what use we might be."

Cedric shivered again.

"It wasn't your fault, lad."

For a while Cedric just watched the condensation collecting on his beer can. He knew that Bagshaw was watching him.

"No. It wasn't my fault," he said finally.

"You saying it was mine?"

Of course it was. Bagshaw had invaded enemy territory with an unnecessary show of strength. He had wasted endless time in taunting Cedric for his own amusement. He had told him to shave and shower when they should have been streaking out like scared trout. He had damned nearly advertised for trouble.

"Who's going to ask?"

Bagshaw shrugged. "Just the Institute."

"No cops? The city? State?"

Bagshaw looked at him as though he were trying to be funny.

"You've got a patron! Probably the best there is! You'll die of old age before any cop gets to lay a finger on you. That's what lawyers are for."

"So a guy works for the Institute, he can get away with anything?"

"Hell, no! The Institute sees to that itself."

Ah! "And who files the report on what happened tonight?"

Without taking his veiled gaze off Cedric, Bagshaw tilted his head back, trying for a last drop of beer. Then he crumpled the can. "I do. You can file one, too, if you want."

"Or countersign yours?"

Bagshaw began to look thoughtful. "You may get asked to . . . this time."

"I could offer?"

The bull head seemed to hunker down into the blanket, as though smelling a threat, and Cedric had a momentary vision of something massive pawing the ground.

"You want to ask for a replacement?"

"Would I get one?"

The reply was grudging. "You might."

Cedric pushed harder. "After tonight, you mean?"

Even more reluctantly, Bagshaw nodded. "After tonight. And if BEST files a complaint, then you will be asked for a report, I guess."

But if BEST complained, then the Institute would close ranks around its own—like little-boy gangs, like the bunkhouses at Meadowdale, each one a separate gang. This was the same, but bigger. And it was not little-boy stuff. It was death, caused by arrogance and rank stupidity.

Gangs had rules, and the first one was always loyalty. But loyalty was a dangerous emotion. It could be turned.

Cedric drained his beer can, too. "No. I'll sign yours," he said. "Your report. Put in all the lies you want. Say anything you need to cover your precious ass, any crap at all. I'll sign it for you, whatever you've said."

Bagshaw bared his teeth. After a minute he said, "You can't back out once you sign."

"I know that." Cedric returned his stare, not caring if he seemed petulant or unmanly.

"Bastard!" Bagshaw said very softly. "Bad as your bitch of a grandmother."

Cedric felt a little better.

"Frigging young bastard! It must run in your bastard family!"

Whatever Bagshaw might make of the rest of his career, from that moment on he would always wonder if he owed his success to Hubbard Cedric Dickson. Nothing could ever hurt worse than that.

6

DAWN WAS BREAKING, and Eccles Pandora Pendor had not been to bed at all. Negotiating, waiting for messages, wheedling and bullying, she had had a busy night. Even had there been a break, she would not have been able to sleep—not when she was poised on the lip of the biggest story in the history of investigative reporting. Hell, it was the biggest story in the history of the human race, and she was going to break it.

A stone ax with blood on it: Cave Men in Space.

Finding that she fretted too much in her office, she had withdrawn instead to her retreat on the eighty-third floor, to spend the night pacing and worrying.

Her apartment was a shimmering cavern of crystal and chrome, all angles and shiny white. The design was the latest and trendiest. To be honest, it gave her the pukes, but she redecorated every three months on principle, so this would soon be gone. Many a girl spent a fortune keeping her body youthful and then gave away her age by going for obsolete decor. Men detected discrepancies. Staying young was a total commitment.

Now and then her pacing would take her past a mirror, and she would pause to inspect her appearance. She was very pleased with her new face. She did not look a day over twenty, and the scars had all gone now, except for a couple inside her mouth,

48

which she could barely feel with her tongue. Even those were fading.

The creep Wilkins had demanded ten million hectos. In official terms, that was exactly one billion dollars. Of course, a billion was not what it used to be, but even a media giant like WSHB could not throw that kind of change around lightly. Although Pandora had a hefty slush fund to call on, hefty was not omnipotent. Approval for expenditure on that scale had to come from higher up, and that meant politics. Frazer Franklin had friends who wanted him to get all the breaks, of course, old has-been though he was—Pandora almost laughed aloud every time she saw that scalp transplant of his. It was going to be as bald as its predecessor in another month or two.

So she had been ramming through an emergency appropriation at the same time as she had been trying to confirm the story and also out-circle the office sharks. Even securing the data was proving to be tricky. She had told Wilkins that he would have to transmit the evidence to her on approval, and he had laughed in her new face—quite rightly so, of course. Getting more serious then, she had suggested that he forget his job, hop the lev, and nip down to Nauc with the coin. He had laughed even harder at that, claiming that then he would be *cut up* instead of *cut out*. He might have had a point there—WSHB's accountants would go a long way to save ten million hectos.

And she had no reliable rats in Cainsville. She doubted that anyone else did, either. Rats did not survive long in the Institute. They just vanished. So, even, did moles. Merely sending a man up there to contact Wilkins had required a good excuse, which had taken time to find. But ten million hectos needed verification of product.

And time was precious. If 4-I made an announcement first, then Pandora's scoop would be dead as the Ides of March.

Of course, the Institute had its own time problems, which was why it had made no announcement yet. The missing explorers had been transmensed to Nile on April first, appropriately. They had planned to overnight until the next window, on the fifth. That was when they had come back dead. Today was the seventh already, and the next window must be due on the ninth, or thereabouts.

She was certain that the Institute would prefer not to issue a statement until it had collected a lot more data, probably not until it had overnighted another team, and that meant the thirteenth at the earliest, if the period was exactly four days. Before then, 4-I would make nothing public—unless it learned about the leak. In that case it would move at once to preempt her and publish its own version.

Pure luck had put Pandora within reach of Wilkins's call. WSHB had a thousand such moles spotted around the world. Nine-tenths of them would never turn up as much as a borscht recipe in their lives, but once in a while a code would twitch in as a mole suddenly decided to rat. Then System would alert the senior news exec within reach. Normally that would have been Frazer Thin-on-top Frankie, but just by chance old F.F. had been interviewing a would-be starlet that afternoon, and the interview had already progressed to the point where F.F. had not been accepting calls. Thus Destiny had laid her hand on Pandora's shoulder instead. Poor Frankie had apparently had a disappointing day all around—he had not even given the lad a training contract. He played dirty even with kids.

So pure luck had taken a hand, but so had virtue, because Pandora's section had been working on an Institute story for months. She had ample background ready to go. The media all took shots at 4-I quite regularly, of course, and had done so for years. Old Mother Hubbard always survived somehow, but now she was at the end of her string. There was no doubt that China was about to recognize the World Chamber. China was still the largest nation-state, the only one of any real size whose government had not collapsed into impotency under its debt load.

If China backed the Chamber, then the long fight would be over, and the U.N. would cease to exist at all. The Institute operated on a United Nations charter, and Hubbard herself was a long-time political crony of Hastings, the S.G. In fact they had been paired once. He had pulled strings to win her appointment as director, and a few years later she had done the same for him. In their case, bedfellows had made very effective politics.

It was all very profound. It meant that Hubbard was going down the sewer very soon, and WSHB was certainly prepared to help all it could. Curiously, this Cave Men in Space story might be enough all by itself. It might even reverse the expected flow of events: Old Mother Hubbard would fall, dragging down Hastings and the U.N. with her, and China would move even faster to throw its weight behind the Chamber. Speaker Cheung would certainly call a world election to confirm his hegemony. It was all very strong stuff, and sweet little Eccles Pandora was going to be a prime mover.

Klaus had called from Cainsville just after midnight. He had

contacted Wilkins. He had viewed the coin. And yes, it was
everything that Wilkins had promised. Anything could be a fake,
of course, but Deputy Director Devlin had been reeling around
having apoplectic fits, his language on the subject of incompetence being hot enough to melt the rest of the polar ice caps. That
alone, Klaus had suggested, might be worth a lot of money.

Klaus had a good reputation in WSHB. Armed with his report, Pandora had bearded the senior lions, rousing them from
their beds—or others' beds in a few cases—until she had her
approval. Ten million hectobucks had flowed electronically from
one account to another, then another and another, destined to rest
at last in one belonging to Wilkins Jules Smuts.

But what was Klaus doing now? Hours had gone by. Had the
Institute's goons discovered the plot? Had Wilkins panicked and
pulled out, or perhaps raised his price? Pandora's pacing grew
faster, although she was bone weary. She began to spend less
time on planning and more on just worrying. Her old, old bunion
operation began to complain, and she promised herself new feet
if this deal worked out.

Ping! said the com. "Secured message, code Honeysuckle
Thunderbolt."

Klaus at last! Pandora made one more quick check that her
hair was in place and had not turned white. *"Code Naples Oc-
tave, accept and record."*

The panel became a window into a grubby little cubicle, with
solid, scruffy, dependable little Kubik Klaus sitting in it. She
wanted to give him a hug. She might just give him more than that
when he got back. He was smiling broadly and holding up a coin.

"What kept you?" she demanded.

He pulled a face. "Our friend had started celebrating already."

"You had to dry him out?"

"Cool him down. He's a plugin freak."

Ugh! Pandora prided herself on being broad-minded, but there
were a few vices she preferred not to think about.

"But the deal's made now, the money spent. So I have a question, sweet lady. Do you still want me to bring this to you, or do
you need it zapped?"

Now there was an almost irresistible temptation. Klaus could
transmit the entire coin in compressed format to Nauc, and the
evidence would be in Pandora's hands within seconds. Unfortunately, that way was risky. Their override codes would mask con-
versations—or so she certainly hoped—but a data transmission
needed higher bands, and the legendary 4-I Security would cer-

tainly be alert for any attempt to zap data out of Cainsville. Its
monitors would detect the sending, and very likely could do so in
time to block it.

There was one entrance to Cainsville, so it was said, and a
million exits. Wilkins and Klaus might find themselves on Nile,
being thumped with stone axes like the previous explorers, or
perhaps somewhere even nastier, breathing the unbreathable.
Pandora did not care a fig what happened to Wilkins, but she
rather enjoyed Klaus once in a while. More important, she
wanted that evidence intact.

"Bring it!"

He nodded in obvious relief and vanished before she could
change her mind.

Finally Pandora could relax. The deed was done, the booty on
its way, and dawn breaking. Today was going to be busy but
joyful. The viewing, cutting, editing, blocking—and above all,
the rescheduling. She would be co-copting everyone down to the
garage flunkies, graciously acknowledging congratulations from
members of the board, bumping Furless Frankie right off prime
time . . .

Oh, bliss!

She decided that for once Eccles Pandora Pendor might just
eat a hot breakfast, and damn the diet. She headed for the bedroom to freshen up and change.

"Call from Dr. Frazer Franklin," the com announced.

Pandora stopped with one foot in the air. What could possibly
be inspiring F.F. to be awake at this time of day?

Worry?

And why would he be calling her? Could it be a surrender?
The white flag? She could think of nothing that he could have left
to lay on the table. By tomorrow she would be the unquestioned
queen of WSHB News. Frankie was going to be back doing cook
shows. She would pick up a Pulitzer and the Nobel Prize for
Espionage and crush his skull between them.

On the other hand . . .

On the other hand the timing was suspicious as hell. The
codes would have kept the Institute out, but of course Razy-Frazy
Frankie had friends in high places in WSHB. He might have been
monitoring her com all night. So he called her *now*, right after
Klaus did?

Pandora backed up, made one more check of that adorable
reflection, and said, *"Accept!"*

And right behind the window was the famous elm desk, in the

exact center of Frankie's opulent and garishly overdecorated office. Behind the famous desk was the famous face. Despite the barbarous hour, he was as smartly dressed as always, freshly shaved and dangerously confident. The deep tan was likely newly touched-up, and so perhaps was the trace of scarring on the cheekbones, the mark of the manly type who spends too much time outdoors. F.F. never went outdoors. His blond hair was most artfully coiffured—of course. Leaning expensive sleeves forward, he was wearing Grave Concern, one of his most effective expressions, normally reserved for minor flooding, or discouraging news on the latest disease.

"Good morning, Panda dearie." He knew how she detested that name.

She registered Bright Amusement. "Hello, Frank. You're up early. Bladder trouble again?"

"Well, I'm a little concerned. Have you completed those negotiations you were fretting about?" He had switched to Polite Interest Only, but he knew the answer. He even knew she knew he knew the answer.

"Oh, those?" She shrugged a Little Importance. "Yes, all done."

"Ah." He conveyed Trace of Regret. "How soon would you be able to actually *use* any of the stuff?"

Pandora fanned through a dozen scenarios in her mind. She could not quite discount the possibility that F.F. or someone in his faction might try to intercept Klaus. It would be treason, of course, but internal gut-spilling could sometimes be carried beyond proper limits. Some things should not be done inside the corporate family, but sometimes some things were.

So don't answer the question.

"Oh, we'll have to decide that at the conferences later today. I'm sure I can count on your cooperation . . ."

He raised an exquisitely manicured hand. "But the deal is complete? The money is gone? It's too late to back out now?"

Pandora felt the ice of terror meet the fire of fury, and did not know which one was going to win. It was like having dangerous revelations emerge during a live interview. Automatically she assumed a Mild Distaste.

"What are you getting at, Frankie?"

Frazer's infinitely spurious face wore an expression that could only be classed as Pontifical Infallibility. "The news conference. It's set for noon. I plan to attend, of course."

Ice won in a landslide. Pandora's hand found the back of a

chrome and cryspex chair, and she deflated onto it. "What news conference?"

For a tiny fraction of a second authentic emotion showed in Frazer's eyes. It was very nasty. Then blandness returned.

"Oh, had you not heard?"

"Heard what, Frankie?"

"The director herself! Old Mother Hubbard's invited the media to a reception. Her first news conference in twenty years. I confess I am curious to hear what the old coot has to say."

Klaus might arrive before noon, but there was no hope on Earth that Pandora could have the story ready to spin before then. All she could do was to follow news of the press conference with a stock "usually reliable sources believe that she will report . . ."

Ten million hectos, and Pandora had bought a couple of hours' rumor—which the other networks would steal away from her at once.

There could be no doubt why Hubbard had called a press conference. Pandora had already researched the figures and knew them by heart. In thirty years 4-I had contacted over fifty thousand worlds. About fifteen hundred had borne life of some form or other, but none had proved in the end to be human habitable. Nor had the Institute turned up any trace of sentience—until that stone ax. Only one of those two possible discoveries could justify a public announcement by the old woman herself, and they could hardly both happen in the same week, not after thirty years.

Scuppered!

Double-cross? How had the Institute known that WSHB knew?

"Do you want to come along with me, Panda dear?" Frazer Franklin asked, drooling syrup. "Or will you be laboring to deliver your billion-dollar baby?"

7

Nauc, April 7

"GIMME YOUR WATCH!"

"Huh?"

The chopper was still heading southeast with its sinister escort swooping around high overhead. Despite a hollow-eyed shortage of sleep, Cedric had been staring out the window with steadily growing excitement. Holos gave sight and sound, but reality was so much more—smells and vibration and the sense of motion. He marveled at the greenness of grass and leaves below the gray drizzle; it made Meadowdale seem like a desert. He had just registered that there was no new building in progress here. The towns were not abandoned, but they had a seedy, neglected look to them, so probably they did not have long to go. Then he had caught a whiff of an unfamiliar scent and decided that it must be the sea.

"You heard me, dummy. Your watch." The thick man had been brooding in silence for a long time and was glowering at Cedric's wrist.

Puzzled and distrustful, Cedric unclipped his watch and passed it over. Bagshaw put both thumbs on it and squeezed, setting his teeth with effort. The watch bent and split, and then spilled parts. Ignoring Cedric's yell of complaint, Bagshaw tossed it into a corner.

"What the hell, mister? Gran sent me that for my—"

The bull grunted. "Babysitter."

Cedric's fair skin tended to flush easily. He felt it do so now. Three times in the last year he had gone over the screens at Meadowdale—small wonder that his freedom had always been so short-lived. "Tracer? That was how you found me last night?"

Hooded eyes gleamed mockingly. "No. I do my own babysitting."

Cedric worked that out and it was even worse. He had behaved exactly as expected—likely they had not even had to call on System for a psychoplot. Sucker! How could he have been so stupid? He felt like a circus animal. He was going to meet his grandmother face to face at last, and now he wondered how he would hold up his head.

So full of shame that he could taste it, he went back to watching the landscape unrolling below, but the magic had gone clammy and sour. Sucker! Sucker! Sucker!

But if he had not ruined everything, what did Gran have planned for him? She had refused to be specific on the com, saying only that there was a job waiting. Rangers must need a long training program, and she had not mentioned training.

Bagshaw had gone back to his brooding, staring malevolently at the shimmer of oil rainbows in a dished floor panel.

Now the land was stark and wasted. The farthest reach of storm tides was marked by long ridges of debris, the remains of buildings and machinery. Cedric reminded himself that those had been people's homes, people's cars and possessions, hopes and dreams. Tree trunks, shattered asphalt, concrete rubble—those told of other damage. In places the piled refuse still smoked. He knew it was fired as soon as it dried out, because it always contained animal carcasses. Or worse. Every storm moved the ridges farther inland . . . and storms were still growing more frequent.

The desolation became worse—barren, salt-soaked flats where nothing grew. Lonely concrete ruins stood in forlorn defiance between oddly rectangular patches of swamp marking choked cellars. In places the ground had been stripped to bare bedrock.

"Why are we coming here?" Cedric demanded suspiciously. This could certainly not be the way to Headquarters.

Bagshaw roused himself from his scowling reverie and gestured idly northward. "Earthfirsters have a missile post thereabouts. Easier just to go around it."

Cedric gaped at him, trying to decide if Bagshaw was stringing him along. "They'd shoot at us?"

"At anything going in or coming out."

"They can get away with that?"

"Sure they can—until we get mad enough to send in gunships and burn their nest. Then they open up another. Crazy boneheads!"

Cedric swallowed his last crumb of pride. "Last night there was no fog on the holo. I saw things I'd never seen done before. I mean like sex. And the news had no foggy bits, either."

Bagshaw glanced at him and just nodded. Then he went back to staring at the floor, a hummock in a blanket.

"They censored our holo? Why?"

The blanket moved in a shrug. "Kids are easier to handle if you keep their minds off that stuff. Especially big kids."

Cedric clung tight to his new humility. "But the news? I never knew that Earthfirsters besieged the Institute. I've almost never heard of Earthfirsters."

Bagshaw gave him a curiously opaque stare. "There's probably a lot of things you don't know, Sprout."

"Like what?"

"It'd be quicker to list what you do know. Did they teach you anything other than skeet lasering?"

"Lots of things. Like farming and riding . . . canoeing and woodsmanship. Like rock climbing."

"You still got forests out west?"

"Some. In the drier parts. Desert trees resist UV, they say. The rain doesn't hurt alkali soils as bad."

"Not like forests used to be, I'll bet." Bagshaw scratched himself. "What good is all this outdoorsy stuff going to be to you? You going to be a cowboy when all the grass has died? More and more food has to be synthetic."

"I want to be a ranger," Cedric began, and wished he had not when he saw Bagshaw's lip twist.

"Ranger? Rangers don't go outdoors, sonny. They stay inside their skivs. Been watching too many holos, you have. *Stone of the Institute*? Or maybe *Ranger Stone and the Killer Cheese*. 'You will thrill as fearless Stone Craig battles the—'"

"Awright! What—"

But Bagshaw was enjoying himself. "You know what *skiv* means?"

"Self-Contained Investigatory Vehicle."

"So? Self-contained! No sane ranger leaves his skiv unless he must. He reads dials and keeps the equipment running and that's all."

"Tell Devlin Grant that!" Cedric said hotly. "Or Baker Abel! Or Jackson Wilbur!"

"Okay. A few. But I know a lot o' rangers. Mostly they're a dull bunch. They're only cabbies for the big shots—the plane-tologists, geologists, and so on. The rangers spend most of their duty time lying around watching holo coins or playing craps. Believe me, I have that on good authority. Can you read?"

"Of course!" But Cedric felt his face warm up again.

Bagshaw wrinkled his dermsym in wry amusement. "And write?"

"Yes."

"Well, or just so-so?"

"Well! Well enough!" But Cedric knew he could not compare with Madge, say, or Ben, at reading and writing. He was much better than most of the kids at Meadowdale, though. No one had ever taught him. He had picked up reading from watching holo, and big words really bothered him. He could write his name and not much more, picking out the keys with one finger. He had always meant to start practicing in earnest, but somehow there had just never been time.

Bagshaw looked skeptical and laughed.

"What of it?" Cedric demanded, angry that the big man could so easily make him feel angry. "I saw a Frazer Frankie special last week that said half the Ph.D.s in the country can't read'n'write."

"Including that slime Frazer himself, I'd think."

Cedric turned back to the window. The copter was curving over the sea, a wide bay dotted with ruins.

"Ranger's gotta be able to read, though," Bagshaw said, "be-cause a skiv can't carry much of a System. Ranging's chicken work, Sprout. It's not exciting and dangerous; it's just dull and dangerous. Stay home and watch it on the holos—you'll see as much as they do from the skivs, anyway. And it's risky."

"Yeah, but how risky?" Cedric was skeptical. "Really—how risky?"

"About one party in fifty."

"Bull!"

"No bull. Not killer cheddar, just broken strings. Next win-dow comes due, and the techs punch in the numbers, and there's nothing there, no world at those coordinates. It happens. Tough if you happen to be overnighting!"

"Maybe overnighting's risky," Cedric conceded. "But how

often do they overnight, though? Surely that's only done if a planet's really got something exciting?"

Bagshaw shrugged. "It's done a lot oftener than they let out. But even quickies can be dangerous. Suddenly there's instability—and if you don't get your ass back here real fast, the window may be gone. And that's it, Sprout! They never find a broken string again. When a world's lost, it's lost. Creepin' rotten way to die."

Cedric was gazing out at the bay but not seeing much. He was thinking of parents he could not remember. He always felt guilty about that, always felt that there should be something there, some vague baby memory of giant smiling faces. But there was nothing.

"So maybe ranging isn't romantic," he said, and felt like a traitor as he did so. "But it's important! We've got to find a Class One world. Even if the worst of the troubles is over—"

"What makes you say that?"

Holo did. Cedric had gotten his own set when Clyde left and he became eldest, and he had been watching all kinds of educational stuff. "The ozone's started to come back—"

"Wrong. The ozone's stopped getting less. That's not the same thing at all."

Why should this beef tub know anything about that? "The ozone was destroyed mostly by fluorocarbons," Cedric said firmly. "And we stopped using them a long time ago."

"True, but all the junk they put up there back last century is still there—still hard at work, catalyzing merrily. We're down to a basic equilibrium now. If it's going up at all, it's going up so slowly it'll take centuries to get us back to where we were."

The copter had crossed the bay and was over land again, rows of shabby houses, each set in a patch of bare mud or rank weeds. Cedric looked away quickly. "And the transmensor's done away with fossil fuels, so we're not stuffing all that CO_2 in the air anymore."

"Oh, yes," Bagshaw said. "Thank God for the transmensor. But it's too late now, Sprout. The damage is done. The CO_2 caused the greenhouse effect, and that screwed up the weather and melted the ice." His voice grew angrier and louder, although he had already been shouting over the engine. "And it feeds on itself now. Plants are the only thing that can take CO_2 out of the air, at least on our time scale, and look what we've done to plant life! Zapped it with ultraviolet, burned it with acid rain, starved it with soil erosion, poisoned it with pollution, shriveled it with drought, drowned it with too much rain there, cut down the forests . . ."

"Tropical forests just ran a rot and grow cycle and—"

Cedric was shouted down.

"But those forests weathered the rocks they grew on, and that gets the carbon out of the air, and they held down a lot of soil that's mostly gone into the sea now, and the seas took a lot of CO_2 out of circulation, too, and we're still poisoning the seas. The weather's gone mad, and every storm removes some more plant life or more soil for it to grow in. Hurricanes in January? *Any* change in climate hurts vegetation, laddie! Species after species is just giving up, and each one takes others with it. So the CO_2 level's still rising, and there's enough of it in the air to do a powerful lot more damage. The ocean's going to keep on rising. We still don't know when the Earth's going to find a new equilibrium, or where. It'll take thousands of years to get back to where we were.

"Furthermore—" He thumped a fingertip on Cedric's chest. "—the fall in population isn't matching the drop in arable land, and the Cancer Curve keeps—"

He stopped suddenly—the copilot had twisted around to watch, then grinned and turned away again. Bagshaw scowled like a constipated gorilla.

"So where did you learn all this?" Cedric demanded, trying not to believe as much as he did. Real world now—don't trust anyone!

Bagshaw grunted. He seemed ashamed of his outburst.

"That's one of the things they kept from us at Meadowdale?" Cedric asked.

"Naw. It's kept from most everyone. Talk like that and you're called an alarmist."

"The Institute?"

"Not many even there," Bagshaw muttered. "See, I'm—I was—pairing with an ecologist. Till recently. She told me. They don't like to frighten people, but she told me."

His manner had changed completely, and Cedric sensed something left unsaid. "It's that bad?"

Bagshaw nodded in silence.

"So we need a Class One world desperately!"

The motor changed its note. The copter was starting to lose altitude.

"Guess so." The sneer crawled back into place. "Then they'll send for you to do the canoeing. Maybe that's the job your grannie's got in mind for you."

Cedric turned his head to watch the fast-approaching ground. There were still six billion people left on earth, though. Transmensor windows were always short, and eventually any string ran out. How many people could you move to your Class One world if you found it?

And which ones?

"What's that?" He pointed down at high wire fences and watch towers. Armed guards were inspecting vehicles at a gate.

"The Institute."

Cedric had never dreamed that such precautions would be needed in Nauc.

"That's just the outer fence," Bagshaw said. "There are two more." The copilot was jabbering into his mike, identifying himself.

"But . . ." Cedric stared at his companion in bewilderment. "If HQ is guarded like this . . . Does it work?"

Bagshaw was in Security. Of course he would say it worked. "Completely. There has been no successful penetration in seventeen years—not in Zone One, anyway."

Cedric shook his head, hurt and baffled. "Then why Meadowdale? Why did she send me there when my folks died? Wouldn't I have been just as safe growing up here?"

"Safe from violence, maybe. But there's other nasty things, that even Security can't keep out."

"Like what?"

"Drugs. Disease. Debauchery." Bagshaw grinned mockingly.

Cedric chewed a thumbnail. "And understanding?"

"Yucch! Know something? You're getting contaminated already!"

The sheer size of HQ was astounding. It was a small city in itself. As the helicopter angled in for a landing, Cedric saw tower after tower, obviously including both offices and apartments, plus canopied playgrounds, an STOL field, and local lev stations. Yet Bagshaw said that it was not especially large, not as HQ's went; not when compared to some of the multinationals', like BEST Place, or Greenpeace Township, or the various media centers. After all, 4-I was only a minor research facility, an arm of Stellar Power, Inc.

If you believed that, Cedric thought, then you'd believe that rainwater's good for you.

This was HQ, Bagshaw added, the political and fiscal end of things. The real work was done in Cainsville, up in Labrador. That was much bigger. And Gran ran all this? Cedric had never realized.

By the time they landed, Bagshaw had donned his bull suit again—probably the easiest way to transport it. Cedric's percy remained on the floor. He felt very vulnerable and shivery as he jumped down onto concrete in the misty rain to find himself facing a circle of armored men, and another fusion cannon pointing at him—he ought to be getting used to that by now. His only consolation was that Bagshaw seemed unconcerned, and even a bull suit would not stop a plasma jet. Apparently this was a standard welcome.

The newcomers were escorted across to a doorway, and then the real trials began. Bagshaw cheerfully relinquished Cedric as though he were delivering pizza, blew into a sniffer to establish his identity, and then departed. His great bulk seemed to fill the corridor from wall to wall. Surprisingly, Cedric was sorry to see him go. The man was sarcastic and offensive, but since falling seventeen stories into his arms, Cedric was inclined to trust him.

His new owner was saturnine, cadaverous, and not much shorter than Cedric himself. He gave no name, but his white coat was labeled McEwan. He was middle-aged and bored; his obvious indifference hurt more than Bagshaw's sarcasm.

The first exercise was to establish that Hubbard Cedric Dickson was truly Hubbard Cedric Dickson. A sniffer matched his exhalations against records that must have come from Meadowdale, or from hospital records of his birth. Fingerprints, footprints, and DNA came next, and then he was told to speak his name, confirming his truthfulness with a polygraph cuff and vocal stress patterns. When he had passed all those tests, the last two armed men departed, looking disappointed.

"Why not retinas?" Cedric asked, but no one bothered to answer.

The ensuing medical outdid any ordeal he had ever experienced, involving a dozen people and a hundred complex machines. They began by removing his clothes and continued by systematically stripping away every last shred of human dignity, as only medics could, stopping just short of skinning and gutting.

With increasing reluctance, he submitted to the escalating humiliations until he discovered that his entire alimentary canal was to be explored in detail. It was not easy to be assertive when crouched on a table in the nude surrounded by several strangers, but at that news he lost his temper. "Why?" he shouted. "I've never been sick in my life."

"That's not what we're looking for," one of the women said from somewhere in the background. "Take a deep breath and try to relax."

"Then what is all this—ouch!—all this about?"

"We just want to be certain," McEwan said.

"Certain of—Ouch! Hell! That hurts!—certain of what?"

"Certain that the Sierra Club has not packed you full of explosives, that you contain no Greenpeace transmitters, Earthfirster receivers, BEST's little silicon wonders, unaccountable radioactive materials, custom-designed viruses, or toxic wastes. Little things like that."

"Do try to relax," the woman said.

And once they had counted and tagged every corpuscle, they made a small incision behind his ear and drove a screw into his skull. That was an earpatch, they told him, so that System could talk to him in private. System was fortunate, Cedric thought, that it could not hear his feelings at the moment.

When all that was over he was sent to a cubicle to dress—a sop to modesty that seemed strangely unnecessary after his public ordeal. He had never worn formal city clothes before. He had known that he would have to do so in Nauc, and the outfit hanging there was worse even than he had feared. System knew his size, of course—System no doubt knew the size and shape of every organ in his body by now—so the fit was perfect. Perfect fit in a business suit meant no room to breathe. Formal clothes fitted tighter than skin. That was okay, Cedric supposed. But the color was an eye-jarring fluorescent green. Hideous!

As he heaved the last zipper closed and straightened up to regard himself in the mirror, the drape over the door was thrown aside.

"Great Merciful Heavens—the leek that ate Denver!" Bagshaw was resplendent in an equally snug uniform of brick red, and Cedric suppressed a comment that his bodyguard resembled a mutant beetroot. Neither of them looked good in skintight suits, he thought, but scrawny was surely no worse than bulging. Bagshaw carried his fearsome Hardwave slung on his shoulder, and he sported several impressive badges. His bald scalp was concealed by a red helmet.

"I could eat a fair piece of Denver about now," Cedric remarked hopefully.

"Your decision. Next thing we have to do is code you into System, but I was told that Grandma's waiting to meet her darling. You decide, after this." Bagshaw wheeled and strode away. A few oversize strides put Cedric level with him.

"What happened to my coins?"

"The data will be inserted into System keyed to your voice, file name 'Baby Talk.' The originals will be destroyed."

"Why? You frightened that they might be booby-trapped, too?"

"They were."

"What?"

Bagshaw glanced up at him with a grimace. "Physically you were clean, but not your coins. We'll be finding out who arranged that, and how. We ran a decon program on them. They were hot. In here."

Computer viruses? Who could have tampered with Cedric's coins? No one. There comes a time when a man just stops believing . . .

"Speak your name," said the tall, saturnine man in the coat named McEwan. He was seated at a comset that seemed more complex than most.

"Hubbard Cedric Dickson."

"In command mode." McEwan was obviously eager to be off doing something else. Rapidly he ran through a routine to introduce Cedric to the Institute's System. Its responses all seemed much the same as Meadowdale's, except its voice was male and had an Eastern accent. It had no trouble distinguishing the intonation of Cedric's command tone. He was given a wrist mike.

"Up in Cainsville you're almost never more than a few steps from a wall unit," McEwan explained in a fast monotone. "Confidential replies come through the earpatch. Confidential questions you input with a keyboard, right?"

"Right." Cedric was careful not to catch Bagshaw's eye.

"You do understand about ranking?"

"He doesn't understand anything," Bagshaw said.

The tall man frowned as though he also was long overdue for breakfast. "There are nine grades. As a beginner you'll probably start as a Nine, but you may have a work grade that's higher, depending on what they give you to do. You'll learn that later."

Cedric had learned one thing already: that he was going to be asking a lot of questions. "What's the difference?"

"You're not supposed to use the higher rank for personal prying."

"Who knows?"

"System does, of course, and your supervisor will be informed. Look . . . say I'm a Five—"

"Not a chance," Bagshaw remarked nastily. "I'm only a Six, and I sure as hell outrank you."

McEwan shot him a glance of powerful distaste. "All right, I'm a Seven. I can call Six-level data, though, if I need it for my job. Sometimes system will ask me to justify my request." He turned to the com and asked in command tone: *"What grade is Hubbard Cedric Dickson?"*

"Information confidential below Grade Three," System told them.

"See? You'll have to ask it yourself."

"What grade am I?" Cedric inquired.

Through the bones of his skull came a spectral reply: "Four."

"What did it say?" McEwan asked innocently.

Cedric might be dressed as a two-meter leprechaun, but he was not green enough to answer that query—not after Bagshaw's careful hint. "Nine," he lied. *"What's my work ranking?"*

Again the hollow voice echoed in his head, creepy but quite distinguishable—and completely unbelievable.

"Eight," he told the waiting men. He might have hidden his shock from McEwan, but Bagshaw was appraising him with eyes like awls.

"Where now, Sprout? Hotcakes, bacon, steak, coffee, toast, eggs—or Grandma?"

Cedric shrugged sadly. "What big teeth you have."

"Right!" Bagshaw wheeled and headed off along the corridor. Cedric followed blindly, wondering if this was a test, wondering again what was in store for him, and totally unable to imagine what sort of job he could handle that would require a Grade One ranking on System.

8

HASTINGS WILLOUGHBY HAD not ridden in a percy since being blown up in one, back in 2036. On that occasion his leg bones had been reduced to gravel and later replaced by synfab, but he had not felt right down there since. He rarely traveled at all anymore, and when he did he preferred a cavalcade of armored Caddies. In any case, other people usually came to call on him. He was Secretary General.

Any message from Agnes carried supreme priority, and that morning he had been awakened at dawn to receive one. It had come in one of their private codes, a code simple enough to require only a pocket computer. Even the smartest Systems still had trouble with homonyms, and the text he finally deciphered said merely, "Cum heer gude noos."

Come here—good news? Come, hear good news?

It had taken even Willoughby some time to work that out. Only when his regular early-morning briefing told him of the media reception she had scheduled for noon did he understand. She wanted him there, but she was not about to tell him why. The cloaking-and-daggering might be to tell him that it was important without saying so over a public com. Or she might be playing some sort of double game.

Even God would never guess at what devious mischief Agnes

66

might get up to. Willoughby ranked her as one of the greatest schemers the world had ever known; he felt privileged to have worked with her for so many years, and the thought of observing her in action just one more time was irresistible. Moreover, in an odd sort of way he still felt affection for Hubbard Agnes Murray. No one else had ever bested him at bedroom politics. Certainly no one else could summon him like a whistled dog, as she still could.

Within seconds of receiving enlightenment, therefore, Willoughby had made his decision, summoned transportation, and canceled a dozen scheduled commeetings. He chuckled when he saw the squad of bleary, half-shaven, half-zipped bulls that gathered to escort him. One of the prerogatives of power had always been the right to rattle one's subordinates. Some men took it as a duty.

His Caddy had hardly crossed the outermost mine field before he began to have second thoughts. Cold introspection soon told him he was indulging in self-deception. He was not rushing to Agnes's side to assist her, nor out of old friendship, nor—truly—to observe her in action one more time. He was going there in the hope that she had found a lifeboat and would make room in it for him. He should have called her first and argued. To seem too eager might arouse her suspicions.

He was old and tired, and he needed solace. Folly, folly! No one appealed for help to Hubbard Agnes. She despised weakness. If she concluded that he had become too feeble to be a reliable ally, she would turn on him herself. Possibly she already had, and he was heading to his own execution.

The sharks were closing. He had known it for months, and this time he could see no raft to hand. China was poised to recognize the World Chamber. Then the U.N. would vanish overnight, or at least as soon as Cheung Olsen Paraschuk had called and won a global election. When the U.N. went, so would Hastings Willoughby; and so, too, would Hubbard Agnes. She must see the danger as well as he did. There was the real reason he was so eagerly answering her call—for comfort, to be told that once again she had found a plan that would save them both.

Sprawled out across the seat at full length, he gloomed for a long while in lonely luxury, ignoring the cityscape hurtling by, debating whether he dared cancel and return. Inevitably he concluded that to start displaying indecision would only make things worse.

It was a fine day: the rain was classed as "harmless," and the

UV flux was as low as it ever got at that time of year. He saw endless miles of shanty towns, and estuaries that had once been valleys, and salt marsh that had once been farmland. None of them warmed his blue mood. He watched holo. He received bulletins from his office. The Indian government in Delhi had announced that it was withdrawing its U.N. delegation and allowing elections for Chamber representation. But the Delhi government controlled little or none of the country, and the other claimants had been Chamber supporters for years. One of the two rival Japanese governments might follow; that would be more serious.

Nor did his first glimpse of Institute HQ do anything to banish his sulks—it all looked so old now. Many of the buildings dated from the early twenties. By the time 4-I had been born, the need for cities to move to higher ground had been obvious, and thus, unlike most other large organizations, the Institute had never been forced into a massive relocation. Its shabbiness was one more reminder of the years that had died since Hastings Willoughby and Hubbard Agnes had together lifted the world by the scruff of its neck and shaken a little sense into it—not enough sense, but some.

The Institute was old, more than thirty years old, and he had already been into his fifties when he slid its charter through an unsuspecting General Assembly one sleepy August afternoon. He could still remember the bulging veins, the purpling complexion on old DeJong, who had been S.G. then.

"I turn mine back for one hour," the fat Dutchman had screamed. But by then the deed had been done. The charter for Stellar Power had been approved, Agnes installed as director.

A few years later she had applied enough bribery to return the favor, pulling strings to install Willoughby in DeJong's chair.

The good old days, alas!

He was old. He would cheerfully retire in a day, except he knew he would be dead in a week. He had made far too many enemies.

Age showed in his sagging belly, pitilessly revealed by the present fashion for absurdly tight clothes. Surgery would help, of course, had he not sickened of surgeons long ago. Modern sartorial engineers could do wonders, but he was old-fashioned enough to despise their mechanized corsets as shameless fakery. So he stayed his own prehistoric shape.

He showed age also in petty irritation at having to wait until the security forces completed their inevitable wrangling. U.N.

cops in sky blue, 4-I's in dark red—bulls well named, they glowered at one another, huffing and puffing and pawing the rug. Legal fantasy made him the director's superior, and inevitably that fiction prolonged the dispute. The arguments were settled at last in the way they always were—his own guards could accompany him, but they must go unarmed, and a batch of 4-I's goons would in turn "guard" them.

Age showed even in his foolish embarrassment when his false bones rang scan alarms, as they always did, requiring explanation. And when at last he limped along the corridor, peering over the heads of a dozen angry young grizzlies, he was very conscious of a steady click from his right knee. His prostheses were aging, too.

The decor was outmoded, almost shabby. Even new it had been little more than adequate, he recalled, and now the executive suite of the world's richest organization seemed blowsy and cheap and old-fashioned. Agnes had never cared much for ostentation. One day some unscrupulous whippersnapper would seize power and clean house. Then she would be gone, and probably Hasting Willoughby also, at much the same time. They had climbed to power on the same rope, and they would fall in the same coup, leaving nothing but their names collecting static in libraries.

He was ushered at last into the big, familiar, five-sided office. How many of the current day's rebels would recognize the deliberate irony in that design? If she had changed the carpet since he had last been there, then she had stayed with the same bland peach, and the ebony pentagonal table in the center was still the only large piece of furniture.

Agnes came forward to greet him. She was wearing powder blue, as she so often did, to match her eyes, and her outfit could only be a Kaing original, or perhaps a Dom Lumi. Her hair was pure white, her gaze as sharp as ever, and her appearance immaculate. She had weathered well, but then Agnes's dislike of ostentation had never extended to personal grooming. Her facial texture would have flattered a woman a generation younger, and modern medicine had preserved her figure.

"Mr. Secretary General, this is indeed an honor." She offered both hands. Her fingers showed her age, though.

"I am a little early, I fear, Director..."

The flunkies departed, the door was closed. He leaned over, keeping his weight off that tricky right knee and touching dry lips to well-moisturized cheek. Then she was all business as usual, waving him to a seat at the table and taking one close by.

He felt very conscious of the bloodless appraisal behind the business-grade smile. As always, she wore a faint aura of impatience, as though she had already foreseen everything that anyone else was going to say and had long since made the right decision on the matter anyway.

"You look as lovely as ever, Agnes. Not a day over forty."

"Rot. It must be five years since you were here." She spoke with more emphasis than he had expected.

"Three and a bit. And we met at the NASA Embassy, remember?"

"So we did. Well, we have a moment before the conference— I am flattered to see I still have the power to bring you running. *File for attention next week.*"

The last remark had been to System, in reply to some private query. She would not stop working just because she had a visitor. It was a widely-used technique, but he had never met anyone who did it better than Agnes, and she faked it less than most. Back in her younger days, Agnes had been able to read eight hundred words a minute and listen to a three-way conversation at the same time.

"Blame it on my insatiable curiosity," he said.

Two of the five walls were floor-to-ceiling holos, displaying incredible vistas of peaks shrouded in pale pink ice, beetling against a violet sky—undoubtedly recorded on some world of lower gravity than Earth. The room was an eyrie perched high above the darkling valley. Willoughby leaned back and regarded her with sudden amusement.

"Why the senile leer?" she inquired acidly.

"Remember skiing? I never thought of it before, but these absurdly tight clothes we have to endure nowadays are almost exactly what we used to wear for skiing when we were kids."

"When I was a kid, you were not. Besides, throughout history, recreational style for clothes has become formal costume a couple of generations later."

"I didn't know that!"

"Well, you do now. Thank you for coming, Will."

"But you're not going to tell me why?"

Compared to Agnes, the sphinx was an open book. "Trust me."

"The last hundred men who did that are long dead."

"Nonsense," she said. "Some of them have barely stopped bleeding."

He laughed—time had not blunted her. But he knew her ways well enough to guess that she was suppressing some strong emotion. The sharpness of her voice was one sign; the way she kept tightening her lips was another. Nothing trivial would so disturb Hubbard Agnes. Big stakes today, then.

"You have the holo channels humming like hornets," he said, probing gently. "Goodson Jason says it's a Class One world at last. Eccles Pandora is claiming you've uncovered sentience, and everyone else thinks asepsis has been broken—monsters have escaped and are eating Labrador."

She shook her head in impatient disbelief. *"Refer to Security."*

"If you're planning to retire, then I refuse to accept your resignation."

He should not have said that. She eyed him with a sharper appraisal yet. "Your presence naturally makes the occasion more solemn, Will. I should warn you, though—your dignity may suffer."

He turned that ominous remark over several times before answering it. God alone knew what was about to happen, then. "Do I come out ahead in the end?"

She shrugged. She was still a fine figure of a woman, and she had to be well over seventy.

"I hope so. There are risks."

"I never knew one of your schemes not to contain risks. I've watched you skirt the jaws of disaster a hundred times."

She pursed her lips again. "I think you tangled your metaphors, there."

"Give me a clue."

Her eyes narrowed, and suddenly he wondered if what she was hiding might be anger. He had never known her to allow emotion to influence her actions, but he could see that she was jumpy about something.

"Cuthionamine lysergeate."

"Never heard of it—wait! LSD? Isn't that something lysergic?"

She nodded, surprised. "Ergot fungus? That fits. There's fungus involved in this ... Well, all will be revealed in due course."

To ask for more would be futile. For a moment they sat in a silence that neither wished to break. Then suddenly Agnes said, "Would more money help?"

He shook his head. "I'd have asked. We've bought everyone except the fanatics. There are too many fanatics, that's all."

Senility had not yet reached Hubbard Agnes. Her mind went to the heart of things like a harpoon. "The Chamber? That self-proclaimed gang of shysters? The elections are all rigged! Besides, it has no legal standing whatsoever, and never had."

"Nor do we, really," he reminded her. "Unilateral abolition of the Security Council was a very shaky move."

"That was long before your time. *Send him in*."

He chuckled. "Why is time relevant?"

She dismissed that argument with a toss of her head, and then suddenly uttered a rueful laugh that surprised him. "You have Cheung and the Chamber. I have Grundy and BEST."

"They're in cahoots, of course."

She nodded. "Probably. But this time it's gone too far—I have a score to settle!"

He shivered at the look in her eye. He had a sudden vision of Agnes with a stiletto, counting ribs. Whose ribs? He could not shake an uneasy suspicion that they might be his.

The door opened. She rose, almost concealing a smile. "Forget them for now. There is someone you must meet."

"Who's that?"

"Your grandson."

Who? "I never... You mean John and Rita..."

But Agnes was already advancing to the door. A massive red-clad bull had entered and was looking around in proper form to confirm that his client might enter safely.

"Dr. Bagshaw!" Agnes reached out two hands in greeting, a personal trademark.

The bull, naturally, looked astonished. "Yes, Director?" That brute could never be any relative of his, Willoughby decided, and was certainly too old to be John's son.

Agnes had clasped his great fists in her thin fingers. She dropped her voice until Willoughby caught only a few scattered phrases. "... only met her once... Christmas party... talked at length..."

The man's face was rigid as a granite boulder, and his voice was a gritty rumble. "Thank you, Director."

"We all share your sense of loss—and outrage."

"Deputy Fish tells me that the matter is not closed yet?"

"It certainly is not."

He nodded, and for a moment the two of them held their pose, eyes and hands locked. Whatever else was being said did not require words. Her ability to enslave men had not faded with age; if this one had not been a devotee before, he certainly was now.

Then a green-clad youth ducked through the doorway and stepped around the guard like something emerging from Sherwood Forest—possibly one of the trees. He smiled nervously down at Agnes. He was very skinny and enormously tall, even taller than Willoughby himself. His brush of tawny hair had apparently missed its daily appointment with a comb, making him seem even taller. Every bone showed through an expensively tailored suit of a screaming green color that suggested its wearer must be color blind.

John and Rita's son?

Possible, Willoughby thought, just possible; but whatever Mother Hubbard is up to with this unfortunate youngster, she is not telling the truth, the whole truth, or anything like the truth.

The bull departed, evidently reassured by those cryptic condolences. The gangling kid received the icy blue-eyed smile and the two-handed greeting. He hesitated, then stooped awkwardly to place a kiss on the upturned cheek. Agnes was a tall woman, but she did not reach his shoulder.

"You had an interesting journey, I hear, Cedric."

He blushed in deepening waves of scarlet. "I'm sorry, Gran. Truly, I—"

"Sorry? What is there to be sorry about?" Agnes turned and headed back to the table.

"I didn't do what you said . . ."

"Of course not. No real man would. I'm glad to see that my grandson is not a ninny."

"Oh!" He grinned in wide juvenile relief and took a couple of long steps to catch up with her. Then he noticed Willoughby.

"You know who this is, Cedric?"

He started to shake his head, but there were some faces everyone knew. He gulped audibly. "The Secre—sir!" He almost bowed. Then realization struck, and all the color drained from his bony face, leaving a faint sediment of faded freckles. "Hastings Willoughby? My father . . ." He looked at his grandmother—the woman he thought was his grandmother, at least. Willoughby was not so sure.

"Your father was Hubbard John Hastings. This is your grandfather."

Willoughby pushed himself to his feet, taking his time. They shook hands.

The kid had calluses, dirty fingernails, and an unthinkingly powerful grip. "I am honored, sir. I never knew!" His eyes were very wide; gray eyes, like John's, and they held an understandable hurt.

"Neither did I, lad. Agnes . . . explain!"

That was another shock, of course, and Willoughby wondered if the old vixen appreciated what she was doing to her wretched victim, God help him. He was very young to withstand such treatment.

She might not have expected him to hear the truth blurted out so brutally, but she recovered easily. "Your father and his father were not on friendly terms, Cedric. So it is true that Dr. Hastings was never informed of your existence. I respected your parents' wishes, but now that you are no longer a child, of course, you must make your own decisions."

With no visible effort, she contrived to seat all three of them in almost a straight line, with the kid in the middle. This was to be a massacre of the innocent, but just to sit and watch her in action felt like the good old days. Willoughby was almost glad he had come.

"I am very honored to have two such distinguished ancestors, Grandmother . . . Grandfather . . ." The lad's head was snapping from side to side, as he tried to deal with an impossible situation. "Tell me about my mother's family?"

"You can get all that from System," Agnes said firmly. *"Begin the commeeting."*

Then she stopped talking—the silence test. Willoughby was busily trying to analyze her play, but old age must have been slowing him, for he was making no progress. The presence of the supposed grandson made a difference to him—she had warned him that his dignity might be in jeopardy. He felt much less happy now about being included in whatever sensation she was plotting. If he withdrew, would that turn her against him? Would it upset her plans? And was that young beanpole really his grandson?

He wondered how many games she was running simultaneously. The curious regrets to the guard, the epoch-making press conference, the sudden revelation of a putative grandson—were those independent or related? And where did the unpronounceable chemical come in? Or Grundy Julian Wagner and his Brotherhood of Engineers, Scientists, and Technicians?

As the silence dragged on, the youngster twisted restlessly, looking from one to the other, white-knuckling the arms of his chair. His Adam's apple bobbed several times before he spoke. "You have a job for me here, Gran?"

"Yes. Some media relations work, I thought."

With great difficulty, Willoughby stiffled a laugh. Agnes's media relations were the worst on the planet, and she liked them that way. Tendons tensed in the kid's stringy neck, but he was not cowed yet.

"I have always hoped to become a ranger like my father, Grandmother."

Ranger? What garbage had the old woman been feeding the kid all these years?

"So you've told me often enough!" Agnes said with distaste. "It must run in the family, then. It was your father's fixation on that which led to his quarrel with your grandfather."

There was a remarkable absence of truth in the conversation, but if Willoughby began throwing denials around, he might spoil whatever Agnes was up to. The kid was easy meat—far too easy for her to be bothering with for his own sake, so she was cooking him up for some other table. Cedric had swung around to look apprehensively at his alleged grandfather; he suddenly frowned, rose, moved his chair back two paces, and sat down again. A little late, but not bad under the circumstances.

"Can you read and write, Cedric?" Agnes inquired brusquely.

"Of course." His knuckles whitened again.

Certainly Agnes had been keeping this unreported grandson— if that was what he was—under wraps, and almost certainly at an organage. Green was an appropriate color for him, then. It was astonishing the kid could even talk in sentences.

"That's good! What I had in mind was some public relations work. The Cheavers report that you are very personable. You were well liked by everyone—from ranch hands to small children."

Hubbard Cedric reddened and squirmed as any young male would under such torment. "But, Gran—"

"To give you an example," Agnes said firmly, "a lot of important visitors call on us. There's a princess arriving here shortly. Someone has to squire her around. That sort of thing. She's about your age."

The boy's mouth sprang open as though he were being throttled, but Willoughby did not hear whatever sounds emerged. Another piece in play! He could guess where that princess came from, and so he knew at least one of the games in progress. He was amazed that the old harridan would dare attract media notice at such a time. She was obviously plotting a diversion—something outrageous. His skin prickled. He must be crazy to trust

Hubbard Agnes when she was in this mood. She was capable of anything.

With a *ping*! of warning, a hologram appeared on the far side of the table—a short, plump man with hair gleaming like black steel and a pudgy face as pale as cream.

"Ah . . . Cedric," Agnes said. "I want you to meet the senior staff. This is Deputy Director Fish, in charge of Security."

Cedric sprang to his feet and leaned across to offer a hand before he realized that he was making a fool of himself.

"Good morning, Mr. Secretary General," Fish's image said in a voice like oil—oil of vitriol, perhaps. "And Mr. Hubbard? I hope we can meet in the flesh soon. Will you be coming up to Cainsville in the near future?"

Crimson-faced, Cedric said, "Er . . ."

He looked at Agnes, who said, "Tomorrow."

"Tomorrow, sir."

Fish Lyle was as mild and inscrutable as a bowl of milk. He peered across at Cedric through thick glasses that likely served no purpose except to frustrate any clear view of his eyes. He was devoted to Agnes. He was also one of only three men in the world whom Hastings Willoughby truly feared, a slick assassin with a silk-smooth smile.

The mutual greetings had hardly ended when another *ping*! produced another holo and the greetings began again.

The new image was that of Moore Rudolph. He was faded and dessicated now, but he had always been unobtrusive—a brilliant accountant and operator of the greatest graft net the universe had ever known. The fires of stars flowed in through the transmensor at Cainsville to power all human civilization, and Willoughby had once calculated that at least a tenth of the proceeds were distributed illicitly by Moore's unseen hands. For a quarter of a century that flood of corruption had helped keep them all—and especially Willoughby—on top of the world heap.

Agnes ruled 4-I through a team of aides commonly known as the four horsemen. The door swung open to admit another—after her bull had inspected the room, of course. In her youth, Wheatland Mary had been an embodiment of the Earth Mother. Huge and black and voluptuous, she had conveyed to every man she had ever met the understanding that she wanted to rape him as soon as possible. It had all been a fake—U.N. Security, which knew everything, insisted that she was still a virgin, even now.

As Willoughby rose to greet her in old-fashioned courtesy, he wondered if women lasted so much better than men did only because they spent more money on repairs, or if the cause was deeper. Age had not withered Wheatland Mary. Her joyful roars of welcome filled the room, her massive arms were outstretched, and an infinite smile spread over her plump ebony face as she flounced across to envelop him in a rib-cracking embrace that proclaimed to the world that they must be fervent lovers. He wondered how he would have reacted had he not been expecting this.

"Good to see you again, Will," she repeated several times, still clutching him like ivy, pressing her cheek against his chest, thumping his back. "It's been much too long! Good to see you . . ."

She broke loose at last and turned to the wide-eyed, wide-mouthed Cedric. "Oh, aren't you gorgeous! Come to Mama, sonny!" When he courageously stepped forward into her embrace, she gave him much the same treatment. Willoughby tried to estimate what the effect would have been on him at the kid's age, but the very idea trashed his mind. Probably Agnes had planned all this.

Was the lad being tested? Tested for what, and why? Tested for whose benefit? Certainly not his own. Willoughby thought of an old technical term from his college days and shivered at the memory: *tested to destruction*.

Wheatland Mary's arrival left one to come, one whom Willoughby had never met. The Institute's original Deputy for Operations, Bieber Marvin, was two years in his grave. That was another sign that time was rolling on. His replacement was . . . Willoughby had forgotten the man's name.

Cedric had not. He had been visibly impressed by meeting so many powerful people—understandably so, for Agnes and her band of helpers would impress anyone—but when another guard had glanced around and withdrawn to admit a fourth deputy director, the kid looked ready to fall on his knees.

Tall and broad, brazenly moustachioed, and immaculate in rangers' safari denims, Devlin Grant was a self-made legend. Unlike Agnes, he was a master of media relations. Explorer of a dozen exotic worlds, hero of fierce battles against carefully holographed monsters, Devlin had been the only possible replacement for Bieber. Without waiting for an introduction, he strode forward to squeeze Willoughby's hand too hard and boom that he was honored. And then he turned his charisma on young Cedric like a battle-ax.

"Hear you're a marksman," he said. "A sharpshooter?"

The boy nodded rapidly, obviously overwhelmed that the great man should have heard of him at all. "I've done some lasering, sir."

"Grant! Call me Grant. That's great! When're you coming up to Cainsville, Cedric?"

"Tomorrow—Grant."

Devlin winked, faking a punch at the lad's shoulder, man-to-man. "How about a little trophy collecting? We usually have a good game world on tap. Big game. *Very* big game! Things that make dinosaurs look like rabbits—"

"Grant, that's not teaching my grandson proper respect for regulations." But Agnes did not seem very disapproving.

"Ah . . . right! Regulations! Can't allow private hunting parties, now, can we?" Devlin winked even more broadly, and Cedric's eyes glowed.

Willoughby decided that he did not care for Devlin Grant, Great Explorer and Mighty Hunter.

The projections of Moore and Fish remained patiently seated at the far side of the big table. The real Wheatland and Devlin edged unobtrusively toward chairs, gently excluding Cedric and Willoughby.

Agnes smiled graciously. "System tells me that the media persons have arrived, Will. Would you and Cedric like to go down? I'll join you in a moment. I need a quick word here."

"Of course," Willoughby said resignedly. He felt a tingle of warning from some ancient instinct.

She turned her imperious gaze back on the youth. "This could be good practice for you, Cedric. I've called a major media reception. Probably all the big names will be there."

His eyes widened. "Really there?"

"They can't guzzle my champagne by hologram."

"No. Of course. But like Eccles Pandora? Quentin Peter?"

"Yes, yes. Everybody. You should meet them. But also, I think you should introduce my speech."

Willoughby saw panic rise behind the gray eyes and felt an odd admiration as he watched it being overcome. "If you will tell me what to say, Gran."

Not bad at all! Faced with four possible replies, the lad had instinctively chosen the right one. If Agnes wanted to break this boy, she was going to have to get much rougher. She would, if that was her purpose.

She merely glanced at Willoughby. "Make up something for him, won't you?" It was a dismissal.

For a moment he seriously considered pulling out. He had never been so vulnerable, and he was starting to have serious doubts about Agnes. Under the cool veneer she was certainly more agitated than he could ever recall seeing her. But then Cedric had sprung to open the door for his supposed grandfather, and the chance had gone.

Someone had taught the kid manners. Not many organages would bother doing that, and if he had picked it up on his own by watching a lot of holo, then he must be brighter than he looked. Limping past, Willoughby felt himself being assessed.

He straightened his stoop. "Two point what?"

The kid stammered, shamefaced at being so obvious. "T-T-Two point oh-five, sir."

In the anteroom red guards and blue guards rose to their feet. "To the press conference," Willoughby told his own party chief, who referred the command to the bulky Bagshaw man by means of a silent glower. As the convoy formed up and set off along the corridor, Willoughby turned back to considering his stringy young companion. "You're taller than I ever was, then."

That earned a satisfied grin. "A little, maybe, sir."

Willoughby chuckled to put him at ease. "A fair bit. I claimed six-foot-six when I was your age—that's a fraction less than two meters—but I never quite was. In the morning I almost made it. A man's taller in the morning—did you know that?"

Willoughby had never been as tall, and certainly never as gaunt, as this human skeleton. The skintight clothes were no help, of course. He looked grotesque in them.

"No, sir."

"Slow down!" Willoughby complained. "Your grandmother will certainly keep us all waiting half an hour at least. There's no hurry. Yes, a man shrinks a little by nightfall. He shrinks as he gets older, too. And I lost a couple of centimeters when I got my tin legs."

Apparently Cedric now noticed the limp for the first time. He frowned and changed the subject. "What do I have to do at this meeting, sir?"

"Just stand up by the lectern. Give them time to notice you. Then say something like, 'Honored guests, ladies and gentlemen —Director Hubbard.' You needn't shout. System'll amplify your voice so everyone can hear you."

The kid's sigh of relief was quite silent, yet as obvious as a cornet fanfare. "That's all?"

No. Almost certainly that was not going to be all.

"It's all I would do."

Cedric nodded vigorously. "Sir—tell me about my father?"

Tricky! Willoughby was tempted to say, "Tell me what you think you already know."

What he did say, to gain time, was: "I wish I had known him better." The convoy had reached an escalator, and the bulls were checking for booby traps. "Your grandmother is a remarkable woman, lad. How well do you know her?"

"I just met her! You saw." Then Cedric bit his lip and protested loyally, "But she's called me often on the holo—almost every month. A lot of the kids never hear from their families at all. Not ever. Not even at Christmas!"

Agnes had been working on this one for twenty years or so, and she was putting him into play now. Important cards were only used to take important tricks.

"Yes, a remarkable woman," Willoughby said. "We really got to know each other back in 'ninety-nine, I suppose it was. It was the year she was nominated for the Nobel."

What a woman! A truly remarkable mind, better than average looks, and a will of steel. Willoughby had possessed far wider experience than she, and yet she had outwitted him.

Those had been exciting times in global politics. The first generation of truly liberated women had been making its mark, those who had been brought up all their lives to expect equality and who had arrived at the top in large numbers. But in Willoughby's experience, any political action always produced side effects. Every blow inevitably boomeranged somehow, and that triumphant female invasion had unwittingly reintroduced sex into statecraft on a scale not seen since the days of Antoinette and de Montespan—not that this gangling yokel would have ever heard of such people.

Willoughby had been thirty-two, tall, and—when he cared to bother—suavely sexy. He had been devious and consciously amoral, playing the lover game. He had also used a couple of legal-term pairings to good effect. He had won promotion in bed, establishing himself as an up-and-coming man at the U.N. . . . marvelous expression, that! And then he had run into Agnes.

Having found neither bomb nor ambush, the bulls waved their clients onto the escalator, standing guard at top and bottom.

Willoughby led the way, chuckling. "We'd spoken a few times at meetings. We met again one evening in an elevator. By the time we reached ground level, she'd told me she wanted a child, she believed in natural insemination, and I looked like her idea of a lover—would I be interested in a breeding contract?"

Young Cedric's eyes bulged at that story. "What did you say?"

"I suggested we have a drink and discuss terms. Your father was conceived about an hour later."

Stunned silence.

Or three hours.

Or ten... "By morning it still seemed like a good idea to me." Willoughby recalled how he had decided that a younger woman would be a form of vacation for him, a well-earned change. "We agreed to set the legal wheels turning, and I left on a trip to France. Neururb, you'd call it now."

They set off along another long corridor.

"And?" Cedric asked in a fascinated whisper.

"I returned two weeks later. By then your father had been pipetted out and installed in an incubation tank. Your grandmother told me the deal was off."

"Off?"

"She had what she'd wanted. Oh, I squired her many times after that. She was always a fascinating companion. Everyone assumed we were pairing. We weren't! No one else knows this, lad... but she never did let me into her bed again."

"Why—Why not?" To be thus taken into the confidence of a world leader was turning the boy an extraordinary shade of red.

Because Agnes gained her thrills from other activities.

"Because she regarded sex as an unnecessary and potentially risky procedure, I suppose. She put her own name first on our son, and she never let me pay any support. She did show me the gene reports. I was his father, no question on that. But I rarely met him until he was an adult—and not much even then." A Secretary General had very little in common with a rodeo cowboy.

Agnes had gained what she wanted in other ways, too. However promiscuous, a human male usually had some regard for the welfare of his offspring, and she had judged Willoughby correctly. He had fostered her career for the boy's sake. Together they had formed an unofficial, political pairing, a mutual assistance society. Young Hubbard John Hastings had been unwitting cement for one of history's most effective partnerships.

"What was he like, sir?" Cedric asked wistfully. "My father?"

Just for a moment Willoughby felt a surge of pity, but he suppressed it quickly. He would really be showing his age if he started letting sentiment interfere with business. This innocent was obviously business, and Agnes's plans must not be warped from their path.

"Not as tall as you and I, but not short. About average. Gray eyes. Talked a lot." Willoughby cut off the next question. "Now it's my turn. I'm a little shocked at running into two meters of grandson that I didn't know I had. Tell me about yourself. Where have you been doing all this growing up?"

The corridor had reached another anteroom, a much larger one. It was a real bull pen at the moment, with about fifty guards in thirty different uniforms spread all over the furniture, even sitting on the floor. They were already rising menacingly, and Willoughby sighed at the certainty that every one of them would demand the right to search him. He waited for the wrangling to start.

With half his mind he was wondering still what devilry Agnes was planning and how this green kid fitted into it. Why, for example, had she not suggested that he comb his hair?

The rest of him was vaguely listening to that same unexplained possible grandson babbling enthusiastically about his life in some place called Meadowdale. It certainly sounded like an organage, but it must have been an unusually humane example. Some of those places confined their victims from birth to puberty in animal cages and, often, in atrocious squalor. Perhaps that sort of treatment was actually kinder, though, considering the barbaric fate awaiting them.

9

ALTHOUGH THERE WERE other urban complexes she preferred—Nipurb, for example—Alya was no stranger to Nauc. Quite apart from many brief social visits and shopping trips, she had lived on campus at New Columbia for a course on crisis ecology. She had even been trapped for two weeks in Knoxville, of all places, during the Florida Panic, when every vehicle capable of moving had been enlisted to help with the evacuations.

She had been dreading the usual bureaucratic trip wires that ensnared travelers at every port. She was pleasantly surprised. An army of red-uniformed, gun-bearing Institute guards boarded the super before anyone could leave, shouldering aside all protest. Alya and her companions were escorted out with no delays at all, and zipped away in an armored Honda the size of a small café.

The leader of the force was a woman named North Brenda. Remembering to think in English, Alya supposed she must be a female bull, except that English was usually a very logical language about gender. North was solid and foursquare, with a face as expressive as tree stumps. Jathro was being alternately obsequious and officious to her; neither approach seemed to produce any special reaction. He did not introduce Alya, but likely that was standard security procedure.

She sat in a corner with her teeth clenched, trying to straighten out a very muddled and unhappy brain. She was certainly jet-lagged—dizzy and displaced, seeing the world muffled and blurred by reflections as though she were living in a glass box. That was normal; she had felt like that before. Her head throbbed, but it had been doing so for almost three days now. The ancestral mutterings had faded when she left Banzarak, seeming fairly content as long as she concentrated on thoughts of Cainsville. The sight of Jathro's river list had aroused them again, but only briefly. Now she could feel another *satori* stirring—somehow she did not think it was the same one, although the *buddhi* was never specific. A sense of imminent danger began to grip her.

She was doing something wrong. Ambush? Could it be an ambush?

The Honda had passed three checkpoints and was slowing down again. That felt wrong, very wrong.

She turned to the North woman to insist that they change course. ". . . knew that the lady would wish to proceed straight to Cainsville," the bull was saying, "but, if you prefer to remain here when we see her off on the lev—"

That was what was wrong!

"No!" Alya said. "I do not wish to proceed straight to Cainsville!"

Jathro blinked at her in surprise.

"Very well, ma'am," North Brenda said, frowning. "I should have asked. Driver . . . the east gate." The Honda picked up speed again and swept by the entrance to the lev station.

Alya relaxed, feeling better.

Jathro looked puzzled and distrusting.

Alya was surprised. The suite to which she was shown was large, but it was drably functional. Even an average sort of hotel would have seemed cleaner and newer. She had expected something more ostentatious, more in keeping with the riches 4-I should have piled up after thirty years' monopoly on stellar power. Of course, the Institute's secret activities must be incredibly costly.

She refused Moala's offers of help, insisting that she could turn her own taps. She settled herself thankfully into a hot tub, assuming that the others were all doing the same. She lay back, prepared to enjoy long, warm decadence.

For the first time in her experience, hot water failed to soothe away the jangles of travel. Definitely, her *satori* had changed—Cainsville was not the answer. As the minutes ticked away, her sense of urgency rose, and rose very steeply. She found she was fighting down a sense of panic that she had never felt in her life before. What in Heaven's name could be wrong?

Angry and feeling cheated, she abandoned the bathtub. Bed? No—standing in the middle of her bedroom, still half wet, still toweling, she was seized by a claustrophic need to escape, at once. The walls seemed to lean in and glare at her. She had felt a little like that before a minor earthquake in Djakarta. Hastily wrapping herself in a loose robe, with her hair hanging limp down her back, she went swooping out into the central lounge of the guest suite.

The threat eased. No earthquake, then. Alya stopped, struggling to consider the new problem rationally—not that anyone ever had managed to explain the *buddhi* rationally. There was nothing seriously amiss with the lounge. Flanked by six bedrooms, it would have housed twelve typical Banzaraki families. It was more dowdy and shabby than she had expected, but that barely mattered—she could be perfectly happy in a student hovel for weeks on end. The roof was not going to fall. The need was not that.

Jathro was still chatting with the security woman, leaning close and staring intently into her eyes. North was short, but solid as a wrestler. Her face was grimly dutiful, denying awareness that Jathro possessed any special charm at all.

Alya told herself not to be catty. The man was merely being polite. He probably always spoke to women that way—all women. And if he seemed pompous, he was entitled to. He bore great responsibility. He had a great future. She shivered.

Now, though, he was starting to grow surly. "Then you have no idea at all when the director will see me?"

North shook her head. She looked less movable than a continent. "I was told to offer you any hospitality within the limits of Zone One, Excellency, and ask you to wait until after the conference."

Alya frowned. Her headache had been there so long that she hardly noticed it anymore—and perhaps it was not a sharp enough pain to qualify as a real headache, just a misery—but now it rapped hard on the inside of her forehead to attract her attention. "What conference?" she asked loudly.

North and Jathro turned surprised faces toward her.

"Director Hubbard has called a press conference, ma'am," North replied.

"Is that usual?"

North shook her head, her placid face showing just a whisper of a smile. "It has never happened in living memory."

Quivers ran up Alya's spine and then down the undersides of her arms . . . curious sensation! She looked at Jathro, who was frowning uncertainly. "Then what is the occasion?"

"No one knows, ma'am." If North had her suspicions, she would clearly not reveal them under penalty of flogging.

Could Alya herself be the occasion?

The same idea had occurred to Jathro. His frown darkened to a scowl, then he shook his head. "I cannot believe that it has anything to do with us." He glanced hesitantly at North, before cautiously telling Alya, "None of the other plantings was ever published."

Not even a funeral announcement . . .

"No, it cannot concern us," he repeated.

But it did, it did!

"I wish to attend," Alya said. The headache retreated a pace or two in approval.

North Brenda pursed her lips in doubt and looked at Jathro, who shook his head.

"I *must* attend," Alya said, and felt even better. "I'll change at once—how long until it starts?" Not long, obviously, or she would not have felt that urgency.

Jathro walked over to intercept her, and for a moment she thought he was going to take hold of her. She stopped, glaring.

"I prefer not to reveal your presence here," he said.

"Then I am leaving!"

"No. You are wearied by the journey. Take some rest—and don't worry about the negotiations. I will handle everything."

Alya attempted a royal manner and aimed it at North, who was being craggily inscrutable. "Please arrange transportation to the port. I am returning to Banzarak."

"You are not," Jathro said, and turned away.

At that, Alya no longer had to feign anger. "I certainly am—unless I am permitted to attend that press conference."

"You can watch it on the holo. I'm sure it'll be on the holo."

"No. I must be there."

"It will be in English. Do you understand English well enough?"

For the first time in her life, Alya discovered that it was truly possible to see red. "Understand ... What do you think I am? Yes, I understand English. I have studied many things under many English-speaking teachers."

Jathro blinked, and suddenly she realized that he had not done his homework—he probably knew nothing about her except her name and rank.

"Political science," she said, with grim satisfaction, "under Bozeman Charles. Economics with Stavely Wills. Superstring theory in Ankara, under Gutelman—in English and Russian. Genetics in Sydney, mycology in Neururb-U.K. ... Yes, I speak English, Dr. Jar. My accent is much better than yours. And I am going to that press conference."

"Why is that necessary?"

"Why?" Alya echoed, stunned. "Why?" Fists clenched, she roared at him. "You have the audacity to ask me why? To ask me why?"

Jathro fell back before her fury. She followed him, screaming at him, wanting to pound on him. Her headache had dissolved and an icy joy surged through her. Here was action! Here was something she could do at last! "You ask me why, you dockside fart, you bastard son of an alcoholic fish gutter, you sleazy, sermonizing, rabble-scratching eel shitter? Me?"

The urgency and the agony of her buddhi had not gone, but they had faded before this immediate task. She had no doubt whatsoever that her duty—her need, her destiny—was to go to that press conference. It was essential, and that slimy tub-thumping turd was not going to stand in her way. And she told him so, in three languages at the top of her voice. She repeated it in two others.

Jathro was backed into a corner, and Alya could barely keep her nails from his eyes. "My ancestors for a hundred generations have seen their children die for this. You dare doubt the verdict of two thousand years? You will question me?"

A century of democracy collapsed before millennia of autocracy. The peasant cowered before the princess. Jathro gasped and shook his head. "No, Your Highness!"

"Oh?" Taken aback by his sudden surrender, Alya awoke to the horror of crooked fingers she was waving in his face. She lowered them quickly and turned away. Moala, enormous in a pink bathrobe and wearing a towel around her hair, was peering out to see what was wrong.

North was not quite suppressing a grim smile. "You have ten

minutes before it is scheduled to start, ma'am. But I doubt that Director Hubbard will be on time."

Alya clasped her hands in her armpits to hide their shaking. "Five should be plenty." She headed for her room without another glance at Jathro.

Fingernails? She had threatened him with fingernails?

After all those karate lessons?

With Moala's well-meaning help, Alya was ready in nine minutes, feeling suave in the gold silk jump suit she had acquired on her last trip to Nipurb, in January. Had that been foresight, perhaps? It was so tight that a bad attack of goose bumps would split it in shreds, and it did astonishing things to men's eyeballs. Silver sandals, silver belt, a slender silver band around her head, her hair hanging loose over Moala's entreaties, and Alya strode out into the lounge, feeling ready to take on the whole of Nauc.

Jathro had changed also and was ready, damn him, and his smile seemed to go right through her outfit and find satisfaction. He was wearing tan corduroy and looking good in it. For his age. Damn him.

North threw open the door and went out to inspect the corridor. Then she beckoned. Just for a moment Alya was amused— guarding her was like waterproofing a fish.

Jathro was close at her side as they set off along the hallway. "Dr. North, would it be possible to preserve our anonymity at this gathering? Can you provide false identities? I am reluctant—"

Never! Alya knew at once that he was wrong.

"I could, Mr. Minister, but it would be an error." North was marching a little in front of her two charges, speaking over her shoulder. "They will run ID checks on you. If either of you has ever been identified in a media holo, even if it was never shown, then you will be memoed in minutes. Deception merely attracts suspicion, believe me."

Jathro scowled. Honesty would be foreign to his nature. "Then how do we explain our presence here?"

My presence, Alya thought. "I met Devlin Grant a couple of years ago," she said on impulse. "We are here as his guests."

North glanced around at her. "That will be adequate, and I can advise him of the story you are using. Between ourselves, though, ma'am, it will do your reputation no good."

"My reputation will not matter very long," Alya said bitterly. "I will use my own name."

Jathro glared. "I hope you know what you're doing."

"I certainly do not."

That would worry him, and of course it was perfectly true. But she knew that her arrogant assumption of authority was wearing thin. This second surrender would be his last.

She had only one bargaining chip left. Of course, she could again threaten to return to Banzarak, but that thought was so nauseating that she was sure her face would betray her. No, her strength lay in that list Jathro had shown her—seven names in pencil and another writ in fire. Only she could see the difference.

There was her value. They needed her *buddhi* to find the silken string among the seven cobras.

The media representatives had brought their own armies. Honored guests or not, Alya and Jathro were searched a dozen times before being allowed to pass through the anteroom. The male guards seemed especially distrustful of Alya, enjoying the journey as they ran their scanners over her golden silk. Eventually North Brenda lost patience. Roaring like a rock crusher, she forced a way through by sheer power of personality and then stood aside and glowered defiance as her charges entered the auditorium.

After all the functional dullness that Alya had seen so far, the splendor of the auditorium was a pleasant surprise. It was a salon, large and bright, vaguely reminiscent of Florence, or what Venice must have been. It glowed with the brazen opulence she had anticipated in 4-I's HQ.

The media had great power, and their representatives expected to be royally treated. Perhaps a hundred men and women lounged on the antique furniture, or stood around on priceless rugs between works of art. Live waiters were circulating with trays of champagne, which seemed surprising. Should not the celebration come after? But no. After the announcement, the reporters and other holostars would have to rush off and tell the world what it should be thinking.

Already Alya had begun recognizing faces. For every holostar personality, though, there would be at least two holographers, commonly known as "owls" because of their two-lensed cameras. Once those had been carried on trucks, but now they were no larger than jewelry and could be worn on a headband. Yet holo work was still more art than science; an owl could make or break a clip, and the good ones were rewarded accordingly. A semicircle of men and women stood strategically poised by the door.

They turned, displaying the twin cameras sitting on their foreheads like unwanted sunglasses.

A girl could feel flattered when a crowded room fell silent at her entrance.

Jathro stepped to her side. "Her Highness, Princess Alya," he explained smoothly. "Sister of His Majesty Kassan'assan IV, the Sultan of Banzarak." As always beyond the shores of Borneo, mention of Banzarak produced only blank stares.

Men rose from chairs and couches. A general drift toward Alya became apparent, each star being tracked by an attendant owl. A beautiful princess was a rarity in the twenty-first century, even if no one had ever heard of her homeland, and a pretty girl was always good copy.

"And you?" someone asked.

Oozing modesty, Jathro introduced himself: Banzarak's Minister for Refugee Affairs, but present that day only as aide-de-camp to Her Highness.

"And what brings Your Highness to Director Hubbard's press conference?"

Jathro opened his mouth again, but Alya spoke first. "Pure nosiness! We happened to be in the complex on a social visit, guests of Deputy Director Devlin. We heard that there was to be an important announcement and came to hear what it might be."

She just wanted to be left alone. Alya had no fear of crowds, no sense of stage fright, for eyes had followed her all her life, but at the moment she was beginning to doubt the hunch that had brought her. The sense of urgency had vanished, so she was on the right track, but she truly did not know why she was there. As Jathro had said, her brothers and sisters had never drawn attention to their missions in such a way. Unease tingled her skin like a rash. Had she made a stupendous error? She had a sense of something missing, and she desperately wanted to hide in a corner and just watch, unseen and unnoticed, until she could work out what it was.

Small hope! But at least her rank and youth gained her respect—beautiful girls were not bullied in public—and the six or seven personages who chose to be recorded talking with her were all polite and considerate. One by one they stepped forward to ask much the same questions. She gave the same answers and gradually convinced them that she had no knowledge of what was to be announced and was certainly not personally concerned. Then little Wok Lee of *Singapore Witness* mischievously asked her a question in Malay. She replied in kind and found herself admitting that she spoke five languages fluently and could get by in several others. That stupid indiscretion revived the interest and prolonged her ordeal.

She thought ruefully of Kas and how horrified he would be if he turned on his holo and saw this appalling publicity. He would think she had gone mad. Perhaps she had.

As a born schemer, Jathro had seen that any interference by him would only arouse more suspicion. He had stepped aside, wrapping himself in silence and a thin, sour smile.

She was rescued at last by Quentin Peter of 5CBC, who liked to think of himself as the dean of the world press corps, even if no one else did. Courtly, white-haired, and wistfully lecherous, he gave her his arm and led her into the center of the room. There the most important personages were trading lies on a horseshoe of soft, chintzy couches amid a sparkle of wit, jewelry, and champagne. Prominent people met so seldom in the flesh that this must be a notable experience for them. With no visible direction, a group of owls cut Jathro off when he tried to follow.

Alya knew that every word she spoke was still being recorded, every eyelash scanned. She knew that every man and woman in the group was trying to calculate how this interesting character could be used to further his or her career by some minute amount, but at least she could sit in comfort and pretend she was merely attending a meeting of the Banzarak Ladies' Refugee Assistance League. But that could never have been so interesting.

She realized with sudden astonishment that she had started to enjoy herself. The Dom Perignon tickled her nose with the audacity of a celebrated vintage, and even a princess could relish being treated as a celebrity sometimes. She was scenting the ozone of excitement that filled the hall, the tingle of suspense. So large an attendance of world-famous faces spoke wonders for the importance of the occasion. A million hectos' worth of tailoring glimmered under the chandeliers.

Her gold jump suit was too bright. Pastels and earth tints were the correct thing, subtle and soft. Probably the gold would have been fine when she bought it, but that had been three months earlier. These were the beautiful people, the ever-young gods of transient fame, and they measured the progress of fashion to the minute. Many of them looked as though they could hardly breathe, so tightly was uplift being impressed upon female bosom and washboarding on male abdomen. Some of the costumes were triumphs of concealed engineering—she watched Goodson Jason lift a champagne glass and saw his biceps bulge as though he were hefting an anvil.

The inner circle to which she had been admitted was composed of the biggest names. Lesser organizations hungered outside the horseshoe; nonentities and the massed owls flanked them.

Non-English media like *Pravda* and *Beijing Voice* were present in the persons of their Nauc stringers, but English was Alya's favorite language for news broadcasts. It just seemed to be the best for the purpose, like Italian for opera or Japanese for poetry. She favored English-speaking channels, and thus she had no trouble recognizing the solid sky-blue pomposity of Frazer Franklin of WSHB. He was older than she had expected, and even a fortune in sartorial cunning could not conceal the breadth of his hips.

Next to him was the deliberate crudity of Crozer Bill, displaying a matted chest above a neckline that plunged halfway back to Australia.

And perched nearby like a resting angel, Eccles Pandora Pendor was the unquestioned belle of the hall in silvery-pale rose. She looked younger and lovelier than ever—and very tense, which seemed odd. WSHB liked to play up the friendly rivalry between her and Frankie. Alya had always been skeptical of that as a mere gimmick, but perhaps it was no less than the truth. They were certainly showing no signs of friendship at present.

And Eccles Pandora, lisping in baby-doll innocence, kept working around Alya like a knife thrower. Had she spoken to Devlin Grant that day? Was he in Nauc, or up at Cainsville? When had Alya arrived? Where had she met him?

Alya dodged the fast-flung queries as well as she could with the minimum amount of lying, while wondering at that curious interest in Devlin Grant—whom she had met for three minutes at a cocktail party in Mecca two years before. She also wondered why Eccles Pandora fidgeted so much; why her voice seemed shriller than it should.

Frazer Frankie, on the other hand, was expansive and jovial.

Then, as Director Hubbard's tardiness was being remarked on and condemned for the fortieth time, the door opened. The gracious, dignified Quentin Peter said, "*Keerist!*" and lunged off the couch with an agility that Alya would not have expected. The whole room followed.

The old man was easy. No one in the room had trouble identifying the craggy dried-leather face, the hatchet-blade nose, and the bat-wing ears. His hair was gray and thin, his back bowed by age, but he smiled the famous ironic smile and raised a hand in greeting as he shuffled toward the center of the room, the lectern in the middle of the horseshoe. He towered over them all, both literally and figuratively: Hastings Willoughby, Secretary General for a generation, political giant of the century.

The room shimmered as excitement crystallized into a sense of history in the making.

"Sentience!" The whisper came from somewhere behind Alya. "It has to be First Contact!"

"Or a Class One," someone retorted stubbornly.

The Institute reported to the U.N., and thus in a legal sense Hastings was Hubbard's boss. His presence at the present gathering was like calling God the Father to witness.

But the young man beside him? He was even taller. Hardly a man—a boy. His hair was a disaster, far too long and standing up in tufts of disarray, and his suit was a sick joke, a ghastly luminous green that screamed at all the pastels and pearly tints. He was as thin as wire rope, and he had a sickly nervous smile on his face as he tried to keep close to Hastings.

Who had let him out? Out of where?

But Alya's heart was racing. She felt the electrifying touch of a *satori*. That was what had been missing—that gawking adolescent beanpole. That boy. Who was *he*?

What the hell did he have to do with Alya?

He burned. Like that one word on Jathro's paper, he glowed for her. She could imagine a fiery aura around him. He had not even seen her and could not know that she existed, but she was certain. *He* was why she had come to the meeting. Centuries of agonized death had led her there, to that awkward, overgrown juvenile.

The Secretary General had reached the lectern, although he merely came to a halt at one side of it and rested a hand on it for a moment. Alya had been almost pushed back down on her couch by the throng as stars and owls crowded in. She squeezed out of the way and moved to where she could see.

Hastings glanced around and was granted instant silence.

"So you are all real!"

Laughter.

"I've always suspected that most of you were computer constructs."

He was old, but he was still good. The room was as quiet as a closed grave. Alya wondered what he had been like in his prime.

"Now, I did not come here to steal Director Hubbard's thunder. She'll be here very shortly, and she'll make her announcement then." A long finger wagged to forestall argument. "And I'm not going to answer any questions on politics, either. I might say something that would upstage her. This is her day."

The calculated pause . . . "I will say this: To accuse women of being unpunctual is rank prejudice and sexism—but I've always found that if you do it promptly, they're never around to hear you!"

Laughter, babble . . . and again the hand. "No questions! But I will accept a glass of champagne—and if you all want to go off the record . . ."

"Who's your friend, sir?"

Alya thought he had been waiting for that—she certainly had. "Who?" Hastings turned and peered up at his companion, whose rich flush was visible to everyone in the room. "Him?" The aw-shucks manner grew more obvious. "Well, now, ladies and gentlemen of the press, I'll be proud to introduce you all. This is my grandson, Hubbard Cedric Dickson."

There was a beat of silence, and then a roar, as every throat in the room seemed to speak at once. Apparently Alya was not alone in finding him interesting.

Hastings raised a hand, and the peace returned—his control was astonishing. "Seems like they got some questions for you, lad. You want to answer some questions?"

Horrified, the youth shook his head so vigorously that his ochre comb flapped. Hastings led the laughter.

Alya elbowed her way between two groups, squirmed around to another couch, and almost threw herself over the back. She was sitting demurely upright, with her hair back in place, when the crowd opened to allow the Secretary General to find a seat, and he arrived at that same couch. Of course—it was easy.

Alya made to rise, but he signed to her to remain seated, and his shrewd old eyes twinkled at her with no sign of surprise.

He knew!

"Princess Alya!" He bowed over her hand. "At last! You have turned out even lovelier than I predicted. How's that bush-bearded brother of yours?" He was showing off to impress the press—but he knew. He had known of her arrival, and he knew why she had come. But of course he would. Hubbard Agnes could hardly have masterminded history's greatest conspiracy for so long without Hastings Willoughby knowing about it.

The Secretary General settled at Alya's side. If she had placed herself to meet his grandson, though, then she had failed. Young Cedric, unable to see a vacant seat nearby, unabashedly settled on the floor at his grandfather's feet like an oversize child. Completely unaware of Alya behind his shoulder, he crossed his grasshopper legs and seemed to go into a trance, staring boggle-eyed at Eccles Pandora.

Alya hardly minded. The mere fact that he was close seemed to have eased her headache and satisfied her sense of something missing. She would not have known what to say to him any-way—but why him?

"I didn't know you had a grandson, sir," Quentin remarked.

Hastings glanced at him over the lip of his glass and then around the company. "We're off the record?"

With sour expressions the media of the world agreed that they were off the record. The owls pointedly turned aside or removed their headbands.

"Well . . ." Hastings paused dramatically and took a deep breath. "Why should you have known?"

Everyone except Quentin enjoyed that. He raised a shaggy white eyebrow and regarded the youth. "How old are you, Ce-dric?"

The boy dragged his eyes away from Pandora. "Nineteen, sir."

Alya was surprised—her own age. She had thought him younger than that, in spite of his height.

"You're the son of Hubbard John Hastings?"

"Yes, sir."

Of course, he must be Agnes's grandson, also! That explained why the reporters had found him so interesting, even if it did not explain why he rang Alya's alarms. Whatever she was seeing in him was certainly not physical—he was immature and awkward and apparently not very bright. Certainly not her type. Why that invisible aura?

The rest of the company were leaving the interview to Quentin but watching the Secretary General's reaction.

When no other question followed, Cedric turned back to gaze adoringly at Eccles again. As though that had been a signal, Quentin spoke. "Your parents were lost through a broken string incident?"

"Yes, sir."

"A world called 'Oak'? That was its code name—Oak?"

"You remember it?"

Quentin shook his head impatiently. "No, lad. You're on file."

North had warned Jathro about just this. Cedric had been re-searched already, 5CBC would undoubtedly have a library second to none, and Quentin would have an earpatch.

"They had been overnighting?"

Alya recognized the cross-examination technique, but apparently Cedric did not, and he continued to agree blithely as detail after detail was cautiously added.

"So—they were overnighting on a Class Two world, code name 'Oak,' a party of six, and the next window failed to appear. Contact was never reestablished?"

Belatedly Cedric reached for caution. "So I've been told, sir."

Quentin sprang his trap. "And what was an agricultural worker doing on a Type Two world?"

"Agri—my father was a ranger!"

Quentin shook his head. "Not according to the files."

Cedric's head swung around so fast it seemed his skinny neck would snap. "Grandfather?"

Willoughby was toying with his now-empty glass, twiddling the stem in his fingers. "He was a ranger trainee." Then the old man chuckled, eyeing Quentin inscrutably. "These youngsters won't remember what it was like, Peter, but you should. The transmensor was very new then. So was the Institute. There was no big corps of professional rangers in those days. First planetfall was only made in 'twenty-two, remember, and we were not as skilled at zapping from one to the other as we are now—as Agnes's minions are, I should say."

He glanced around the group. Cedric was nodding, and so were some of the others. "We kept finding all these juicy little worlds, and every one was always going to be the Second Earth. You hotshots used to announce them on the news programs! When's the last time you mentioned a Class Two world, Peter, huh?"

He had them grasping at every word—true mastery! "So all sorts of people got involved that wouldn't nowadays. My son was a rodeo cowboy, as a matter of fact—not an unbroken bone in his body. Nor in his head. But Oak had big grassy prairies that we thought should be looked at, and some horse-type beasts." He paused, then added quietly, "It also had lethal concentrations of antimony everywhere. We didn't find that out until too late, after the string broke."

Quentin stayed with easier prey. "But you, Cedric—you don't remember any of this?"

"No, sir. I was only a baby."

"Were you, though? The Oak disaster was in 2026. That's twenty-four years ago, sonny."

Some of the listeners seemed surprised, but most of them had obviously been waiting for it. Again Cedric's head flashed around to look at his grandfather . . . who was accepting a refill of champagne. And sipping it.

"That's right, Peter, now that I think about it," the old man replied. "It happened while the second South African thing was on—2026."

"But, Grandfather—"

Hastings stopped him with an uplifted palm. "This is no time for a lecture on the birds and the beasts, Cedric. Ask your grandmother—she's better on that technical stuff, anyway."

Cedric recoiled, staring, amid the laughter.

Cruel! Alya thought. How could the old man treat his own grandson like that?

Who else could he be?

There was a resemblance, certainly, yet not as much as she would have expected if Cedric was what the media people obviously suspected he might be. Illicit cloning was a major crime, and greatly condemned, since only the very rich could afford it. There would be an enormous scandal. Hastings would fall, and he might well drag down the whole fragile structure of U.N. hegemony.

The old man had put this off the record. He could hardly put Cedric himself off the record, not now.

So the boy could not be a clone—but he might not know that, for he had gone very pale.

Then pompous, balding Frazer Franklin intervened. "You seem to be a bit of a mystery, lad." Cedric turned toward him, much more warily now. "Since we are off the record—where have you been all these years?"

The question fetched a few angry mutters, but Cedric did not seem to notice. "A place called Meadowdale, sir. Out west, in the mountains."

Frazer nodded meaningfully. "What state?"

"I don't know. They wouldn't tell us."

There were a few smiles at that, and again they were lost on the youth. He looked to Eccles Pandora, and Alya saw a dreamy expression soften his bony profile. "I know Glenda, of course, Dr. Eccles. How is she?"

Eccles Pandora dropped a canapé. Mild confusion upset the conversation for a few minutes while a waiter arrived with a napkin and Pandora twittered about how careless she was. Then order was restored. "I just cannot *stand* this suspense!" she proclaimed. "The excitement is—"

"Answer Dr. Hubbard's question, Panda dear," Frazer said loudly. It was the first time he had spoken to her, so far as Alya knew.

"What?" Pandora seemed to flutter feathers. "But I want to ask the Secretary—"

"Cedric asked you a question." Franklin's voice was louder. "About someone called—Glenda, was it?"

Cedric nodded, his coxcomb waving. "Garfield Glenda, Dr. Eccles's cousin. We were close . . . we were friends." He blushed scarlet and gazed hopefully at Pandora.

Pandora had turned pale. The room was very still.

If the youth had begun to sense the tension, he was merely puzzled by it. "She left about six months ago. She sent word the next day that she was going on a world cruise." Abruptly his voice went very small. "How . . . is . . . she?"

Pandora was chalky white. Faint pink scars showed on her neck.

Franklin took a celebratory sip of champagne. "Six months ago? Is that where you disappeared to, Panda? I knew you'd been on vacation somewhere. We all thought it did you good. You came back looking like a new woman."

In the awful silence, Pandora raised shaking fingers to her cheek, and surely did not know she was doing so. Alya felt sick. Cedric had also gone pale—very pale.

"Oh . . . oh God," he whispered. "God God God *organage*! That's what it means . . ."

Had he gazed into those eyes? Alya wondered. Had he kissed those lips?

He made a choking noise, as though he were going to throw up.

Only Frazer Franklin was smiling.

And at that moment the door opened to admit Hubbard Agnes.

The director's powder-blue suit was not as clinging as most in the room, but it was snug enough to show that she had kept her figure. Her complexion was beyond reproach, and her coiffure might have been freshly crafted on a silversmith's bench. Age showed only in a certain cautious rigidity, and perhaps in the arrogantly upright way she held her head. Hubbard had Presence, and the company rose to acknowledge it. Alya had seen fanatic Banzaraki royalists fall on their faces for her brother, and yet she was impressed by that unrehearsed compliment from an antagonistic, hard-headed group.

Cedric had farther to go than anyone, but he sprang from the floor in a whirl of ungainly green limbs and crossed to the lectern in four enormous strides like an alarmed giraffe, starting to speak almost before he had turned.

"Honored guests ladies and gentlemen Director Hubbard!"

He flashed his grandmother a shaky smile and began to move. Stepping forward, she stopped him with a magical gesture like a witch in a children's holo fantasy, rooting him to the floor and freezing an expression of dismay on his face.

Hubbard had no notes. If there was a prompter in the lectern, she did not seem to use it. She laid her hands there and nodded. The world's press sat down obediently to wait for enlightenment.

"Ladies and gentlemen of the media." Her voice was high-pitched but incisive. "I must begin by thanking you for coming at such short notice. It seemed appropriate to me for personal reasons to hold this meeting today, April seventh."

The only person who did not seem to be hanging on her words was Cedric. Smile discarded, he stood restlessly a couple of strides away from her, glooming anxiously at the audience and belatedly running fingers through his hair.

"To review very briefly the history of the International Institute for Interstellar Investigation—"

Someone at the back groaned, but she did not seem to hear.

"...although superstring theory had been developed as a branch of particle physics as early as the 1980s...in 2002 the work that established the theory of the transmensor...classic paper in *Physical Reviews* by Chiu Pak and Laski Jean-Marc..."

She swept a professionally catered smile around the room like a flashlight. Alya could hear nothing but a quiet rattle of breathing from Hastings Willoughby at her side.

"The possibility of interchanging one of the familiar four dimensions of space-time with any of the additional superspace dimensions not normally expressed..." She droned on. Some men at the back started coughing. She raised her chin like an archetype schoolmarm and waited until they stopped.

Once, while visiting West Africa, Alya had experienced the

hot wind called the harmattan. It had brought enough static electricity to make her hair crackle. She was reminded of that now—the room was becoming charged. These people were not accustomed to being treated in so cavalier a fashion. She was convinced that Hubbard was deliberately baiting them. And so were they.

". . . may remember the furor when the General Assembly granted our charter." She smiled briefly over heads at Hastings Willoughby. "That was in 2020, so this year marks our thirtieth anniversary. It was on June third that the resolution was ratified and I was appointed director."

She paused momentarily to relish the puzzled frowns. "But today happens to be my seventy-fifth birthday."

The applause was thin as skim milk.

"This is obviously an opportune moment to review what has been achieved; and what must be achieved in future."

No! If Hubbard was about to announce her retirement, then all Alya's future might change. She might never see what lay behind that word of fire on Jathro's paper. She might have to stay here —but then she realized that no *satori* had come to warn her of danger ahead. So the news—when it finally came—would not be that.

". . . have never had a destructive accident, nor a power failure. We have grown until we supply the entire Earth through a complex of twenty-four microwave relay satellites. Our research arm, the International Institute for Interstellar Investigation, has identified over fifty thousand nonstellar bodies. As of today, 1502 of these NSBs have been found to contain some form of life, and ninety possessed surface conditions so Earthlike that we categorized them as Class Two worlds."

Somewhere a faint whisper said, "Get on with it!" But Hubbard was not to be hurried.

"Not one of those ninety proved capable of supporting human beings for any extended period. You all know the problems and disappointments we have encountered—heavy element contamination, dextroamino acids, virulent allergens. Personally, I know that time and again I have believed that I was on the point of making that long-awaited, epochal announcement, and every time some new, diabolical danger has surfaced in the lab reports."

What of Etna? Alya thought. Or Raven? What about Darwin, and Halibut?

"The world we called 'Paris,' for example, taught us about

carcinogenic pollen. 'Giraffe' had a complete absence of zinc, an essental trace element. We don't know why. 'Dickens' was a world so like our dreams of Eden that it was unbelievable—and its primary was violently unstable. If you think our present UV problems are serious, you should see some of the radiation profiles we encountered there. Sol is a benevolent star compared to most.

"And our terrestrial mosquitoes are much friendlier companions than the lethal bugs on 'Beaver.'"

"It has begun to seem, over the years, as though nature has been conspiring to lock us up in this one sick little world."

The listeners fidgeted slightly as she seemed to draw near to what they were waiting for. Alya heard "Class One" being whispered in several directions.

"This is also an appropriate moment," Director Hubbard proclaimed, "to pay tribute to the eighty-six courageous men and women who gave their lives in this search . . . including my own son."

She glanced around at Cedric, who nodded.

And then she took off on another slant altogether, as though all of her preceding remarks had been only a feint.

"You are aware, I am sure, that the Institute is organized in four main divisions, each having its own deputy director. Dr. Wheatland handles Personnel—our most precious resource, as you may guess. Dr. Moore, in Finance, and Dr. Fish, in Security —all these people have served long and loyally and well."

She had to raise her voice slightly, over the hiss of puzzled whispers, growing angrier and more persistent.

"Dr. Devlin Grant is a relative newcomer, but he is doing great work as deputy for Operations.

"Nevertheless, it had been suggested to me several times recently that the Institute could do more to cultivate good relations with you, ladies and gentlemen—with the information business, the media. Some unkind persons have even suggested that I myself might have given you cause for annoyance on some occasions in the past."

That fetched an ironic laugh, and Alya smiled, remembering stories that Kas had told her of the director's abrasive tongue. Hubbard Agnes beamed blissfully at the reaction.

"I invited you here today, therefore, to meet my grandson, Hubbard Cedric Dickson, whom I have just rescued from an undeserved anonymity. And I also wish to announce that in future the Institute will have five deputy directors instead of four, and I have appointed Hubbard Cedric Dickson as the first deputy for Media Relations. If you have any questions, please direct them to him.

"Thank you for your attention."

Then she turned and strode from the room.

10

Nauc, April 7

A FOURTEEN-YEAR-OLD CAN almost always beat a ten-year-old, even if the ten-year-old is bigger. In Cedric's growing days his height had been a challenge to older boys; it had brought him much sorrow. Although he himself had never started fights and had always hated even having to defend himself—for his leverage could cause real damage, and Ben and Madge had reacted with great fury to broken teeth or damaged noses—Cedric knew what brawling was.

So he knew what it was like to be banged in the nuts. And this felt just like that.

The whole room was stunned.

Then realization began to come. The first spectator to recover roared out in a strange, harsh accent, "Tell that sheila that April Fools' was last week!"

Hubbard Agnes had apparently treated herself to a birthday present at the expense of this audience.

Then everyone was roaring. Cedric saw fists being shaken at him. He stumbled instinctively to the lectern, putting it between himself and the angry mob, and gripping it tight while trying not to show his nausea. His head was swimming, and he could not think. Why would Gran have done such a thing? Why insult all those important people? Why then throw *him* to the dogs? He did not know what he could have done to deserve this sort of punishment.

He looked up, and the room was full of eyes. Dozens of eyes, angry eyes, hundreds of eyes, and all those goggle camera lenses, all glaring at him. And behind those would lie millions—no, billions—of other eyes, all over the planet. All watching *him*.

He gripped until his fingers hurt, and he forced himself to return the stares. He could come to no harm. No one was going to kill him before such an audience. He felt a little better when he had worked that out.

Then there was sudden silence. The crowd opened to let the Secretary General come shuffling forward. His face was a wan gray shade, and he seemed to have shrunk—and aged. He stopped beside the lectern, peering up at Cedric with an inexplicably bleary gaze. The room was as silent as the moon.

"You want to come back with me, lad?"

Cedric tried to swallow the rocks in his throat, without success. He looked into filmy eyes the exact shade of his own. Was this really his grandfather? Could such a man truly not know he had a grandson? But if he was not Cedric's grandfather, then Cedric must be his clone, and if Hastings had been cloned, then he should certainly have been aware of the fact. That made no sense, either. There was no sense in any of it. Cedric had expected the world to be a more logical place. He shook his head.

"She's mad!" Willoughby said wearily, and all the cameramen were watching. Hundreds of millions might have heard those words. Billions would hear them later. "There's no way that this could help anyone. She'll have to be replaced. She's gone crazy!"

Cedric tried to speak and could not, suddenly choked by sorrow at the old man's distress—or perhaps by fear.

"You better come with me," Hastings said throatily.

He had tin legs. Cedric's flesh crawled. *Freezerful of spare parts*, Ben had said—warning him of what? Cedric did not want to donate his legs to anyone. They were too long and ridiculously skinny, but he wanted to keep them. He wondered what had happened to Hastings's own legs, and when. About nineteen years ago, perhaps, or twenty? He shook his head.

"I swear I didn't know..." The old man's voice faded away.

"I think I have a job to do here, Grandfather." Cedric's voice was little better, a dry rasp. "Thank you."

Shaking his head like a tortoise, the old man shambled to the door.

Other people were dribbling out, also.

"Job to do?" The shout came from Frazer Franklin, who elbowed his way forward to accost Cedric across the lectern. His face was almost purple above his sky-blue tunic, his jaw thrust out far enough to look bony. Owls shimmied and jostled, hunting a good angle. "Did you know that this was going to happen?"

Cedric licked his lips. He should have known. Dr. Bagshaw had said that only Gran and the deputy directors ranked live bodyguards. System had told him he had Grade One access. He might have guessed, had the idea not been so crazy.

"The director told me I would be doing media relations work, but not that she—not that I would be a deputy director, no."

"Awright, sonny! Where'd you get your doctorate?"

Cedric felt an insane desire to weep. "Nowhere."

"Masters, then?" Frazer shouted with disbelief.

"I don't even have grade school. You know where I came—"

"Never mind that! Have you any qualifications for this job at all?"

"None." Cedric shook his head and hoped that his misery would show enough to cool the rage that the mob was radiating at him.

"Tell me what you want," he said suddenly. "What do you want from me?"

A stunned silence was followed by drumrolls of laughter.

Then the man with the funny accent shouted, "We want you to comb yer hair!" The laughter swelled.

"We want to know why!" Frazer Franklin bellowed, raising a roar of agreement. "Why'd she sucker us all like this?"

It did help to be able to look down at them—Cedric raised a hand in the way he had seen his grandfather do, and there was a momentary pause. He must assume that this was some sort of insane test. He could not win, but he had nothing to lose.

"Did she? Did she really? Was your name on the invitation?"

The sound rose, and then dwindled further, and his heartbeat surged in excitement as he saw that his guess might be going to work. He raised his voice and heard it echo as System amplified.

"It was a mistake! I don't think she meant this to happen. She was trying to offer—to make friends. She invited the networks to send people to a meeting to tell you that she'd appointed a media deputy. That was all! She didn't expect all you high-power types to come!"

Skepticism rumbled like summer thunder in the background. "It was you that jumped to conclusions!" Cedric shouted desperately. He wished he believed that himself. His grandmother had looked so smug when she talked about the champagne . . .

"So try it! Pretend it's for real!" he begged. "Tell me what you need from me."

He won a stunned quiet then—for a moment.

"You wouldn't last long working for your precious grand-mother if you gave us that!" Lacking much of his usual dignity, Quentin Peter had arrived mysteriously before the lectern and was brazenly trying to ease Frazer aside.

Cedric shrugged. He was on the right track, even if he could feel sweat dribbling down his neck. "Fine by me! What do you want?"

"Access to System!" several voices shouted.

"I'll ask. If not that, then what?"

"Hold it!" Quentin held up a hand for order and had to settle for shouting. "You're serious? You think this is on the level?"

"If it isn't," Cedric said, gathering strength from somewhere, "then I don't know otherwise. What I mean is . . . When I'm given a job to do, I try to do it." Oh God, that sounded prissy! "If Gran hasn't been releasing the data you want, then maybe she'll let me see to it. Tomorrow . . . let's set up a commeeting in the morning, and you tell me how you think I should try, and what you'll need from me. Ten o'clock?"

The hubbub faded, the audience exchanging puzzled looks and incredulous shrugs. Their fury had faded to a bitter, shame-faced resentment. Further show of anger would merely increase their absurdity.

"It's worth a try, isn't it?" he pleaded.

"Right!" Quentin said. "Ten it is. I'll put someone on it—but I'll believe the results when I see them!" He headed for the door, and the crowd began to disintegrate, angry and baffled.

Cedric clung tight to the sides of the lectern, ignoring the hot glares going past him. He heard angry words coming from the anteroom as bulls and clients argued about precedence. He ig-nored those also. He hung his head and sucked in long, deep breaths, feeling dampness cool on his forehead. He had not been lynched, anyway. Was he really supposed to try this job? It needed a Ph.D. Nowadays any job needed a Ph.D. Even a short-order cook required a masters. Deputy director of the Institute was no chore for a dumb hayseed who moved his lips when he read and chewed his tongue when he wrote.

More likely he had just been set up to annoy the media super-stars. Anything he tried would fail—and would make matters worse.

He wanted to be a ranger and go exploring.

He heard the door slam behind him, and then he thought he could relax. He looked up and wiped his brow. Only a dozen or so people remained.

One of them was Eccles Pandora Pendor. She was standing slant-hipped before him, a cherub in ghostly pink, smiling with Glenda's smile.

"Dear Cedric!" She fluttered eyelashes.

Suddenly his nausea and weariness had gone and he was choking with rage and hatred. "Dr. Eccles?"

"You'll be watching the holo tonight, I expect. Part of your job? You'll be on all the newscasts."

"Big deal." Even fifteen minutes ago he would not have believed that he could ever speak to the great Eccles Pandora in that tone. His hands were shaking with fury.

"Watch WSHB. I've got something special. More than the others."

"Right."

She moved enticingly closer and peered up at him. "Don't you want to kiss me goodbye, big boy?"

Mockery! His fingers were hurting again—maybe he would break the lectern. "What did you do with the rest of her?"

She pursed her lips—Glenda's lips. "In storage. I'm thinking of using the tits next. Nice tits. Firm—right?"

"Go away!"

"So brusque?" She waggled a finger at him. "You know, my property had been damaged? It wasn't quite as—perfect—as it should have been. Were you the naughty man who did that? Did you have help?"

Cedric raised a clenched fist. He had very large fists. "Go away," he said, as quietly as he could manage. "Just go away."

"Oh, my! This is not good media relations, Cedric."

He thumped the lectern. "Go—away—now!"

Eccles sniggered triumphantly and sauntered toward the door, swaying her hips. Two guards were standing there—Bagshaw and a short, thick woman. They closed the door behind her, and again Cedric relaxed with a rush.

For a moment he closed his eyes. If prayer does any good, he thought, then this is a prayer for Glenda.

Madge had wept when Glenda left. That was almost worse. Madge and Ben had known what they were rearing in their *organage*.

Glenda . . . Glenda . . . Glenda . . .

Was he different from the rest? Madge had not wept for him.
Joe . . . Bruce . . . Janice . . . Meg . . . Shaun . . . Liz . . .

Butchered, wrapped, and stored until required.

He raised his head, and it weighed a ton. The room had the used, shabby look that parties always left, with empty glasses everywhere and crumpled paper on the rugs. Waiters were moving around, clearing up.

Food!

"Hold that!" he shouted, and strode over to a man bearing away a tray big enough to bed a horse. Cedric grabbed it from him and carried it to the nearest chair. Sitting, he laid the tray across his knees and began to stuff himself with handfuls of tiny triangular sandwiches. There were little sausages and things wrapped in bacon. Lots. Cheese and crackers. He was starving, absolutely starving.

"When did you eat last?" a voice inquired.

A girl in shiny gold had just settled on a spindly, fragile-looking chair beside him. She had gleaming hair like a black waterfall all down her back.

He pondered, gulped down his cud, and said, "A pizza—last night."

She laughed. "And before that?" Her skin was cocoa-colored, the sort of skin that looked smoother than anything else in the world, that a man wanted to stroke very, very gently with the side of his finger. Her eyes were deep, dark, and twinkling; her thick black hair was long and unbelievably enticing.

A gorgeous girl. With dimples.

"An apple, in the morning." He felt his face returning her smile. "I was in a hurry to get away."

"Then carry on! Don't let me stop you." She helped herself to a slice of peach from his tray and grinned at him as she bit it.

A man in a tan-colored suit came and stood behind her. He had a narrow beard and a green turban. Cedric went back to sneaking glances at the girl's slender arms and legs and thinking how gorgeous she was. She did not bulge in front as much as the women on holo shows did. She had small breasts that came to points, and they looked firm and very nice indeed. Yes, he would not change a thing.

"Er . . . ma'am?" the man behind her said. "I'm told that the director will see us now."

"In a minute." She did not look around. She seemed to be returning Cedric's detailed inspection, and that was a rather alarming experience for a man.

He tried to speak, and his mouth was full again. Trying not to be too obscene, speaking mostly in sign language, he mumbled, "Who're you?"

She had a round, happy face, and yet very delicate features. Her nose was small and perfect. Her lips were made for smiling, and she had the cutest dimples he had ever seen.

"Princess Alya of Banzarak."

Cedric said "Oh, shit!" very messily, and felt himself starting to go red.

"You're an antimonarchist?" She raised very thin eyebrows in mock alarm.

"No! No! But Gran said there was a princess around, and I was to—oh—" He swallowed and said carefully, "Oh *bother*!"

She laughed again, but she seemed to be laughing with him and not at him, although he felt all gangly again, all arms and legs like a dumb kid. And pink.

"Highness!" the man said warningly.

"In a minute! May I call you 'Cedric'?"

"Of course, Your Majesty!"

"Call me Alya!"

"Yes, sir!"

She grinned again. He would do anything to earn another smile. But he was feeling better. It must be the food. Then he pulled a face. "Ugh! This jam's gone bad!"

"I think it's caviar," the princess said seriously. "Try those— they're shrimp."

"Not bad."

"They used to grow wild."

"What's this?"

"Papaya, looks like." She edged her stool closer and began naming the things he did not know as he tried them, sometimes sampling them herself. Princesses were apparently very friendly folk. He did not think this one had stolen any bits of other people.

Musn't think about that.

Someone held out a glass of orange juice. Surprised, Cedric looked up and saw that it was Bagshaw, grimly inscrutable.

He realized what Bagshaw had guessed—eating was making him thirsty. He said thanks and looked around. Bagshaw and the security woman; the turbaned man in tan, who had a narrow, dark face and must be in attendance on the princess—all clustered around him, as though his feeding habits were something remarkable. The waiters had gone. The five of them had the enormous place to themselves.

"I think you did wonderfully," the princess said. She seemed to be serious, but she saw his skepticism and smiled. "Jathro?"

"Highness?"

"How would you rate Doctor—Mister—Hubbard's performance?"

"He astonished me," the man with the beard said. He was trim and smooth and dapper, everything Cedric was not. "I thought the mob was going to riot and throw things. He didn't lose his head at all. I was impressed."

"Jathro knows," Alya said. "He's a politician. He makes his living rousing rabbles. Don't you, Jathro?"

Jathro responded with an exasperated sigh. "Highness . . ."

"But was Cedric right," Alya asked earnestly, "when he suggested that this shambles of a meeting was a big accident? You're the political expert. Tell us."

"Princess! Anything said in this building will be monitored. The director—"

"This," she told him sternly, "is important!"

He blinked at Cedric with doubt. "It is?"

"It is."

Doubt became strong dislike. "You're sure?" he asked the girl.

"I'm certain! Now tell us."

Jathro scratched his beard, glanced at the watching guards and the distant doorway, and then sighed again. "Very well. No, he was wrong. Dr. Hubbard is one of the great minds of our age. She does not make mistakes on that scale. She was thoroughly enjoying herself. Didn't you see how she was enjoying herself? Whatever happened, she had planned it down to the last cough. It was a deliberate slap in the face for everyone in the room—including her boss and former lover, the Secretary General. She spat on the massed media of the world. Incredible! I would not have believed it possible. Did you choose that suit, Deputy?"

"Huh?"

"That green monstrosity—did you choose the color?"

"Er, no."

"Don't be jealous, Jathro," Alya said sharply. "Cedric didn't ask to be made a deputy. He wasn't told anything about this in advance—were you?"

"No," Cedric said, stuffing lettuce in his mouth with the enthusiasm of a caterpillar. He liked lettuce. It had been underneath the fruit.

Jathro nodded. "The hair was just luck, I suppose, and the fingernails; but the bright green was a masterful touch. In English the color green carries connotations of immaturity, Highness. You were sent up as a human insult, Mr. Hubbard."

Cedric sneaked an unobtrusive look at his nails. They were even worse than usual. Damn! Girls noticed hands.

"Why they didn't tear you in half I can't guess," Jathro added with interest. "But tonight's newscasts will."

"Why?" Alya asked. "Why did she?"

Again Jathro sent a fidgety glance toward the door. "I have no idea. I am completely baffled. BEST is reported to be stepping up the pressure on her, and the Chamber is threatening to replace the U.N. altogether. If Hastings Willoughby and the U.N. fall, then 4-I will certainly go also. BEST and the World Chamber will take over. Hubbard Agnes will be lucky to reach jail in one piece."

Cedric exchanged puzzled stares with the princess.

"Then how did today help?" he asked. "Why did Gran do this?"

"I told you—I don't know. Short of public murder, it was about the worst thing she could have done. She played right into Grundy's hands. Remember, while the General Assembly is officially a collection of government representatives, in practice the delegates and their backers are bribed and coerced into giving Hastings his own way. He is puppet master of the world—or he was, until today. Now he's a public sucker."

He pondered a moment. "Grundy's ambition is to unionize 4-I. For years BEST has been urging the nations to replace Hubbard as director. Hastings has defended her, using the money she plucks off Stellar Power. They have been a great partnership, those two, for most of this century. After today's performance, though, he will not be able to resist the pressure. The media will be after her scalp, claiming she is senile or insane. Him, too."

"Hastings was not part of it?" Alya asked.

"No, no! He blanched when she sprang the trap. White-eyes' faces are very revealing. You saw—he was a broken man. He could not have known what she was planning. She duped him more than anyone. He must have expected something else, probably something that would help him out of his own troubles. Instead she will drag him down with her." Jathro shook his head sadly; but he had enjoyed his own lecture.

Alya beamed up at him in reward. "How do you know all this?"

"I watch the news as you do," he said sourly.

"Newscasters don't report this sort of thing!"

"Listen to what they don't say and watch what they don't show."

"Great! I'll remember. And our business?"

"I would guess that we have about a week. I give her that long, but very little more. Grundy will be starting his moves already."

"Grundy is BEST?" Cedric was struggling to follow it all. The information was interesting, but not immediately helpful.

Jathro nodded. "Grundy Julian Wagner. He and your grandmother have been deadly enemies for years. She will not allow a member of BEST into Cainsville."

"BEST's only a union," Cedric said, crunching celery. There was nothing else left on the tray. "How can a union—"

"Grundy can. Five years ago he withdrew all technical expertise from Italy. He threw the whole country back to the Middle Ages inside a week. People were dying in the streets."

"I didn't know that!"

"It wasn't reported—the media need engineers and technicians, also. Since then, though, no government has argued with Grundy. Nobody can."

"And now he's going to make them vote against Gran, and the media will help?"

Jathro barely nodded at that repetition of the obvious.

"Maybe she has gone crazy," Cedric said glumly. "Seventy-five?" That seemed an incredible age.

"Trust her!" Alya said firmly. "We'll all have to trust that she knows what she's doing."

Cedric was not sure he could do that—not after what had just been done to him.

"Then let us go and see what she wants with us!" Jathro said urgently.

Alya rose and lifted the empty tray from Cedric's knees. "What are you going to do?" she asked.

Muttering thanks, he clambered to his feet. She was not as tall as he had hoped—but not small! And still delicious. He ought to be feeling nervous around a princess, but he could not help wondering if that smile meant that she liked him, too. Dreamer! "I don't know. Try to do the job she gave me, and see if she was serious."

Jathro began to walk, but Alya did not, so he stopped.

"Where are you going to begin?" she asked Cedric.

"With System, I suppose."

Then they all moved, Bagshaw and the other guard, also. Cedric was trying to plan what he must do in the absurd job he had been given, but it was not very easy to concentrate on that with a scrumptious princess walking at his side. They could have held hands—her elbow was very close to his wrist. Then they reached a comset on the wall. The Jathro man had arrived at the door. Finding himself alone, he growled and strode over to join them. "Highness! Director Hubbard—"

"Oh, plug up!" Alya said absently. "You go talk to her."

Jathro took a very deep breath, as though dealing with a wayward child. "She has eight candidates for you to choose from."

"So? I already know that. I know which one I'll choose."

"You do? That list? You said—"

"I lied." Alya was keeping her eyes on Cedric—which was flattering, but too distracting to be much help.

He chewed a knuckle, wondering where to start. He would have to have something ready for ten o'clock the next morning, even if it was only a suicide note.

And Eccles Pandora had hinted at some extra treat up her sleeve. He must not forget that nasty threat.

"Even so," Jathro said. "Common courtesy—"

Cedric looked to Bagshaw. "How do I go up to my work grade?"

Most of the bull's face was hidden by his helmet, and the rest of it was just shiny plastic, too. "First time it balks you say, 'Override.' But anything you do after that may get tattled to your granny."

"How do I turn it off again?"

"Say 'normal grading'—or wait five minutes. It downgrades automatically."

Cedric nodded. Then his eyes went back to Alya. "Oh—sir?" Her dimples did lovely things when she smiled. "I'm supposed to play host for you, Alya. I'm not doing a very good job, am I?"

She smiled. "How long have you been here?"

Again Cedric looked to Bagshaw, who said, "About three hours."

"Then we arrived at about the same time. You can't know this place any better than I do."

"True. But—"

"Your Highness . . ." Jathro said.

Alya nodded. "I must go."

She took Cedric's hand and squeezed it. "See this?" She

pointed to a brooch on her left breast. It showed a double helix, outlined in gems. She clung to his hand still.

"Pretty," Cedric said doubtfully. "Looks like DNA."

"It's the—" Alya gave him a puzzled look. "For someone who claims he doesn't have grade school, you know some odd things."

"I watch a lot of holo. There's educational stuff there, if you hunt for it." He felt his face go pink again, because that sounded as though he were trying to sound smart. He knew he was not smart.

"Mmm. Well, this is the national symbol of Banzarak, a cobra and a silken rope."

He stooped to peer at it, less conscious of what it looked like than of where it was. The snake was done in emeralds, and the rope in diamonds.

"It's a very old symbol," Alya said. "It—"

"Highness!" Jathro growled a warning.

Alya hesitated.

"That is not your secret to reveal!" the bearded man said sharply.

Her chin came up and she met his eye, but she seemed less certain that she had been before. "I think it's important!" She turned to Cedric again. "For hundreds of years there was a tradition in my family. When a prince or princess came of age, and again whenever the throne came vacant, then he or she—"

"Highness, please!" Jathro stepped close, openly threatening. "There are others present."

Alya ignored him, fixing Cedric with her cryptic dark eyes and speaking rapidly. "He was presented before the people—or she was, originally. After Islam came, it was only the men."

"Islam?"

"In 1413. Never mind that. There were two clay pots—"

Ping! A holo of Hubbard Agnes glared out from within the comset. "That will do, Princess."

She had changed from her blue suit to a looser one in gray. She sat in a swivel chair with her back to the big pentagonal table that Cedric had seen earlier. Her expression was frosty, to say the least.

Alya flinched and then raised her hands to her face and bowed. "God be with you, Director."

"And with you, Your Highness. You were about to be indiscreet."

Cedric had thought that eavesdropping was not good manners. Apparently grandmothers had other rules.

Alya hung her head, avoiding the older woman's cold gaze. "It seemed important to me."

Then it was Cedric's turn to endure the freezing inspection.

"Indeed? That is a complication I had not anticipated. You must not let recreation interfere with business. Moreover, there are others present. I have utmost confidence in the discretion of both Dr. North and Dr. Bagshaw, and I admit that Cedric's brief career seems impressive so far. But there are some secrets that it is dangerous to know, Your Highness."

"Yes, Director."

"You will do nobody a favor by sharing that one."

"I am sorry. I will be more cautious in future."

"Very well." Hubbard Agnes seemed pleased. The tip of her tongue moistened her pale, dry lips. "Cedric, you handled those nerds much better than I expected."

"You hoped they would eat me alive?"

The cold blue eyes snapped him a look that felt like a slap in the face. "If you don't want to paddle, you can always swim."

"I'm sorry, Grandmother."

"Very well. What are you planning?"

"They want access to System."

His grandmother winced as though in pain. "Talk to Lyle."

"Lyle?"

"Dr. Fish. The one you tried to shake hands with when he wasn't here, remember? If I allow those busybodies into System, then they'll flood us with computer viruses. But if Lyle says he can do it safely, then go ahead."

Cedric's heart jumped. That felt very good indeed. "And I need advice! Aren't there consultants—"

"Talk to Personnel."

That was the lecherous bouncy black woman, Cedric remembered—Dr. Wheatland. Just thinking of her was enough to make him squirm. But Gran had not thumped him down yet; he began to feel hopeful. "Money? How much can I—"

"Spend whatever you can justify. You have credit now—for God's sake get some decent clothes."

That was deliberate unfairness. "And get my hair cut?"

"If you hurry, you can do both before the four o'clock lev."

"The lev?"

Obviously he was being stupid. She was not giving him time to think straight.

"You have taken on a commitment for ten o'clock tomorrow, so you had better go on up to Cainsville tonight. Princess Alya—we expect a window to Rhine at about two hundred hours. I want you to inspect it."

Alya flinched and glanced at Jathro, who said nothing.

"I do not think Rhine is important, Dr. Hubbard."

Hubbard Agnes rose from her chair. She was taller than Alya. "Are you quite certain? It is a very promising candidate."

Alya hesitated.

"You know the stakes, child."

Alya nodded unhappily. "I had best be certain." She glanced at Cedric, but was given no chance to speak.

"Come to my office and we shall discuss the next few days' program. Cedric—do whatever you feel is right. If you make a mistake I will throw you away like a gum wrapper."

Cedric boiled over. "Toss me out a seventeenth-story window?"

"That might be a kindness," his grandmother said calmly. "If you lose this job, you can anticipate a career in organ donation."

"Grandfather—"

"He is a rusted bucket. Your High—"

Cedric raised his voice over hers. "But is he my grandfather? How come I was born five years after my parents died?"

She looked at him as though he had just puked all over himself. "Your father's estate came to me. It consisted of six dirty shirts and a frozen embryo. I had that thawed out and put in a utervat to see what it might grow into. That was twenty years ago, and I am still waiting for the answer."

"Oh."

"Is that all?"

"All?"

"I just thought," his grandmother said, "that you might want to thank me."

"Thanks for everything."

His sarcasm was ignored. She smiled in mirthless satisfaction, and her eyes went back to Alya. "Come to my office now, Your Highness. We have much to discuss."

Alya reached out and squeezed Cedric's arm and walked away without looking at him. Jathro and the female guard followed.

Just in time, Cedric remembered another problem. "Gran, Eccles Pandora hinted that she has something special planned for tonight. It sounded like more than just your press conference."

Agnes sniffed. "Indeed? Well, I don't think we need worry

about it yet. WSHB management will certainly run it through their System. The strategy routines will recommend waiting until tomorrow, or later. Two bombshells in one day would be a waste."

"You know what it is?"

"I can guess. I knew a coin has been stolen. I wasn't certain who had bought it. Again, talk to Fish."

The door had closed. Only Cedric and Bagshaw remained in the big room.

"Gran?"

She sighed a *what now* sigh. "Yes?"

"Why did you do that to me? Why make a fool of me like that, and of all those important people, too?"

For a moment he thought she was not going to answer at all. Then she said, "I can't explain. If it makes you feel any better, you almost ruined everything."

"What? How?"

She replied with grim amusement. "By being a lot more of a man than I expected. I was really hoping that you'd start weeping. Try to do better in future."

"You wanted me to fail?"

She shrugged and vanished. The comset was a gray blank.

"Bitch!" Cedric said.

"You just worked that out?" Bagshaw said.

"Yes." Cedric sighed. He had a lev to catch; no time to rest or relax. "I need clothes."

The bull nodded impassively. "Nobody carries your size, half-pint, but you can choose style and fabric here, and they'll be made and waiting for you in Cainsville." Yet he did not move. He was waiting for Cedric to do or say something more.

Of course.

Cedric switched to command tone. *"System. Is my DNA on file?"*

"Nuclear DNA and mitochondrial DNA both," the twangy Eastern voice said.

"Do you have DNA for Hastings Willoughby on file?"

"I have three persons by that name on record." There was a hint of smug satisfaction in the tone. This System had traces of personality; it made Meadowdale's seem very primitive.

"The Secretary General."

This time the answer came in a hollow echo through Cedric's ear patch. "Information confidential to Grade Two."

Cedric was graded to One. *"Override."*

"Affirmative."

"Analyze his chromosomal DNA and mine. Report how similar they are."

"Stand by." He heard quiet resignation—much work to do.

Cedric waited, his heart thumping. If his grandmother had lied to him, and if his use of override was reported already, she would surely intervene. He twitched impatiently. Why so long?

"DNA's pretty complex stuff," Bagshaw remarked. "It'll take a while."

"Comparison complete," the ghostly voice in Cedric's ear said. "Analyses are identical to three decimal places."

Clone! He was Hastings Willoughby's clone.

Bagshaw could not have heard, but he apparently saw Cedric's face change, for he turned away toward the door so quickly that he might have been hiding a smile.

11

FOR SOME TIME Alya had been walking alongside Jathro, following the solid bulk of North Brenda, but she had been lost in thought, unaware of her surroundings. An escalator broke the steady pace and also broke her reverie, and it was then that she noticed the expression on Jathro's face.

"It was not sex!" she snapped in sudden fury.

His moustache writhed in a sneer. "Oh—forgive me!"

Damnable male pig! He looked so smug, so sure of his erroneous presumption, so unbearably superior—and then her anger turned and slashed back at herself. Why should she care what that grubby hack was thinking? Let him wallow in his prejudices! Let him assume that every woman was a natural wanton, and that this one was planning to jump into Hubbard Cedric's bed at the first chance she got. Why should she care?

Of course, she had chummied up very close to the boy—but never mind! Jathro repelled would be one less worry. It would take him off her hands—and vice versa.

Normally she would not have given a second thought, or even a first thought, to what might be churning inside Jathro's narrow little mind. Today she was just edgy because she was jet-lagged, and because she was tired, and because—because the pain was coming back. The *buddhi* had its claws in her again. Every step away from Hubbard Cedric was making it worse.

She felt a need . . .

It was not sex! He was an ungroomed, overgrown wisp, ungainly and immature. Alya had enjoyed men in the past and hoped to try out two or three more before she made a final selection, but she could guess how that young giant would approach lovemaking. Mud wrestling would hold more appeal.

It was certainly not a desire for friendship. They had nothing in common. She could converse on almost any subject on Earth, and Cedric would be ignorant in all of them. Not his fault, of course, that he had been reared inside a crate. But not hers, either. Buddies they could never be.

It was not some perverted mother instinct, either. He radiated loneliness and rejection. He needed somebody to comb his hair and pat him on the back when he tried hard, and steer him toward civilization. But not Alya! Motherhood and its troubles could wait.

It was not even admiration, although he had displayed an astonishing courage before an angry mob. Despite his youth, his ludicrous costume, and his jungle hairstyle, that boy had been more impressive than his grandfather, Hastings Willoughby, the celebrated political wizard. Boys did not do what he had done . . . but admiration would not explain her strange longing.

No, it had to be the *buddhi*. Close to Cedric it let her breathe again. Away from him, it tormented her. Somehow he was important.

She could not help that.

And then Cedric was driven from her mind as she found herself being ushered into the spine-chilling presence of Hubbard Agnes.

The office was large and five-sided, containing only the wide pentagonal table and some chairs. Two of the walls were comsets, the biggest Alya had ever seen. They displayed a breathtaking seashore—majestic high waves breaking and hurling spray, rolling up on a glistening beach that curved away into far distance. She could hear a very faint soundtrack, as though muffled through thick glass, and the effect was so realistic that she could almost smell the salty tang. A backdrop of high frondy trees looked like palms tossing in the wind, but the sky behind them had an uncanny purple tinge.

"You like it, Your Highness?" the director inquired, somehow managing to make the simple question condescending.

"Very much. Not Earth, though. That's a stable beach profile. I'm too young to remember those."

Alya thought she had won that round.

She took a chair next to Jathro but did not move it close to his. She had no intention of letting Hubbard Agnes intimidate her. Well, not much, anyway. She tried not to remember that Director Hubbard ate presidents and generals raw.

There were six of them gathered around the big table—Alya herself, and Jathro, and his two political sidekicks from Banzarak, who were staying silent as nonentities should. Moala had been left outside. For the Institute there was only Old Mother Hubbard—but then the door closed behind Dr. Devlin Grant, the King of the Rangers himself.

He bent low to tickle the back of Alya's hand with his moustache. He *smiiiiled* at her. He looked her over with much the same analytical, speculative gaze that Cedric had used. In Cedric it had been a curiously innocent and unconscious lechery, and rather flattering. In Devlin it was not innocent, and it made her flesh creep. Compared to Devlin, Jathro was a blushing virgin. Kas had warned her about Devlin.

The door was closed, the meeting brought to order. Bargaining was about to begin. That was Jathro's problem. There were some preliminary pleasantries: inquiries about Piridinar's health, and about Kas . . .

Alya wondered what color would seem best on two meters of mop handle with ochre hair, and how that hair would look if decently styled. Then she saw that Hubbard was addressing her.

"Your brother's call was not unexpected. We have a feast of Class Two worlds on our hands just now, a surfeit. We have never had so many. The last three years have been sparse, and suddenly we are deluged. The obvious problem is—which one do you want?"

Tiber.

"We are using river names again now. We have eight worlds under scrutiny—Nile through Usk. Grant, would you review them quickly for Her Highness?"

Blue-gray, to match his eyes, Alya decided; those big round Nordic eyes.

Devlin showed teeth from ear to ear. "Delighted! With the exception of Rhine, most of these seem to be short-period bodies. You do understand, Princess, that since both the Earth and the target world are moving, and since certain wave functions must be in phase, our effective access is restricted to the brief repeating periods we call 'windows'?"

Alya nodded again. Of course, Cedric might look real cute in dark blue, to set off that baby's-bottom complexion.

". . . estimate Rhine at eight days, approximately. That's why we are anxious for you to take a look at it tonight—last chance for a week. Po is the shortest—it's lining up at twenty-hour intervals, and the windows are already shrinking. If you choose Po, then you'll give me serious problems." Devlin *smiiiiled* again.

"What Dr. Devlin means," Hubbard interrupted acidly, "is that we just do not have time to run a thorough check on Po and later transmense a significant number of people there. We believe that three thousand is about the minimum viable plantation."

Alya shuddered. She was to be responsible for three thousand lives?

"More is better, of course," Devlin said, keeping his glittery snake eyes on her. "We managed forty thousand for Etna."

"Omar?" It had been Omar who had gone to Etna, five years before. Happy, laughing Omar! She had never known anyone more stubbornly joyful than Omar—until his call had come. Like her, he had endured a day or two of moping and rising strain, and then he had been gone, and Oh, the hole his passing had left in her life! It had been then, at fourteen, that Alya had first really felt the agony of the *buddhi*, the first time she had truly understood that one day it would carry her away also.

"Yes," Hubbard agreed, her blue eyes lancing across the table at Alya. "Prince Omar. We must assume, Your Highness, that he lives on, that the colony prospers. We have no reason to believe otherwise in his case."

Alya shivered again. "Do you sometimes?"

Hubbard pursed her lips, then spoke cautiously. "Never since your family became involved. In a couple of our early attempts, before we knew all the gruesome tricks that Nature can play—Oak, for example. You have heard of Oak."

"Cedric's—your son?"

It was old history—but had Hubbard ever shed tears? "Yes. My son. We were almost at the end of the string. The planting was complete—sixty-five hundred and supplies. Then the lab reports showed excessive concentrations of organic antimony compounds. No one had thought to check for those. Antimony is an element similar to arsenic in its toxic effects."

After a nasty silence, Alya said, "You could not bring them back?"

"There was no time." Hubbard was being clinical, as emotionless as stainless steel. Was she testing? "We had two more windows, of a few minutes each. We sent all the relevant information, of course, and what supplies we thought might be effective. Then contact was lost. We have never reestablished contact, with that or any other world. Our probing is basically random, you know."

She was trying to frighten Alya, or judge her dedication.

"And the antimony would poison them?"

"Unless it was a local problem and they managed to move to some other area free of the contamination. We never have time to explore more than a tiny fraction of a world."

"But you had time to say goodbye, in effect," Alya said, wanting to crack the metallic facade. "Why did you not at least rescue your own son and his pair?"

"I tried. Of course I tried! They refused to leave the others."

There was no feeling there at all, except maybe contempt for stupidity.

"So today, when you reported that eighty-six people have died in the Institute's explorations—"

"The true number can never be known." Hubbard Agnes smiled her ghoulish smile. "Other plantings must have failed after we lost contact. It is inevitable. I am surely one of the great mass murderers of history."

"So you see, Your Highness," Devlin said in his greasy voice, "how vital it is that we investigate these candidate worlds as quickly and thoroughly as possible. Nile we may discard. It is strictly Class Three, of scientific interest only. Orinoco looks good, very good. I am inclined to think that Po is hopeless— there just is not enough time. Even leaving Po out, we face a severe shortage of equipment and trained personnel."

"Tiber," Alya said miserably. "It's Tiber." Jathro's shoe slammed hard against her anklebone, too late.

Devlin and Hubbard glanced at each other.

"You are sure, child?" the director said.

"Certain. I saw the list. That name crawls off the paper at me."

The old woman nodded in clammy satisfaction. "And your brother called a few hours after we made first contact. Usk came later. Well, that helps. Grant, you had better keep your best for Tiber. But do not neglect the others."

Devlin leaned back and beamed toothily. "Who knows? We may have hit on two Class One worlds at once?"

"Possible, I suppose."

"I had better get away to Cainsville as soon as possible, then?" Alya resisted a temptation to push her chair back. "If I am to do whatever it is you want with Rhine in the middle of the night. I'm feeling jet-lagged."

"I was hoping we might have dinner together. You can go on the ten o'clock lev." The snow-haired bitch smiled her thin-lipped smile.

Trapped! "I was hoping to travel with Cedric," Alya admitted.

"Wait, please!" Jathro said angrily. "We have certain arrangements to negotiate yet."

But Alya had cut the ground from under him by revealing that name.

Dr. Hubbard made a faint shrugging gesture. "The arrangements are fairly standard now, Your Excellency. You choose the first five hundred, and we the next five thousand . . . We can discuss this again when we know which NSB we shall be colonizing—how long its windows are, how frequent, and how stable. What is the Tiber schedule, Grant?"

Devlin had his facts to hand. "We caught a shadow contact on April second. First focused contact at those coordinates came on the fifth. We opened a Class Two file right away and transmensed a robbie. It's very Earthlike—gravity, oxygen, temperature. In fact, next to Orinoco, it's the obvious candidate. We expect to meet up with it again tomorrow, around noon."

"Waxing or waning?" Jathro asked.

"Can't tell yet." Devlin favored Alya with another leer. "He means, are the windows growing longer or shorter?"

"I know." She did not care about any of that. She cared about Tiber, and the thought of seeing it tomorrow was like air to a woman drowning. But mostly—right now, before anything—she wanted to go in search of a certain overgrown adolescent. She wanted to hold his hand. She was crazy. He was leaving on the four o'clock lev.

Jathro was glaring murder at her. Poor Jathro!

"We'll have every telemetry gadget ready to go," Devlin promised Agnes, "plus a full overnighting expedition. I'll rip that planet to shreds for you."

Dr. Hubbard rose gracefully. It was impossible to believe she was so old. "I expect no less. Thank you all. This meeting can adjourn, but I wish a private word with the princess."

Two thousand years of royal blood be damned—princess be damned—there was no doubt who ruled here.

"Wait!" Jathro banged a fist on the table. "We must discuss this matter of refugees. Banzarak is a small and a poor country, Director. It has suffered grievously. Yes, many of its citizens have been allowed to emigrate to better worlds—but it has done far more than its share for refugees from other lands. We have almost a million in our camps now. They outnumber the natives! Yes, the Institute has helped generously, but money does not solve everything."

Hubbard frowned, as though that were heresy.

"It is essential," Jathro protested, his voice rising, "that the refugee portion of the planting this time be taken from camps in Banzarak. We can no longer—"

"Talk to Dr. Wheatland!" the director snapped, cutting him off without mercy. "I repeat that details can be better discussed when we have more data."

Jathro tried to protest more, but Devlin's powerful hand assisted him from his chair. Willing or not, he departed, his two flunkies scurrying after, not having spoken a word. Alya felt like a gnat stuck in a web as she watched the door close, leaving her alone with the all-powerful Hubbard.

The director sat down and stared thoughtfully at that door. "Your friend shows great compassion for refugees," she murmured.

"He has ambitions," Alya said.

Hubbard studied her for a moment, and then something like real amusement touched her face, revealing ghosts of excised wrinkles. "Do they include yourself, by any chance?"

"Yes."

"Oh, really!" Hubbard shook her head in disbelief. "Tell me!"

"He has a big following in the camps," Alya said glumly. "And in the country. If he can arrange for a large contingent from both—and all others will be fragmented, is this not so? Many groups from many places?"

Hubbard nodded, still amused. "So he will have a working plurality? He thinks that that, plus a royal wife . . ."

Alya nodded, and found herself returning a smile. "Exactly."

"I do not think he quite appreciates the problems he will face."

"Probably not," Alya said. "He's smart, but very limited—a child of the slums. He cannot imagine a world that is not confined and bounded. I mean, people don't live under demagogues from choice, do they?"

In frontier worlds there could be no kings, no tyrants; barely even civic mayors. Anyone trying to seize power would find himself a leader with no followers.

Then Alya realized that she was next item on the agenda. Hubbard was evaluating her, not Jathro. She dropped her eyes and vowed to guard her tongue more carefully.

The carpet under the table showed patches worn by years of feet. The office was unusually austere and frugal for a person as prominent as the director of 4-I.

"Your presence at the news conference today was a surprise to me, Your Highness."

Not since she was a tiny child being handled by gigantic adults had Alya felt so helpless, so conscious of unlimited power. That dangerous old woman could do whatever she chose—and would. Alya kept her head down and said nothing.

"What provoked your attendance? Intuition?"

Alya nodded.

"And what exactly has my grandson got to do with you?"

"You treated him abominably." Alya forced herself to meet the basilisk scrutiny.

"Yes, I did. What has that to do with you?"

"I don't know. But it has."

Hubbard's eyes narrowed and she tightened her lips.

"What were you doing?" Alya demanded. "Testing him?"

The old woman breathed a ghost of a laugh. "He hardly ranks a test on the scale of what happened today. Did you understand his remark about seventeen stories?"

Alya shook her head.

"Last night he blundered into danger. Early this morning Dr. Bagshaw rescued him, but in the process he was forced to drop Cedric fifty-five meters out a window. He was strapped inside an armored box at the time, yet that sort of experience could easily turn a man into a gibbering moron. Cedric, I am informed, merely complained that he had not been warned what to expect."

"Is that what you're trying to do—turn him into a gibbering moron? Because you made another try at it this afternoon, didn't you?"

Hubbard's thin smile mocked Alya's anger. "In Cedric's case it would seem to be impossible."

Time was running out—Alya could feel it. The lev would go without her. But she had to ask. "What do you mean?"

"It is a complex story. May I offer you some refreshment? Coffee? Wine?" The old witch was picking at Alya's impatience like a hangnail.

"No, thank you."

"Very well. What I told Cedric was the truth. He was sired by my son on Dickson Rita Vossler. As a zygote, he was removed from his mother's uterus and frozen. Common enough procedure nowadays, of course. In Cedric's case, his parents went to Oak, where they almost certainly died. Most of our clients simply vanish, but in John's case I had already arranged a cover story about a broken string and a lost expedition. We do that for anyone whose absence may be noticed."

The Banzaraki royal family did the same. Omar had "drowned while fishing." In a few days or weeks, Kas would find a convenient air crash or hotel fire, and the country would officially mourn Alya.

"So, ironically, John did die—and in what may have been the only sentimental action of my life, I had the embryo thawed out and brought to term in vitro." Hubbard smiled that razor-thin smile of hers again. "A foolish impulse? You think I felt a debt to my son?"

"I doubt that my opinion is relevant, Director."

"Or welcome. Anyway, I had Cedric salvaged and reared."

"Reared in an organage!"

"Don't jump to conclusions!" Hubbard's voice cracked like a rifle. "There are a thousand worse places for a child than Meadowdale. It is one of the best foster homes in the country. Some of the children are exactly what they seem—the offspring of prominent persons who cannot otherwise guarantee their safety. They are given a very healthy upbringing, with as much outdoor activity as modern climate permits."

Alya's temper sprang up and trampled caution underfoot. "Some are? But most of the inmates are clones, aren't they? Being raised as meat, as spare parts! And the healthy exercise is designed to produce strong organs for autografts!"

Hubbard dismissed that irrelevancy with a shrug. "Buying organs on the open market is expensive. Rejection is always a danger. So is disease. The children are well looked after."

"Physically!" Alya shouted. "Looked after physically—fed and exercised like horses! But their minds are deliberately retarded. You almost won a Nobel Prize, and your grandson probably can't even read!"

For the first time she had penetrated the ice—Hubbard had felt that thrust, but her voice went quieter, not louder. "His father wrestled livestock. I told you that Cedric was a foolish impulse on my part. I threw out my son's old underwear; I should have had his genital excretions flushed down the sewer."

Alya was beyond speech.

Hubbard leaned back in her chair and studied Alya thoughtfully. "This intuition of yours—have you ever heard of GFPP?"

"No."

"It is a relatively new technique, Genetic Factor Personality Prediction. It seeks to estimate a person's character by analysis of his genotype."

"Does it work?"

"Within limits. About three years ago I thought to run it on Cedric's DNA."

"And?"

"He scored high on intelligence, and sociability, and several minor factors. He was low on ambition. Very low on aggression."

Even when Cedric had been angry, he had barely raised his voice. Alya could not imagine him wanting to hurt anyone. "A gentle giant!"

"Sentiment! I am talking science. The truly remarkable feature of his profile was tenacity. There he registered as high as the test results would go."

"Tenacity?"

"A complex of perseverence, single-mindedness, and stubborness."

"Courage? Why not say it—'courage'?"

"Portmanteau term. Can't be scientifically defined."

Alya was being provoked to lose her temper. Trouble was, she was going to. "I know what it is, even if you don't. What about Cedric's tenacity?"

"I admit I wondered then if I might have wasted a valuable resource."

God in Heaven! Why can't she think of him as a person?

Hubbard chuckled soundlessly, as though she had heard that thought. "I said that GFPP has limitations—that is because inheritance is not everything. We are molded by our environment, also. Indeed, the usual estimate is that nature and nurture play a roughly equal role in making us what we are."

"You can quantify environment?" Alya did not try to hide her skepticism.

The old woman nodded. "We think so—in this case. Cedric's background has been very impoverished in stimuli. Dr. Wheatland has been encouraging this research, you understand. It is useful in evaluating potential employees. She set up parameters to model a deprived institutional upbringing, and we ran an HCP —that's a Holistic Character Prognosis."

"And what were the results of the experiment this time?"

"Very interesting!" Hubbard spoke as though she were discussing something pinned to a specimen board. "Apparently organages develop self-reliance. His tenacity estimate went right off-scale."

"So?"

"So I can use Hubbard Cedric Dickson without fear of reducing him to gibbering moronship. Drop him out windows? No problem. Set an angry crowd on him—why not? He has tenacity, he hangs on. He continues to function. You saw him today—he's virtually indestructible."

Alya felt ill. She pushed herself to her feet, determined to leave before she blurted something dangerous. "I shall go to Cainsville now."

Hubbard stayed sitting, staring across at her with what seemed to be quiet contempt. "You have missed the point, child."

"What point?"

"That I have plans for Cedric. He is a pawn, but an important one."

Alya leaned heavily on the back of the chair she had just left and stared into the hateful, mocking eyes of the evil old woman.

Mad as a moray eel.

"A pawn you plan to sacrifice?"

"Possibly."

"Literally? Literally sacrifice? Kill him?"

"If necessary," Hubbard said flatly. "I play for high stakes. This is the high table, Princess. No nickel bets here. And sentiment is a small-denomination chip. That is the point you missed. Don't throw your heart at my grandson. You'll only get hurt."

"I shall go to Cainsville now."

"I'm not finished. I have a question for you. This family intuition of yours—I understood that it only detected personal danger?"

Alya could guess what was coming. She waited, pretending that the question had been only a statement.

Hubbard frowned. "Well? Is it also self-referent?"

"Self what, Director?"

"Oh, don't play dumb bunny with me, girl! Does your inherited intuition also pick out breeding partners to enhance itself?"

Kas thought it did. Alya shivered. "If it does, then I am nothing but a pawn also, a puppet of the *buddhi* talent, and anything I say on the subject might be a falsehood."

"I see." Hubbard considered that, showing her lower teeth in the nastiest smile Alya had seen yet. "Well, enjoy my grandson while you can, Princess. I saw how you kept trying to paw him. But remember that he won't be available for very long. You can't have him to keep. He is not going to Tiber with you, or whatever world you choose. He is mine to do with as I please."

She rose, tall and straight in her gray suit, and deadly like a sword. "I shall give you a world, Princess Alya, and you may play Ms. Moses and lead your people to your promised land. But Cedric stays here. I caused him to be. He is mine."

"You're crazy!"

"Many have told me so. Most of them are dead now."

The Institute had its own lev station, on a spur from the main tube. It ran private cars nonstop between HQ and Cainsville every two hours, thereby creating massive inconvenience for every other user of the artery.

Alya reached the platform with minutes to spare, flushed and puffing from an entirely unnecessary sprint. Flanked by his guard, Cedric stood among the crowd, as inconspicuous as a palm tree in a rice paddy. He was wearing a pale blue poncho, and his hair was neatly set in tawny ripples. The doors had just opened, and he was watching the passengers emerging, so he did not see her until she reached him. He looked down then, and joy blazed in his smile.

Alya's heart rolled over and submerged in a swamp of guilt and dismay. She should have guessed what would happen! His grandmother had lied to him and betrayed him, his foster parents had been revealed as murderous ghouls, his childhood friends were all foully murdered—but a pretty girl had smiled and spoken kindly. If he was really nineteen, then he could not be more than eight months younger than she, at the most—or even slightly older. He must be forty centimeters taller. Yet compared to her, he was only an overgrown child.

He smiled sheepishly. "Hope you don't mind the work clothes. The store had nothing in—"

"Anything but that green! Blue suits you."

He blushed, as she had known he would.

And she felt better already, as she had known she would, just being near him.

She felt mean, using him as an antidote.

Then he shyly pulled a single red rose from under his poncho and offered it to her without a word.

Mean? She was as bad as his bitch of a grandmother.

The Institute's private lev cars were considerably cleaner and more comfortable than Nauc's usual. Furthermore, a deputy director had status. The little VIP compartment at the front was snappily appropriated by a group of venerable scientists who thought they deserved it more than Cedric did. His burly bodyguard explained their error. When words failed to convince, he led the eldest out by the ear, and the others followed meekly. Then Jathro tried to accompany Alya, and the bull threatened to burn off his beard with a torchgun. She suspected that was the bull's own idea, not Cedric's, but Cedric was grinning gleefully and obviously not averse to having her all to himself.

Even first-class seating would not normally have been adequate for his legs, but when acceleration was over and the seat backs reversed, he stretched out and laid his astonishingly large feet on the opposite bench. Alya raised the armrest between them, expecting him to accept that as an invitation, but he was apparently too shy to believe the signal. At first he made no move. Still, just being close to him relieved her pain.

Supported on magnets and flashing through vacuum at a thousand miles an hour, a lev was normally a smoother ride than even a super. The Cainsville express was an exception because it ran nonstop in a tube designed for stops. The curves were all gentle, but not all had been designed to be taken at full speed, and some produced a crushing gee force. On the first bend Cedric tried to keep his weight off Alya, but on the return she just relaxed and leaned. He caught the message and encircled her with a long arm. She fitted neatly into the crook of his elbow, his shoulder a good headrest, if bony; giants did have their uses. Thereafter they rocked in unison.

And that was the cure she had needed. The long arm banished the ghosts. The gnawing of her intuition died away at last—she was traveling to Cainsville and cuddling as close to Hubbard Cedric as decency permitted, and for the first time in days she felt peace. A *satori* never explained, so she could not guess why he should matter, but she was very relieved to know that mere proximity was enough. Whatever the *buddhi* wanted, apparently it was not going to drive her to coitus with him. She was relieved to make that discovery—bedding Cedric would be child molesting.

The comset was showing scenes of the daylight world above,

and being ignored. They talked. She queried him about Meadow-dale, and was impressed by the range of skills he claimed—tracking and shooting and rock climbing and horses and canoeing and cattle. There might have been more, but he grew shy and asked to hear about Banzarak.

"It's a silly little kingdom," she told him. "Too small to stage a musical comedy, Kas says. According to legend, it was founded by a refugee prince from India, a Buddhist fleeing the Brahmins of the Sunga dynasty. That's not very likely, though. How would he have got to Borneo at that early date?"

"When?"

"Heavens knows! The timing is all confused, but it would have been before Rome became an empire. The real records only go back a thousand years—"

"Only?"

"A little more. Ninth century in European tally. Anyway, whenever it was, we've managed to maintain our own identity ever since—"

"How?"

The aptness of his queries surprised her. His ignorance concealed a good mind, and his naiveté let him batter questions at her like a child. "The sultans were smart, of course."

"And the princesses beautiful?"

"That helped sometimes." She told how the land was threatened now by the rising sea, as well as by the diseases and famines, radiation and refugee hordes that were the bane of the century. She was reluctant to talk about herself, but he pried, with sly, penetrating queries. Soon she had admitted far more than she had intended about the extent of her travels, her experiences, and even her studies.

"But I'm like you, really," she said. "No doctorate; in fact not even a master's. I'm ashamed! I'm just a mental bumblebee, buzzing around collecting knowledge."

"What else," he asked, "apart from nutrition, soil chemistry, marine biology, and meteorology?"

"Oh, that's about it."

"No genetics?"

She knew he must have felt her twitch. "How'd you guess?"

"Just seems to fit. Parasitology?"

"Cedric! How?"

He smirked down at her. "Pilgrim clubs. I've seen documentaries on them. They have a list of recommended skills much like that. But why should a princess need to know any of those?"

"I know one skill that you have and didn't admit to," she said. "Cross-examination!" And she reached under his poncho and pinched him.

"Arrh!" he said. "Do that again—lower."

Obviously here was one child who would not object to molestation. Alya withdrew her hand quickly.

An attendant brought a snack and offered drinks. Alya stuck to coffee to combat her drowning sense of fatigue, while Cedric downed three large glasses of milk. He watched surreptitiously how she ate; he copied her. He had had a manicure, as well as a haircut.

They talked more. He wanted to be a ranger, he said, even if his father had not lived to be more than a trainee. She did not repeat what she had been told about his father.

"Maybe," he said wistfully, "if I do a good job at this media thing for Gran . . ." He fell silent, in an uncharacteristic brooding.

Tenacity, Alya thought. In one day he had already withstood shocks that would have broken most men twice his age.

Then her subconscious mind gave up chewing over a problem and tossed it up to her to deal with.

"How," she asked, "did you know I was going to be on this lev? You bought a rose."

Cedric grinned pinkly. "I knew Gran wanted you to look at something called 'Rhine.' That had to be a planet—NSB, I mean. That meant the lev. I wasn't sure you'd be on this one."

"If I hadn't, would you have waited for the next?"

He turned pinker and nodded.

And likely the one after that—Cedric was in love.

Bagshaw stuck his head in the door. "Evening news coming up. If it's anything like what they ran earlier, it's a hoot. Wonder where they dig up these clowns?" He leered, and was about to disappear—

"Wait!" Cedric said. "Anything about the President Lincoln Hotel?"

"No." The bull looked blank. "Should there be?"

Cedric pouted, but he voiced the holo on and tuned to 5CBC. They caught a brief glimpse of Quentin Peter, and then a clip of the disastrous press conference. It was just as bad as Alya would have guessed—Agnes behaving like a madwoman, and Cedric's shocked young face showing white above the mob of angry reporters, like a child standing on a table in the middle of a riot. The clip was cut off as soon as he admitted having no formal schooling, and before he asked what the media wanted from him.

That was blatantly unfair, but only to be expected.

"So far," a grim-smiling Quentin Peter told the world, "Director Hubbard has failed to refute her grandson's own assessment of his qualifications. Her other deputy directors are believed to earn in the neighborhood of two hundred thousand hectos a year. Not bad for starters, you'll agree! Now, for reaction to this extraordinary appointment, we go—"

With a snort, Cedric shouted the set off. Perhaps he thought he had suffered enough for one day. "If I'd known I was being paid that much," he said, "I might have bought you *two* roses."

"Easy come, easy go," Alya said. She picked up his hand and kissed it, then laid it firmly back on the seat.

She wondered if the cabin was bugged and decided it certainly could be. "What are you going to say at your commeeting tomorrow?"

He brightened. "I was thinking . . . What those guys really want is the romantic stuff, right? Gallant rangers adventuring on Class Two worlds, or even Class Threes. System can sort that out and then feed it into a subsystem, another computer hook-up altogether!" He was obviously excited about this brainwave.

"How would that help?" Alya asked cautiously.

"It can be done on a *one-way* download. Then no one can access back up to System itself. We had a gadget like that at Meadowdale to stop the small fry scrambling the main board."

She thought about that.

Obviously he had hoped for more enthusiasm. "Of course, we could add other stuff—life stories of the rangers; that sort of thing."

It would never work. One thread would unravel a sweater. Given a single bone, a paleontologist could reconstruct the whole animal. With detailed information about 4-I's explorations, the media would soon penetrate the secrets that Hubbard Agnes had defended so long—computers were very good at that sort of analysis. And of course it was for just that reason that Hubbard had fought her bitter lifelong battle with the media.

But Alya could not tell Cedric all that without revealing the great secret itself. And she was not going to—not because his grandmother had forbidden it, but because of what he would say: *Take me with you.*

He was not going. The director's word was law.

"It sounds good on the surface," she said. "Do you want my advice?"

"Please."

"Don't commit to anything at your commeeting. Just listen. That's what it's for, right? Why you called it? And don't make any announcements that your grandmother hasn't approved first." She meant *in writing*, but probably even that would not help much.

"You think she'd cut me off at the knees?" he asked after a while.

"I'm afraid I do, Cedric."

"And I think so, too!" He sighed. "I wish I knew why she's doing this to me."

So did Alya. Insanity still seemed the likeliest explanation. Hubbard Agnes had murdered her son and was punishing her grandson because of it.

But if Hubbard was insane, how long could she keep control of 4-I? And would Alya be able to escape to Tiber first?

Somewhere before it reached the St. Lawrence River, the lev supposedly surfaced, but it still ran in a tube and it still had no windows. Cedric called for exterior view on the com.

"No vid available," he was told.

"Why not?"

There was no reply—apparently the car's System was not up to such complex conversation.

"Nothing to look at, I expect," Alya said sleepily. "It's all dead rock up here now, I'm sure." Why bother fitting cameras to look at that?

And she settled deeper into the crook of Cedric's arm.

She awoke with a start and looked up to see his smile hanging over her. "I slept?"

"About an hour."

She straightened, rubbing her neck. Usually napping like that made her feel terrible, but she felt very good, refreshed, calmer. Lord knew she had needed the sleep. "Did I kill your arm?"

He smiled blissfully. "Total gangrene! But the other's long enough for two. I'll get half transplanted."

They had to be almost there—Alya saw what could only be Cainsville in the com screen. The Institute was an impressive complex, as big as a small city, but it was all one giant machine, a conglomeration of spherical domes and dish antennae, mysterious towers and ring structures—a thing unworldly, a dream of aliens.

"That's a sim," Cedric said. "Faked. Aerial view, see? But

nothing can fly over Cainsville, because of the microwave beams. It doesn't even have an airport."

Alya yawned, which saved her from having to comment.

Some hoaxes succeed by their sheer enormity: If no one can see more than a small part of it, no one can comprehend the whole. As Kas said, an elephant sitting on a skylight is invisible.

It had been the start of deceleration that had wakened her. The lev was arriving at Cainsville.

12

Cainsville, April 7—8

NOT LONG AFTER she arrived in Cainsville, Alya made an alarming discovery. She might have made it sooner, had she been given a chance to think.

But she had no such chance. A phalanx of red-suited bulls whisked her through security with a minimum of investigation—the whole complex was classified as a safe zone, she was told; she would need no bodyguards while she was there. Deputy Director Fish Lyle met her at the gate. She did not like him. He smiled with his lips, while the eyes behind his thick glasses looked long dead. Possibly she had merely been prejudiced by Kas, who claimed that Fish could raise goose bumps on him at fifty paces, and who muttered dark tales of mysterious disappearances at Cainsville.

Deputy Devlin would be her official host, Fish explained, but he had been delayed in Nauc and sent his apologies. Alya offered a silent prayer to several deities, giving thanks that she had been able to spend the last two hours with Cedric, rather than with the toothy Devlin Grant.

And then she was introduced to a young man in ranger denims, fair, fresh-faced, and superficially like an older version of Cedric, but thirty centimeters shorter, twice as wide across the shoulders, and probably considerably shrewder. Baker Abel was his name, Fish said, and he would be party leader for her expedition to . . . to wherever she chose. If either Fish or Baker had been told that Tiber was their destination, they did not say so—but Baker did say almost everything else imaginable. He started talking while shaking her hand and did not seem to stop thereafter. He had a cocky manner, an erratic limp, and an unending line of banter and commentary that would have done honor to a bazaar horoscope huckster.

Rangers were supposed to be strong, silent types, Alya thought—slayers of fearsome monsters. This one could have sold the monsters real estate or talked them into vegetarianism. He never paused for a reply, so she was relieved of any duty to make conversation. Yet he registered her fatigue without commenting on it; he deftly extracted her from the mob of obsequious officials and doting spouses without visibly offending anyone, and by snapping a few sharp words of command, he organized her and her companions and their baggage and attendants onto a caravan of golfies and got them moving at once. She detected a real competence behind the juvenile facade.

With Alya at his side in the lead golfie, Baker began a rapid commentary on the Cainsville complex, scattering bad wisecracks like a tour guide—see the pyramids by moonlight, and they're even better with your eyes closed . . . more than eighty hectares enclosed at Cainsville . . . nowhere to walk a dog—and he effortlessly spun webs of statistics.

Despite a heavy traffic of vans and bicycles and other golfies, the little cart built up a considerable speed on the straights, with Jathro and the others zipping along behind. System did all the steering.

"Just tell it where you wish to go, Princess," Baker explained, "and it'll get you there. Hang on for this curve. Lots of curves, because so many of the buildings are domes. Forty-two geodesic domes, and another thirty in plain chocolate . . ." He prattled on as the caravan wound and twisted along a bewildering variety of busy arteries. Most were large enough to rank as city streets, but sometimes Alya found herself hurtling at high speed along narrow passageways like hotel corridors, hoping that nobody opened a door in front of her. After the sharper bends, she would listen for Moala's screams, far behind her.

"This must be a shortcut," Baker remarked cheerfully. "Can't say I've ever come this way before. I expect Livingstone Dome's busy just now, with everyone heading home—whoops!" The golfie skittered on two wheels around a right-angle bend and shot through a doorway that was still opening. "Now this is Lewis and Clark Dome . . ."

Alya tuned his voice out, hanging on tight and holding a starched smile on her face to hide pure misery. Jet lag was really rattling her now. She had been up all night, in effect, and this was early morning, Banzarak time, and—and that was when she made the alarming discovery.

She was in Cainsville, and there was nothing at all she could do about Tiber until its window opened the next day. That should have been enough to satisfy the most relentless intuition. But it was not. Somewhere during her arrival she had become separated from Cedric—who most likely had been officially met also, to preserve the fiction that he was a deputy director. So now he was gone and her dread had returned. She felt a gnawing urge to ask Baker to turn the golfie and go back; she twitched and itched with the need. Apparently Cedric had become a permanent addiction for her.

She wondered with sudden dismay if her intuition could be faulty, if it might be misleading her and everyone else. That could happen. The history of Banzarak held many tales of sultans or their children being driven mad by a *satori*. The warnings were not specific, and they never gave reasons. A simple aversion was easy enough to understand—don't take that plane, you don't want the fish sauce, stay out of the water today—but sometimes the urge was not just a negative, it was a positive command to *do* something, a something that was never specified. Then the victim could only thrash around, trying everything possible in the hope that something might relieve the premonition. The urgency might be extreme, the directive incomprehensible—and that combination could bring on insanity very quickly.

That was the dark side of the family gift, an instinct for self-preservation bred into her genes by generations of clay pots and cobras, silk ropes and royal inbreeding. The people of ancient Banzarak had wanted sultans who were guided by the gods to make correct decisions, and so they had devised the puberty rite of the deadly snake and the harmless string. The youths who had chosen wrongly had died. Those with the right hunches had survived to bear children. Genetic selection had done the rest, and in time the Draconian test had created what it sought to find: an inherited intuition.

The sultans had served their land well, and their family, too. By repeated inbreeding, they had strengthened the gift and also retained it among their own relatives. None of them, it was said, ever swallowed a fish bone. None ever met with accidents—except for Alya's own parents, who had died while rescuing people during the floods of 2040. Kas swore that they had known what was going to happen and had stayed on to prevent a panic that might have killed thousands more.

Yet sometimes the intuition went beyond the mere avoidance of danger, as Hubbard Agnes had guessed. All afternoon Alya had been trying not to think of Kas's account of his first meeting with Thalia. "Instant bird song" was the way he described it.

Cedric had worn an aura of fire.

Oh, hell!

He was a nice kid, but unlucky, unpolished, uneducated . . . He had nothing to offer except mere physical satisfaction. And probably little of that—finesse would not be his forte.

Couldn't her genes have found someone her own size?

And he was not available anyway.

"Columbus Dome," Baker Abel said, bringing Alya out of her black reverie. The golfie had come to a stop before a narrow doorway that led into a stairwell—containing a very curious staircase.

"You're not familiar with spiralators?" he inquired as Alya hesitated. "Just reach for the handle at the back and jump in. Now!" He took her by the waist and lifted her bodily inside. Then he moved to follow, tripped, and landed on his knees on the tread below her.

He rose, grinning up at her rather sheepishly. "Gimpy leg," he explained. "Not quite healed yet. Got bitten by a rock. Well, it looked like a rock. There should have been a sign: 'Danger: Do not feed the rocks.'"

Alya was certainly not familiar with spiral escalators. She watched with interest as a doorway to the next floor went curving by and vanished downward. "What happens at the top?" she asked.

"Not sure at all. We sent a guy up to find out once, but he never came back. Expect he's still going."

"Smartass!"

Baker grinned. "This column in the middle is the newel, okay? Well, there is a school of thought that says that at the top the steps level out like an ordinary escalator and then curve around and vanish into the newel. The treads are sliding up vertically on the newel tube, you see, and it's the newel that's doing the turning. The theory is that they flip over and come back down inside the tube. I don't believe a word of it. It's done with mirrors. Next door's ours. Stand by to leap . . ."

Alya stepped out nimbly. Baker stumbled again and would have clutched at her to steady himself—had she been there. Moreover, in her hasty efforts to help him, she ineptly thumped him on the back of the neck with one hand and behind the bad knee with her foot, and thus spread Baker Abel flat on the rug. And then she trod on his fingers.

"Oh, I am extremely sorry," Alya said. "That was clumsy of me."

He scrambled up, completely unabashed. "Black belt?"

"Brown."

He grinned with no trace of a blush on his pallid Nordic face. Cedric, had he tried that and been caught out, would have glowed like a neon lamp. Baker Abel was little older, but infinitely more confident than Cedric, and his foolery was hiding arrogance, not shyness. As he turned to help Jathro and the others emerge from the spiralator, Alya allowed herself a small smile.

Baker enjoyed watching her, and she knew that he would certainly accept the challenge and try again for a fast grope as soon as he got the chance, but her instincts told her that his intent was not serious. His real interest lay elsewhere; his heart was already mortgaged.

She did not know how far other women could judge men's intentions, but she had never been wrong yet, so perhaps the *buddhi* helped. Baker would play for fun, with no attempt to follow through. The antler-moustached Devlin Grant had been calculating when he could make room for her on his calendar. To Jathro, she was a potential meal ticket. All three men looked upon her differently.

And Cedric had fallen hopelessly in love the moment she had spoken a kind word to him.

Baker made a sweeping gesture at the room. "Circular. You get sick of circles in this place. This is the guest lounge. Eating machines over there for snacks. Bar over there. Full cafeteria two floors down. You get Room One, of course, Your Highness. Dr. Jar, Room Two. Grant said he'd call for you at 0200. Until then, what pulls your string? Food, rest, dancing, swimming, exercise, stamp collecting?"

"Sleep," Alya said.

"Alone?"

At that, of course, Jathro exploded in roars of pompous indignation, which was exactly what the jokester had intended.

Baker's juvenile silliness was going to be a pain in the posterior, but he had his moments.

Just after two A.M., with the lights dimmed to a moody gloaming, Alya found herself being graciously assisted into the down spiralator by Devlin Grant. Her efforts to sleep had been fruitless. She felt at once hungry and nauseated, exhausted and feverish. She had a headache again, and a hollow, used-up feeling. This journey to inspect a world called Rhine was a totally useless exercise, she was certain. It did not frighten her, nor did it excite her—it was merely irrelevant. The thought that she would see Tiber later in the day had power to stir her, but even that seemed less urgent than something else . . . someone else . . . someone she should go looking for. She cursed herself for being a brainless infatuated ninny even as she knew that what she was feeling had nothing at all to do with conventional physical desire. She certainly had no patience for the bedroom eyes and predatory scrutinies of Devlin Grant.

Jathro sat in glowering solitude in a second golfie, while Devlin squired Alya in the first. He chattered, although much less painfully than Baker Abel would have done. The golfie ride itself was considerably more sedate—Baker must have given System some very unorthodox instructions on the earlier occasion.

"We shall be using de Soto dome, princess," Devlin explained. "We actually have six transmensors operational at the moment."

That surprised Alya. "I thought one was the limit?"

He flashed his teeth at her. "We can only use one at a time. Prometheus Dome is the power source. About once an hour System turns on that equipment for a moment and cranks the temperature up a few thousand degrees. Stars are easy to find. You would never want to visit Prometheus.

"For exploration work, though, de Soto and David Thompson are our largest and best equipped, but with so many NSBs to investigate all at once, we may have to use Bering and van Diemen, as well."

Under the orange dimness the passages and halls were eerily barren of traffic. Alya struggled to suppress yawns. Her eyelids weighed a ton apiece. The golfie halted at a door for an automated identity check, and Devlin paused in his lecture until they were under way again.

"We picked up Rhine's shadow on prelim scan back in February—we always have a hundred or so leads ready to follow up.

We've only made one real pass at it, and that was more than a week ago. The specs looked good, and we dropped a robbie. We'll see what it has to tell us."

The golfies came to a halt at an armored door. If the whole of Cainsville was regarded as a secure area, then some parts were more than just secure, for certainly the men who were rising from their poker game to inspect the passengers were guards, and there were two more checks before the drive ended.

Eventually Alya found herself being assisted into a person-shaped plastic bag. Apart from its sickly chemical odor and a tendency to whistle when she walked, it turned out to be surprisingly tolerable. Its air supply was cool, and it muffled voices slightly, which was not all a bad thing. It also fended off Devlin's wandering hands, which was a very good thing. She shuffled along between him and Jathro, both similarly garbed, heading for the next stage. She thought she would give anything in the world —in any world—for about a week's sound sleep.

They passed through two successive airlocks with circular doors a meter thick, like those on bank vaults, through a decon spray, and finally entered a gloomy, red-lit control center, loud with anonymous voices. Devlin guided Alya to a couch and then excused himself to go and attend to business. Fine by her.

Jathro sat on her left, being darkly inscrutable, either suppressing excitement or possibly just sulking over Alya's continuing lack of interest in him. She did not care which. He did offer to find her a coffee. She declined, without asking him how she could drink one when sealed inside a bubble suit.

The room held half a dozen people seated at coms, all in the same sanitary packaging, half of them jabbering into mikes over other voices coming from speakers. Two walls were transparent and showed larger and busier rooms beyond, where more troglodytic shadows moved in ruddy-tinged dimness. Another wall held a giant circular window, and after a moment Alya guessed that the blackness beyond must be de Soto Dome itself. The glass— or whatever the port was made of—could probably withstand anything up to and including stellar infusion.

A constant rain of voices splattered through the air around her, individually quiet and calm and confident, but in the mass conveying a sense of turmoil and confusion. Once in a while she recognized Baker Abel, sharp and imperative, devoid of jocularity. Often the voice was the nasal twang of System.

"Four-seven . . . four-six . . . four-five . . . Stand-by, Prometheus. Three-five . . . three-six . . . Bering finalizing, Prometheus engaging . . . calibration, is that a shadow on seven? . . . Confirming shadow on seven . . . shadow noted . . . mark two-nine."

What did it all mean? Did anyone know?

Did anyone care?

"Prometheus counting . . . three . . . two . . . one. Stellar infusion."

Machines clicked and clattered somewhere in the dimness. She yawned until her jaw ached. Her interest in Rhine was absolutely zero. Tiber, fine. Tiber felt good. And at the moment a certain long young man would feel good. She wondered where he was billeted. Her head was clogged with fatigue.

Devlin reappeared and settled on her right, too close. "Just a minute or two, now. We're stoking up Prometheus to heat Nauc's morning bathwater. Rhine's next, if it's there. Abel's laying bets that Contact'll be around on the night side this time. Lord alone knows how anyone can tell, but that guy's right more often than he's wrong."

"Perhaps he has intuition also, Dr. Devlin."

Devlin flashed a big smile to show he was unwounded. "Grant! Call me Grant. I doubt it. You are unique; a unique woman." If he was trying one of his steamy glances, the dim lighting masked it. "Baker's goddamn baby sense of humor riles me, but he's a good operator."

Voices weaved and twined in intricate polyphony.

"Perhaps I should explain some of the physics here," Devlin remarked, sliding closer and laying his arm along the back of the couch.

She made a noncommittal noise.

"Her Highness studied superstring theory under Gutelmann in Ankara," Jathro said with satisfaction.

"The hell she did!" Devlin said, and for a moment he was speechless.

Except that Her Highness has forgotten every integral and fractal tensor she ever knew, Alya thought. Four-dimensional space-time was a special case within ten-dimensional superspace —that much had been known by every schoolboy for sixty years —but the way in which the Chiu-Laski transmensor realized one of the normally nonoperational dimensions by exchanging it for one of the three spatial dimensions was something that could only be expressed in math.

And the resulting string could be regarded as being of either infinite length or of no length at all. That had never made any sense to Alya, but as Gutelmann himself had said, "Just because we don't understand it doesn't stop it working." On a clear night a telescope swept across the heavens would catch a million stars. So the transmensor could sweep a string through superspace, finding stars whose location relative to the Earth could not be expressed in real quantities. A transmensor gave strings, not answers, Gutelmann said—*more knots than yesses*. Baker Abel might appreciate that one.

"Four-two... elevation..."

Prometheus had disengaged. Alya gathered that much. Just as well, or it would have melted the planet. She heard a sudden tremor of excitement in the dryness: "Response at predicted coordinates. A little high on *tange*... No rippling."

Pause...

Tange?

"Ah! Here we go," Devlin said with satisfaction.

The voices began picking up again, muttering their incomprehensible muddle of sounds.

Then she sensed a sudden crackle, and everyone seemed to look toward the window. Was that a faint bluish tinge she could see?

"Young devil's right again," Devlin said. "That's moonlight out there. Two moons, both a fair size. Come!"

He rose and insisted on assisting her. They went over to the port and peered through.

There was nothing startling, for Alya had seen such places on a hundred holodramas and even a few newscasts. The sheer size of the dome impressed her. It was larger than any stadium she had ever seen, and she had seen many. Of course, its relative emptiness was making it seem larger. The floor saucered down to flatness in the center, where an indistinct clutter could just be discerned as a ring of armored skivs like patient dinosaurs, plus a blur of other equipment, anonymous in the muddled glow of red lamps high above and moonlight blue streaming up from the middle.

It was all irrelevant. If they suggested Alya go out there and take a look, she would obey without argument and it wouldn't make any difference. Tiber. Not Rhine, *Tiber!*

The voices rose again, and then fell still, listening to a warbling rattle on a solitary tinny speaker.

"They're picking up the robbie!" Devlin explained tensely.

A robbie would be a robot of some sort, some gadget that for the last seven or eight days had cruised around—crawled?

flown? swum?—and now was radioing in its findings.

"... at mean sea level point nine nine nominal ... variance subnominal ... oxygen one point one nominal ..." That was System, relaying.

Alya wandered back to the couch. The rustle of excitement came again. The rest of the people in the room were grinning at one another.

"... noble gases nominal ... deuterium point ..."

"Looks good!" Devlin said.

Then ... she had missed it, but others had not. Devlin muttered "Fart!" under his breath.

"Grant, you read?" That was Baker's voice.

"Yeah, we got that, Abel."

"You heard? She's bassackward." Disappointment.

"I heard."

"Suggest we throw out a couple o' mark fours and a seven-eighty-eight, and strike our tent here. Pick 'em up next window."

"Fine," Devlin said. "Go ahead."

"What's wrong?" Jathro asked, petulant at being out of things.

Devlin yawned and stretched. "Right-hand thread. Amino acids—they're what make up proteins, okay? All terrestrial amino acids are left-rotary. Almost all Class Twos are the same—you'd expect half and half, but that's not so. But a few have right-rotary isomers, like this one."

"So?"

"So they would mess up your body chemistry something horrible. I'm not sure what happens, but they plug the works. We've tried hamsters and we've tried mice. They don't last long on a bassackward. You were right, Alya—Rhine's not important."

Tiber ...

Devlin escorted Alya back to Columbus Dome, with Jathro scowling along in the background like a distrustful maiden aunt. She felt groggy and weary beyond caring about anything, and yet a sudden spasm of ... *something* ... struck her as the spiralator brought her to her floor. She stumbled as she stepped out, just as Baker Abel had done earlier in the evening.

She thanked her escorts at her door and closed it in their faces. The clock showed exactly 0400. By Banzarak time it was afternoon, and she ought to be wide awake.

She leaned helplessly back against the door and stared across at the oversize bed, which was grotesquely rumpled by her earlier attempts to sleep on it. If she did not sleep soon, she would collapse. She felt near to tears with exhaustion. She would do anything for a good night's sleep.

Anything?

Yes, she decided. Anything. The *buddhi* was completely unyielding, completely immoral. It would give her no peace. Not here. But she had slept like a baby in Hubbard Cedric's embrace. She had been right about Rhine. She had no cause to doubt her intuition.

Torn between relief and disgust, she went back to the spiralator. Two floors higher felt right to exit. The circular lounge was the same, and she walked around, studying doors, until she found one that—again—felt right.

She had no doubts that this was where she must come, of all the rooms in Cainsville. Nor did she doubt that he would have left his door unlocked. She did not knock.

She was surprised, however, to find a light on. He was sitting up in bed, bare-chested, reading a magazine. He laid it down as she entered, his face so shadowed that she could not see his expression. She had hoped for darkness to hide her shame, but there could be no pulling back, although surely hordes of royal ancestral ghosts were petitioning all the gods in history to hurl thunderbolts at her. Pretending a calm that her knotted stomach and dry throat belied, Alya walked across to him.

"Can't sleep?" she asked.

He adjusted the covers around his waist in an oddly defensive gesture. "Bed's too short. And I was checking on Rhine, like you."

"You saw me?"

He shook his head vigorously, registering alarm. "Wasn't spying on you—just the data. But I knew that's why you'd come."

She was surprised that he had gained access. Illiterate or not, he was skilled on a com; she had forgotten. Holos had been mother and father to him.

Now what? He was staring, naturally—wide-eyed with hope, starting to blush, and yet not able to believe his good luck. All she wanted was to lie there beside him. That was the only place in the world she would be able to sleep. Fair enough—but first she would have to pay the rent.

The preliminaries were over and each was waiting. Surely he would not make her beg? Then he pulled back the edge of the covers, but not far enough to expose himself. It was an invitation to sit and talk, as if ladies really did visit men in the middle of the night for conversation—perhaps he thought they did. Or it was an invitation for more, if that was why she had come. The gesture was oddly touching, a good solution to their problem.

Well! If this was what Alya must do, then she would do it properly. No cheating—the works. She smiled as though she expected to enjoy herself. She kicked off her shoes and reached for her zip, and saw his ribcage heave in a deep sigh of wonder.

And suddenly she was certain that this was not going to be child molesting. He was watching her intently, eyes glittering with excitement, but a man was supposed to react like that. He was not squirming, or making nervous jokes, or smirking a juvenile leer. His unpredicatable boy-man transitions continued to surprise her, but the manual for the act of love did not require literacy. Cedric had done it before—she was sure. And then she felt less guilty.

"You want the light off?" he muttered, his voice thick.

"Not unless you do?" Dumb question.

She took her time, dropping her clothes deliberately, letting him look. Even naked, she found that she could take his gaze without flinching—it was flattering to be so obviously appreciated. Then she took time to unfasten her hair and shake it loose. Pale skin was very revealing—his flush of arousal was spreading over his chest.

Then she was ready, and he seemed to think that it was his turn, or that she might be equally interested. He took a deep breath and threw off the covers completely. He slid down, flat on his back. He was not wearing anything, either.

Alya slipped into his embrace. The body contact sent a delicious sense of peace rushing through her—Safety! It was dry land in a flood. It was slamming a soundproof door on a clamoring factory. It was all she needed.

It was not, obviously, all she was going to get.

"Just hold me first," she whispered, melting against him. "Not yet! Just hold me for a minute." Then you can collect the rent.

13

SHAVED, SHOWERED, DRESSED, and feeling quite extraordinarily pleased with himself, Cedric set off down to the cafeteria in search of a hearty breakfast, and for the first time managed the spiralator without banging his head. He felt faintly fuzzy after three sleep-shy nights—excitement on Tuesday, terror on Wednesday, and now miracles. What miracles! Were it not for his extremely smug sense of well-being, he might have concluded that she had been only a dream.

Crazy! When he had bought all his new clothes the day before, he had forgotten underwear. At night, therefore, he had rinsed out his briefs and hung them up to dry. For the first time in his life he had gone to bed in the raw. Then the most beautiful girl in the world had come and climbed in beside him and let him make love to her. He must remember to buy some shorts, but he would certainly sleep that way from now on. It paid off!

He wished he could share that joke with—but he had decided not to think about Meadowdale.

And good guys did not tell tales, anyway.

There were a dozen or so people eating, but no one he recognized. They would all know him, after yesterday. He was not inconspicuous. Some of them, he noticed, were reading as they ate. He had not brought the magazine he had bought to practice on, and he was not going to try reading in public, anyway.

So he thought about Alya instead. He had been careful not to ask her why she had come there all the way from Banzarak, but he was beginning to guess. Last night he had done some research on the traditional ritual with the cobras. System had coughed out clips of it, because it had survived into modern times as a tourist attraction. Of course, the whole thing was a fake, the reports said, and always had been—the snake was defanged and the prince or princess was warned in advance which pot to choose, anyway.

Cedric did not think Alya would have cheated like that. Some people were born with a good musical ear, some were born to grow tall, and Alya's family all had a sort of second sight, handed down from the distant past. Everyone knew that the East held mysteries that science did not understand yet! She must have been hired by the Institute as a consultant seer. The Institute was supposed to do scientific research, and would never admit that it was using mystics. That explained why System was treating Alya as a secret.

And the previous night the hope had been to find a Class One. Devlin himself had been there with her—in the middle of the night—but the party had dispersed as soon as Rhine had turned out to be a mirror world. Everything else about it had been fine, apparently.

Obviously they had been hoping for a Class One. After thirty years of unsuccessful hunting for Class One worlds with science, his grandmother was trying with mystics, obviously. He had put that idea to System, but all he had discovered was that there must be a Grade Zero confidentiality, higher even than his own Grade One. But if he could get so close to so stunning a secret so quickly, then the media would do the same, sooner or later, and the more information they were given, then the more sooner and the less later. His grandmother would not tolerate that—she dared not. Small wonder that she did not get along with BEST! Conventional scientists would denounce her as a charlatan. That was what Alya had been hinting at on the lev, when she had warned him not to make any announcements until Gran had approved them.

Breakfast was good and there was lots of it. He would have liked a third helping, but he had an appointment with Dr. Fish to talk about the ten o'clock commeeting. In the cruel light of morning he thought he had been absurdly snotty to issue that invitation; but Gran had given him a job to do, and he must try his best.

He found a golfie and told it to go to Philby Dome, where the offices were, and he arrived right on nine.

Dr. Fish's room was small and plain and starkly tidy. Along one wall stood a row of metal cabinets, and the two drawers that were open were full of papers. Cedric wondered what sort of records could be too secret to store in System.

He liked Dr. Fish, who was short and almost plump and much less intimidating than, say, Devlin Grant or Hastings Willoughby. His hair gleamed like black plastic, heat-molded to his head, but there was no gray in it. Cedric had seen people wearing glasses in historical holodramas often enough, but never in real life. Funny things, eyeglasses—they made Dr. Fish's eyes seem as though they never blinked. The deputy for Security reached across his desk to shake hands, and of course that reminded Cedric of how he had made a fool of himself in Gran's office.

Dr. Fish had soft white hands, with extremely short fingers, and he waved his visitor to a plain, hard chair.

"Now, Deputy," he said with a smile that did not crease his pudgy face at all. "What can I do for you?" His voice was an elusive murmur; it required a listener's full attention, and it made everything sound like a secret.

Cedric laid his right ankle on his left knee. "Dr. Fish, would you please call me Cedric? I'm not very comfortable being a deputy." He paused and then decided to take a chance. "And, sir . . . why did Gran do that to me? They thought she'd gone crazy!"

"They've been thinking that for thirty years."

Silence. Apparently that was an answer.

"Oh. Well, what I need is some advice."

He outlined Gran's instructions, and what he thought the media would want, and his own idea for a one-way download. Dr. Fish listened to the whole thing without moving at all, his hands lying limply on the desk, his eyes so still that they might have been painted on the backs of his glasses. So attentive an audience was very flattering, and Cedric could feel himself relaxing. At the end he switched—left ankle on right knee—and waited for reaction.

"That would work, Cedric. Will you announce it today?"

The answer should have been yes, and Cedric was relieved that Dr. Fish had approved of his idea, but he remembered Alya's advice. Alya did not trust Gran, and Alya knew a lot more about the world than he did, even a lot more about the Institute.

So he said, "No. I think I should listen to what the media want, and then I'll call Gran before I make an announcement. Maybe she should make it, not me."

Dr. Fish pursed fat lips. "She's on her way—she'll be here by noon. But a quick resolution of the problem would enhance the viability . . . make you look good. A definitive statement of your proposed methodology would be welcomed by the press. It would do a lot to ameliorate—take the heat off the director."

"I'll see, sir. When I see what they ask for." But it was a tempting thought, to be able to help Gran so soon.

"I'm sure you've already guessed their requirements and have elicited—found the answer." Dr. Fish smiled again.

"One other thing, sir. I need some expert help! Surely there must be consultants that I could hire to advise me?"

Distaste showed on the clay-white mask. Dr. Fish curled his lip. "They might be members of BEST."

"Huh?"

The curvature increased. "Members of the Brotherhood of Engineers, Scientists, and Technicians are not allowed into Cainsville under any circumstances."

Oh! Cedric put both feet on the floor. "Well . . . thank you for your time, sir."

"There is one other matter we should discuss."

"Yes, sir?"

Fish's tiny voice crept over the desk like lurking spiders. "Dr. Eccles Pandora, of WSHB."

Cedric winced and said nothing.

"She is planning a special tonight. Normal programming has been canceled to make way for it."

Gran had foretold that it would be put off until tonight. "What sort of special, sir?"

Dr. Fish smiled more broadly than ever, and yet somehow his face held no amusement at all. "That is not quite certain, but as deputy director for Media Relations, you should be standing by to make a quick rebuttal."

Gelded with a rusty saw . . . Cedric gulped and took a couple of very deep breaths. Why did it have to be Eccles Pandora? "How can I, sir? I'm new on the job, and I don't know the truth. It would be the truth, wouldn't it? I'm not a very good liar."

"Certainly the truth. Come and see me this afternoon—I should have amassed more data by then. We can draft something up together, or perhaps even prerecord it." Dr. Fish blinked for the first time. "We might enlist some help—from Frazer Franklin, for instance."

Cedric felt confused. "He's WSHB, too! Why should Dr. Frazer help us, sir?"

"Because I can blackmail him."

Dr. Fish's face was as deadpan as ever, but Cedric knew when he was having his leg pulled. He laughed appreciatively and unfolded himself from the chair. The deputy for Security rose also. Perhaps it was because Cedric was then so very much taller than the dumpy Dr. Fish, or just because he trusted the man's gentle benevolence, that he found the courage to ask, "Is Pandora's show likely to be about Class One worlds, sir?"

The glasses gleamed up at him inscrutably. "No," Dr. Fish whispered. "No, I don't think it's about Class One worlds, Cedric. Just between ourselves, I think it's about murder."

The commeeting was not as terrible as Cedric had feared. Only about a dozen companies had bothered to participate, so System was able to arrange full-size images around one big table. Most of the representatives were very junior, chosen to show how little faith their employers had in Cedric's abilities or prospects. At least half looked no older than himself, and a couple were strikingly female into the bargain—not in the same league as Alya, of course, merely stunning. Some looked almost as scared as he felt.

But he soon realized that this was much like being back in charge of the dining hall at Meadowdale, and then he felt better. He bade them all welcome, asked their names, and told them to do the talking. He was going to listen and their words would be recorded, he said. They must assume he knew absolutely nothing, and if they wanted to call him nasty names, then that was fine by him—he was trying to broaden his vocabulary anyway. Soon they were all relaxed enough to start kidding around, and after that things went okay.

The main complaint, one he heard six or seven times, was that the Institute held back information and then edited it. The media wanted to elect their own heroes—they were tired of having Devlin Grant and a few others thrust down their throats.

And Cedric would never have guessed how much Gran was hated. The trick she had pulled the day before had been merely the last and greatest of many provocations she had used to bait the media over the years. Being a genius herself, she had no patience with stupidity in others, but there had to be more to it than that. He was certain that she had been deliberately keeping the media at bay, and if that were so, then he was wasting his time. Any proposal he came up with would go squasho.

Around eleven the meeting ended, and he found himself alone at the end of the table again, the ghosts departed. They had not seemed like ghosts, and he would have enjoyed trying to make friends with some of them, especially that slinky auburn fox from NABC.

Now what? Fish had said Gran would be arriving before noon. Likely she would have bigger balls to juggle than Cedric, but he decided he would try to stay out of her way. In the flesh she was lots more scary than she had been in the Meadowdale com. Fish himself had designs on Cedric for later, and he would rather not think about those at all.

For a moment he considered calling Meadowdale, but the thought of facing Ben or Madge was nauseating. They must have known. All the adults must have known—teachers and nurses and instructors, even the farmhands. How could they live with themselves? How did they justify their own lives when they looked in a mirror? *If I don't do it, someone else will?* That would cover any crime at all.

Now Cedric understood why nobody called back after leaving Meadowdale. Either they had been butchered and used for autografts, or they had discovered the truth about that and could never bear to talk to the ghouls again. And obviously they would never be allowed to talk to the kids. He shivered and tried to put it out of his mind.

Which left Alya.

"System, where is Princess Alya?"

"No such person on file," the nasal voice said sniffily.

Gran had said Cedric was to play host for Alya, so she was business. *"Override."*

"She is in the command room for David Thompson Dome."

"Am I allowed to go there?"

"Grade One rating allows physical access to all parts of the complex except—one: the personal offices of staff members ranking higher than Grade Three; two: those parts of the stellar..."

The list unrolled for a while, until Cedric told System to shut up and send him a golfie. He would try it and see.

When small, Cedric had almost killed himself a few times by putting a plastic bag over his head and pretending it was a bubble suit. Most boys did that, and some were less fortunate than he. Growing older, he had come to understand that bubble suits were not especially glamorous garments. They were not designed for real exploration; they were lab clothes, overpressured to prevent invasion by gas or dust or microbes, the last line of defense against accidental contamination. Yet they were still not much more than plastic bags, fitting closely over shoes and hands, and usually belted at the waist, but otherwise ballooning everywhere else. They were not elegant.

Nevertheless, he felt a satisfying little thrill as he was assisted into a real bubble suit for the first time. The technician who helped him muttered darkly about how old that one must be, speculating that it might not be safe after so long in storage. No demand for that size, he explained, and he insisted on testing it to well beyond the required pressure.

But the seals held, and Cedric's irresistible authority as a deputy director won his way past successive layers of sullen guards until at last he was ushered into the command room of David Thompson Dome. It was large and dim, with many people sitting around muttering at coms. Voices wove in and out of the red darkness in a basketwork of sound, while a spectators' corner of comfortable couches held Devlin Grant and the man with the turban—and Alya.

Cedric's deputy-directorship was not going to frighten anyone very much with Dr. Devlin there.

But Alya gave a shout of joy. She ran forward to meet him and threw herself into his arms. He had thought a princess would keep her love affairs secret, but apparently that was not so. Kissing through two thicknesses of crysfab would be low in satisfaction, so he just swept her off her feet and hugged her mightily. The bubble suits bulged and rippled and made little squeaky noises.

Then he took a harder look at her through the plastic. "What's wrong?" he demanded.

She laughed breathlessly and made ashamed sort of sounds. "I'm being silly, I think." She seemed to draw a deep breath. "*Oh, God*, but I'm glad to see you, darling." Then she hugged him again.

Darling? Much more of such royal appreciation would do terrible things to his lovable boyish humility.

"Don't start sniveling inside there," he told her. "You can't wipe your nose." And he led her over to the corner, where Dr. Devlin and the Jathro man were standing and watching blackly.

"What the hell are you doing here?" Dr. Devlin snapped.

"What the hell have you been doing to Her Highness?" Cedric countered. There was a brief silence marked by astonishment all around. Cedric himself was as surprised as any.

Devlin's moustache writhed. The day before, he had been unexpectedly friendly. Obviously that policy had been revised. "Get out of here! Operations are my turf, sonny, and you're trespassing."

Cedric could not argue with that. He looked down at Alya and decided that she was frightened about something. "We'll go, then," he said. "Come along, *sweetheart*."

But apparently that was not what Dr. Devlin had in mind, nor Dr. Jathro. They choked, then both tried to speak at once.

Alya grinned up rather wanly at Cedric and then turned to the others. "If Cedric can come with me, then I'll do it."

"Do what?" he asked.

Devlin looked blacker than ever in the reddish glow. "Your Highness, the director herself warned you—"

"But I already know what you're up to," Cedric said loudly. "You're looking for Class One worlds, and Alya's helping you." He felt her start, and then she hugged him comfortingly.

"I didn't tell him that," she said. "He's a lot smarter than he—than you might have expected."

Dr. Devlin made an angry growling sound.

"What's more," Alya said sternly, "if you value my opinions at all, then you must value all of them. Tiber I don't mind—I've told you what I think of that. But I'll look at the other if Cedric is with me. Else not."

"We're wasting precious time," Dr. Devlin shouted. "Would you feel happier doing Tiber first, Princess?"

She nodded quickly, and Cedric thought she looked relieved. "Good idea!" she said.

"Right! *Message Baker Abel*. Abel, we'll head along to de Soto and do Tiber first. *Com end*. Let's go!"

Back out in a main corridor, Alya urged Cedric over to a golfie and slid in beside him. Devlin and Jathro had to settle for each other as company, and neither looked very pleased. The two carts hummed off together, with the men's leading.

"Now..." Cedric said.

Alya chuckled and hugged him. "I was having another attack of the jimjams. I'm better if I'm with you, somehow."

"It's mutual!"

She shook her head and leaned her head against his shoulder

as the golfie cornered. Obviously Devlin had ordered top speed. "Not the same, I think. Cedric darling, you do understand why I'm here, don't you?"

"You have second sight."

"Well, not quite. I have a special sort of intuition. Most of my relatives have it. It runs in the family. It warns me, that's all, warns me of danger. In English you'd call it 'intuition.' We have a couple of words we use. The gift itself we call the *buddhi*. That's a very old word, and a presumption. It means 'enlightenment.' Buddha was the Enlightened One. We say that so-and-so has the *buddhi*—not everyone in the family has it, but most do. The other word is Japanese: *satori*. It means much the same, a flash of understanding, but I say I've had a *satori*. Right? A premonition, a warning from the *buddhi*? That's all. In English you might call it a 'hunch.' It's not really second sight. It's just that if something is dangerous for me, I get bad vibes about doing it. That's all it is."

"It's no great secret, Alya. System has pix of it."

"The ritual isn't secret. What is secret is that it's for real."

"I expect it is. I can't see you cheating."

She glanced up at him oddly. "You don't get creepy feelings? Some people react like I was a witch or something."

"You give me lots of creepy feelings, but not that sort. You have no idea how much I want to kiss you! Do you suppose they have bubble suits for two?" He was getting all hot again, just being near her.

"Later—I promise."

He felt very creepy then. Lordie, but she was gorgeous! How could he have ever been so lucky? He remembered playing with all that hair on the bed, and the way she had trailed it over him a couple of times. Down, boy! he told himself. "And this intuition can warn you about worlds?"

She agreed with a nod as they cornered again. "Yes, it even seems to work on that. You know how many things can be wrong with a world, like too much of this element or not enough of that. People evolved here on Earth. We're very well-adjusted to this planet, and not many others will do instead."

"But the robbies and gadgets—"

"Yes, but there's so little time, ever. Windows of a few hours at most, and not very much of those, and then they're gone. The planetologists can measure everything, but it takes time, and there's always the chance that nature's found a new trick to play and they've overlooked it. My . . . hunches . . . are quicker."

The golfie slowed down to climb a long ramp.

"Of course, the scientists pull their tricks, too," Alya said. "I'm just a backup. But none of us has ever been proved wrong."

"Us?"

She winced slightly. "My brothers and sisters all had the gift also."

"But—you mean there have been—Class One worlds?"

She nodded, looking puzzled.

"You mean," Cedric said, unable to take it all in, "there really have been other Class One worlds, kept secret? I mean, I know that some people say . . . I thought that was just crazy talk. Kept secret?"

"That's right."

Incredible! "So Gran has been using you—your family—to find Class One worlds—"

"No, not quite," Alya said. "We don't *find* them, we just inspect. My *buddhi*'s completely selfish. It only works for me, my own safety. Same with them."

He felt a sudden chill. "So?"

"The Earth is very sick, Cedric dear. We've poisoned it. It may be dying—at least as far as people are concerned. Life will go on, and in a million years or so everything will be back to normal again, but all the predictions now are that a big part of the human race is going to die very shortly. No one knows how many. The numbers are dropping fast already. It's snowballing, too—look at the Cancer Curve! We've even polluted our own germplasm." She stared up at him solemnly, as though doubting his comprehension. "And my family intuition tries to make us go to other worlds. That means it thinks—not thinks, really—oh, damn—it says that this world is unsafe for us!"

"Floods, famine, disease, storms—Bagshaw Barney told me."

"Right. Dangerous. But other worlds may be even worse, you see? There are some real horrors hiding out there. And that's where I come in. I can tell a world that looks like a better bet than this one."

"Oh!" Now it made sense. "Pilgrim clubs? Ecology and nutrition and—"

She smiled, he thought rather wistfully. "That's right!"

"But . . ." He thought his brain would overload. "But if it's better for one of you, then why not all? Why don't you all choose the same world?"

She squeezed him. "Clever man! It does work that way, but

your grandmother made a rule: only one of us for a world. Kas
—he's my brother, the king—he feels the same way I do, but
she'll still only let one of us go. And the *buddhi* seems to know
that. Only one of us gets the full *satori* each time. It's quite
complicated, really."

"And then you inspect the world?"

"Yes, but you see, it's purely subjective. I have to be involved. I can't just say, 'Yes, that's a nice little planet you have
there.' I can't just walk around for twenty minutes and put a seal
of approval on it. My *buddhi* would only worry about those
twenty minutes, and some dangers may not show up for years. I
have to be going myself—to live there for the rest of my life.
The gift only works if I'm in danger—me, myself."

"I want to come with you!"

The words were out before he had time to think about them,
but he knew that he meant them with all his heart. He had no
desire to be media flunky for Gran, with no chance of doing any
good in the job. His grandfather had offered him help—but
Hastings was not his grandfather. Cedric was Hastings's clone.
The Secretary General might be the deadliest danger of all, and
Cedric had not had time yet to think about that problem. What
rights or choices did a clone have? Legally he did not even exist.
He had wondered earlier if Alya might be able to give him em-
ployment—not as a lover, obviously, although he planned to be
available for that as long as she wanted him, and he also hoped
they could stay friends afterward—but he had hoped that perhaps
she could find him a living somewhere in Banzarak. He was not
qualified to do much more than rake leaves off the palace lawn
—not here, in this world—but on a frontier planet . . .

Then there was an interruption, as the golfie reached a check-
point. The concern was not over identity, but safety. Once both
bubble suits had been tested for pressure again, and their air
supply inspected, Cedric and Alya were waved through.

"Last night," he said, "you found my room. Was that intuition? And if it was—"

She squeezed his hand. Crysfab squeaked on crysfab. "We
don't know exactly how it works. In fact, nobody has any idea. I
tried to analyze it with superstring theory once—switching one
of the unexpressed dimensions with time—and all I got was a
headache. Two or three hundred years ago one of my ancestors
fancied himself a philosopher. He said it was like a spinning a
yarn. Have you ever seen a spinner at work?"

"No," he said. The golfie was slowing down for another

ramp. Cedric did not care if it took forever to go where it was going. He could sit there forever very happily. Except, of course, that she had promised later...

"Well, think of it this way. The past is fixed, right? The future we can't tell. There's one *me* in the past, and lots of *me*s in the future. There's a *me* who invites Hubbard Cedric into her bed tonight. There's a *me* who doesn't. And a *me* who—"

"I like the first one much better."

"Yes, but—"

"I would make that one very happy."

"Yes! Now, stop that! I promised you—later. But all those future *me*s somehow become just one present *me*. You understand? The future has lots of *me*s, like all the threads that are to be spun into the string. The present is the point where they all come together. In that past, there's one *me*, one rope."

He nodded, thinking of the feel of her nipples against his tongue in the night.

"So what the *buddhi* does, this old graybeard said, is tug on the strings in the future, and pick the string that's the longest. The longest lifeline, the longest-living *me*. Understand?"

"I understand that I love you very, very much, and I don't care if you can turn yourself into a black cat." She had not explained how she had found his room in the night, so she obviously did not want to.

Alya smiled and squeezed his hand again. "Later, then."

She had not said she loved him, either.

The golfie rolled to a halt beside the other. Jathro was already holding a door open.

"What's the rush?" Cedric asked as Devlin handed Alya down.

And Devlin neatly cut out Cedric on the way in. "Two likely worlds, Tiber and Saskatchewan. Their windows are due at about the same time."

They stopped at a second, massive armored door, standing open. Waiting beside it were three men in ranger denims and bubble suits. The two at the back were grizzled-looking veterans holding Beretta 401 torchguns. The other was a stocky, broad-shouldered young man gabbling into his wrist mike. He looked up in surprise at the stranger.

"You're Hubbard Cedric!" He grinned, holding out a hand, studying Cedric with obvious interest. "I'm—"

"You're Baker Abel!" Cedric was thrilled. First Devlin Grant and now Baker Abel! Baker was only twenty-three, and already he had done some great exploring. "You discovered the man-eating boulders on Marigold!"

Baker laughed. "They discovered me first! We're all ready to go, Grant. Why the change of plan?"

"Her Highness will inspect both NSB's," Devlin said pompously. "But she is apprehensive of Saskatchewan."

"The name alone scares me," Alya said.

"Rightly so!" Devlin's attempts at humor were ponderous. "I must find out who picked that name, so I can can him." Apparently, jocularity was back in vogue, now that he had returned to being Alya's escort. "It should have been something easier, like Susquehanna."

"Or Syuyutliyka?" Baker remarked. "That's a river in Bulgaria." He got some irritated stares but no answer.

They filed into the airlock and the door clumped shut with satisfying finality. Cedric slid close to Alya and took her plastic-wrapped hand in his to squeeze. She seemed perfectly calm, though.

A fine decon mist fell from the ceiling, but no odor could penetrate a bubble suit.

"Activate," Baker told his wrist. "Window's open, right on spec, friends. *Take her up about five hundred meters if you can, Clem.*"

"Why did we have to come to another dome?" Cedric asked. He knew there were several domes, although only one could be used at time. Two transmensors working at the same time would create interference, even if they were a whole world apart, it was said. Everyone knew that.

None of the men replied, so Alya said, "Special equipment. They have extra stuff standing by for this one. I've told them that this is it, that Tiber's the one."

The far door hissed, the bubble suits crackled, and Cedric's ears went dead. He swallowed to get his hearing back and noticed how his heartbeat was picking up. This was no holo show, no make-believe for the small fry on a boring afternoon too sunny to play outside. This was for real! Those guns certainly were.

"Gravity's a trace lower," Baker said, "and air's higher in oxygen. The suits'll mask that, but this'd be a great world for wild parties. This way to the promised land, lady and gentlemen." He led them out into de Soto Dome and started down the gentle slope toward the center.

"Cedric!" Alya exclaimed.

"What?"

"You're hurting me!"

Hastily Cedric eased the pressure on Alya's hand and apologized. Idiot! He had been trying too hard to seem calm and relaxed and not babble "Wow!" noises.

The sheer size of the place was overwhelming. The roof curved far overhead like a metal sky, lit by a bright glow pouring up from the central pit. Most of the dished floor was empty, curving gently down to where the pit itself was hidden by a collection of machinery ringed around it. Motors were revving and crane arms flexing; mechanical spiders rippled along high gantries and lights flickered on and off as the rangers ran through test routines one more time. All that stuff would need an army to run it—Cedric tried to count and ended with a wild guess of at least fifty operators. Clearly Alya's opinion was valued, and Tiber was going to be investigated very thoroughly.

Some of the units were small, some high, some just plain enormous. Two things like rows of houses must be SKIV-10's, which were the biggest made, despite some fanciful holodramas Cedric had seen. A hangar-size door had opened in the far wall, and another of these monsters came rumbling out, heading for its mates like a sociable condominium. The closer the watchers came, the more crushingly huge the equipment seemed.

Baker continued to lead the way, muttering into his handcom and presumably receiving replies in his earpatch. Belatedly Cedric remembered his duty again and glanced at Alya. She was holding on to him tightly, but her face glowed with happiness and an excitement as great as his own. On her other side, Jathro was watching her carefully. The guards followed, with guns at the ready.

"First scan of the robbie data's fine," Devlin announced. "No mirror-image crap this time. Trace elements are okay. Orbital parameters good. This looks very right, Princess."

"We have enough altitude to launch aerials," Baker announced. *"Proceed when ready, Clem."*

Mechanical things moved in the clutter around the pit. Metal arms lifted and swung. Cedric saw something rise from the far side, saw wings unfold and brighten as they caught the light, and watched it swoop down and vanish into the pit. Other aerials swung for a moment from the gantries and then dropped.

Baker knew exactly where he was going. With the others trailing in single file, and the gunmen still at the rear, he led a winding course between giant wheels and throbbing behemoths, finally attaining the edge of the pit, at a clearing where rails

marked off a spectators' gallery—not that the railings would
have lasted long had one of the skivs made a wrong turning.

And there was another world, floating below them, hot with
sunshine and gaudy with fall colors. Copper and gold trees filled
a valley floor, flashes of silver showing where a stream wound.
The flanking uplands were gentle, and greener than any hills
Cedric had ever seen. As though he were riding in a balloon, he
watched the landscape slowly twist, drifting by in silence below
him. He searched in vain for signs of animal life, wondering how
he would feel if a road or a barbed-wire fence came into view.

"Bring her up!" Baker's voice said, but the result felt more as
though de Soto Dome were dropping. The ground rose and began
to turn more quickly. Baker shouted about that, and the twisting
slowed. Then a dark shadow came crawling over the woods and
Cedric's heart spasmed. No one commented, and at last he
worked out that it was the shadow of the pit, the transmensor
string itself, the hole between worlds. How could a hole cast a
shadow?

"Get away from these damned trees!" Baker shouted into his
com. The woodlands began to twitch sideways in uneven jerks,
even as they continued to rise toward the viewers.

Alya squeezed Cedric's hand. "That's impossible, you know?"

"What is?" The disk of shadow was growing larger, and
closer.

"It's theoretically impossible to move Contact around!" She
sounded just as thrilled as Cedric was. "The 4-I people can do
it—a little, they can—but theory says they shouldn't be able to.
Math insists that a transmensoral string must end at a null value
on the first differential of a gravity gradient, which means the
surface of a planet, or some dense body. Maximum gravity will
always be at the surface of the geoid, so that's why Contact is
always close to sea level. The surface is sharper on a solid, which
is how they tell NSB's from stars, and it's why they usually find
dry land and not ocean, but there is no theoretical way they can
shift around and change the location of—" She stopped and bit
her lip. After a knife-twisting moment she said quietly, "Sorry,
Cedric!"

"No problem," he said, and managed to smile. He thought
there would have been less of a problem if she had not said
"Sorry" quite so intensely. Obviously Alya was a genius. She had
studied everywhere and everything. She knew real science, and
all he knew was science fiction—he was ignorant. He could
barely read. They had nothing in common except the physical

attraction of healthy young animals. He was just a stud to her, a pleasant and conveniently malleable male, a well-equipped, clean-limbed country lad to play with. She was royalty, rich and well-traveled, probably accustomed to having a gigolo on call wherever she happened to be. She must regard him as nothing more than a mental health measure, like a masseur. He just hoped he had satisfied her—he had tried as hard as he could in the night. He thought he had been quite impressive, but of course he could not be sure. No matter. He would accept whatever she offered. Nothing as good as Alya would ever happen to him again.

"Hold it there!" Baker said. The field of view had cleared the trees and settled lower, almost to the grassy surface beyond. Pocked with low bushes, it lay only five or six meters below the watchers, almost all of it in shadow. The edge of the pit was a shallow steel bevel above a dangerous blur, a roiling hazy contact between light and dark. The wise stayed well away from the edges of strings. A man who strayed too close might find his substance spread over a billion light-years.

Contact! Two ramps roared out from the sides of the pit, just above the ill-defined edge. They touched down on the grass, not quite facing each other.

And something like a haze rose from the ground, as though at a signal. Baker yelled a warning, and the two armed rangers whipped up their weapons—but there was no target, only a mist. Cedric moved to pull Alya back from the rail as the fog streamed upward.

"Butterflies!" she cried, and Cedric stopped to stare.

The cloud of butterflies distilled, condensed into a smoke, and came whirling upward, sparkling in a million hues. They ranged in size from mere midges to beauties as large as dinner plates. Peacock blue and ruby, pearl and amethyst and chrome yellow, they spun in a multicolored helix.

"Beautiful!" Alya said. "Oh, they're lovely!"

"Don't be sure, Princess," Devlin growled. "I've seen beauty that could kill."

"It's a welcome!"

"As long as they don't drink blood or something."

But the butterflies seemingly meant no harm. They circled and danced, and gradually sank back down to their own world and dispersed. Soon they were gone. If they had been an omen, it had been a very touching one.

Now the skivs were rolling, roaring down the ramp and rocking off across the grass, raising faint dust. Some of the other vehicles were of types that Cedric did not know, although he could make easy guesses at the rocket launchers and the trailers bearing sail planes. And silence descended again. Soon the great dome was empty.

"Well, my lady?" Baker Abel wore a puckish grin on his homely face. "The string seems stable. The window will be open for hours yet. Would you care for a stroll on Tiber?"

"Yes," Alya said fervently. "Oh, yes!"

"Hold it!" Devlin boomed. "Regulations, Abel!"

Baker donned an expression of great innocence. "It's good grassland, Grant. Nothing sharp that I can see."

Devlin seemed to chew his moustache in doubt. "You understand the risk, Princess?"

"Bubble suits?" Alya said, looking woebegone.

He nodded, visibly wavering. "They're not certified for surface. One tiny puncture and you can't come back—not without a two-year quarantine!"

"I'll risk it," Alya said defiantly.

Cedric made a quick move before he could be displaced from his position as escort. Holding her hand, he led the way around the lip of the pit to the nearer of the two ramps. Together they strolled down into another world.

14

SOON THEY STOOD on the grass, and all that remained visible of
the world that had birthed them was a vast circular darkness
overhead, mysteriously balanced on its two ramps, seeming to
contain nothing but a few lamps gleaming high on the gantries in
the dome. Cedric led the way forward, out from under the
shadow of that dark umbrella, until they reached the sunlit grass
and could walk beneath the clean blue sky, frilled with new-
washed white clouds. Soon the window was invisible, and the
ramps seemed to end in midair.

The guards looked around longingly for something to shoot at,
but no threat showed on Tiber.

There should have been a fresh smell of crushed grass from
the skiv tracks. The bubble suits masked that, and they masked
the wind also, diluting it to a mere crackly flopping of their own
material. But they could not conceal the warmth of the sun, or the
lushness of the hills, or the autumn glory of the woodland in the
valley bottom. Far off to the east lay a hazy blue range, snow-
capped. Baker announced that there was an ocean westward—
the aerials had photographed it already, and didn't the clouds that
way have a maritime look to them?

Cedric did not care. The one lush little valley looked

166

good enough all by itself. Four head to the hectare, easy. He would settle for this—and Alya, of course.

A circle of skivs had settled down as a camp near the edge of the wood; already suited rangers were out, peering at trees. Technicians fussed around the rocket launchers on a grassy hillock a safe distance away. Another group of vehicles was just disappearing over the skyline upstream.

Cedric crouched to poke at a tire scar. The soil was dark and rich, but the grass looked a little strange. The ground was peppered with flowers and feeding butterflies. He found a flower with two red heart-shaped petals and rose to offer it to Alya.

She took it and thanked him with a look that needed no words.

And then he held out his other hand to show its contents, starting with Jathro, who glared and spat out an unintelligible oath.

Cedric was startled and then started to laugh. "No offense meant, sir! I just wanted to show you. It's animal dung."

"I can see that!"

"But don't you see what it means? Not more than two days old, and obviously something big." Cedric glanced at Devlin and Baker, and they were way ahead of him, of course.

Baker was grinning. "Herbivore. Could be edible, maybe."

"Well, something's keeping the grass cropped," Cedric said, "and on Earth I'd have said these were horse buns."

"Want to domesticate it, do you?" Baker asked. "As the sun sinks slowly in the north, gallant Sheriff Cedric forks his trusty seven-legged feathered warthog and gallops off in a shower—" He dodged as Cedric threw the specimens at him.

Alya's face was glowing, but they all felt it—peace and freedom and boundless opportunity. The new world, Eden regained.

Thunder rolled over the meadow, and they turned to watch the first rocket scamper up the sky on a rope of white light. Following it with his eyes, Cedric noticed the sun. It was too yellow and too large, and he could look straight at it. There seemed to be shadowy markings on it.

"Smaller than Sol," Baker shouted, having seen his attention. "But closer. Also safer. No UV to worry about. You could sunbathe here!"

Cedric shivered at that idea. All his life he had been nagged about goggles and blocking cream and told to keep his skin covered.

"It's looking good," Devlin said as silence returned. "No

problems so far. Your intuition seems to be working, Highness. Almost I can envy you . . . and you, Abel."

Alya smiled at Devlin, and at Baker.

She did not look at Cedric.

Suddenly System's metal voice twanged in Cedric's ear. He jumped. He had not realized that he was still within range, and yet Devlin and Baker had not lost the preoccupied looks of men half listening to other voices.

"Message for Hubbard Cedric Dickson from Deputy Director Fish. Text as follows: 'Come to my office as soon as possible.' Text ends."

"Message received," Cedric told his wrist mike. He did not add, "and ignored." Duty and pleasure required that he stay with Alya.

"Time to go," Devlin said. "If the old woman hears about this, she'll have my hide for a rug. And we have another world waiting."

Alya seemed to shrink, her happiness dissolving like a mist. She moved closer to Cedric. He put an arm around her for comfort.

"Don't worry, my lady," Baker said. "This one'll be back in another three days."

"We can start the planting then?" Jathro asked.

Devlin shrugged. "If the overnighters don't turn up anything unexpected, and if the princess still feels that this is the one she wants. . . . Yes. Why not? The sooner we start, the more people we can move before we lose the string."

Alya nodded reluctantly and let Cedric urge her forward; but as they walked back toward the ramps, he could almost feel that he was having to push her.

There had been one decon chamber going in to protect Tiber; there were three on the way out, and the brew in the first was powerful enough to wilt Alya's flower into a smear of brown slime. Cedric could not be sure through two thicknesses of streaming plastic, but he thought she dropped a tear over that.

With the outside of their bubble suits still glistening and doubtless reeking of diabolic chemistry, they mounted golfies again for the trip back to David Thompson Dome. The joy that Tiber had produced in Alya had withered like the blossom; she sat tight against Cedric with her fists clenched, biting her lip.

He decided that conversation was required. "You said you had brothers and sisters with the same intuition?"

She nodded. "And cousins."

"But it only works when you—they—are in danger, personally?"

"Ten of us have gone. I'll be the eleventh."

"My god, woman!" he exclaimed. "How long has this been going on?"

"Twenty-five years at least. Ask your grandma. I don't know all of it. She hinted that there had been two others before we got involved, but there could have been more. One of them was Oak, Cedric."

"My parents?" But Cedric was a clone of Hastings Willoughby, so his father would have been his son, and his mother no relation at all—hell! When he thought about that, he felt as though he did not even exist. He was not anyone.

"Yes, your parents," Alya said. "They were part of a plantation, apparently. The tale of a broken string was a cover, but the antimony business seems to have been real, so they did die. Maybe! As I said, only your grandmother knows for sure."

"And System."

"I doubt if even System gets all the truth." Alya was staring straight ahead, and her chin had taken on a determined set. Cedric had a curious feeling that her soul was somewhere else, that her voice was speaking words she hardly heard. "The deception is staggering. How she's kept it going all these years is beyond imagining. It helps to have unlimited money, of course."

"Where does she get the bods—from Pilgrim Clubs?"

"Pilgrim Clubs?" Alya snorted. "They may have meant something once, when the transmensor first started up and everyone had hopes. Maybe a few are still legit, but most of them are nothing but gun-toting, wife-swapping, screaming racist religious fanatics."

Cedric started to laugh. After a moment she looked at him with hurt puzzlement, and then seemed to realize what she had said. She smiled sadly. "On alternate days, I guess."

The train of golfies whizzed eagerly down a long ramp and cornered on two wheels at the bottom. Devlin must have pulled some potent override code to pry that kind of speed out of them.

A shaky image of the *Mayflower* and Puritans in tall hats had faded from Cedric's mind, giving way to pictures of giant skivs and mobile laboratories, of shining city towers rising amidst the virgin beauty of a paradise like Tiber. Of course, the line between habitable world and Class Two was so fine that a single number in a report could make the difference. "BEST!" he said. "That's why Gran won't let BEST people into Cainsville! To keep the secret."

Naturally Alya knew that. She nodded distractedly. "And nothing defines loyalties like a good feud."

"So where do the people come from?" Cedric asked again. "Who runs it? The Institute, obviously, but who? The rangers? How big is this?"

"Very big. Most come from refugee camps, I think. There are so many disasters these days—floods and famines and mass evacuations. No one can keep track of all the millions."

"But there must be a core of scientists for each new colony, surely? Engineers and doctors and—"

"Perhaps a few," Alya said with a shake of her head. "But they wouldn't be much use. Any plantation is going to start from where? The bottom, right? You don't need doctors. First you need peasants to till the land. Civilization is always built on the peasants."

And Cedric's visions of futuristic science-cities were replaced in turn by remembered newscasts of endless dusty shantytowns under deadly sunlight, of dark brown men with ribs like picket fences, of bloated starving babies.

"And they'll scatter," she said, "spread out in search of the best land. In ten years they'll cover a continent."

"Huddled masses! The homeless! Chinese and Bangladeshis? And Africans, of course. And I suppose lots from Central America, the flood running before the plagues?"

Alya agreed. "You European types are being shortchanged on this round, I think."

"We did better than we deserved on the last one."

She smiled, her distress momentarily forgotten. "That's true, although not many of you would admit it. Some must get to go—Dutch, maybe, and Afrikaans survivors. I suppose her choice is largely dictated by the timing—by wherever there happens to be a good disaster going on and enough confusion that a few hundred or thousand won't be missed."

It was staggering. "Thousands? They're doing it on that scale?"

"Tens of thousands. So far as I know, the last Class One world was Raven, three years ago. My sister Tal chose it—I think she had a choice of one, but her *satori* wanted Raven. Before that was Etna, and my brother Omar. You would have liked Omar—I remember his last call home. He mentioned Japanese—that was the time of the Nipurb floods. There would be doctors and so on in that lot. The Institute moved forty thousand to Etna; so Devlin told me yesterday."

A voice spoke in his ear. "Call from Deputy Director Fish Lyle for Deputy Director Hubbard Cedric."

Cedric ignored it.

The golfie skittered around a corner and the parking hall was right ahead, with Devlin and Jathro dismounting.

"Forty . . ." Cedric's mind whirled at the revelations.

Alya smiled in bitter amusement at his expression. "Of course, for its size Banzarak has sent more colonists than anywhere else has."

He frowned, at first puzzled and then with growing distaste. "What exactly does that mean?"

"The Institute needs my intuition, or thinks it does, or else it just likes to have its own judgment confirmed. I have to be prepared to go, or my *satori* won't work. I buy the tickets—five hundred of my countryfolk for every five thousand others."

"That's horrible! You're being bought!"

She smiled and laid a tiny hand on his much larger one. "I minded more being sold! I hated to leave Banzarak. I hated to come here—and yet I couldn't resist my kismet. It drove me. And you saw what happened today: I could hardly drag myself back from Tiber." She squeezed his hand squeakily and sighed. "Now I want to go! I will scream and fight to go. Standing there under that fat yellow sun, I felt as though I were free for the first time in my life, as though a great curse had been lifted from me. I shan't rest until I return."

Cedric's wild longing almost choked him, but he fought it down. Time enough for begging when he knew a little more.

"But if there really are all these Class One worlds, then why keep them secret at all?"

"Isn't that obvious?" Alya said bitterly.

The com on the golfie went *ping*!

"Call from Director Hubbard Agnes for Deputy Director Hubbard Cedric."

The cart parked itself and stopped. He grabbed Alya's hand and jumped off, hauling her behind him. "Run!" he said, and they raced for the door where Devlin and Jathro were disappearing. Baker and the armed rangers were on the golfie behind.

"Before noon," Deputy Fish had said, and Cedric realized that he was famished again. Lunch must be hours overdue—where had the day gone? So his grandmother was in Cainsville, and almost certainly she was waiting at that very moment in Fish's office with her glare turned full on the comset, ready to fuse its circuits. Cedric knew he could not evade her for long, but he was going to stay with Alya while he could. She seemed to want him around. Nothing mattered more than that.

Behind them Baker shouted, "Heh!" He came up at a limping run, with his two gun-bearing buddies close behind. "What's the screaming hurry?"

Cedric could hear his golfie still squawking; he hauled the door of the decon chamber closed as soon as the others were inside. "Just want to get it over with."

But Alya obviously did not want to get it over with. She was hump-shouldered and hugging herself. That seemed like a waste —Cedric put his own arms around her also as the chemical drizzle began to fall. The runnels on the plastic made her look as though she were weeping, and she cuddled into his embrace.

"This is crazy!" he said, peering out at Devlin through his own streaming cover. "She's frightened to death. What are you doing to her?"

Devlin tried to rub his moustache through the crysfab of his bubble suit. He scowled. "We just want her to take a look. She doesn't have to go down to the surface. She'll be perfectly safe."

"Saskatchewan window's open," Baker said. "Skivs're on their way already. No problems so far." He paused, listening. "Not as pretty as Tiber, but robbie data register nominal across the board."

"But if Alya likes Tiber—"

"We've got five or six likelies out of eight," Devlin said. "It may be that more than one's okay. She can't cut herself in half, but we could use two worlds, if the windows fit. Okay, sonny?"

Cedric was about to protest, but Alya spoke first. "I'll look. I just want Cedric with me, that's all."

The light went on at the far door, to indicate decon was complete.

"And that's another point," Devlin added sourly. "The way she clings to you like tired ivy doesn't exactly reinforce my confidence in this famous judgment of hers." His voice grew angrier as Baker swung the door open. "Sure, I've seen the records on the others, and I saw her sibs pick Raven and Etna. But there can be black sheep in any family."

"Now, look here—" Cedric began, trying to disengage himself from Alya's embrace.

"No, you look here!" Devlin's square face was growing ruddy, and he thrust his chin out as he glared up at Cedric. He was a big man—Cedric knew how big men disliked him. "I'm not going to risk hundreds and thousand of lives just on the word of a dippy, slant-eyed floozy unless I believe in it, and if she picks you as her ideal of manhood, then I don't think she knows what's good for her, which is what this exercise is all about. If she can show me what there is on Saskatchewan to be so all-powered scared of, then I—"

Ping!

Lost in the argument and growing hotter by the minute, Cedric had not noticed that there was a comset on the wall of the decon chamber. He spun around and was surprised to see a red helmet and red uniform and the familiar scowl of Bagshaw Barney.

"Hugging's more fun without those suits on, Sprout."

"Go away. I'm busy."

Bagshaw shook his massive head like a bull aiming a charge. "You're crazy. You know damned well your grandmother's been trying to get through to you. Nobody—*but nobody!*—keeps Old Mother Hubbard waiting, laddie. She'll pop your balls in the stellar converter if you don't smarten up fast."

Cedric could see the area behind Bagshaw, and he recognized the waiting room outside Dr. Fish's office.

Baker had gone on into the dome. The two guards hovered by the door. "Come on, Princess," Devlin said.

Alya clutched Cedric's arm harder.

"You go ahead, sir," he told Devlin with all the calm he could muster. "Give me two minutes to settle this, then Her Highness and I will be right with you."

Devlin shot him a flinty glare. He turned and strode through the door without a word. The two rangers hesitated, then followed him. Cedric turned back to the com, but Bagshaw spoke first.

"Listen, kid, this is important! Eccles is going to blow up bridges tonight on WSHB."

"Okay, okay!"

"It's dangerous and it's all wrong. We can't stop her, but we do have a chance to put out the real story right afterward—and Fish has pulled more strings to get that chance than you could believe. But there's not much time. You've got to be briefed before she even starts. And get your hair combed this time."

Cedric felt as though part of his intestines had fallen loose. "Why me?"

"It has to be you, Sprout."

Twice in two days? "No! No! No! I'm fed up with being a

comedy act. I don't know the first damned thing about appearing on holo shows, or media relations, or whatever this scandal of Pandora's is all about. Gran's just setting me up to look like an idiot again, the way she did yesterday. Tell her to go find another sucker."

Bagshaw's lashless eyes narrowed to slits.

"The last man who said something like that to your grandmother got a whole world all to himself."

"Bugger off!" Cedric said shrilly. "Oh, hell—tell her I'm escorting Princess Alya, as she asked me to. We're going to go and take a quick look at Saskatchewan, and then we'll be all through for a while." He hoped that was correct. He wondered if he dare mention his long-overdue lunch, and decided not to. "Then I'll come right away—just give me ten minutes."

"And you'll do this interview?"

"Not that! I told you—I'm sick of being the world's joke of the day. Come, honey."

"Wait!" Bagshaw seemed to hesitate. His eyes flickered momentarily.

Alya uttered a little wail as Cedric released her and made a seven-league sideways leap to catch another angle in the holo. As he had suspected, Dr. Fish had been standing just out of view. Cedric pulled a face at the pair of them and went back to Alya.

Bagshaw's expression became blacker than ever. "You fallen in love, Sprout? The old hormones really perking? That must be what's made you so god-fired uppity, 'cause you were a nice, quiet, polite boy yesterday. You're rutting!"

"Yes," Cedric said. "I'm rutting. In heat. I have fallen in love. Madly. It's crazy time. I'll come in ten minutes." He turned to the door.

"I was in love, too," Bagshaw said softly, and something in his voice stopped Cedric faster than a shout would have done. "Can you believe?"

"Huh?"

"Remember in the chopper I lectured you about the environment?" The guard's voice had gone strangely flat. "I told you I was pairing with an ecologist? We'd been together about a year. Cute little thing, soft and graceful and gentle . . . amazing she'd fall for a lunk like me."

"And?" A cold finger stroked the back of Cedric's neck.

"She's dead."

For a moment Cedric wanted to doubt, but Bagshaw was not the sort of man who would easily seek sympathy. He would not easily bare his soul, either, and to do so falsely would be even more out of character. And the topic lay too near his manhood for begging. Bagshaw believed he was tough; he had to believe in his own toughness.

So Cedric had to believe his story. "And?"

Bagshaw took a deep breath, as though his next words were going to hurt. "She was murdered. Raped and then murdered. I want justice, Sprout—revenge! Need your help. I'd appreciate that."

This was the man who had saved Cedric from BEST's agents in the Lincoln Hotel, the man who had caught him when he fell seventeen stories.

Of course, he was also the man who had pushed him out the window to start with, and the man who should have sneaked him quietly out the front door an hour earlier with no trouble.

Maybe it was just flattering to have a man like Bagshaw ask for his help. Cedric looked at Alya, but she was obviously suffering her own torments and not paying much attention. He did not turn to the com.

"Why me? Why do I have to look like an idiot?"

"Because you're so well suited to the part! Yes, you were set up yesterday. So today who's going to believe you?"

"No one!"

"Exactly."

Cedric spun around, feeling a quiver of rage raise goose bumps on him. "Are you saying that I was made to look like a lunkhead in front of the whole world yesterday just so I wouldn't be believed today?"

"I didn't say that, but—it could be. Could well be. It's necessary that we give out the truth, but that the truth not be believed—we have a trap to spring. It has to be you, Sprout."

"Because I don't know enough to see through your lies?"

Bagshaw roared. "We'll show you holos!" He lunged forward, as though about to fall right out of the comset. "Take you down to the morgue and let you smell the bodies. Is it blood you want?"

"Just the truth." Cedric wondered if anyone in Cainsville knew what truth was.

"You'll get the truth. And tell the truth. And you'll not be believed—that's the meat of it." Bagshaw brought his temper under control with a visible effort. "Listen. I've sweet-talked a lot of girls in my time, but I've never asked a favor from a man since I was old enough to stop wetting the bed. I'm asking you now, Sprout. And if you won't do it for my revenge, maybe you have some good times of your own you'd like to remember?"

Oh, God in Heaven!

Cedric's lips moved. "Glenda?"

Bagshaw smiled softly and nodded. "Fish can show you how to sink Eccles Pandora's dinghy, lad. She'll be all through, all washed up."

Cedric swallowed something that wouldn't go away. Oh, Glenda! He owed that much to Glenda. "Ten minutes."

"You'll do the interview?"

Glenda, sliced and wrapped in little paper packets.

"Sink Eccles Pandora?"

"Dead in the water. Your doing. Promise."

Glenda!

"I'll do anything you want," Cedric said.

The set went blank instantly.

David Thompson Dome was even larger than de Soto, or perhaps it just looked that way because it was empty. The central pit glowed with a muddy red light, like a sunset under rainclouds, but the skivs had all gone and the gaunt superstructures of cranes and gantries were still.

Cedric paused and waited for his eyes to adjust to the dimmer light. He could see only one ramp extended, and he recalled that Tiber had been given more than the standard treatment. Three men stood lounging on the rails of the spectators' enclosure at the near edge of the pit. Two carried torchguns slung on their shoulders. The other was too tall to be Baker, who must have gone down to the surface.

"Let's run," Cedric said. "We'll belt down to the rail, and you take a quick peek and say 'wrong color,' or whatever you fancy. Then we'll scamper like hell back here again. Okay?"

Alya nodded, staring down at the pit. "I feel such a fool! I'm really not this sort of sniveling idiot most of the time."

"I know you're not. And you'll be all right in two minutes when we're back here again and it's done."

She nodded, shivering. "Just keep hold of my hand."

"Ready? Go!" They took off down the slope together.

Considering relative leg sizes, she ran well. Cedric loped at her side, hanging on to her hand. Devlin had turned and was watching them come.

Panting, they reached him and flopped against the rail to peer down.

Below them lay a leprous swamp of rocks and scummy puddles, with scrub and tufty vegetation in lurid yellows and browns. Rain was falling—which was a paradox—and wind ruffled the more open parts of the pools. Soupy mud bubbled in the tracks left by the wheeled vehicles at the end of the ramp, while right below the viewers was the largest growth of all, a lumpy thing like a pallid barrel, which instantly squirted upward, extending into a high, thin column like a palm tree that simultaneously curved over, directing down at the viewers a hollow crown ringed with stubby knobs; and those in turn stretched out into long white ropes to reach over the railing and wrap around Alya, scooping her up high, tearing her hand from Cedric's grip before he had even registered what was happening. The two guards unslung their guns. Devlin yelled at them not to shoot, and their sudden movement attracted the attention of more of the white ropes, which flashed out to entangle the weapons also.

Cedric made a standing leap up on the rail, and his outstretched hands caught hold of Alya's ankles just before she was elevated beyond even his long reach. Wildly off balance, he hooked one toe under the rail, and then his other foot as well, for he, too, was now swathed in tentacles and being hoisted and pulled outward. Grips on his legs were probably human hands. He thought he heard his joints crack as he stretched out like taffy. He dared not release his hold on Alya—who was screaming and cursing in a dozen different languages, and that was a good sign because it meant that nothing had wrapped around her neck yet. He cried out at the pain of the rail on his feet and an already unbearable tension that kept on increasing, trying to tear him in half.

Then buildup of air pressure in the top of his suit made his ears go suddenly dead and plunged him into choking, stuffy-headed silence. Gradually he was tilted from near vertical to horizontal as the ropes tried to carry their prey back home. Their grip tightened mercilessly around him, squeezing his bubble suit out in ridges, crushing his chest so he could not breathe. The ends of the ropes bore mouths or teeth or eyes of all of those; butting and pummeling at him, they tried vainly to chew through the crysfab. But his feet were slipping, and between the agony in his feet and the effort of keeping his toes up to maintain his hold, he could hardly think of anything except to wonder whether Alya's knees would come apart before his arms were pulled from their sockets. If the railing came loose from the floor, he was lost.

He was stretched out flat, staring down at the rocks and pud-

dles far below, and also seeing the deadly blur that surrounded
the pit. Even as he watched, a stray rope touched it and was
severed in a flash and a crackle. Cedric was going to be dragged
down, and when he was standing on his head, he would be
crushed against the edge of the string, and that was death.

Then a coil twisted around his neck and that was much
quicker death. It began to tighten.

As the ropes shortened back toward their source, they were
growing thicker. The trunk had contracted almost into its original
barrel shape. In a moment or two Alya was going to be sucked
completely inside the monster. And he was going to be strangled.

Darkness!

Everything went black, and he dropped a meter and smashed
his face into a steel floor. His feet were still hooked over the
railing.

The ropes and the bubble suit had cushioned most of his fall,
but his nose had taken the rest of it. Damn, but that hurt!

His bindings lashed and buckled in death agonies, which
slowly stilled to small twitchings. Dim lights appeared, or his
eyes adjusted. He was still clasping Alya's ankles. Dazed and
giddy, choking on blood, he disentangled himself and thought he
saw her trying to sit up. Then more lights and lots of people—
and of course what had happened was that Devlin had ordered the
window closed, and the rope plant or herd snake or whatever
it/they was/were had been cut in half, and Cedric and Alya were
lying on the steel object plate of the transmensor, barely lower
than the rest of the dome floor, and all sorts of medics and
rangers were flocking uselessly around, and Cedric's ears popped
back into life again with a sudden influx of shouting and babbling
voices, and his face and throat were full of blood from his god-
damned nose, and perhaps he was just a little too close to losing
control . . .

He took a firm grip on himself, and the world stopped spinning.

He retched and spat blood and wished he could wipe the tears
of pain from his eyes. He could barely see out of the suit because
of the blood smeared on the plastic, and his nose throbbed as
though someone were standing on it.

He pushed hands away and sat up. "Quiet!" he roared. "You
all right, Alya?" Then he coughed frantically because he had
inhaled some blood.

"I think so."

He felt a great rush of relief. More pains were coming to his attention—crushed ribs and scraped feet and one elbow. Mostly his nose—he tried to pinch it through the plastic to stop the bleeding, but it hurt too much.

"Just sit a moment," a voice said. "We're trying to check you for broken bones. Your suit's intact, so there's no contamination."

"Never mind me—the princess . . ."

But there were others looking after Alya.

"You were right, Highness." That was Devlin, standing over them among the twitching white ropes and the bustling medics. "I'm sorry. Damn, I'm sorry ! You too, Deputy. Great work!"

"Why?" Alya asked shrilly. "Why did it pick me?"

"Fast movement," Devlin said. "And size. The rest of us would be too big for prey. It went for the guns, too—they're small. I've seen variations on that pattern before. A good thing you didn't get sucked into the core, or it would have crushed you."

"Baker?" Cedric mumbled.

"He walked right by the damned thing. He must have been too big, or moving too slow. Lucky bastard, though!"

Pushing medics aside, Cedric crawled over to Alya and took her hand.

"You're hurt!" she said.

"It's just my nose."

She squeezed his hand in both of hers. She was shaking. So was he.

"Of course, every world has dangers," Devlin said. "We'll have to see how you feel about this one . . . later."

No one was listening to Devlin. Alya tried to sit up, and Cedric helped her.

"Darling, I'm sorry," he said.

"Sorry? Sorry, for God's sake? Sorry for what?"

"I let go of your hand."

She put her arms around him and laughed aloud. "I think you'd have pulled my arm out otherwise. I'm fine, fine! Oh, your poor, poor face! You're all bloody!"

"Bloody poor guardian."

Alya shook her head and mouthed a kiss at him. She was happy again. The danger had gone. Her *satori* had warned her—had Cedric not been right there at her side, she would have been sucked down into the heart of that *thing*.

"Call for Deputy Director Hubbard Cedric from Director Hubbard."

Cedric struggled to his feet, knocking away hands that tried to help. He swayed, wincing at a whole new world of bruises and strains. With his luck he would probably find he was ten centimeters taller yet.

"Call for—"

He raised his wrist mike to his mouth. *"Tell her I'm on my way."*

15

AFTER TOO MANY sleepless nights, Dr. Eccles Pandora was running on little blue wheels—chemical wheels, one every two hours. Anything that brushed against her nerves made them twang so loud that she was surprised when other people did not look around. As long as she concentrated, she was fine, but at the slightest trace of relaxation she began to drift off into weirdly rippling hallucinations. She would survive, though, and playbacks of the clips had convinced her that the overload was adding a special luster to the coy sparkle that was her own distinctive style.

About fifteen minutes more would do it. Then champagne and celebration. The plaudits would be flowing, the world at her feet. When she would get to bed, she neither knew nor cared. This was her triumph, her apotheosis. Move over, gods, Pandora had just inherited Olympus.

"Stand by!" said the voice in her ear.

She dug fingernails into her palms and straightened up in her chair, forcing away the wavering shimmer that was trying to settle between her and the studio. She ran smoothing white hands over silver silk, then reached for the glass hidden under the table at her side. The damnable thing was empty, so she palmed one more blue disk and forced it down dry.

Ready for the big windup.

It had gone without a flaw.

The cameramen fussed in the gloom before her, gesturing for infinitesimal changes in the lighting. Up in the control room, Maurice gave her a thumbs-up. A classic, this would be. People would be watching this a hundred years from now. Universities would grant doctorates for analyses of what she had wrought tonight—of how Pandora changed the world.

In the tiny cage of the monitor, her image was concluding the interview with the xenologist from Harvard, Dr. Whatsisname. He had not contributed anything factual, but he had been so excited he could hardly speak, and that had come across beautifully.

The billion-dollar coin had been worth every hecto, every cent. A viewpoint inside the skiv would have been better, of course, and more than one viewpoint would have improved the artistry. The coin had come from one of the fixed cameras inside the dome—they thought it was van Diemen Dome, but that did not matter—and it had been beautifully positioned to watch the door of the skiv.

Higginsbotham had vouched for its authenticity—WSHB's resident expert on trickery swearing that if it was a fake, he would emasculate himself by hand. "After I do," she had warned him.

And the technicians had done a lovely job on cutting and extracting close-ups. Lovely, lovely, lovely. Stop that! Concentrate! She glanced at the monitor, where a female hygiene ad was running. Thus was history financed . . .

Concentrate!

She had begun with a few teasing references to the search for extraterrestrial sentience, with a brief clip of some brainy types from the Sagan Institute.

None ever found, they had said.

Stay tuned, she had told them.

Establish friendly contact, they had advised.

But what, she had asked, if they're killers, too?

The coin had shown nothing of Nile itself—the Nightmare Planet she had named it—but Moscow had told them what they needed. The mycologist van Schoening had come from Moscow, a consultant brought in to study the fungoid vegetation. He had been supplied with all sorts of preliminary data by 4-I, and had left all that lying in his office. It had not come cheap, but what the hell? Surely Dr. van Schoening Mikailovitch would have died happy, had he known that he was making his secretary a rich man.

So there had been interviews with planetologists from JPL about Nile, a dark and poisonous world where rain never reached the surface, a surface of slaggy black rocks hot enough to cook meat.

There had been an interview—she had done that one live—about the toadstool and puffball vegetation. That had perhaps not been a total success; the woman had used too many big words. Of course, the resemblance to terrestrial fungi was merely "convergent evolution of saprophytic organisms"—meaning they lived on a fallout of organic debris from the airborne algae in the cloud layer. Pandora had cut that off as soon as she had established that fungi could be edible. Food is food. Likely there was something there eating the yeasts and mushrooms. So there was no water? Let them drink beer.

And then she had moved on to the record from the coin—the skiv being retrieved and hauled up on the crane; the scurrying, shouting, near-hysterical people climbing all over it and peering in the windows; Dr. Devlin Grant making a total ass of himself. He had always been one, of one sort of another.

And then . . .

Pièce de résistance!

Then the skiv doors had been opened, with more excitement and shouting until the bodies had been brought out. Pandora had demanded close-ups and had been prepared to scream for them, but Maurice had agreed without a murmur, bless him. The Institute medics had not even put sheets over the stretchers, so bless them also—and she had given the viewers a good look at two naked male bodies, slashed and ripped, with their heads battered to pulp. Strong, strong stuff!

She had taken a brief detour through the men's life stories and then zeroed in on the missing woman, ecologist Gill Adele. WSHB's library had turned up a half-decent file shot, too. Cute little twist—any half-decent surgeon could have made something really great out of her face. Missing . . . presumed carried off by . . .

. . . wait for it . . .

. . . the ultimate! . . .

Cave men in space—zoom in on Devlin Grant holding a stone hand-ax, crusted with dried blood and brains.

Pandora had called witnesses on that ax, too. Early Acheulian, the experts had agreed, an example of cultural convergence.

What they had meant was that if one battered up a rock to put
sharp edges on it, one finished up with a battered rock with sharp
edges on it.

Her ear said, *Ping*! She jumped. Signal light on camera
one . . .

She smiled to the Folks Out There. "So now we come to some
different sorts of questions. The pictures we showed you were
made on April fifth, and this is the eighth. As yet the International Institute for Interstellar Investigation has made no announcement about these tragic deaths. In three days it has
released no information at all about Nile or its sinister inhabitants. We obtained our data from unofficial sources. You have
heard how important this discovery is—'epoch-making' was the
word, wasn't it? So why is it being kept secret?

"Why the cover-up?

"Why did the next of kin in all three cases refuse to talk with
us?

"To help us with these questions, we have Doctor—"

For a moment her head went blank—total whiteout. Panic
burned in her throat like acid. Such a thing had never happened to
her before, in twenty years' broadcasting. The prompter blurred
before her eyes.

"Jenkins Wanda," her ear said.

"Dr. Jenkins Wanda, Professor of Political Science at the University of New Orleans." She recovered and carried on, keeping
her hands clasped to hide the trembling. Too little sleep, too
many pills! But not long to go—she must not falter.

A chair containing Jenkins Wanda appeared on the other side
of the table. Jenkins was a dream. A tall and striking black
woman, she was as smooth and deceptive as a jungle stream. She
had suggested most of the questions they had selected, offering
up some startling implications and innuendos that even Pandora
herself had not seen.

"Good evening, Wanda."

"Good evening, Pandora."

"Now, Wanda, you've been watching . . ." Gaining strength as
she swung back into action and squeezed out a few last drops of
adrenaline, Pandora started serving the lines.

Jenkins returned the expected responses. ". . . but, of course,
after thirty years it is a shock to find evidence of sentient life. Of
course, after so long the Institute is old and hard-arteried. Of
course, its experts could panic . . ." And so on.

"Now," Pandora said, leaning into a Between Ourselves

mode, "you may recall a curious thing that happened yesterday. The Director of 4-I . . ." Behind her, she knew, a mirage cut of that disastrous press conference would be reminding viewers of Hubbard's catastrophe, and the human celery she had left behind, leaning on the lectern.

"Oh, I think you're right," Jenkins said, although Pandora had actually made no statements at all. "The original intention was to announce what you have shown tonight—the discovery of sentience on Nile. There can be no doubt of that. Obviously Dr. Hubbard then changed her mind. *Something* or *someone* changed her mind, but too late to cancel the announced reception. So she improvised that absurd excuse about appointing her grandson as a deputy director. Quite clearly, the director herself has panicked, also. The confusion seems to run right through the Institute's organization, from top to bottom. She made a public idiot of herself yesterday. She is getting on, you know," she concluded with a slyly feline smirk that even Pandora could envy.

Pandora had thus been granted a clear fairway for the next drive. She swung. "But why, Wanda? First contact with a sentient species is staggering news, a historic event. We all know that the transmensor allows us only very brief access to other worlds, so we have very little time. Surely we should be making the greatest possible effort to learn more about these stone-age beings, whatever they are. Why, we don't even know yet what they look like! So why this cover-up by the Institute? Why did Director Hubbard panic and change her mind about making an announcement?"

With an eerily sinister smile, Wanda prepared to sink the ball. "Well, remember, Pandora, that Hastings Willoughby himself, the Secretary General, was also at that meeting yesterday. I think it's a fair guess that it was he who ordered the cover-up, because what may seem to be a very academic scientific discovery will certainly have a real impact on global politics."

For a moment she lingered playfully on the lip of the cup: such scandalous incompetence had been revealed by the triple tragedy, that a major shake-up . . .

And then she dropped it neatly: however short-lived it might have to be, contact with another intelligent species would certainly cause the human race to close ranks at last. The World Chamber with its elected delegates would prosper, because it was the only body with a legitimate claim to represent the human race. The United Nations, a discredited and outmoded collection of ineffective governments, would wither to dust. Hastings Wil-

loughby and Hubbard Agnes would be drowned in a political
tidal wave, and they knew that.

A lovely piece of work, Pandora thought. Of course, it was
only valid if one did not know too much about Chamber elections, but she could save that problem for another day, another
show, another night . . . Gods, but she was tired!

Wanda had finished her razor job on Hubbard Agnes and was
waiting for the next question. Was there a next question? Pandora
fluttered her eyelids as though they were not made of lead and
sneaked a glance at the prompter. No, they were finished.

"Dr. Jenkins Wanda, Professor of Political Science at—at—
Wanda, thank you very much for being with us this evening."

"It was my pleasure, Pandora." Jenkins dissolved into the air.

Now, just a few closing words . . .

Ping!

Maurice was giving her the sign for a commercial! What the
hell was that for? But Pandora's well-honed instincts spoke up to
assure the world that she would be right back. She was hoarse.

The signal light went off.

"Maurice!" She began to push herself up out of her chair and
then realized that the floor might not be steady enough to stand
on.

"Ten more minutes, Panda." Frazer Franklin's voice! She
would know it anywhere, even in an earpatch. "We have a—"

She leaped to her feet. Swaying, glaring up at the control
window, she started to scream. "Frankie, you stay out of my—"

"We have a rebuttal, Pandora."

"Rebuttal? What in the name of God is there to rebut?" She
was too tired. There was nothing left. That damned-to-a-
thousand-hells pervert and his accursed friends had no right to
tamper with her triumph. "I won't," she said. "I won't—"

A chair appeared, with occupant.

Pandora collapsed back on her seat and for a moment could
only gape. "You!" she said. "Oh, sweet merciful . . ."

It was the human celery; except that someone had taken him
in hand and the luminescent green was gone. His hair was
combed. He was wearing a pearly-gray jump suit in a frilled
bow-bedecked style that was just being adopted by the frantic-
fringe youth cults and would not reach the adult world until late
summer at the earliest. Damn him, but he could get away with it!
It played down his binder-twine skinniness, at the cost of making
him seem even younger than he must be. The size of him . . . But
his sandaled feet ended a couple of centimeters below floor level,

she noticed. Was that Maurice's doing, or was someone at 4-I trying to shaft the kindergarten deputy? And weren't his cuffs riding just a little high at ankle and wrist?

Pandora wanted to laugh, and dared not start in case she never stopped again. Human sacrifice! She had uttered challenge at the gate, and the knight had ridden forth to slay the foe. Oh, jewel beyond price! Perfection—the final touch to add to her glory.

"Cedy! Does your grandmother know you're out this late?"

He flushed, and Pandora finally managed to bring his face into focus. Great Heavens! This was even better than she could have dreamed of. She felt a tremor of almost sexual excitement run through her. Her fatigue vanished in the thrill of the chase—of the kill. Bless you, Frankie! The final dish tonight, ladies and gentlemen, is human head, served hot and weeping.

"What happened to your nose, Cedric?"

"I had a run-in with some exotic plant life." It was puffed and purple and probably packed with surgical gauze, because his voice sounded as though he were speaking underwater. By the next day he would have black eyes, also.

It was all just so delicious.

The massacre of the innocent.

But she had watched that kid face a mob the day before. For an amateur, a beginner relying only on native courage, he had done not badly at all, until Pandora herself had sharpened an experimental claw on him. She knew his chinks, maybe better than he did. Very likely better than he did—there could not have been many women in so brief a life. Quite likely only the one.

His eyes flickered sideways to look at nothing, and then moved back to Pandora. Of course he was seeing someone else in the same room he was in. To him Pandora was the projection, the intrusion. But the great unseen audience would perceive such flickers as shiftiness, and they showed his lack of training.

She glanced at the monitors. She had about ten seconds to soften him up. It was not essential, but genius never overlooked an opportunity.

"It's too bad about that," she said. "Your nose." She dropped her voice to Husky, Full Strength. "Because you're a very good-looking young man."

He had been about to say something else. His mouth opened and stayed that way.

"I wish you were here in the flesh. We could have gotten together afterward, maybe?" She sighed. "Oooh, I would have liked that."

Color was rising in his face like that red stuff in thermometers. His knuckles had gone stark white. Good.

"I must admit that I'm curious," Pandora said. "You do have the advantage of me, you know."

"Ad-Advantage?"

"You already know what I look like stripped, don't you? I can only guess about that strong young body of yours."

The color all drained out again, leaving the swollen nose like a petunia on a snowbank. His lips mouthed something that might been "Bitch."

"Tell me: are you well . . . proportioned? You're one of the tallest men I've ever met, and a girl can't help wondering—"

Ping!

"And finally, friends, to wrap up tonight's astonishing revelations, we have here the famous Hubbard Cedric. Good evening, Cedric."

He had to swallow twice before he could return her greeting.

"Cedric, of course, is with the Institute. Only yesterday his grandmother snatched him off the company basketball team and appointed him deputy director for Media Relations, which was quite a surprise to all of us . . . and to you, too, I think, Cedric?"

He nodded.

She waited.

"Yes." Anger and hatred burned in his eyes. She felt a sudden lurch of desire—those damned pills always did that to her. But she did enjoy her men young. She loved to lead them on . . . and on . . . watching their lust rise until it was an agony, until they were driven beyond endurance, either lashing out in frenzy or suddenly humiliating themselves by ending before they had begun—that was glorious. And to start with one who already felt such savage anger . . .

Business before pleasure. Concentrate!

"And tonight Cedric has been sent along to give us the official word from his gran—from the Institute. Haven't you, Cedy?"

"That's correct, Dr. Eccles."

She shivered at the intensity of his contempt. It was arousing her. She would be doing the blushing next. "Do call me Pandora, please. All right, then, why has the Institute been keeping this story secret? Why has it not admitted the truth before now?"

"What truth, Dr. Eccles?"

"Evidence of sentient life forms!"

Then she saw the triumph flower in those big gray eyes, and all the world seemed to explode in alarm bells.

"There is no evidence of sentient life forms."

"No evidence?" She must play for time—but she must also speak without any sign or doubt, or hesitation. "Are you suggesting that the records we showed tonight are faked?" Not that! Oh please, not that! The people are missing, their families are mourning—it can't be a hoax. Please, God, let it not be a hoax.

"No. The coin was stolen, but it was genuine. Everything you showed was genuine."

Relief! And before she could speak, he plunged ahead. He had been well briefed.

"But you only saw a tiny portion of the data. We have evidence from more than twenty cameras, not just one, and from other sources also. For example—"

"But the window was open on April fifth?" She must get the ball away from him. If she could pull the kid off his rote briefing, then he would flounder.

"Yes." He paused a fraction of an instant, and she pounced.

"So the Institute has had three whole days to start producing fake records. How can we possibly trust anything you show us?"

No—they had thought of that. "I'm not offering to show you any records."

More relief! Could it be that the whole rebuttal nonsense had been the long whelp's own idea? She raised her brows in Obvious Skepticism. "So we are expected to take your word for it?"

"For now you'll have to."

She was running the predicted track, damn it! But she had no choice of move. "And why should we?"

"Because this is under investigation as a criminal matter."

"Criminal?" That one threw her on the ropes, and in fact she had fallen back in her chair. "You are planning to arrest these stone-age inhabitants of—"

"It was murder!" His eyes glinted with genuine, youthful outrage. "A horrible, premeditated murder. That's why I can't show you the holos. The records have been seized—attached, I mean—by the authorities, as evidence." Then he smirked at her and waited expectantly.

"What authorities? You're not suggesting that the cave men on Nile have police?" No, levity was the wrong tack. She was blundering. Criminal crap! "Never mind that for now. You've got two dead men and a missing woman to explain, boy. Whodunit? Was there a fourth person in that skiv?"

He shook his head and settled in to tell the story, a faint smile of triumph on his big mouth. "Have you ever heard of—" He took a deep breath. "—cuthionamine lysergeate?"

"No, but I'm sure I'm about to."

"It's a poison. It's powder, but the fumes are deadly. It drives people mad."

"Fungus derivative, Pandora," said her earpatch.

"What sort of mad?" she asked. She was so weary. Even one conversation was almost too hard to handle, without having to work out why Maurice was blathering about fungus derivatives.

Cedric adjusted himself in the chair, moving stiffly. What other injuries were hidden under that fancy tailoring? Bruises, welts? Pale skin with red weals—no, she must keep her mind on business.

Obviously he thought he had her now. "In women it causes extreme confusion and certain libidinous tendencies."

"Oh, gimme a break! Who's been teaching you the big words? It makes them horny, you mean?"

His Adam's apple jumped. "I guess so. It has that effect on men, too, and it also makes men violent. Women usually less so, and after a few hours it rots the higher centers of the brain, and it causes a mental degeneration and regression, and in a day or so it will kill—depending on the concentration, you know."

"So the Gill woman killed the men?"

"It's obvious she must have killed at least one of them."

"And where did she get the stone ax?"

"van Schoening made it."

"Oh, really!" Pandora tried a laugh, and it sounded screechy even to her. She needed time to think—days. "Well, tell us the official story, then. You've seen these forbidden records?"

Again he registered satisfaction—the interview was following the script he had been given. "No. All I can tell you is what I've been told. There will be a trial, and the jury will get the evidence. But this seems to be what happened. The skiv went—was transmensed—to Nile on April first, with the ecologist Dr. Gill, and Dr. van Schoening from Moscow, who was an expert on funguses, and a ranger, Dr. Chollak John, as operator. You know all that. Well, everything went fine for two days. They drove around, taking pictures and collecting samples. They found nothing unusual. They did not go outside, because of the heat and because the air is not breathable."

"We know all that."

"You don't know the rest of it. It was on the fourth. That was when the poison hit. It was very sudden. Dr. Chollak and Dr. van

Schoening started to fight. Chollak won, because he was younger and bigger."

Through the deadening fog of fatigue and confusion and anger, that image registered with Pandora. "He won the woman? He raped her?"

Cedric pulled a grimace as well as he could around his swollen nose. "It wasn't rape. We wanted to spare the families this— but Dr. Gill was affected as much as the men were. Partly she provoked the fight. I have to mention that, because of what happened later. After the fight, Dr. van Schoening went into the lab room at the back of the skiv. He took out some rock samples and made a hand ax."

This time Pandora let the laugh come, to show scorn. Then it became ridicule. She howled. She felt tears come, it was all so silly. After all her work and all the evidence, to have this bimbo come along and spin cobwebs on her shiny triumph . . . Maurice shouted something in her earpatch, and she did not listen. And then she saw the amazed expression on the kid's face and coughed herself into silence.

"I told you that the poison causes mental regression," he said sternly. "It can have that effect, depending on which parts of the brain it affects. He regressed. There were lots of better weapons around—he even used a hammer at one point—but he smashed at a rock until he got an edge on it. Then he went into the room where the other two were, and he battered Chollak to death."

Obviously Cedric himself believed that crud, and he was young enough and innocent enough to be very convincing to the viewers.

"That's when you get your rape scene!" he said.

"Pan," Maurice told her. "Cuthionamine lysergeate is extracted from fungus. The external atmosphere was overpressured."

Cedric was waiting for comment. Pandora was floundering between his story and Maurice's nonsensical babblings in her ear. When she did not speak, Cedric continued.

"And then the second murder. Yes, it had to be the woman. She got revenge."

"And then went out to find a cop?"

He shook his head, his calm rebuking her stupid levity. "Then she began hunting—she seemed to realize that something was wrong. The poison is so random that it's possible she could still think after a fashion, even if she could not control her emotions. You understand?"

"Hunting? What had she seen worth hunting?"

He blinked. "Sorry—I didn't mean that sort of hunting. She began ransacking the skiv. Because this was the third day, remember? The poison hadn't shown up earlier. There had to be some sort of booby trap, or time bomb, to release it then."

"And what did she find?"

Cedric showed wariness again, as if he had been warned of bad footing ahead. "We don't know. She was holding it tight against herself, and none of the pictures showed exactly what it was. But she tried to throw it outside. She opened the—"

"Well!" Pandora spoke loudly. The time had come to win back control of the interview. "You think she found some sort of time lock that had spread poison? It must have been small, this contraption, or they would have seen it sooner. You haven't explained why she didn't just toss it in the disposal chute, or seal it up in a sample locker."

"Her brain was half jelly by then. She put on her EVA suit, but she forgot the helmet. She must have used an override code to open the airlock, because normally it wouldn't let her out without approving the readings on her suit monitor. She would have died at once, and the outer door was self-locking . . ."

Pandora began to speak, but he shouted the end of the sentence.

". . . and the inside door she propped open with her helmet!"

That was the sort of pathetic detail that Pandora did not need.

"Wrap it up!" was the order from her earpatch.

But she could not wrap it up and let all this hokum spoil her lovely special. She had pulled out the rug, and she was not going to let them lay it again so easily.

"Well, so that's the Institute's version, is it? But you're only reporting what they've told you, and you have no evidence!"

He flushed and just shook his head.

"Conveniently, the evidence is all sealed away by the law. Whose law applies there, on Nile?" Again she saw wariness.

"Cainsville law. And that comes under a special agreement between the U.N. and the government of Canada." He tried to say "extraterritorial" and stumbled over it.

She saw an opening and flogged her tattered brain through it. "What government of Canada? Well, never mind. Isn't it convenient, though? The Institute has its own security people looking into this supposed murder. The evidence is all locked away for months, by which time the string to Nile will have been lost. So no one will ever know the truth! Very handy! How many other secrets has the Institute buried over the years?"

Hubbard Cedric had opened his mouth to say something. He started to stammer, and his face went chalky pale. That was puzzling. If she had not been so battered and flattened, she might have tried to follow that up.

"And I don't suppose there will be any more expeditions going to Nile in the meantime, just in case they might run into some stone-age beings?"

Maurice was jabbering at her. "Pandora, if it was a voice-operated airlock . . ."

Cedric was gabbling: "There will be evidence! Tomorrow!" A joyful gleam came into his eyes. "The window'll be open again tomorrow, and we're going to go and recover Dr. Gill's body. It should be lying right where the skiv was parked. There's a responder on her suit, so we can locate her. And whatever it was she found should be right there, too!"

"When you say 'we'. . ."

The years fell away; the grin would have graced a twelve-year-old. "I've been promised I can go along! No overnighting, just a quick trip. I wasn't in Cainsville before this happened, see, so I'll be an independent witness when they find the body."

"You? Independent? You think that you're independent?"

"You are calling me a liar, Dr. Eccles?"

"I'm saying that you're not my idea of an independent witness."

He shrugged, exultant. "Well, I am. I happen to be honest! There are some of us honest men around, you know. And I'm going along with Dr. Devlin, and tomorrow evening we're going to hold a press conference. Tune in and see what we found!"

They were stealing her triumph. She wanted to scream. Maurice was babbling in her ear, and the king-sized cherub was openly smirking at her. They'd had days to plan some sort of trickery to hide the truth. Of course there were sentient aliens out there! Hastings Willoughby had ordered a cover-up. Hubbard Agnes had buried much worse truths than that in her time.

"You and Devlin? Just the two of you?"

He shrugged. "Maybe a ranger, or another witness."

"I'll tell you what witness!" Pandora shouted, suddenly inspired. "A truly independent witness. Me! I'll come along and keep your friends honest. Show *me*! I dare you!"

The big kid started to laugh—and stopped, his mouth hanging open. Then his head twisted around and he glared at the blank space he had watched earlier. The nape of his neck was as hair-less as a baby's.

"You're joking!" he told it.

He turned back to Pandora, suddenly red and glowering and mutinous. "You really want to come?"

For a moment she wondered if she might have stepped into—no, this rube could never fake a reaction like that. "Yes, yes!"

He pouted. "They say there's one spare seat. Be at Cainsville at 0800."

Triumph! Victory snatched again from the jaws of whatever. . . . "Okay?" Hubbard Cedric asked grumpily.

"I'll be there!"

Without even a good-evening, he started to rise. He and his chair vanished.

That was a surprisingly abrupt ending.

Pandora found the blur that was the camera, although she could not bring it into focus. The room was swaying and weav-ing, and there was a throbbing sound in her ears. "Well, it's certainly been an interesting evening! Maybe tomorrow we'll know some more . . . and . . . wish you all a very . . . all wish . . ."

"Relax. You're off."

The signal light had gone out.

It was over, thank God. Over. She felt sick.

She tried to stand, and darkness poured into the room and the floor tilted. Take another pill—no, don't.

How curious! She thought she might be going to faint.

Not surprising. She was not as young as she looked.

16

"YOU PLANNED THAT!" Cedric shouted, hurling the door open. In his fury he almost forgot to duck under the lintel. This was the closest to real anger that Alya had yet seen in him. "You set that up!"

All through his ordeal she had been sitting in a corner of the control room beside Fish Lyle. Bagshaw, the beefy security man, had been leaning against a wall behind them in silence. They had all been watching through a window. Fish had not spoken and had barely moved, an inscrutable gnome. Only once had he used his mike to prompt Cedric, and that had been right at the end, to extend the invitation to Eccles Pandora. Now Cedric crossed the room in two long strides and glared down at him, and was rewarded with a bland smile from the round, pallid face. Lights glinted on Fish's shoe-polish hair and turned the thick glasses into empty patches of brightness. His face was a jack-o'-lantern carved from a grapefruit. He bore a scent of cologne.

"You did very well, Cedric." His voice was a rustle of leaves.

"Well done, Sprout," the security man growled. "Thanks."

"Almost too good," Fish added. "You almost convinced her."

Alya stood up and smiled.

Ignoring her, Cedric again shouted at Fish. "But you knew she would want to come along on the trip tomorrow! Why let her?"

195

In another corner the technician arose and stretched. He was a sallow, spotty youth who had done nothing at all that Alya had seen except looked bored and pick his nose—System ran everything. He headed for the door, thumping Cedric on the shoulder in patronizing approval as he went by.

Fish rose also. "You overestimate my precognitive abilities. But yes, I did run a prediction . . ." He chuckled inaudibly. "System said that if you played your part as we discussed it, then there was a decimal seven three chance that she would react that way. I'd have guessed higher."

"But why let her? Why do we want her?" Cedric had so far afforded Alya no more than a nod. That was a measure of both his anger and of a self-confidence that was growing astonishingly fast. In two days he had visibly matured, throwing off the childish cocoon in which he had been kept swaddled so long. He was filling in the holes in his knowledge, finding his strengths, and measuring them against the world. He had rolled with some of the roughest knocks she could imagine and gained strength from every success. It was a fascinating process to watch, but it did raise problems—such as the problem of where he was going to be allowed to sleep that night.

As though he had read her thoughts, Cedric turned with a shamefaced smile and hugged her, very softly. He was not always so gentle.

"You did beautifully!" she told him. "That horrid woman! You tied her in knots."

"Did I?" He did not look totally convinced. Cedric being skeptical? That was new, and he was even eyeing Fish more suspiciously than he had before the interview. Obviously the unexpected ending still bothered him. He tugged at a cuff. "And this suit! I feel like I forgot my guitar somewhere."

"I didn't know you played the guitar!" she said.

He grinned. "I don't, really, but—"

He pursed swollen lips and kissed her cheek. Again she wondered where he would sleep. She was badly bruised, as he was. Bruises could be used as an excuse for a night or two, maybe, but after that she might well be gone, never to see him again. A man who had saved his lover's life might reasonably expect more than a peck on the cheek for thanks.

"Call for Deputy Director Hubbard from Dr. Quentin Peter of 5CBC," System announced.

Cedric shied like a startled horse. "Yugh! Of course!"

Fish had already reached the outer door.

"Wait!" Cedric yelled, and lunged over to grab his arm.

"Correction," System said. "Calls for Deputy Director Hubbard from Dr. Quentin Peter of 5CBC and Dr. Goodson Jason of NABC."

"They'll all want to come!" Cedric yelled.

Fish gazed up at him in opaque silence until Cedric released his grip. "I expect so."

"What am I going—"

System interrupted. "Correction. The following five persons are standing by on calls . . . Correction. The following eight . . ."

Cedric howled. Fish made another attempt to slip out the door, and Cedric squeezed in front of him. Alya, impressed, wondered if the reptilian little man was surprised by the sudden new assertiveness he had provoked.

Cedric glared down at the chief of Security. "Not so fast, Doctor! You cooked this up! Why let Eccles Pandora have the scoop? What's the purpose? We can't take the entire world media along on—"

Ping!

System's mindless recitation of celebrated names was ended by an override and the furious image of Devlin Grant. One look at the inflamed beefy face, and Alya could imagine sparks flying from the moustache.

Devlin roared. "What the hell is going on? Hubbard, what right have you to make announcements about me going to visit Nile?"

Cedric put his arms akimbo, completely blocking the doorway. He stared down darkly at Deputy Fish's shiny black hair, as if hoping to see through it to whatever sinister brew seethed within. "I was given to understand that it was all arranged."

"Oh, you were, were you? Lyle?"

Fish looked from holo to Cedric and back again in surprise. "Has there been a misunderstanding? I assumed, Grant, that you would wish to handle the matter yourself, but I certainly suggested that Cedric check with you before making any announcement."

Cedric's expression showed that he might be recalling the conversation differently.

"Did you, now?" Devlin said through his teeth. "Well, I hadn't even been advised that there was going to be another mission to Nile at all."

"We must try to recover the body. We promised Gill's next of kin that we would make the attempt." Fish looked very innocent, very shocked by the disagreement. Doubts were already gathering in Cedric's face like mud rising in a stirred pond . . .

And Devlin still resembled a volcano in the most unpredictable stage of an eruption. "I was not aware that my authority over operations had fallen into question."

"Of course not!" Fish sighed. "Well, I surely do hope we don't have to start going to formal memoranda and requisitions in this organization after so many years of striving to minimize red tape. As chief of the investigation into Gill Adele's death, I requested that an attempt be made to recover her body. I would have sworn that the matter was discussed at our first board meeting after the tragedy. And I'm sure that Agnes told me she'd mentioned it."

Devlin chewed his moustache. His tunic was unzipped, his hair awry, and the room behind him was a very frilly, pink bedroom. "She may have," he admitted cautiously.

"Well, then!" Fish beamed. "And all I told Cedric was that he would make a good independent witness, since he had never had a chance to tamper with the equipment that killed the three victims, and that *I was sure* that you would not mind him coming along, but that he should check with you. He may not have heard me clearly. Well, the man's had a busy day; we shouldn't be too hard on him."

"I—" Cedric said.

"What exactly are you demanding, Lyle?" Devlin asked.

A string of glowing words floated along past his knees: 16 INCOMING CALLS WAITING FOR DEPUTY DIRECTOR HUBBARD CEDRIC—CORRECTION: 21 INCOMING CALLS WAITING FOR DEPUTY DIRECTOR HUBBARD CEDRIC. Cedric stared at them angrily and began gnawing his lip. Even if he could not read fast enough, the voice coming through his earpatch must have been making the message abundantly clear.

Fish shrugged. "Just that you send out a skiv fitted with those grapple things for collecting samples. The body must be lying where she fell. Even if there are predators, they will not have destroyed the suit. Theories of cave men we can forget, but Eccles Pandora will not believe us unless she sees with her own eyes."

"That slut!"

"Exactly. I thought we might make her eat a little crow, that's all. Now, if you are too busy with the princess's affairs, I see no reason why some junior ranger can't drive the equipment. You must have some young lunk you can spare?"

Devlin's image scowled, obviously thinking hard.

"There are twenty-one—no, twenty-seven—calls waiting for me," Cedric said. "Every other network wants to send someone along, too. What do I tell them? And when? Can we have a press conference in the morning? Dr. Fish? If I let them all come up to Cainsville, can you handle the security?"

Fish beamed paternally. "Certainly! You have promised Eccles the seat, so the rest will have to be content with watching you leave and watching you return. Grant, what do you think?"

Devlin ran his fingers through his hair. "Damn you for a sly, creeping toad, Lyle! Well, I am very busy, but this won't take too long."

Alya mused that Devlin's fondness for headlines was no great secret.

"But, as senior investigator," Devlin added darkly, "you probably ought to come along with us yourself."

"My doctors have advised against excitement," Fish said sadly. "You will have Cedric."

Devlin's eyes narrowed. "I think maybe Baker Abel, also."

Certainly there was some cryptic undertone there. Alya wondered why the glib-talking Ranger Baker should be significant. Cedric had not noticed—he was scowling at the visual message as it came around showing 32, then dropping back to 31. Someone had gone away mad.

"Your decision," Fish said with a shrug. "We'd better let Cedric answer his mail, here. By all means, let them all come."

"I'll handle the press conference!" Devlin snapped.

Either Cedric's assertiveness was not yet developed enough for a head-on confrontation with Devlin, or he just did not care. "Fine!" he said. "You can have 'em. 0700?"

Devlin grunted, then vanished.

System spoke at once: "Calls for Deputy Director Hubbard from the following thirty-one persons . . ."

Fascinated, Alya moved back out of the field of view as Cedric stepped to the com, biting his lip and tugging his cuffs down. Fish vanished out the door.

"Collective reply," Cedric said.

"Go ahead."

He took a deep breath, ran a hand through his hair, and then put on an extremely convincing little-boy smile. "Hi! Sorry I can't take your calls one at a time, but you're all stacked up like firewood. There isn't another seat available on the skiv, but anyone who wants to come to Cainsville to see us leave and then see us come back is welcome to do so." He paused and gulped for a moment, then forced the smile back. "You'll be able to watch us on monitors, I guess. Dr. Devlin will be available for questions both before and after ... Let's say 0700 hours? And we'll provide breakfast. Thanks for being so patient. That's all. Oh—no, I don't know why Dr. Eccles got preferred treatment. It just happened that way. Good night. *Com end.*"

Bagshaw had neither moved nor spoken throughout the Devlin-Fish argument, but now he broke the ensuing silence. "You know, Sprout, there are times when you don't act nearly as stupid as you look."

"Like now, for instance!" Cedric said, wrapping Alya up in his arms and starting serious kissing procedures. He began as if he were planning to go a full three-minute round with her, but he broke off halfway through, gasping for air.

"Damned nose!" he said thickly.

"I'm bushed!" he said as the two of them climbed into a golfie.

Perhaps he was going to be tactful and considerate.

No, he was not. "I'd like to go to bed *very early*," he added, and hope was written all over his face in flashing neon. *"Columbus Dome!"* he told System, wrapping Alya in an arm like a garden hose.

"I'm tired, too," she said, and they fell to arguing over who had had the least sleep lately. It seemed they had both been missing out.

As a child Alya had been allowed to run wild in the Residence grounds, often unattended. With the *buddhi*, no guardian was ever necessary. For as long as she could remember, she had trusted her intuition to see that she came to no harm. Thus she had been an unusually vulnerable thirteen-year-old when a thick-shouldered, broad-smiling gardener twice her age had led her into a dusty, cobwebby summerhouse and taken her virginity. That had been a shock—but not truly harmful. In fact he had been a very slick performer and the education likely valuable.

There had also been a rather wild party when she was sixteen, and the captain of the school basketball team—but she preferred not to remember that.

Since then she had been more discriminating, but she had paired briefly twice; and she had terminated both affairs as soon as they began to turn serious. She had known what her kismet was, and neither man had been the sort to take along on a one-way journey to another world.

So she'd had experience of four men before Cedric, but none of them had been as boisterous as he. He was big and powerful, and last night he had been extremely enthusiastic. She still felt sore inside, and her later encounter with the rope plant had left her bruised all over outside. She was not in the mood for love.

Cedric obviously was.

"Let's eat," she suggested, and they stopped at the cafeteria. He ate four times as much and as fast as she did, but he never took his eyes off her.

"Window to Orinoco at five," she said. "I have to get up early."

"I'll nudge you," he said, and waited hopefully.

She let that one go, but her conscience was squirming: He had saved her life, and paid for it with a smashed nose and all-over bruises. Injury deserved compensation.

They walked back toward the spiralator. "When you go to Tiber," he said, "then you won't be a princess anymore, will you?"

She agreed, automatically thinking of Jathro. She did not know where Jathro had got to, but his absence was a welcome improvement. It was true that the people of Banzarak had a strongly held belief in the infallibility of their royal family. Alya was not going to be a princess, but her opinions would continue to carry much weight with at least the ten percent of the colonists who came from her homeland. That was a good start on having a lot of influence in a society that would of necessity be fragmented and lacking overall leadership. That was Jathro's assumption.

"I want to come, Alya," Cedric said. "Even if you—if I—if we are only friends, I want to come to Tiber with you."

Oh, those enormous, innocent, round eyes!

How could she explain? Last night she had been driven by the *buddhi*. It had been completely unscrupulous, telling her to bind this unusually tall, agile young man to her as a lover, so that he would be at her side and willing to risk his life for her. She had gone to his bed. She had accepted his lovemaking. She had even pretended to enjoy it, just to hurry him along.

So she had fashioned Hubbard Cedric into her devoted slave. When the time came, he had leaped to her rescue without a second's pause to weigh the risk. He had been fast enough and tall enough to catch hold of her, strong enough to keep her away from the core of the rope plant while Devlin closed the window, and tough enough to endure the punishment involved. Cedric had been available and malleable, lanky and steadfast—nothing else.

And now?

Now the need was past. She felt no more than casual friendship for him. They were the same age; they had known the most intimate contact possible, the most potent experience that two people can share. He had been a virile performer. Nothing more than that.

But just because the *satori* had been completely amoral did not mean that she could be. "Cedric, I have no say in who goes to Tiber. Yes, I'd love to have you come with us, but you'll have to ask Devlin, or Baker, or your grandmother."

He swallowed hard and nodded.

He handed her courteously into the spiralator and followed. Even when he was standing one step lower, his eyes were still much higher than hers. With a hard squeeze, he could encircle her waist with his hands, middle finger to middle finger, thumb to thumb. He had discovered that last night, and it fascinated him. He did it now.

"Ouch!"

"Sorry!"

"I'm very bruised, Cedric," she said.

He pulled a face, then nodded. She thought of whipped dogs.

"Tiber on the eleventh?" he asked.

"Day after tomorrow," she agreed. Two more days only. Of course, in theory it all depended on what the overnighting expeditions had discovered, but Alya had no doubts. Tiber it would be. Probably Jathro was already off somewhere, organizing the first planeloads.

The spiralator brought them to her floor, and they stepped out. Cedric walked her to her door in hopeful, attentive silence.

She had used him as unscrupulously as Fish had, or his vixen grandmother, or several others. Was she no better than they? Why did everyone *use* him? He deserved any reward she could give.

She opened the door and paused. "How're your bruises?"

Smiles dawned again. "I could cope. Yours?"

"I'm not sure. They should be looked at, I think."

Relief! "Very closely?"

"Very! There's a whirlpool tub in my suite."

His eyes widened. "There is?"

"Have you ever made love in a hot tub?" She never had. Cedric moaned and reached for her.

She slipped from his grasp and headed across the room without looking to see if he was following.

Cedric took less than five seconds to unzip, tug, balance on each foot in turn a few times, tug some more, and then he was in the water, waiting for her. He was as badly roped by bruises and welts as she was, and they showed up far worse on his milky skin, but obviously they were not going to dampen his fires.

Alya took longer. Then she sank down beside him and pushed his hands away. "Wait awhile. Just soak."

He had probably never soaked in a whirlpool tub before. It eased the aches, but he would not know how enervating it was.

After a while she let him fondle her, but then he began to grow urgent. "How do we manage this?" he muttered into her ear. "I'll drown you!"

"Like this!" She slid into his lap. "My turn to drive!"

She had never been so blatantly aggressive at lovemaking. It was obviously a new experience for Cedric also, and Alya found a strange wild joy in her power to take a being so much larger and stronger than herself and almost immediately reduce him to a gasping, spasming, slack-jawed jelly. She worked him savagely, until he was drained and spent and yelling for mercy.

They cuddled longer in the sensuously swirling water, but soon his eyes began to wobble out of focus. She sent him off to dry himself and wait for her in bed; and she took her time. When she went to him, he was stretched out like a major highway, fast asleep.

Easy.

She slid in beside him, and for a while she lay and studied his astonishingly innocent face, his battered nose, and the spread of his hair on the pillow, shining bronze in this light. Then she whispered for dark to come and turned over to go to sleep herself.

She, too, was spent. It had been a hell of a day.

But sleep did not come rushing down on her as she had expected. That mean little seduction had been too cheap and easy. Certainly he had no cause to complain that the brave had not received the fair, but she knew he would have wanted more. He meant well, but he was clumsy, inexperienced, and altogether too rampageous. In her present condition he would hurt her without meaning to—he had done enough of that the previous night.

Yet she found that she was fighting a fierce desire to wake him up and tell him to do his damndest. That was her conscience speaking, not her intuition—the *buddhi* no longer seemed interested in Hubbard Cedric, tall or not. There were lots of good men around.

Partly she was feeling her own unslaked lust. Partly she was feeling guilty for being a selfish, conniving slut.

And partly, she knew, she was wondering in a purely cerebral fashion whether she would be an idiot to let this one get away.

17

"GOOD MORNING, MY lady." Baker Abel's voice was sickeningly cheerful. "I wish I could say that you were looking well, but I'm not looking at all, if you follow me. I'm sure you are, anyway."

His cocky, impudent face peered out through the holo, but Alya had specified voice-only reply. Beside her, Cedric moaned softly and pulled the covers over his head.

"What's the time?" She rubbed her eyes. Lord, but every bone in her body ached.

"Just before 0600. Your judgment on Orinoco was confirmed, so we let you sleep. The lab reports show something badly wrong there. The mice are growing tumors. Grant's decreed complete embargo."

Orinoco had already been overnighted and given a provisional Class One rating before Alya had even reached Cainsville. So her intuition had a range of several days—but was it reliable on a scale of years? When would human colonists on Tiber start developing tumors?

She prepared to throw off the covers and then decided not to. People facing blank screens usually had a fixed, glazed look about them, and she was not sure that Abel's sparkly eyes were quite glazed enough. There were a lot of sneaky override codes in the Cainsville System.

205

He babbled on. "So you have the rest of the day off, Your Largesse, at least as far as Operations is concerned. Quinto and Usk show up tomorrow, then decision time for Tiber. I wouldn't have called you now, but we seem to have mislaid a couple of meters of deputy director, and I wondered if you might have seen any, er, lying around?"

Smartass! "You could ask System."

"Ah, well, I did. Never mind, but if you do happen to . . . lay your hands on him, tell him the media are on their way. Nice room you've got there." Baker Abel vanished.

"Saints have mercy!" a male voice groaned from under the bedclothes.

"He's a kindergarten dropout. I swear it."

Cedric rolled over with grunts of pain. "Oooh! Pity the poor cripple, beautiful lady. I'll never walk again."

Nothing wrong with his hands, though. Alya removed them and rasped a fingernail over his cheek. "Sandpaper! And you have work to do."

He wailed. "Sadist! I hadn't finished—I just took a rest at halftime.

"Tough."

"You'll make me wait until tonight?"

"Abstinence makes the lust grow stronger."

Tiber was due just after midnight the next day. Tonight would be his last chance.

Evidently Cedric had pandered to his ambitions when ordering his Cainsville wardrobe. He returned from his own room bedecked in ranger denims, grinning and strutting like a kid with a private moonship as he escorted Alya to breakfast. She wondered what the real rangers would think, and concluded that a deputy director need not care about their opinions.

When they reached the cafeteria she saw no rangers around, but she did notice people sending Cedric nods and small smiles of acknowledgment. His performance against Eccles Pandora had apparently met with approval. She was surprised, for he was still the boss's grandson, who had been brought in over everyone else's head. Yet he was doing astonishingly well. Was it possible that Hubbard Agnes had been serious in giving him the job? What other destiny did that sinister madwoman have in mind for him?

They ate and then still had time to spare before the lev arrived with Eccles and the rest of the media stars. Cedric suggested a quick inspection of the equipment. He was bubbling with excitement over his coming exploration. In Alya's opinion, considering what she knew of planet Nile, he was nutty as a palm grove.

"*De Soto Dome,*" Cedric told the golfie, adjusting Alya in the crook of his arm, where he preferred her.

"Access to de Soto Dome is restricted at this time," he was told.

Cedric frowned.

"Devlin's probably being careful," Alya said. Someone in Cainsville was a murderer—or so Fish had said. "The last skiv was booby-trapped, remember."

"Right, so it was! *Override!*"

In a moment Cedric's easy grin vanished. The reply had been through his earpatch, and Alya did not know what it said. She could guess.

He pouted. "I was told my grade was the highest there was. Little did they know . . . Well, let's think about arranging the party."

He should have been thinking of that anyway, Alya decided. He was obviously annoyed at being refused by System, but the extent of his authority over it had always seemed extraordinary to her. Indeed, she suspected that the rating he had been granted might have come automatically with his nominal rank of deputy director and was an oversight that Hubbard Agnes would surely correct as soon as she discovered it.

Alya left him jabbering to a comset and went back to her room, feeling oddly unneeded. Her intuition seemed to be content with the way things were progressing. Tiber still felt right, and none of the other names did. Cedric was no longer important.

Moala had not returned. She had gone off in full war paint the previous evening, admitting with much giggling that she had somehow contrived dates with no less than three handsome young rangers—because of the language problem, she claimed. That was not a very credible excuse when System could translate anything. Alya had advised her to choose the largest and let him worry about the other two, but she was curious to know how things had turned out. Moala would certainly tell her, in brightly embroidered detail.

And Jathro's continued absence was odd. Alya settled herself before the comset and called him. There was a noticeable delay before he appeared, looking annoyed and even more self-important than usual.

"I am in conference, Your Highness." The view around him

was masked, but Alya could see a corner of the table at which he was seated. It was not rectangular—probably pentagonal, for the director and her four horsemen. Most likely Hubbard Agnes had the same sort of office in Cainsville as she did at HQ in Nauc.

"I am so sorry to intrude," Alya responded. "Do let me know if I can help in any way. Rinse your socks, maybe. *Com end*."

She glared angrily at the blank screen. Two-anna conniver! Slimy tub thumper!

Now what? Well, it was about the time that Cedric would be welcoming Eccles and a trainload of reporters from all the other networks and media, a real invasion. Alya did not particularly wish to watch.

Kas!

She had been neglecting Kas. This would be early evening, Banzarak time. She placed the call.

He answered at once, as though he had been waiting for her there, in his familiar, shabby old office with its book-strewn desk and battered leather chairs of unknown antiquity. She saw at once the ravages of strain on his face, and she could have believed that his beard was grayer than it had been two days before.

Was it only two days? It felt like a lifetime.

"Little sister!" His smile was forced. "How do you fare?"

Her eyes filled with tears. "Kas, darling! I'm fine."

"The doubts have gone?"

"Yes! Yes!" She could barely recall the anguish that had racked her when they parted. "Oh, yes. I'm fine. It's beautiful, Kas!"

"You've seen it, then?"

"Tiber. It's called Tiber. And yes, I've seen it, briefly. Glorious! So many butterflies!"

"No more regrets?"

"Only about you . . . and Thalia and the kids." How could she have been so selfish as to forget them? Thalia was a distant cousin; she also had the *buddhi*. So did all their children, so far as could be told. They would still be suffering, feeling the siren call of an open door, a safer, finer world available. "Kas, is there no chance that you, too—all of you?"

She thought he shook his head—she could not be sure. Then he said, "This is your kismet. Maybe next time."

"But this—" She recalled what Jathro had predicted about Hubbard Agnes after her folly at the press conference. Jathro, a shrewd politician for all his sleaze and pomposity, had said then that the director could last no more than a week before the hounds

pulled her down. Alya had been overlooking the scheming and
intriguing that must be under way. "This one may be the last, Kas
dear."

He coughed meaningfully—there could be listeners on such a
call. "I saw you on Thursday."

Kas was no mean twister himself when he wanted to be. He
must have been sorely puzzled, though, by Alya's appearance on
the holo. None of her brothers or sisters or cousins had ever gone
public like that.

"Oh . . . I don't know what came over me."

"Then I am sure it was the right thing to do. I would only
worry if I thought you were trying to be logical."

She laughed. "Beast! But—I think it was because I had to
meet someone."

"Tall, dark, and handsome?"

But she dared not try to explain about Cedric. He was not
relevant anyway. His grandmother had other plans for him. "Tall,
fair, and looks lost?" she tried.

"Then I can guess. He was impressive, Alya. Don't stop to
think, whatever you do."

Her mind whirled. Kas . . . and Cedric. Damn! Maybe that
long string of innocence was important, after all. She wished she
dared confide in Kas.

"But is this farewell?" he asked. "I'll get the others—"

"No! I'll call again." She thought quickly. "Thirty-six hours
from now?"

"We'll be waiting," he promised.

There was more, all told in hints and half truths in case of
listeners, mingled with unimportant precious things. The hibiscuses were dying, Kas said. She told him she had been given a
flower with two heart-shaped red petals. Afterward she sat and
wept for a while. The future could wait; the past deserved tribute.

"So that's SKIV-Four," Frazer Franklin pontificated. "Can
you tell us exactly what that means?"

"Well, 'SKIV' stands for 'self-contained investigatory vehicle,'" the tame expert explained. "The 'Four' simply means that
it will support four people."

Everyone knew that, Alya thought. Not wanting to leave her
room with her eyes still red, she had turned to WSHB to see what
was going on. The expedition ought to have been on the move
already, but obviously there was some delay, and the anchor was

filling in. His guest was a vague, dried-out ancient. Not impressive.

"For how long?"

"Well, if needs be, almost indefinitely. I admit recycled solids and water don't sound appetizing, but as long as you have power, then you can distill . . ."

Alya changed channels—and got more filler.

"Impossible to tell. Certainly one stone hand-ax is not very impressive evidence on which to presume sentience."

"And this cuthionamine lysergeate that we've all heard so much about—it can produce homicidal mania?"

"Oh, very definitely. The regression to an innate stone-working behavior is more speculative, but there have been reports of . . ."

She tried yet another channel and was rewarded with a shot of de Soto Dome and the skiv.

". . . sometimes known as 'beetles' because of the three sections." The female voice was nasty, like fingernails on silk. "The front is the driver's cab. The middle section is the living quarters, and the rear portion the working part—the lab, and so on. Of course they're modular, and in this case that rear part is quite small, because they're only going out to retrieve the, er, body. Those tongs on the back are very remarkable tools—sensitive enough to pick up a hecto coin, yet strong enough to lift a house. Now, if we could get a close-up . . ."

Alya went back to WHSB.

"And we do seem to have some action now," Frazer remarked with ill-concealed relief. But the great dome remained deserted. In the center the metal object plate of the transmensor was as blank as a skating rink, while the giant three-module skiv brooded alone in a stark puddle of light beamed down from the impossibly high roof. The only action that Alya could see was that one of the gantries was trundling back into the shadows, as if to leave room.

Likely Frazer had been tipped off, for suddenly the window was open. The object plate had become a circular void, pure darkness. Nothing more happened.

"I expect they're adjusting Contact," Franklin commented off-stage. "As you can see, the surface of Nile is dark. That's normal—the sun never penetrates the— Ah . . . did you notice that, Jimmy? There's quite a wind blowing down there, and I'm sure that was a cloud of dust we just saw coming up through the pit."

Open the champagne, Alya thought.

"More likely a cloud of spores," someone else said. "There's a circulation—spores and dust carried upward to fertilize the cloud tops, and the fallout—"

He was cut off by a burst of excited chatter from Franklin as a ramp ran out from the edge of the pit and settled down into the dark. There was no mistaking the swirl of dust.

Covering another pause in the breathtaking activity, Franklin began asking his expert witness about decontamination. Nothing simpler, he was told—the Institute was meticulous. The dome would be opened afterward to a stellar corona and washed with high-energy plasma and hard radiation.

Alya switched channels.

But every station seemed to be carrying the same picture, and variations on the same talking heads.

At last the skiv began to move. Looking very much like a giant insect on its outstretched wheels, it flexed over the lip of the pit and rolled smoothly down the ramp. She sent a silent blessing after Cedric. She could imagine few things she would enjoy less than a visit to such a hell planet, but he was probably having the most exciting experience of his young life. She wished that her intuition would guard other people as well as herself. She told herself that he could come to no harm, that such feats were commonplace to the wizards of Cainsville.

And then there was a tap at the door and Moala was back, bubbling over with good humor and bursting to recount all her adventures. Alya was surprised at how good it felt to have some female company, and Moala was always good company. She was much less stupid than she liked to pretend, and could certainly not be one-tenth as debauched. But she told a good story, and after recounting her arduous experiences with a hairy-chested ranger named Al, she went on to invent sequels, introduce new characters, and turn her evening into a continuing saga of unbridled lust. How much came from her own imagination and how much from other sources Alya could not guess, but the end result was both mind-boggling and side-splitting. Moala especially approved of hairy chests.

At last, though, she ran out of either breath or invention. "But you?" she asked. "That *big* young man of yours—never have I seen one so tall! Did you let him bed you again? Is he good? And tell me exactly what he looks like."

Alya fought a tough withdrawing action before a barrage of questions, admitting to having been intimate with Cedric, but refusing to discuss his anatomy, stamina, or technique.

"Then I will borrow him and see," Moala said complacently. She peered sideways into the holo. "There he is, no?"

And there he was, yes. As long as the window was open, then signals could relayed from the skiv, and at the moment the com-set was showing the inside of the cab as if through a viewport behind the occupants. Devlin was driving, with Eccles Pandora beside him. In the rear seats, and only visible if one stood close and peeked in at an angle, were Baker Abel and the unmistakable shape of Cedric. This would be the third consecutive day that 4-I had dominated the world's news, and Alya could not recall ever seeing a planetary excursion given such massive coverage; certainly not for a Class Three world.

Despite its cantilevered wheels and complex suspension, the skiv rolled and pitched. The view in the headlights showed the surface of Nile to be a jumble of boulders and ridges, largely hidden by the bloated globes and spires of fungoid vegetation, with only the steeper pinnacles emerging as completely bare rock. Some of the growths were as large as houses; some were shaped as grotesquely as floating seaweed. Any touched by the skiv exploded like puffballs into dust, which was whipped away by the wind, although Devlin had to keep using wipers to clear the sticky stuff from his windshield. Beyond the lurid, scabrous jungle, where the headlights could not reach, world and sky were black. The only thing similar on Earth would be a view from a submarine.

Somehow Alya had come back to the WSHB channel, and Pandora was piping a commentary in her sweet voice, occasionally flashing a question at Devlin.

Their destination lay about ten kilometers from Contact, Alya gathered, at the spot where the first skiv had been parked when the disaster occurred—it had been brought back to Contact by remote control. The detectors were picking up response from that area, from Gill Adele's suit. So the sentience theory was looking shakier by the minute. Of course, if the suit had been moved—if it were set up on an altar, with offerings laid before it, for example—then a further search for stone-age beings might be justified.

Alya wondered if Cedric was regretting so much breakfast, with all that bouncing. And—

And the scene rippled.

Pandora's childish voice faded and returned, marred by a faint background crackling. Devlin must have seen the danger right away on his instruments, for he ripped out a screaming oath that stopped whatever his companion was saying. He revved the motors, spun the wheel, and the cab tilted almost on its side. Spires and trellises of fungus flashed by the windows, or erupted in blizzards of dust. The view shimmered again.

Then the scene was WSHB's Nauc studio, with Frazer Franklin registering concern. "We have a minor transmission problem there, as you may have noticed. We ..." He paused, raising a hand to his ear in a dramatic but completely unnecessary gesture. He let the suspense grow. "Apparently the problem is a little more serious than just—"

Alya knew how much more serious, but she was surprised to discover that she had her arms tight around Moala, who was in turn hugging her.

"System!" Alya shouted. *"Have you direct transmissions from that skiv on Nile?"* She wished Cedric were there, with his higher rating, but apparently hers was adequate. She had expected a refusal. Instead she was shown the cab again. If it had rocked before, now it was leaping, while the bloated jungle danced insanely before the plunging headlights, whirling from cellar to sky and back again. The motors' roar was audible under Pandora's screams. Could any machinery withstand such pounding for long? The transmission rippled, twisted, then stabilized again.

Cedric! Oh, Cedric!

Moala was shaking her. "What's wrong? What's wrong?"

"It's the string!" Alya said, fighting to keep panic out of her voice. There was nothing she could do. Nothing anyone could do. "The string's become unstable."

"Why?" Moala yelled, sounding prepared to go in search of whoever was responsible for the problem and make him stop it or rue his folly.

"Insh'Allah!" It is the will of God.

Another gravitational field was interfering, some other mass approaching the line of the string. If it were very small and moving very fast—an asteroid, for example, close to either Earth or Nile—then the effect might pass in a few minutes, without damage. If it were larger, like a star, then the string was going to be broken. A broken string was never found again.

Alya began shouting orders at the set, switching views, jumping from the commercial channels to Cainsville's own System and back again.

She saw the dome, vast and empty, but with the edges of the pit marked by a flicker of blue light like St. Elmo's fire that could only be Cerenkov radiation.

Frazer Franklin was explaining about string instability and gravitational masses.

She demanded to see the control room and was denied by System.

On NABC, Goodson Jason was displaying a sim map showing the original destination and Contact and the present position of the skiv. At least ten more minutes to reach Contact, he said.

Alya tried to call Hubbard Agnes, and the call was refused.

She went back to the dome, and the pit was a seething mass of blue. She wondered if even a skiv could protect its occupants from radiation so fierce. If the window were still open when the explorers reached Contact, they might be fried coming through. The instability was growing.

Frazer Franklin was showing a sim map also. At least six minutes . . .

Alya wanted to scream.

She flipped back to the cab. Continuous stomach-churning ripples made the occupants look as if they were dissolving in turbid water. Pandora was mumbling in terror, not making sense. Devlin was doing little better, growling curses, fighting to make the best speed he could over the impossible terrain. Even a skiv had its limits. Even a skiv was not indestructible.

Pandora and Devlin were being bounced right and left and up and down in their safety harnesses, their voices being drowned by a steadily growing crackling roar.

Moala tightened her grip on Alya. "You love that long young man, then?"

Love? For a moment Alya was speechless, as though a dinosaur had appeared in front of her. Love? Was this love? "I must," she said. "Yes, I must. I wouldn't be sniveling like this otherwise, would I?"

"But where is he?"

Cedric and Baker had gone. Her eyes were so blurry that she had not noticed the two empty seats.

"Show me Hubbard Cedric Dickson!"

She thought it would not work. Almost she could feel that the response was slower than normal, as though System were mulling over confidentiality, weighing internal priorities against a visitor's rating. Then she was granted a clear view back from the cab, toward the rear of the skiv. Cedric, followed by Baker Abel, was working his way along the corridor. There was a railing attached to one wall for just that purpose, but they were making slow progress, gripping with both hands, edging sideways. Half the time they must have felt as if they were standing on their heads. Cedric buckled and almost fell, then pulled himself upright, and a moment later Alya saw his feet leave the floor.

"Move it, fatso!" Baker's yell was just audible through the scream of static. "You're plugging up the works. Suck your gut in!"

Cedric grinned back at him. He did not look especially frightened. He never would. Oh, that grin!

Perhaps he was even preparing a suitably insulting reply. The scene was shimmering constantly, with patches of fog walking around in it, so Alya did not see exactly when it happened, but a door flew open between her and the two struggling men. Out hurled a pillow, a chair, and then another man. He came out half crouched, struck the opposite wall, rolled, and then spread out, flat on his back. He had no clothes on.

"Who's that?" Moala barked. She was still hugging Alya like a hungry python. Baker and Cedric seemed to be wondering the same thing. They had stopped to stare.

And Alya certainly was wondering. The first skiv to visit Nile had been booby-trapped with poison. Now the second contained an unauthorized passenger. Why would anyone stow away on a trip to Nile?

Blur . . . shimmy . . . steady again. Whatever Abel and Cedric had said about the intruder, Baker was clearly urging Cedric on toward the rear, while Cedric wanted to go back and aid the unconscious stranger.

He was a smallish man, dark and hairy. Moala would approve of his chest, Alya thought irrelevantly, but probably not of much else, for he was thin-shanked and scrawny. As the skiv lurched, he was bouncing and sliding, at times coming right off the floor and then flopping down again like a tossed pancake.

Baker was roaring. With obvious reluctance, Cedric had begun moving rearward again.

Disconnection—

Silence.

The holo contained only a featureless whirl of gray snow.

"Transmission interrupted," System said.

Alya wailed. Moala hauled her over to the bed and sat her down.

If needs be, almost indefinitely—the skiv would keep them alive until they died of old age or went mad. Trapped in hell. But there were five people, if that fifth one was still alive and if he survived the beating he had been getting. How long would a

SKIV-4 support five? And who was the stowaway?

Alya called for WSHB, and there was Frazer Franklin, gazing solemnly straight out at her.

"...by the authorities at the Institute that the window has been closed. The instability had reached the point where the string was unusable."

He sighed. Behind him a mirage display showed a ghostly replay of the four explorers as they must have been shown earlier, lined up in front of the skiv door: Devlin's unctuous toothy grin, Pandora's simper, Baker's leer. Behind them, shining over their heads like a sunrise, the juvenile glee of Hubbard Cedric.

"This means that the four explorers have been lost. You all know that a broken string can never be recovered. Even if Nile were by a miracle located later, it would be on a different string altogether, and might be removed by thousands or millions of years from the world that these four brave explorers were visiting. And, with or without a time anomaly, Contact could be half a world away from their present location."

He observed a few moments' silence.

"To me personally, and to all of us in WSHB, this tragedy—"

Ping!

Override—

Alya found herself facing the December stare of Hubbard Agnes. "You know what has happened?" the director inquired.

"I offer my deepest sympathy on the loss of your grandson, ma'am."

Hubbard pouted. She was wearing an elaborate outfit in corn-flower blue, with a high lace collar, almost a ruff. Her hair, as always, was a perfection in ice sculpture.

Fifty-six years from now on Tiber, Alya thought, I will not look as good as that.

"It was unfortunate. More unfortunate from your point of view, Highness, is that we also lost Deputy Devlin and Ranger Baker, party chief for your mission."

"What—"

Hubbard's thin white eyebrows rose in ridicule. "You were mourning the wrong one, perhaps? I have no choice but to close the Tiber file, Princess."

"No!"

"Oh, yes. Deputy directors are not readily replaced. Baker was in charge of all the arrangements. By the time we can reorganize for a planting, Tiber will be long gone. Maybe later in the year, or next year, some other world . . ."

"Who was the fourth man?"

After a perceptible pause, Hubbard said, "What fourth man?"

"There was a fourth man on that skiv. One woman and four men. He fell out into the corridor near the end, when Cedric and Abel were—why were they going to the rear, anyway?"

Hubbard shrugged narrow shoulders. "There could have been no fourth man, Princess. The imaging was very poor, right at the end."

"I saw him!"

"No, you didn't. There was no fourth man. You must know enough about our procedures to know that a skiv is never loaded above its rating. *Never!* There could have been no fifth person on board. I can't imagine why the other two might have left the cab, if indeed they did."

She would certainly have the records wiped, though, just in case anyone tried to check.

Alya bowed ironically. No one would ever know what sinister plans that iron-hearted woman had prepared for her grandson. But she had known about the fourth man, and she knew why Cedric and Baker had left the cab.

Cedric, oh Cedric! Who could think of a more hellish end?

"If you will please have your packing attended to as soon as possible, Your Highness?" the director asked icily. "The lev leaves in thirty minutes."

"No!"

"Yes." Vindictive triumph played over lips as old as China. "The planting is canceled. Cedric is lost forever, and you are going back to Banzarak."

18

WAY BACK IN 2042 or 2043, Hastings Willoughby had made a tour through Southeast Asia and called in on the sultan of Banzarak. Although young and still new on his throne, Kassan'assan had impressed the Secretary General as being already much more than the figurehead his constitutional position decreed.

Just as Banzarakian culture was a mishmash of many elements contributed by its neighbors—Christian, Islamic, Buddhist, Hindu, and even jungle animism—so the people themselves comprised a blend of many races. Normally they tended toward a nondescript average, but occasionally the melt would throw up someone quite extraordinary. Kassan'assan was one such, and so was his youngest sister, Princess Alya. Her beauty had been obvious even then, when she could not have been more than twelve—slight and dark, already sporting a cataract of heavy midnight hair and eyes enshrining all the ancient mystery of the East. Willoughby had prophesied that she would break men's hearts.

At the moment she looked more ready to break heads.

The U.N.'s new HQ building was provided with an imposing grand entrance for receiving distinguished guests: marble steps and high pillars of porphyry. Willoughby had selected the design himself and it was a fraud, being located safely indoors, out of the dangers of weather. Somehow that seemed symbolic. So far it had been reserved for ceremonial welcomes to heads of state or heads of government, but today he had decided that youth and beauty should be given the honor they deserved. To the great disgust of his protocol staff, he decreed that he would greet the princess there.

His life had been extremely hectic during the last few days, and he was feeling his age. He thought that a couple of hours entertaining a pretty girl was exactly what the geriatrician ordered. He had even indulged himself in a cane to lean on, but he rather regretted that as he watched Alya come striding up the shallow steps in a very unladylike march, her small entourage hurrying behind her and red-suited bulls from the Institute in escort. A bearded *hajji*, who must be her political case worker, was whispering urgently in her ear, undoubtedly trying to slow her down. Princess Alya was in no mood to heed his cautions.

Yes, a heartbreaker. She was clothed in skintight opal white, an outrageous choice and a stunning success. Tiny ripples of fire flowed over her as she moved—ruby and leaf green and king-fisher blue. She was taller than she seemed at first glance, and slender. She could almost have been taken for a boy, so unobtrusive were the curves of the hips and the conical breasts, but few youths could have ever matched that neck, or the tiny waist, or the raging arrogance that burned in every move.

Willoughby was amused. Agnes had warned him that there would be tempests.

Cameramen fluttered around like moths as he bowed over the royal hand. Age honoring youth—her slender beauty and his sagging decrepitude—he knew they made an incongruous picture. That, and Alya's looks, would ensure them a few seconds on the evening news, which was all that mattered.

He had not prepared a speech; after the first few thousand, speeches came easy. He bid the princess welcome, as the honored representative of her brother. The bearded man held out a paper for her to read. She accepted it graciously, then crumpled it with one hand and threw it at his feet. Was he the cause of her vexation, or only the butt? Then she spoke clearly and in perfect English, saying no more than necessary and barely enough.

She was extremely mad about something. She was also very young. Willoughby decided that further ceremony would be an unnecessary risk. He led her inside and skillfully engineered her away from her companions and into a private room. As the door closed, he caught a glimpse of the hairy-faced hack grinding his teeth.

The Banzaraki royal house, as he recalled, was pretty well agnostic in private, in spite of its many public roles. "I would not offend if I offered a sherry before lunch, Your Highness?"

She was glancing around the little office. It was cozily furnished and cunningly littered as though in constant use. Probably no one had been in it for weeks, but the disarray suggested informality and invited confidence. And none of the imposing documents lying around was of any importance whatsoever.

She released a long breath. "A sherry would be very welcome."

"Anything else?"

"Some answers."

"As many as I can find."

Her reply was a look of skepticism. Agnes had that effect on some people.

He saw her comfortably seated; he poured the sherry. Then he settled into an oversize, oversoft chair that disguised his height. He raised his glass. "Your health and that of your royal brother, and his family."

They sipped. She was eyeing him like a fencer armed with a real saber. He smiled. Pretty girls had that effect on him.

"First question? No, I'll start. Did you have a good journey?"

"No. It was a zoo." The way she bared her teeth tended to confirm the legends of headhunters in her family tree, and not very many branches up, either. The lev must have been packed with reporters returning from Cainsville, and a beautiful princess would have been a welcome diversion.

He laughed aloud. "Your turn, then."

She studied him for a moment. "Why do you not mourn your grandson?"

"Oi! Your claws draw blood, ma'am."

"Is it thinner than water?"

"I commend your grasp of English idiom."

"I admire your skill at deflecting inquiry."

He regarded her while he took a sip of sherry, amused by the youthfully aggressive questioning. "Untimely death is always a tragedy, but I would be hypocritical to pretend any special sorrow for a young man I did not know existed until two days ago. I met him only once, for less than an hour. You had become friends?"

"Lovers." She hoped to shock him, but Hastings Willoughby had lost all his shockability long before this razor-tooth tigress cub was born. Still, his grandson must have been an extremely fast worker. Or she was. He felt a pang of envy at the thought of being nineteen and admitted to her bed.

Her poise was remarkable for her age, but that was a family trait. Willoughby had met most of the royal Banzarakians who had passed through Nauc in the last twenty-five years en route to Cainsville and worlds unknown, and he recognized the innate arrogance—but who would not walk tall after being reared on royal jelly and guided by the *buddhi*, the finger of God?

Yet there had been exceptions. A few had still been unsure of exactly what their inner demon was demanding, and those had been very scared young aristocrats indeed, meeting the unknown for the first time in their lives. Alya's eyes had borne traces of that dread two days before, at the press conference. It had gone now. It always did, as soon as they saw their path clear ahead again.

"Are you certain," she inquired sweetly, "that Cedric is dead?"

Willoughby had not thought of that alternative, and did not try to conceal his surprise. "I had never . . . You think that the Institute can recover a broken string? They've always denied—"

She shook her head vigorously, spilling plumes of peacock and hummingbird over her shoulders and breasts. "No. I've seen the math. The solutions are infinite. A string is only straight in theory. In practice it's bent by gravitational anomalies, just as light is. When they move, it moves. It wriggles, but you never know even which dimension to adjust, let alone—" She smiled, and for the first time she looked her age. "Sorry, Mr. Secretary General! Kas is always lecturing me for lecturing. No, when contact is lost, it's lost for good. But the break could have been faked. Stability is hard to achieve, instability is easy. The next window may still be available on schedule, four days from now."

Willoughby pondered that. "I swear to you, ma'am, that I honestly don't know. Agnes rarely takes me into her confidence. Almost never. I can see why she might fake a disappearance for the ranger, if he was the one who was going to lead the colonization."

"But the others are harder to explain?" The beat of Alya's heart showed just below her left breast, a faint rhythmic violet twitch on the opal cloth.

"Yes. Well, I suppose Cedric had become an instant celebrity, so she might fake a death for him also, if she were planning to send him off to another world with you."

"She wasn't." The violet beat had quickened. He waited, and after a moment she said, "And in four days I will not be on this world to find out—to know if he does come back."

Willoughby shrugged. "And Devlin Grant? His ambitions are no secret. He hopes to succeed Agnes. If she sneaks him back in four days, he will not remain incognito. As soon as any one of them reappears, then the secret is out. Dr. Eccles? She would certainly not stay out of view."

"No." The girl sighed very deeply and averted her eyes. Young Cedric must have done a fair job of winning her affections as well as her favors.

Momentarily Hastings wondered what sort of man could ever hope to bind this wildcat to a long-term pairing. She would never tolerate less than equality in a partnership, and would then instinctively seek to dominate it. Very few men could ever hope to match her in brains; she had beauty and spirit galore. She might select a milksop, of course—he had seen strong women make that mistake often enough—but he rather thought that Princess Alya would know better. Yet she would have trouble finding a man with enough durability to tolerate her flame without being consumed by it. He wondered what she could possibly have seen in the Cedric boy. Only physical size, surely, and therefore she had been after recreation, nothing serious. Not lovers—playmates.

"I had not thought of the accident being a fake, Highness. Certainly with Agnes anything is possible, but I really cannot comprehend how that particular fraud could have worked, or what it would have gained her."

"There was a fifth person on board, a stowaway. A man."

"How— I wasn't watching, I was working. Are you sure?"

She nodded. "You wouldn't have seen on public holo. I'd been given an honorary ranking on System. It let me see more than I was supposed to see, I think." She had changed position slightly, and the cloth below her breast was no longer tight enough to show the violet beat.

A stowaway? She was waiting—waiting for him to catch up with her own thinking. He had not matched wits with anyone so young and unpredictable in many years. He was getting too old for it. The last couple of days had been crushing.

"There is—or was—a murderer on the loose in Cainsville?"

"And also a spy, who sold the coin to WSHB. Not likely the same person, but possibly so."

Anyone could have worked out such things, given time. It was not this slender vixen's comments that revealed her brainpower, but the way in which she made them. He had never had patience with stupid women, or women who pretended to be stupid, or men who preferred either.

"You suspect execution?" He shook his head. "If there were a murder, then I am sure Fish already knows the culprit. Certainly Fish and Agnes are capable of dumping the scoundrel on the first handy planet. I'm certain that they've done such things in the past. They're quite prepared to take justice into their own hands."

"But not with four others aboard?" She wanted to be convinced.

"Never! I mean, Eccles purchased a Cainsville secret, but that was her job. I can't see Agnes being vindictive enough to kill her for it. The traitor who sold it—well, that might be another matter. Devlin has ambitions, but she could throw him out on his ear anytime. And the two youngsters... No. I can't explain the stowaway, but I think you are pushing suspicion a little far, Your Highness."

She sighed again and sipped more sherry.

"I have always understood," he added, "that breaks were not predictable."

She nodded sadly, keeping her eyes down so he could not see them. Even to him, unexpected death was always a shock, but the old had learned how to accept such things. Alya was much, much younger and was clutching at every thread of hope she could find.

"You seemed very annoyed when you came in," he ventured.

"I was. I am."

"Why?"

She shrugged. "All the stupid mystery." She looked up with the sort of smile that had once launched ships. "No—mostly I was mad at myself for being so dumb. I was halfway back here to Nauc before I realized the real reason I had been shipped out in that carton of monkeys. Hubbard Agnes lied to me, and I believed her!"

Willoughby chuckled, hoping to keep that smile alive a little longer. "She often does, especially if she thinks you should be able to work out the truth for yourself."

"It was my own fault for showing up uninvited at her press conference, I suppose. But she told me that the Tiber planting was canceled and I was to return to Banzarak!"

"She's a bitch," Willoughby agreed calmly, remembering Agnes's amusement when she had called him to drop this tangle in his lap. "When did the fog lift?"

Again a smile laid magic on the café au lait face. "Not soon enough! I should have known right away—if the Nile expedition had put Tiber at risk, I'd have got bad vibes as soon as it was suggested. I suppose I only notice when the *buddhi* speaks, and don't notice when it stays silent. Even Jathro knew! He brazenly told me that I was to come here and make a speech—and I still didn't catch on!" Of course, that was what was annoying her most—that the hack had seen what she had not. "Finally one of the reporters' questions made me mad, and I began to wonder what I was doing traveling with a circus . . ."

She shook her head ruefully and drained her glass. "My fault —I advertised my presence at Cainsville. Now I must make an equally public exit."

He nodded. "But my good fortune! We shall feed you a small lunch—about fifty guests. You will address the Refugee Authority, outlining all the priceless work that little Banzarak is doing for refugees, and tonight there will be a dinner."

She groaned. "Can I settle for a public flogging instead?"

"You have stepped in at a moment's notice to replace a South American vice-president suddenly indisposed. We are very grateful."

She grinned. "I trust his indisposition is not serious?"

"You are confusing me with Dr. Fish. No, he is just suffering transportations of delight over a delightful new transportation he has just acquired. It came with a blonde in it."

"And I go back to Cainsville—when?"

"Tonight, about midnight. You should arrive about 0400. More sherry?" The first glass had improved her disposition remarkably, unless that was an effect of his brilliant conversation.

She shook her head. "We should probably rejoin the world before your reputation is ruined, Mr. Secretary General."

"Probably. But ruin all you want."

Her eyes twinkled—moonlight on jungle pools—and then sobered. "One last question?"

"Of course."

"Two questions, I guess. But related. First, why did Hubbard Agnes pull that idiot stunt with Cedric at her press conference? Eccles thought it was because she had planned to announce something else and then changed her mind. But there's no sentient life on Nile—is there?"

"Not so far as I know."

"Then that idea doesn't work. It was not a change of plan!"

"And secondly?"

"You said right afterward that you thought she was mad. She knocked the wind out of you, and yet today you're as chipper as a cricket, and entertaining her discards. Explain, please."

"I fear that secret is not mine to tell."

Her eyes glinted. "For as long as I can remember, I have been entrusted with a greater."

True! Well, he had never promised Agnes that he would keep it secret, and he would like to provoke a few more smiles. At his age there could not be many more to look forward to.

"You should be able to work it out, as I did. I have known Agnes for a very long time. She is infinitely devious. Her stones are never aimed at less than two birds, usually more. But some of it you should be able to work out. She pretended to behave irrationally, and nothing so confuses the strategic-analysis routines as that does. That's why a good poker player likes to be caught bluffing from time to time—it is an investment. She even fooled me. And she publicly made dolts of the media, so their next attacks on her can be blamed on bias."

"I thought of all those points. They are not enough to justify the risks."

Were Alya not so lovely, he would not tolerate that tone from her. "No? Well, I knew the answer by the time I had returned here. When she pulled the idiot stunt, as you phrase it, what questions came to your mind?"

A crease formed between the exquisite eyebrows. "Who is he? Why is she doing this?"

He waited.

"Where has she dragged him from . . ."

He waited.

The royal eyes widened. "The organage!"

He nodded somberly. "Organ replacement, as it is practiced now, is a despicable business. Autografts are the safest, but they must come from clones. It is a secret, of course, but a widely known one. The cost is enormous—not the initial procedure, but the covert raising of the child to adult size. Only embryos can be grown in tanks. A body contains a brain, and a brain contains a person. Diabolic. A huge and bestial industry."

"Why is it not exposed, then, and wiped out?"

"Because it is the prerogative of the rich and powerful, Eccles Pandora and those like her. The minor flunkies in the great organizations know the truth and detest it—perhaps they would do the same if they could afford it, but they cannot."

"And Agnes was threatening to reveal the truth! It was blackmail!"

He smiled and reached a long arm to lay his glass on a paper-strewn table. "You have it! And she did it on world holo—the biggest, most blatant blackmail threat ever made! The secret has survived so long only because no one with real influence has chosen to fight it. But Agnes has unlimited influence. By the time I returned to Nauc I knew—mostly, I admit, because the calls had started already. The phone was ringing, as we used to say. Friends—I use the term in the widest sense—friends I had not spoken to in years were calling me to ask the price. I expect Agnes has been even more popular."

There was another factor, of course, one available only to someone with power like Hubbard's, but the girl had apparently missed that, so far.

"And these minor flunkies you mentioned . . ."

"They dared not expose the truth openly, but they slanted the reports—some of them. Enough of them. 'A hitherto unacknowledged grandson of Hastings Willoughby, raised on a secluded ranch . . .' And so forth."

"And your reaction—that was why she included you!"

He nodded guilty. "Even I was taken in for a while—and if even I assumed that Cedric was my clone, no wonder the rest did! She has never hesitated to use anyone, even me. Especially me."

Alya smiled into the distance, nodding. "So where mere bribery was no longer enough, you have been threatening ruin, you and she." Her face darkened again. She turned her cryptic oriental gaze on him, and it was deadly. "Then the two of you will hang on to power—and the organages will remain?"

He shrugged. "We shall see. Negotiations are still in progress, as the saying goes." He chuckled and pulled himself forward in the chair, preparing to rise.

Centuries of absolute monarchy blazed at him out of those eyes. "I am not sure that I appreciate the moral distinction, Mr. Secretary General. To prolong life at the expense of those other young lives is an unquestionable evil. You just said so. To prolong your own power at that same cost—is this ethically superior?"

How easy it must seem from the vantage of youth!

He rose stiffly, feeling his tin legs quiver. "I said that the game is not over, Highness. You must be satisfied with that. For now."

She wasn't—but then her anger faltered as her Toledo-sharp mind slashed through to another layer of truth. "There's more!"

she said. "It wouldn't work without . . . There has to be more to it than that?"

"Luncheon, Your Highness?" Willoughby said.

They had luncheon, with speeches and more media coverage.

Alya attended a meeting of the U.N. Refugee Authority and read a text that was excessively dull, having been written by a computer.

There was a grand dinner in the evening, and the media were there again. There was talk of the princess's world tour being extended to include Latin America—and all this just to conceal the secret connection between Banzarak and Cainsville.

She was whisked away in a helicopter, one of a half dozen flying in variable formation. At an isolated and well-guarded airstrip she boarded an unmarked plane, followed by Moala and the two political nonentities and Jathro—who had become an intolerable pest again, now that his rival Cedric was dead.

In the black heart of night, while aurorae danced their spectral measures in the uppermost silences, the plane descended along a complex path into the unreported airstrip at Cainsville.

The size of it staggered Alya, but then she recalled that thousands, and hundreds of thousands, had come the same way during various brief periods in the past. If all went well, the salmon run would start again, very soon. Salmon? Lemmings . . . locusts?

Bees! A swarm of bees, and she was the queen . . .

She was rambling. Her mind had been tattered by another brutal day.

The Institute's passion for security showed again. Despite the remote location and the lateness of the hour, the plane was not unloaded until it had been towed into a hangar. With her eyes smarting under the arc lights, Alya picked her way cautiously down the steps to a reception party headed—again—by the inscrutable Dr. Fish. Everyone else looked as though they had just crawled out of bed, she thought. He looked as though he had just left a grave. He whispered polite queries about her journey and then murmured an almost inaudible introduction of Ranger O'Brien Patrick.

"Since yesterday's tragedy, ma'am, Ranger O'Brien has been appointed to take over Baker's duties. Dr. Devlin's are being administered by the director herself, pro tem."

O'Brien was lanky, middle-aged, and lugubrious. He shook

Alya's hand, but it was hard to tell whether he bowed over it, or
if that was just an illusion caused by his stoop. "The hour is late,
Your Highness."

"Very."

"A quick update on tomorrow, then," he said. "There are still
two worlds you have not seen. Quinto has been on our list for a
while. It has already been overnighted. Like Orinoco, it is showing some disturbing features. We have colonies of fruit flies in
the lab, containing planetary material. They're not thriving as
they should. We don't know why yet."

What was bad for a fruit fly might not be much good for a
queen bee, Alya thought muzzily. Lord, but she was weary!

"Usk's due in mid-afternoon. I can't tell you much. This is
only its second window. We transmensed a robbie the first time.
The data from that will determine what we do next."

She nodded, wondering why they had to hold their conversation in a vast and dismally echoing hangar, a dozen weary people
standing around at an hour so godforsaken. "Tiber?"

"Tiber will be accessible early the following morning. The
overnighters' reports will, of course, be critical."

Shivering with the dank dejection of the small hours, Alya
was thus reminded that her time of decision was almost upon her.
She had sworn to make absolutely sure. But how could she ever
recognize absolute certainty? She might beg another three days,
until the Tiber window opened again, but how could that help? If
the instruments and measurements and analyses all said that Tiber
was safe; if her intuition about it remained unchanged; if Hubbard
and her experts then turned to Alya and said, "Well?"

Well? What then?

"I need bed!" she said firmly, and headed for the line of waiting golfies.

She trailed into Columbus Dome with Moala and Jathro and
the other two, and they were all silent and morose and weary
beyond care. Alya surprised herself by stopping off at the cafeteria and gulping down three straight cups of rank black coffee. It
was 0414 hours. She needed sleep and lots of it, not coffee. She
was nutty.

When she went for a fourth cup, Moala begged to be excused.
Her eyes were red as embers.

"Of course!" Alya said, cross at herself for being so inconsid-
erate. Moala smiled, rose, and headed draggily for the spiralator.

But Jathro's two sidekicks went with her, and that left Alya
alone with the lizard himself.

He—damn him!—barely looked tired at all. A faint leer of satisfaction twitched his beard. He slid a sticky hand over hers.

"Alya, my dear!"

"Dr. Jar?"

He shook his head. "When we are alone like this, you may call me Jathro. Of course, I realize that the sad loss of your young friend has been a great shock to you. You know I am always at your service, and if there is any way in which . . ."

Evidently even Jathro could read expressions sometimes—his voice trailed off as he registered hers. She hoped, though, that he had not been about to suggest what she suspected he had been about to. She would certainly have maimed him.

"You have my leave to withdraw, Dr. Jar."

The bright eyes flared dangerously. Then he rose to stalk away in a sulk. She was alone at last.

She sipped at her cup and then put it down angrily, spilling half the contents.

She did not *need* more coffee! For a moment she laid her face in her hands. It had been an utterly inhuman day. The only good thing about it had been that she had been granted very little free time to brood over Cedric. Merciless Heavens! Trapped, maybe for years, in a cell in hell with Devlin and that awful Eccles woman!

Why had her intuition not warned her? True, it never worked for other people. Only her own interests provoked a *satori*. Cedric had gone. She had used him, yes—or her *buddhi* had—but now that he was no longer available, she was sure that what she had begun to feel for him near the end had been something she had never felt for a man before. It must have been love, or at least the start of love. Certainly he had been eager to offer her all the love she would accept. Potent stuff, love—it was sticky on both sides.

Had he not been important, then, that almost-lover, that potential future mate? On a frontier world his outdoor skills and his courage—even his size—would have been invaluable. He would have been a good protector for her, devoted and competent. If his destiny had been to die on Nile, then why had she not received a warning to save him? Would that not have been to her advantage?

Or had his real destiny been that his grandmother had other plans for him and would never have released him to accompany Alya to Tiber anyway? To her *buddhi*, Cedric had been important no longer. He had outlived his usefulness. She shuddered and drained the last of the coffee.

Her *buddhi* had been having an off-day, obviously. After so many centuries of shunning cobras, it had not twitched when Hubbard Agnes had pretended she was sending Alya back to Banzarak.

No, that was not fair. She had felt no *satori* because her intuition had not been fooled by a lie. She rose. Her feet bore her to the spiralator, and it carried her up.

What happens at the top? she had asked Baker that first day. As she reached her floor she felt a sudden urge to find out for herself what happened at the top.

She watched the exit go by and did not move. The coffee was pumping life back into her, making her heart thump. Round and round . . . and that was fitting, because her head was starting to spin. Up and up, and she began to sense a soaring excitement.

Her intuition was not fooled by a lie.

Her intuition was not fooled by a lie.

Doorways slid by, curving downward. There were more levels than she had expected, dimly lit as befitted the middle of the night. Then the confining cylindrical wall vanished. The steps flattened out level with the floor, curving around to vanish into the side of the central pillar, as Baker had said. She stepped off.

The circular hallway was much smaller up near the top. There were numbered doors. Conscious of the wild beating of her heart, of a strange warmth that had started in her loins and was raging through her like a forest fire, she walked around until she found the one that felt right.

It was not locked.

The light was off and he was asleep.

But even in the dark, she knew. Her heart was trying to beat its way right out of her chest. She shivered with desire like a fever. She was reaching for her zip even as she closed the door, and she crossed the room without a stumble, undressing as she went.

Most women would hesitate to climb naked into a strange bed, but she did not. She knew who was breathing there. She was almost sobbing with happiness and excitement and longing.

He was important! He was, he was!

19

Cainsville, April 10

HUBBARD CEDRIC D. had had a rotten day. Bored, angry, and frustrated in everything he tried, he had finally decided to catch up on his sleep. He had gone to bed early. Perhaps, therefore, he had been sleeping lightly. But he had certainly been dreaming of Alya—dreaming she was in his arms and kissing him. And suddenly it was no longer a dream. It was really Alya—and this time he was on top again and right away he—oh glory!

"You're quite sure you're not a dream?" Cedric mumbled a few minutes later.

"Do I feel like a dream?"

"You feel marvelous. Soft and warm. Dreamy."

"Would a dream be weeping all over you like this?"

"Maybe a wet dream. *Ouch!*"

Now he knew. Dreams did not pinch.

She had been a dream, though. Now she wasn't. He had not been really awake, but he had been very ready, because he had been dreaming of her. He hoped he had not been too rough—those were real tears on his chest. He had been dreaming, and she had suddenly been there . . . He wondered if maybe he had established some sort of world record. He knew that a man was supposed to take more time than that and be more considerate. He

231

just had not been properly awake. He would be more careful in future. But, oh, what a way to waken!

"I didn't hurt you?"

"For the third time, darling: no, you did not hurt me. I wish it was always so good. You hear me. I wasn't faking that, I swear."

Wow! "You weren't?" He sighed and adjusted his hands slightly. "I was ready."

"So was I. Now, tell me." The question seemed to be addressed to his left nipple.

"Tell you what?"

"How come you're not trapped on Nile?"

"I don't want to talk about it. *Ow!*"

"You will tell me, or you will suffer a grievous mutilation."

"Let go—no, don't," he added hastily. "Just don't squeeze. All right, it was a fake, a fraud. There was no broken string. All they need do, Abe says, is twiddle the knobs a bit and the window goes unstable, as though the string's about to snap."

"I saw you and Abel heading along the corridor. I saw another man."

He grunted. "Did you, now? I wonder how many others did." He shivered at the memories. "It's not a very nice story."

"I want to hear it, anyway."

"Well, Abe warned me even before the press arrived. 'If I give you a signal,' he said, 'like this, then do as I say, and no arguing!' I said fine. Funny, you know I trust him? I trust you, of course, but not anyone else. Not in Cainsville."

"Wise, I think."

He tried to kiss her, and she told him to finish the story first. He wondered how short he could make it.

"I'll be quick, then! But when Abel stops smartypantsing, he's all right . . . So we were about halfway to target and suddenly Devlin began cursing, and turned us around and started back toward Contact. The radar was showing instability. Did you know that a window shows up on radar? I didn't. But I could see over Pandora's head—the echo had started to, well, sort of wriggle. Like a shimmy, you know? We began bouncing pretty bad."

"I saw."

At the time Cedric had not realized he was being watched. He should have done. Quite likely he was being watched right now, by infrared maybe, lying in bed with a beautiful girl's head on his chest and torrents of her hair spread all over his belly. Let them weep their eyes out!

"Go on!"

"Mm?" There were so many better things to do with lips than talk ... "Then Abel gave me a tap and jerked his head. So we unstrapped ourselves and headed back to the rear. It was a pretty wild trip, and he wouldn't say why."

"And then the other man fell out of the door."

"Yeah. He had nothing on. He must have been lying on the bunk and just bounced off. He was out cold by the time I saw him."

"Who was he?"

"Abe told me Wilkins something." Cedric had wanted to go and try to help, but Baker Abel had insisted that it was too risky, he would just get himself hurt. So they had gone on into the lab module at the back.

"It was bouncing even worse, but there was another radar there, and Abe turned it on and we strapped ourselves into a couple of operator chairs and watched."

She squirmed. "And you saw the window close?"

"Well, Abe was grinning and telling me not to worry—but it was a nasty feeling. And everything happened at once. We got to Contact—there was a lot of blue light coming down, showing up all the jungle in creepy colors—and the ramp had gone. And then the window closed. And Abe pulled a switch, and that disconnected us."

She lifted her head, as though trying to see him in the dark. "Disconnected who?"

"The lab cab. The third module of the skiv. He shut the doors between and unhooked us from the rest of the skiv. Then the window opened again and a crane reached down and lifted us back up, but it was into David Thompson Dome, you see. They'd faked the broken string in de Soto Dome, with all those reporters watching, and then opened up the same string from Thompson. By the time everyone realized what had happened, we were back already."

"But Devlin?"

That was the bad bit. Cedric wished he did not have to tell her, because he was feeling guilty and dirty, although there had been nothing at all he could have done. In fact he had begged Fish to open the window again and rescue the others.

"They're still there—him and Eccles Pandora and the Wilkins man, if he's alive. It was only me and Abel came back, the rear cab."

He felt her shudder in his arms. "No! Oh, Cedric!"

"Yes. Bad."

"But why?"

"I don't know. They wouldn't say."

There had been about six people waiting when Cedric and Baker Abel had come out of decon. Fish had been in charge, but Bagshaw Barney had been there, grinning like a big ape, and a ranger called O'Brien, and some others Cedric had not recognized. They had cracked a few jokes, and there had been a smell of satisfaction around, but the mood had mostly been grim—as it damned well should have been. That planet was real hell.

"Fish said something about letting them meditate on their sins for a few days. Then he went away. I did ask, darling. Even for Eccles. I begged!"

Worst of all had been something Bagshaw had said: "You ought to be feeling good, Sprout. Your Glenda's been avenged. That Eccles woman deserves what she's got."

He told Alya as well as he could, thinking he was not doing it very well.

"I don't feel that way at all!" he said. "I don't know why. It won't bring Glenda back, I guess, and I expect Glenda had a lot more peaceful death than that. I don't feel good about it."

"Not your fault," she said. "They used you. You didn't know."

That helped a little. But he had agreed to appear on Pandora's special because Bagshaw had said he could avenge Glenda. He had, and now he wished he hadn't.

"Fish said they'd be rescued at the next window?" Alya asked.

"Not exactly." Fish had just been shutting him up, giving him time to get used to the idea. Of course, Eccles was not going to be brought back! What could they say to her? "Oops, sorry over that?" The Institute could never admit what it had done. There could never be a rescue. If he had worked that out, then Alya certainly would. She was a lot smarter than he was.

"But why? Why leave them there?"

"Well, the Wilkins man was the spy who sold the coin to Eccles. So Fish said. But I was told not to worry about him. He was almost brain dead anyway."

He felt her shudder again, harder. "How brain dead? What did they do to him to make him brain dead?"

"They did nothing. So Fish says. He was a plugin freak, and he'd got a heap of credit for the coin. He took an OD. Fish says if he ever does wake up, he'll be a raving lunatic from the pain, because of the way it burns the nerve ends." Cedric hoped he believed that.

"And Devlin?"

None of them had been willing to talk about Devlin, Cedric said.

"He was after your grandmother's job."

Cedric knew a lot more about his grandmother than he had a few days earlier, but even so . . . "Surely she wouldn't kill a man just because of that?"

"God, I hope not!" Alya said.

"And why Eccles Pandora, anyway? There must be hundreds of people in the world with clone organs in them, or stored in the icebox."

"I don't know, dearest," she said. "But—I think you're right. There must be more than that to Pandora. She was deliberately snared. So was Devlin."

Snared by him, by Hubbard Cedric Dickson. For a moment he lay in silence, softly kneading the marvelous woman beside him. Then it was his turn to shiver. "The Judas cow!" he said. "The one that leads the herds to slaughter!"

She punched him. "Stop that! You didn't know! And there's obviously a lot we don't know yet. It's hard to see how they could have organized this without Devlin's help. He was a sleazy type, but he wasn't dumb. Could he had been sneaked back the same way you were, leaving just Pandora?"

Cedric shrugged. "I suppose." Fish and Bagshaw had been very uncommunicative about Devlin.

"After all," Alya said, "if he did suspect, then he would have made certain he had a return ticket. Devlin looked after his own skin. He was no kamikaze fanatic dispensing justice like—"

"Arrh!" Cedric bellowed. He spasmed as if he had been electrocuted, hurling Alya off him. Terror! Pain! He howled and curled up and clamped his hands over his ears to stop the screaming—a child's voice screaming: *I won't! I won't!*

The voice in his head dwindled away into whimpers and then silence. Someone—Alya—had spoken the lights on and was pulling his hands away from his ears. At least his legs had stopped thrashing. She was trying to hold and soothe him—not too easy with him wrapped up in a ball like that—and she was cooing like a mother to a baby: "It's all right . . . you're quite safe . . . I'm here . . . nothing to be afraid of . . ." Then she went back to the beginning again. How many times had she repeated that refrain?

He straightened out, realizing that he was soaked in sweat and yet his teeth were chattering with cold.

She sighed with relief, got an arm around him properly, and pushed his hair out of his eyes. "Cedric? Darling?"

"I'm all right, I think." But he wasn't. He had a horrible feeling he might be going to weep—what would she think of him then? He burrowed down, and she clasped his head to her breast and held him. Long silence . . . heart thudding . . . shakes getting better . . .

"What startled you?" she asked softly.

He stuttered—he did not know. Idiot! Ninny!

"I can't remember." He uncurled himself again. "I must be going crazy!"

"No. No, you're not that." But she looked worried. "Just a reaction to the hard day, I think—lots of hard days. Nobody's indestructible, Cedric. But don't let it bother you." She grinned and placed a very careful kiss on his throbbing nose. "Let's think about tomorrow! Abel's back, so he'll still be leading the Tiber expedition?"

"I guess so."

"He has to! And you, too—you've got to disappear, too! You're an unperson, darling!" She must have seen his doubts. "No?"

Bagshaw had turned strangely shy when Cedric had asked about Tiber—not his usual self at all.

"I hope so," Cedric said. "Oh, I do hope so!"

She sighed and squirmed against him sensuously. *"Lights off!"* The room went black, leaving just Alya's faint, fast-fading afterimage. "Now forget all that!" she said. "Because I love you. I love you madly and I've got some wonderfully decadent things I am going to do to you."

But he still felt shaky from that weird fit he'd had, and memories of the skiv, and Fish's expression when— "I'm not sure I'm in the mood anymore," he said. "But I love you."

"You'll come around," she said, chewing his ear. "Depravity is lovely—try a little foreplay and see what happens."

How little a woman had to do to take a man's mind off his troubles! "Sandpaper? I'd better go and shave."

"Doesn't matter."

"How about your bruises?"

"Forget them. Forget everything. Just start."

His fires had begun to glow already. "You're not sleepy?"

"I've been drinking liters of coffee. I'm going to keep you busy till noon, and anything you've ever dreamed of—just ask! So come on, lover—no holds barred. Do your damnedest."

He felt excitement and desire explode inside him. "Sign this release then," he muttered hoarsely, and kissed her.

Any day that had started that well could not improve as it went along. Cedric was wakened by a kiss. A gray dawn showed in the skylight, and Alya was already dressed. He felt bad about what he saw then—her lip was swollen and her cheeks scraped. He had some scratches and nibble marks here and there himself. Some of their lovemaking had been gentle and soft, some wild and jungley, but all of it had been sweet beyond longing.

She slid away before he could grab her. "Clean up and join me for breakfast in half an hour."

"Wait!" he said. "I can't."

"Can't what?"

"I'm in jail. A prisoner."

He thought he saw fear then, swiftly covered by anger. "How can you be a prisoner?"

"You may be one, too!" He sat up and looked around for clothes. "We're at the top of the dome. The only way out is down the spiralator, and if I get on it, it reverses."

Bagshaw had explained very patiently. "Step on there," he had said, "and System will know. It'll reverse the motion and run it as fast as necessary to keep you where you are. Don't even experiment, because anyone else using it may get hurt."

Wondering why getting dressed in front of Alya somehow seemed more embarrassing than just being nude, Cedric pulled on pants while telling her what Bagshaw had said. There were at least three cameras trained on the spiralator. Cedric had tried going near it, and that had made the lights flicker. The cameras were tamperproof. He had no tools.

Alya showed her teeth. "We'll see about this! I'll talk to your grandmother. Or O'Brien. Or somebody. I'll come right back, or I'll call you."

"Maybe not. I can't call out. I don't know if anyone can call in."

"I'll tell them that I'm not going without—" She stopped suddenly. "You do want to come with me, darling?"

How could she doubt? He was vertical and decently clad by then, so he clasped her tightly to him. "Of course I do. I'll follow you anywhere. Pick a world, any world."

It took some time to say goodbye after that. He insisted that she go to Tiber without him if necessary and let him find his own way there. She was determined not to go without him. They almost ended up back in bed again, to settle the argument properly, but obviously they had to discover whether Alya was a prisoner also. Apparently not—Cedric watched from a safe distance as the spiralator bore her swiftly down and out of sight. She had not been supposed to find him; she might not be allowed near him again. They had both known that. He sighed and wandered around the little hallway to the food machine. He punched for orange juice. He was chewing a breakfast of nut bars when he heard the com bell in his room and went in to see.

In the holo, Bagshaw Barney was stripping off his uniform. His face had a shocked, sleepless look to it.

"Just checking on you, Sprout. Need anything?"

"Liberty. Explanations. I'd like to be treated with a little consideration for my feelings once in a while."

"So would we all, son. So would we all."

"How long am I going to be here?"

Bagshaw's face was smudged and haggard, but it bore no sign of needing to be shaved. He stepped out of his pants and from somewhere produced a suit of vast purple pyjamas. "Lad, I don't know. But I think just till tonight. I know it's rough. I don't like it, but I gotta obey orders."

"Do you really? That makes you feel all right?"

"Aw . . ." The big man gave him a look of pure exasperation. He started to speak, and it became a cavernous yawn. "Look, I'm bushed. I'm just going to bed. I've hardly slept in a week. You think I'd do this if I didn't feel it was important? There's a lot more folks than you involved in this—half of the world, seems like. I think you'll be out tonight, for better or for worse, but I'm not certain. And you're happier there than on Nile."

"For sure," Cedric said. "I expect it's quick."

Bagshaw took another look at him. "What is?"

"'Better or worse,' you said. The worse part would be handing me over to Hastings Willoughby, wouldn't it? Or is that the better part?"

The bull sighed heavily. "Sprout, what in hell are you getting at?"

"You know! He said he hadn't known he had a grandson, because he never did. I'm his clone. He lost most of his own legs years ago, and now the replacements are ready. Custom-made legs."

"Aww . . ." Bagshaw shook his massive head as if to clear cobwebs and dead leaves out of it. "Sprout—no! I don't get involved in shit like that. In fact—well, believe me. You are *not* Hastings's clone."

"System said I was."

A faint mockery crossed Bagshaw's face. "I don't think so. Ask it to explain your ears. Now I'm going to bed. Good night!"

The screen went blank before Cedric could inquire whether Alya had been thrown in jail also.

Angrily he called up System and again demanded a comparison of his DNA and Hastings's. He got the same answer as before—identical to three decimal places. Obviously no two things could ever be exactly the same. The lab guys might have added a few improvements, even. His greater height could be just an effect of childhood nutrition, and even Hastings's flappy ears might be a birth defect or something. Cedric was still a clone, a nobody.

He went back out to the hallway and began to run. The space was too small to be a decent track and he became dizzy, even though he reversed direction often, but he needed the release and ran until his sweat glands were pumping and his heart thumping and the hallway spun circles around him. He stopped and flopped down on the floor just before he passed out from giddiness.

He had spent all the previous afternoon in this prison, and if they were going to render him down for parts, he wished they would get on with it. Apparently even incoming calls were blocked, for Alya did not call, and she did not return. He could not contact anyone or influence the spiralator, but he could play with the holo, for System still responded to him. Apparently his Class One priority remained intact for everything except making calls. He had a choice of every holodrama ever made, uncut. Three days earlier he would have jumped at the chance to see some of the things that had been censored at Meadowdale. Now he wanted none of them.

He reviewed all the Class Two worlds presently accessible, as far as he could understand the technical data—which was not very far. When he had thoroughly confused himself, he asked System for its opinions and discovered that Alya's intuition seemed to be right on track so far. Orinoco contained carcinogens as yet unidentified, and Quinto's life forms were based on exotic polymers whose building blocks were not the usual amino acids. Those were little understood, but known to be deadly. Rhine's stereo chemistry was inverted. Usk was still an unknown. Tiber would be much better understood by next morning, after the overnighters' reports came in, but further analysis of the early robbie data had found nothing suspicious. Po had been struck off the list; it was waning, its windows already very short. That left only Saskatchewan, the world that had almost killed Alya. She might reasonably hold a grudge against it, although every planet contained local dangers, but apparently even System did not care much for Saskatchewan. Its isotope ratios were unusual—unique, in fact, and the background radiation count was high. That might be another local phenomenon, or something to do with the isotopes. The unexplained was always suspect.

So Tiber was still the most likely. He located satellite images that had been taken by one of the rockets and radioed back just before the window closed. Brown and blue and white cloud—Tiber had the colors of Earth but not its shapes, and Cedric spent an hour or so naming its continents and oceans and ranges.

Abandoning science, he switched to criminology. He discovered that the records of the Nile disaster had not been locked away as Fish had told him—they were merely confidential to Grade One. So Cedric viewed them, both the scenes that Eccles Pandora had shown and also others that she had not received. He even skimmed over the murders of Chollak and van Schoening, and thereby almost made himself throw up. He saw the crazed Gill Adele reeling out into the deadly, unbreathable inferno of Nile, wearing a suit but no helmet. Then he knew that he had unwittingly lied to Eccles Pandora.

Gill Adele had not ransacked the skiv before leaving. She had not gone looking for the booby trap. She had not been carrying anything with her when she left.

Fish had given Cedric a lie; Cedric had given it to the world —and so he had deceived and snared the real murderer.

Cedric replayed scenes of the skiv's recovery. He watched Devlin screaming and ranting in the dome. He watched a party of rangers led by Devlin force a way in, and Devlin himself discover the bodies. And somehow Cedric was not very surprised then to see Devlin shouting orders to his companions that would keep them distracted while he himself rushed into one of the bedrooms. What he did in there had not been recorded, but with the benefit of what he now knew, Cedric could guess. Obviously Devlin had not found what he sought. Someone else must have found it later.

Cedric could not imagine why a man might murder his own subordinates, but he had figured out why Devlin Grant had been left behind on Nile.

* * *

At 1516 hours the window to Usk was opened. Cedric scanned the operations and the data coming in from the robbies. It was all over very soon—Usk had two suns, a fact that had escaped notice on the first brief contact. Close binaries rarely had planets, especially Class Twos, but apparently the Institute had long ago experimented with the weirdly variable lighting that must result, and concluded that neither people nor their domesticated plants and animals were likely to thrive. Binaries were out; strike Usk.

But he had been able to monitor the conversation in the control room, and he had heard Alya's voice. He felt better just knowing that she was all right.

He lay down on the bed after lunch and, much to his surprise, went to sleep. He awoke feeling musty and foul and bad tempered. He said, "What? Er, *repeat*."

System spoke again. "Message for Deputy Director Hubbard Cedric from—"

"*Accept*."

It was his grandmother, stiff-backed and cold-eyed as always. His viewpoint was at the far side of her great table, so that there was an expanse of polished wood between them. Somehow that seemed like a defense, as though she wanted to keep him at more than arm's length. Stupid! He was not awake yet, not thinking straight.

"Good afternoon, Cedric."

"Is it?" He sat up and put his feet on the floor.

She gave him the same sort of look Bagshaw had, full of weary exasperation. "Oh, don't start behaving like a fool. I'm fighting several life-and-death battles just now. I have no time for childish tantrums."

"You tested me once to see if I was a ninny. I'm not, but you treat me like a rat in a lab cage. This is not a childish tantrum."

"Yes, it is." She paused to rub her eyes with finger and thumb, and he noticed that she looked almost as weary as Bagshaw had. He had not seen her show human frailty before. Cedric took the chance to yawn and stretch and work a bad-tasting mouth. Sleeping in daytime always made him feel as though he had been thumped with a rail.

Hubbard Agnes blinked a few times, as if adjusting her vision. "What do you want?"

"What do I—Tiber, with Alya."

His grandmother studied him for a moment, and a wisp of a

smile congealed on one corner of her mouth. "Who seduced whom? Who is the fast worker?"

"That is none of your business."

She raised faint white brows in mockery. "My! We're growing brusque. Very well. I have invested almost half a million hectos in you, over the last twenty years. Do you feel that I have been adequately repaid in the last three days?"

How could anyone ever answer that sort of question?

"What's left on the bill?" he demanded.

She nodded appreciatively. "Businesslike! I approve. Just this: I need one more service from you, tonight. Then you're free, at least insofar as I'm concerned."

"Who else might be concerned?" he asked, knowing that he would not have talked that way or thought that way three days before.

"Ah, you misunderstood me." She looked him over as if he were an unusually dull catalog. "I mean I shall not stand in your way if you wish to go with the princess."

"What's the service?" he asked. "Another murder?" She had evaded the question.

"That is exactly the sort of juvenile smart-aleck remark I do not need!" She paused then, as though waiting for an apology.

"Tell me the service," he said. What service could be worth half a million hectos?

"To accompany me to a meeting. To look intelligent and say as little as possible. Can you manage that?"

"That's all?" It was far too good to be true. She was going to throw him into another lions' den; maybe a snake pit.

"That is all. I need a witness. No reporters, just a private meeting with two men. Private, and secret."

"Obviously."

She frowned. "Why obviously, pray?"

"Because I'm an unperson, aren't I?"

"Ah, yes! Is that some of your hot little princess's thinking? It sounds too shrewd for you."

He thought about it, sitting on the edge of the bed, wriggling his toes and feeling hollow-headed and bad-tasteish. It did not make sense.

"I'm an unperson. You must send me away with Alya, or kill me, or keep me locked up forever—or else bring back Devlin and Eccles. I'm a witness to their murder. What use can I be as witness to anything else?"

She covered a yawn. "You're as damnably pigheaded as your

father was. No, a witness is not what I need. I don't have time. But I'll have to make time, won't I? All right—I'll run through it quickly. Important people almost never meet in person. It's too dangerous. But this meeting is so vital, so confidential, that these two men are coming here, to Cainsville, in the flesh. They don't trust me; I don't trust them. I am old and getting frail. They are both much younger, and male. I want a bodyguard."

He was about to snort out some skeptical reply when second thoughts prevailed. It was so absurd that it might even be true. She could certainly have invented something more plausible. He spoke softly then. "Why me? Bagshaw weighs twice what I do. He must know a million combat tricks I don't."

She nodded, but her eyes were annoyed that he had not worked it out properly. "And therefore *they* would not trust *him*! The sides must be about evenly matched. You underestimate yourself. I've seen the reports on you, and you're much stronger than you look. I'm sure you could handle two middle-aged amateurs, long enough for help to arrive. Besides, our talk must remain secret."

Why not Dr. Fish? "You've been setting me up as the court jester, haven't you?"

His grandmother threw her head back in a flicker of earrings and laughed aloud. He could not recall ever seeing her do that. "Court jester? That's very good! I admit it. You have a curious innocence about you, Cedric. Even I keep underestimating you. So they will underestimate you also."

"Like Pandora?" he demanded angrily. "Why her? Just because she did a special and called you names—"

The director's eyes dropped to stare at his chest, but he could guess that she was merely reading messages he could not see. "If you only knew how many people you're keeping waiting," she said. "You don't mention Devlin? So you've uncovered that part of it." She sighed impatiently. "It's Eccles that bothers you?"

"Both of them."

"Guilt is something you get used to. All right, I'll explain quickly. I'm not in the habit of justifying my actions, Cedric."

It would be good for her to learn, but he did not say so.

She leaned her elbows on the table. "First, as you know, she had herself cloned. She had the clone reared and then harvested. I see that as a particularly despicable, premeditated, cold-blooded murder."

He wanted to say, You're not the law. But maybe she was justice. Bagshaw had told him how the law had long before been strangled to death by lawyers. He just sat, meeting the old woman's sinister gaze.

"Secondly, no, I don't slaughter reporters who file unfavorable stories about me or my Institute. I've been tempted often enough."

Nor did Cedric treat that remark as being funny.

"But people can be superstitious; it gets noticed that badmouthing the Institute is unlucky. She was not the first, I admit. There is suspicion in the air. I know this, but it wasn't really a reason. That would make me worse than she was, and I assure you that my conscience is very clear."

Still he did not comment. If personal grudge had not been a factor, then why deny it at such length? His lack of response was starting to annoy her.

"Secondly, therefore . . ." His grandmother sighed. "I'm crazy to waste time on you like this. Secondly, Pandora's death was the price demanded by Frazer Franklin for his continued cooperation."

"What!?"

She shook her head sadly, and sapphire earrings glittered. "Oh, Cedric, Cedric! The world is a much more complicated place than it must seem from Meadowdale. Now you know our big secret—that we've been finding Class One worlds, that we've been planting people on them. If Tiber goes ahead, it will be the thirteenth. So far we've transmensed nearly three hundred thousand. It's not very many, really, when you think of the hundreds of millions in refugee camps, or when you think of the floods and plagues, but it's been a superhuman effort, Cedric. My life's work. And it's given humanity a lot more chances to survive." She sat back and folded her arms and waited.

So he threw the questions she expected. "Why you? Why keep it secret? Who are you to play God?"

She nodded approvingly. "You do understand how we've done this? We vet every candidate world as thoroughly as we can. We never plant a world unless it has passed every scientific test we can think of. Since the Oak affair, I've also required that one of the Banzaraki psychics approve it. We don't know how their intuition works, but it's never clashed with our final conclusions. And we don't sell tickets to the rich, Cedric."

For a moment he thought he detected an appeal in those cunning old eyes, an appeal for his approval. Absurd! He told himself not to be taken in by tricks.

"Our colonists are always drawn from the camps, the hopeless," she said. "We send along everything we can think of that they may need to become established. I must seem an evil old woman to you, but I have nothing to be ashamed of in this."

"But why you—you of all the world? Who are you to choose who lives and who dies?"

She had begun to tap fingers on the table. "Are you truly so naive? Can't you imagine what would happen if the politicians got their hands on this? Are you so very innocent? The refugees would be marching though the transmensor fifty abreast, as fast as they could be shipped in here."

Yes, he could imagine. "To where?"

"God knows. Class Two worlds are common as mosquitoes. And refugees more so—they're a blight. Every authority on Earth is perpetually beset by refugees. The chance to ship them all off elsewhere with no complications later . . . that would be an irresistible temptation. It would throw us back a hundred years, to the death camps of the Nazis, but worse—not millions, but tens or hundreds of millions, and a slow death."

Her voice had grown sharper, harder. Cedric had never known his grandmother to speak with such vehemence. She must believe very strongly in what she was saying, mustn't she?

"And the real gems, the ones we call Class One—those would be reserved for the elite, and very likely for their clones. They would spread their own germ plasm throughout the universe on all the best worlds. They would use the others for dumping peasants. I know this! I know how they think! The Earth is very sick, but it's still habitable. Just. It may remain so. The Banzarak intuition says it's still a better bet than almost all the other worlds we find. Only twelve in thirty years—"

"Including Oak?"

She winced. "Not Oak. Eleven worlds, then. Even with the very best of intentions, at least one of our plantings was an error."

For a moment there was silence. Cedric felt far too young and simple to argue with her. He stared morosely at his hands, clasped on his knees. He had been unconsciously picking at a callus with a thumbnail. He was glumly sure that he was about to be suckered again.

"That's why Frazer Franklin," his grandmother said. "The plantings themselves have been easy compared to the problems of keeping them secret. We have many sympathizers, in key places."

"Spies? No, agents. You pay them with murders?" He did not look at her, just his finger.

"With many things. Money. Some, like Frazer, want favors. Some just approve of what we are doing. Many accept immortality."

Then he did raise his head, and she smiled mockingly at his incomprehension. "The instinct to procreate runs very deep—as you should realize, *Grandson*—and I can offer them a chance to propagate throughout a universe. It's often the most potent bribe of all. And it's good for us—we gain valuable breeding stock for our plantings."

"Cloning?"

"Sometimes. Nothing wrong with cloning if the clones are treated as people."

"So you do sell tickets to the rich?"

"In that sense, I suppose I do. When I must. Or murder when I must. Or blackmail, or deceive, or threaten. But I have populated worlds that will bless my name for thousands of years."

She was convincing, and he supposed he owed her his loyalty, even yet.

"If I refuse?"

"Don't. Don't ask the alternative, either."

He shrugged. "All right. What do I have to do?"

Satisfaction thinned the pale lips. "Make yourself respectable. It will not be until late; midnight or after."

"And then?"

"Just stay close to me. Be yourself, but don't speak unless I ask you a question."

"And then I can go with Alya?"

The smile grew wider. "Are you certain she wants you? You may have been only a passing amusement. But if you choose to go to Tiber, I won't stand in your way. *Com end.*"

Not stand in your way . . . Again she had slid around that point. But she had gone. He thought she had shown him one glimpse of a tree and hidden a forest.

He sat and picked at the edge of the callus until he made his finger bleed. He counted his troubles, and the list was crushing. His strengths were only two: that Alya loved him, and that System still obeyed his commands with very few limits.

"*I want to set up some codes.*"

"Stipulate whether codes are for general use or voice specific."

"*Voice specific.*"

"Proceed."

"If the instructions represented by those codes require an override command, you will assume the override command, but not make it effective until I activate the code. Is this understood?"

"Affirmative."

"First code word: 'Palomino' . . ."

20

ALYA, ALSO, HAD been placed under house arrest. The Institute had taken considerable pains to sever all public connection between itself and the princess, and was not going to let her be seen around Cainsville now. Like Cedric, she was confined to one floor of Columbus Dome. The impassive, impassable North Brenda guarded the spiralator, letting no one in or out. System refused to place calls.

A day of playing cribbage with Moala was relieved only when Alya was taken by O'Brien Patrick to view Usk—and that was the briefest planetary inspection yet. Binary suns cut Usk from the list and sent Alya back to jail.

She swore a lot, especially when she realized that Jathro must be wandering loose, not confined as she was. None of her brothers or sisters had been insulted in such a way by Director Hubbard, but then none of them had seduced Hubbard's grandson, either.

And she worried intensely about Cedric. His unexpected fit in the night had terrified her. He was supposed to be the indestructible man, yet something had driven him completely catatonic for a couple of minutes—going cold, heartbeat dropping and fading. Then he had shuddered and sprung back in typical Cedric style. But something had done that to him. Almost certainly Alya had unwittingly said something to trigger a post-hypnotic code implanted very deep inside his mind. She could not have spoken the whole code, obviously, just enough of it to bring a partial memory up near the surface—and that partial memory had hurled him into psychic fugue and catalepsy. It was a tribute to his incredible toughness that he had recovered so easily.

Who had managed to tamper with his head? BEST? Or—Alya kept remembering Hubbard's sneer that Cedric was only a pawn, and a pawn that might have to be sacrificed.

If what had sent him into that fit had been something Alya had said, then the only word that could possibly have done it was *kamikaze*.

She fretted more when she remembered her promise to call Kas and Thalia and the kids that evening. The time came and went with System still uncooperative. Kas would have certainly tried to call her, and had obviously been blocked. Frustrated, Alya decided that she might as well go to bed. Tiber was not due for hours yet, and the previous night had been strenuous in the extreme—Cedric had wonderful stamina, bless him. *Oh, Cedric!*

Much to her surprise, she felt herself sliding into sleep almost at once.

The disadvantage of that, of course, was that she felt so unholy awful when she was wakened by a *ping!* from the com, and Baker Abel's voice.

"We expect Tiber in half an hour, ma'am. Transportation is standing by."

"I want—" Alya said.

"Caller has disconnected," System said.

Escorted by a squad of unfamiliar bulls, Alya was golfied over to Philby Dome and delivered to a big, pentagonal office. It was an exact replica of Hubbard's office in Nauc HQ, or perhaps slightly larger. The big table was heaped with papers; a dozen men and women were slouched around on chairs, all looking totally exhausted. There was no sign of Hubbard Agnes. The two giant com screens were unrolling screeds of multicolored data: text and three-dee graphs, maps, and images. Nobody seemed to be paying any attention.

Alya sped around the room like a ballistic missile aimed at Baker Abel, who was leaning against a wall, rubbing his eyes. His denims were rumpled, his tawny hair mussed and limp.

"Where is Cedric?" she demanded.

Baker peered at her blearily. "I don't know. System won't tell me. I don't know where his grandmother is, either. Or anyone." He started to say something else and it became a yawn.

Suddenly Alya felt sympathetic. Baker was hard to dislike.

"You haven't been to bed recently, have you?"

He shook his head. "Thanks for the invitation, but you'll have to clear it with Emily. I'm supposed to be pairing with her, and it's getting so I can barely remember why." Then he grinned.

"Like hell you can't," Alya said, returning the grin. She glanced around and was annoyed that Jathro was missing. Where and what was he doing, and why? "What's happening about Tiber, Abe?"

Baker shrugged and heaved himself off the wall. "About ten minutes until window. Another ten to run all the data into System. Most of it'll be precooked already, so five for analyses. Then decision time."

An unpleasant quiver ran through Alya. "Who makes that decision?"

He blinked bloodshot eyes at her. "You do. Unless there's something obviously wrong, of course. Them's my orders—go or no go comes from Princess Alya."

"And I lead the parade?"

"Waving your baton."

Her palms were clammy. "And if I want more time to consider?"

He frowned and shook his head. "No instructions. My guess would be that Mother shuts the file. If you're not certain, right away, then it'll be no go."

"I won't leave without Cedric!"

Baker shrugged again. "I can do nothing about that. I'm telling the truth. I—you okay?"

She nodded, angry that a princess could be so transparent. "I think I need to freshen up."

He pointed in silence at the wall beside them, and she saw the almost-invisible door in it.

The washroom was garishly bright and decorated in holographic tiles, a style briefly popular long before Alya had been born. Some of them had fallen off and not been replaced. Mother Hubbard had been economizing behind the scenes, obviously.

Alya washed her face and combed out her hair, and began to feel better. A couple of cups of coffee and perhaps some of the curly-dry sandwiches she had seen out there, and she—

The comb slipped from her fingers. She felt herself bowled

over by a great cold wave of terror, and all the holo tiles seemed
to gape and wink like fanged mouths as the walls rushed at her.
She stuffed a knuckle between her teeth and fought for control.

Danger! it was saying. *Go now! Escape!*

And the *Escape!* seemed to echo, over and over.

She backed up against the wall, sweat streaming down her
face. Never had she felt a *satori* so strong. It was crushing, overpowering. She could no more think straight than if she had seen a
bull charging straight at her, or a man coming with a knife—it
was as irresistible as that. A screaming sense of danger choked
her mind, making her heart race and her hands shake.

What had happened? Cedric? Was something threatening Cedric?

Or Tiber? If the window was open, then the choice was
clearly available to her at last. That was it! All she had to do was
walk out of there and say "Yes!" and she would be whisked away
to a safer world. Relief! Cedric might be important, but obviously he ranked a distant second as far as the *buddhi* was concerned.

Alya forced herself to pick up the comb. She struggled to
compose her face before the mirror—she thought she resembled
a terrified coconut—and then she squared her shoulders and tot-
tered back into the big, pentagonal office.

She sensed the satisfaction at once. The people had all collected before the two big coms. One was still rippling data, much
faster now. The other showed three men in a very cramped interior. They wore denims, and the close cram of instrument boards
and controls around them identified the locale as a skiv lab module. The men were laughing and all trying to talk at the same
time. Sunlight was streaming through a window behind them.

One of the women in the office said something that provoked
more merriment. Baker Abel slipped out of the group and came
around to Alya. He was grinning broadly and had lost most of his
tired look.

"Hundred percent on science!" he said. "System needs a few
moments yet, but the team commander says it's a big improvement on Earth itself! You ready to lead that parade now?"

It was the hardest thing she had ever done in her life.

"No!" Alya said. Every nerve screamed.

Baker's jaw dropped, and for a moment he reminded her again
of Cedric. "No?"

"I need Cedric to help me decide."

Baker frowned, studying her, then gestured to a couple of

chairs. Alya perched on one, and he pulled the other between his legs, so that he sat on it backward, arms folded, his usual flippancy gone.

"I swear," he said quietly, "that I don't know! She's gone off on some mysterious project of her own, and Cedric's probably with her. I know he was locked up on the top floor of Columbus. He's not there now, 'cause I looked."

"Keep looking. He hasn't left Cainsville?"

"How should I know? System won't talk. I can't even get through to the deputies now. Something odd's going on."

Alya leaned back. "Then we'll have to wait, won't we?" She hoped her trembling was not too obvious.

"Alya, please! Believe me—I'm on his side! Truly, I want to help Cedric. I'm delighted that the two of you are pairing. He's a great kid! But I can't find him for you right now."

"Then I shall go and look for him myself."

He shrugged, baffled. "Swell! Meanwhile I've got two thousand refugees and three thousand tons of supplies and trucks and more teams of rangers. Three hours, ten minutes left on the window, maybe. What do I tell everyone? What do I do with them, Alya?"

Rising, she smiled her meanest smile. "Set them to work looking for Cedric!"

"Hold it!" He seemed to be thinking very hard, chewing his lip and staring at her with calculating gray eyes. If he made a wrong decision, Baker Abel was going to be in very deep trouble. "You can find him?"

"I can try." Actually, Alya was not sure she could even find her left ear—the sense of imminent danger was beating on her like a steam hammer.

"You want help? Bulls? No—you don't need bulls, do you?"

She shook her head. Baker was obviously looking for a solution and willing to risk his neck for her.

"If I call 'em off for—an hour?"

Alya nodded with sudden relief at having a workable compromise.

"You'll come back and tell me in an hour?" he asked. "Promise?"

"Yes! Thanks, Abe. I—thanks!" She marched to the door, and he let her go. Bulls sitting in the corridor started to climb to their feet and then settled back, exchanging puzzled glances.

Alya headed for the spiralator. At ground level she climbed

into a golfie. She closed her eyes for a minute to think—or feel, maybe.

"*That way! I mean—what way is this golfie facing?*"

"The personnel cart is pointed west."

"*Then make it go north.*"

After that it was all either *right, left,* or *straight ahead.*

21

LONG AFTER MIDNIGHT Cedric was summoned by an anonymous voice on the com. He headed for the spiralator with his mind churning an immiscible mixture of relief and apprehension. There was no more nonsense of flashing lights. He was borne swiftly and silently down to ground level.

He was at once surrounded by an armed escort. They were all large-economy gorillas; even the women among them looked tough enough to snap him with one hand. Nor were they an honor guard—they gave him a thorough body search. He could almost find that amusing—him, dangerous? He knew none of the faces, but he saw some of those faces register shock when they recognized his, for he was a celebrity. He had died tragically on world holo the previous day, lost on a nightmare planet of a distant star. His presence back on Earth was a physical impossibility.

The mixture of uniforms told him who was going to be at the meeting. Four bulls wore Institute red, four grass green, and four shiny gold. The greens bore shoulder-patch logos of a stylized, five-line house containing a globe, and that was the symbol of the World Chamber. The golds' shoulders said simply *BEST*.

He was more surprised to see that the visitors were armed. That was a major breach of standard practice. That explained why the four Institute bulls were glowering so resentfully, why hands hovered so obviously near holsters. Eight Daniels and four lions—and all of them so tense that they almost crackled.

He had expected to be led to a meeting room, but nothing like that happened at all. He was crushed into a two-man golfie, with a gold bull on one side and a green on the other. He tried making conversation, and neither would speak a word.

Soon he was in unfamiliar territory. The streets and corridors were deserted. He would have expected to see at least a few people around, even at that hour. He wondered if Cainsville could be under martial law.

Other golfies raced ahead and behind and, when the road was wide enough, kept pace on either side. He found such celebrity treatment ridiculous, and in a brighter moment would likely have found it amusing. Of course, he was not being guarded for his own sake, but rather to protect others, as if one moment's lapse in vigilance might let someone turn him into a walking bomb.

Ridiculous or not, the possibility was being taken seriously. His destination turned out to be a medical facility like the one when he was first admitted to HQ, back in Nauc. He groaned loudly and said, "Not again?" No one registered that he had spoken. The reception room held at least twenty people in lab coats, but even they were color-coded, with green and gold outnumbering red. They all turned to look at him and waited expectantly. Resignedly, Cedric began to unzip.

If possible, the ensuing examination was even more thorough than his ordeal of four days earlier. The visitors took at least an hour to satisfy themselves that there was nothing inside Hubbard Cedric's skin except Hubbard Cedric and one earpatch. They struck a piece of shiny metallic tape over that to inactivate it. When at last they could find nothing more to scan, poke, or measure, they reluctantly allowed him to dress himself again. His clothes had a rumpled look, and he could guess that they had been inspected also. When he asked for a comb, his request was brusquely debated and then refused. Not only did the greens and golds distrust the reds, they obviously distrusted each other also. Who could say what infernal machine might be hidden inside an innocent-seeming comb?

After that nasty tribulation, he was taken to a waiting room and told to sit. He sat on a hard bench and leaned against a hard wall while another half hour dragged by in sickening small-hours lethargy. His questions were ignored. His only diversion was dabbing tissue at his wretched nose, which had started dribbling blood again. The medics had done that while exploring his sinuses.

He had known that there was another victim being examined at the same time as himself, for he had heard voices from cubicles he had recently vacated, but he had not been sure who it was. Finally the door opened, and he saw Gran standing outside. She was thin-lipped and flushed, much less spruce and poised than usual. Sauce for gander is sauce for goose now? Cedric began to grin, shaping a wittily catty remark, but the look she gave him caused it to die of an attack of discretion.

Again he was crushed into an overloaded golfie as an enlarged procession took off on an even longer journey. Again the road was unfamiliar to him, and deserted. The hour was late, the lighting dim. The prospect of meeting two of the world's most powerful men held no attraction. He was sleepy and hungry.

He mooned gloomily over Alya. The window to Tiber might be open at that very moment. She might already have departed, never to return. He remembered the look in her eye when she spoke of her new world. He hoped it had checked out well. He hoped she had not been so stupid as to wait around for him. He did not think he was going to see that new world again.

Then he felt cold air on his face. The corridors had taken on a functional, echoing, rivets-and-hard-shadows look, and the temperature had dropped. The train of golfies trundled through a high metal doorway and Cedric snapped alert, astounded at what lay before him. The great dome was huge, larger even than de Soto or David Thompson, but it could not be a transmensor facility, for the floor was flat. In icy air, under a hard actinic glare, stood three great winged monsters. The smallest was a Boeing 7777, and the other two were supers, a Hyundai Six and a Euro Starscraper. All loomed enormous. He felt like a mite on the bottom of a bird cage, but it was not their size that astonished him as much as their mere presence. He had always understood that there was no airport at Cainsville.

With wheels drumming on rows of rivets, the golfies raced across the steel prairie of the floor toward the Boeing, which bore the house-and-globe logo of the World Chamber on its green tail. By the time Cedric was delivered to the steps, his grandmother was already halfway up. He thought despairingly of Alya and wondered where he was going to be taken.

The answer, apparently, was "nowhere." The plane was outfitted like a home, or even a palace. He followed his grandmother through to a very luxurious lounge and there folded himself into a thick-pillowed armchair. Red, gold, and green guards all remained standing, all watching one another as much as the prisoners.

Prisoners?

"Gran? What the hell is going on?"

His grandmother pursed her lips, as if he were speaking out of turn. Then she said, "Look!" and pointed at a window.

Cedric swung around and peered. He was just in time to see the great exterior doors slide open. Snow and even darkness itself seemed to pour into the hangar and swirl around the floor—or at least the snow did. He watched the guards stagger as the wind struck at them. He moved to a closer chair and, in his eagerness, jostled his tender and swollen nose against the plastic. In a moment another giant Boeing emerged from the night, advancing under its own power. It was painted gold and bore BEST's logo. The doors slid shut. A rumble of titanic motors died away. Even with four such monsters present, the dome was still not full.

Steps were wheeled forward; guards took up position. Cedric saw two men descend, saw them board golfies, saw those carts head off in procession through the interior door. One of the two men had been squeezed between a red guard and a green, the other between a red and gold.

Cedric sat back to study his grandmother's coldly angry face across the room. "We're hostages?"

She nodded.

"That's crazy!" he said.

"Of course it is." She smiled grimly. "Bulls are worse than lawyers."

That remark had been aimed at the guards, obviously, but Cedric asked, "How?"

She sighed. "Everyone does it. Accountants did it to bookkeeping, lawyers did it to the law, teachers to education."

"Did what?"

"Tangled it all up so it became meaningless," she said sourly. "It's the search for indispensability—and ninety percent of them are busy playing job politics most of the time, anyway. When I was younger—" She stopped, with a brief glare at the nearest guard. "We have two guests here tonight, but if I wanted to kill one of them during his visit, I could do so easily, in spite of all this tomfoolery."

And that remark, although directed at Cedric, had been most certainly intended for the guards. Even her own reds scowled.

"How?" asked the one she had looked at, a bull-necked gold.

The director smiled frostily. "Watch closely and maybe I'll show you."

That ended the conversation.

22

Cainsville, April 11

"RIGHT! NO! STOP! I think . . . Yes, *right!"*

Alya's head was splitting, ready to fall apart. She seemed to
have been wheeling and spinning around Cainsville for hours.
Time had lost all meaning. Corridors and echoing tunnels and
open plazas had come and gone by the thousand, and she had not
the faintest clue where she was. She had no idea how much
remained of the hour Baker had promised her. Any minute now
he might call her in, and she was certain that he could override
her commands to the golfie. Urgency ate at her like acid. She
teetered on the brink of panic.

Finding Cedric was turning out to be impossible. She was
running two *satori* at the same time—that was the problem. She
had never heard of that happening to anyone in her family before,
not even in any of the strange old tales.

Tiber's was the stronger, by far. Time and time again she
arrived at de Soto Dome, where the window was waiting for her.
The surprised guards had moved to challenge her the first time,
but she had merely referred them to Baker Abel. They had
checked in, then shrugged and let her go. By her fifth or sixth
visit they were openly laughing at her.

Eventually she had learned to stop at every branching, every
choice, and ask System which way led to de Soto. Then she tried

259

to compensate for that in her hunches. but sometimes the right path—if there was a right path—had to be in that direction.

There might not even be a second *satori*. She might be fooling herself. She might have gone crazy, like all those terrified schizophrenic ancestors.

Then the golfie emerged from a narrow passage into a much larger one. Cold and metallic and sinister in the dim night lighting, it stretched off endlessly in both directions. It had rails on the floor, which she had not seen before.

"Does either of these lead to de Soto Dome?"

"Negative."

She cringed, puzzling. Left? Or right?

She was going mad.

She did not know.

"Left," she whispered. System ignored that tone. *"Left!"*

The golfie swung left and hummed along the big tunnel. The walls and floor were bare metal, rushing past. Lights streamed toward her and vanished behind. Her shadow leaped and leaped, hiding from the lights.

Then the little cart slowed and came to a stop before a large, implacable, circular steel door. Corridor and rails ended also.

"What's this? I mean, *What's inside this door?"*

"Bering Dome," the golfie said.

"Am I allowed inside?"

"Affirmative."

There was no decon, so Bering was not one of the transmensor domes. She sat and stared at the forbidding door for a minute or two, wrestling with indecision and self-doubt and that overpowering hunch that she must hurry back to de Soto and the safety of Tiber.

There was no comset on the wall. The round door was not of standard type and did not quite reach the floor—there would be a sill several centimeters high. *"What is this door used for?"*

"Data confidential."

But she had no choice, except to retrace her path. She dismounted and felt her knees shake with fatigue.

"Open the door!" she told the golfie, and walked forward as the great circle swung inward. She stepped over the lip, noting how very thick the wall was. She strode a few paces down a sloping floor before she realized that despite the lack of decon facilities, the place looked very much like a transmensor dome. Perhaps it was an old one, now used for something else? The inside was even dimmer than the corridor, with lights twinkling

near the center, filled with a quiet murmur, as of many people. She caught a curious odor of—of curry?

The door thumped closed behind her, and she wheeled around in alarm. Damn! Now she'd done it! There was no comset on the inside, either, and she had no wrist mike.

She began to separate out the threads of noise: muttering voices and babies crying. Her eyes were adjusting, too, seeing a huddled little settlement down where the floor was flat. The central object plate was blank, but the railing around it seemed to be hung with laundry. Ramshackle fences of canvas zigzagged around, providing some minimum privacy. She could hear a guitar strumming, and a distant group seemed to be chanting prayers. The baby noises were the worst, though—crying babies could drive anyone mad. Kiosks on the far side were obviously portable toilets.

Sadly, Alya started down the long slope. She had stumbled on the secret refugee entrance to Cainsville, and here were Baker's two thousand. Bering Dome was a refugee camp. And when she gave him the go-ahead, all Baker would have to do was to close the window in de Soto Dome and open the same string here. She had failed! This was another door to Tiber, and the Tiber *satori* had won out over whatever she had felt for Cedric—which might have been all self-delusion, she supposed.

The scents and sounds were becoming clearer—and more familiar. Hubbard had played fair so far, for she could hear distinctive Banzaraki voices, her own people. That explained so much activity in the middle of the night—they were in the wrong time zone. Any minute now she would be recognized, and quite likely Jathro was somewhere in the mob, demagoguing, building loyalties.

The clamor of babies was as nerve-scratching as a nettle rash. And older children—from the noise, there were an awful lot of children. And the guitar . . . someone singing.

She knew that voice! With a cry of joy, Alya began to run, seeking that guitar.

She raced along pathways lined on both sides with bedrolls, sleeping people, people sitting cross-legged, people talking, people weeping, people looking up in astonishment, people calling out. She zigged and zagged, ever drawing closer. She ran around the central object plate with its fence of drying diapers. She could *smell* babies now! She began to notice paler faces. Not all Banzarakis, then.

And there he was!

He was standing with his back to her, but his height was unmistakable. Strumming inexpertly on a guitar, he was singing to a semicircle of seated children.

"Cedric!" She rushed up and grabbed him. She hauled him around, ending the song in a discordant jangle as she threw her arms around his skinny neck and kissed him. The children yelled delight.

Appalled, she backed off and stared.

It was Cedric! And Cedric's blush. But not quite tall enough? His hair was too long. His nose was uninjured. He was maybe a couple of years younger, and he was aghast at this aggressive female who had just kissed him.

Her *satori* had not found Cedric after all. It had found a Cedric clone.

23

CEDRIC WAS SHOUTED awake before he was even aware that he had started to nod. The ache in his neck said he had slept a long time. He lurched up, woolly-headed, and lumbered after his grandmother as she headed for the door. Shivering mightily, he stumbled down the steps behind her and stalked at her side across the great bare floor of the hangar. The guards stayed by the plane.

The two men had returned, presumably explored and inspected inside and out just as thoroughly as Cedric and Gran had been. They were advancing toward four chairs that stood in the center of the dome, but they, too, had left their escorts behind, so the meeting would be watched by the three private armies from a respectful distance; it would not be overheard unless there were trick mikes aimed at it. Then Cedric remembered Dr. Fish—of course there would be trick mikes, and probably the visitors' aircraft had some, also. The low-rank muscle round the edges would not hear, though.

"Grundy Julian Wagner, of BEST," his grandmother remarked as they walked. "And Cheung Olsen Paraschuk, speaker of the Chamber."

"Okay. And I say nothing."

"That's right. Your name may not even be Cedric."

Then they had reached the chairs. The men were already

seated. The only greetings were nods of recognition.

Cedric sat with Gran on his left and he recognized Cheung on his right: heavy, sleek black hair, eyes so padded they were hardly visible. His face had been carved from brown butter, and he might be any age from thirty to seventy. Cedric felt none of the thrill he had known four days earlier, when he had first met the Secretary General. Either he was growing blasé about celebrities, or he just was not properly awake yet.

"I understood that the fourth person was to be Hastings Willoughby?" Cheung's voice was extremely low and measured, as profound as an underground river.

"This is my grandson, Hubbard Morris."

"And I understood your grandson's name was Cedric." Grundy, opposite Cedric, sounded high-pitched and unpleasantly nasal. He was hunched and leathery, his hair thin and colorless, and even his hands seemed curiously elongated. He was not tall —not by Cedric's standards—but he seemed spare and fleshless. He smiled ironically, revealing long yellow teeth.

"That was another grandson," Agnes said evenly. "He was lost yesterday on the world we call Nile."

"Identical twins?" Grundy chuckled, showing his teeth again.

"At least. Spontaneous cleavage of the ovum is not uncommon during defrosting. He—they—were a posthumous gestation."

Cedric was cold. He resisted a desire to shiver, wishing he had a coat. He could only admire his grandmother's brazen falsehoods—he could hardly disapprove of them on moral grounds when she so obviously did not expect to deceive anyone. He wished she had chosen a better name for him than Morris.

"How many grandsons do you have, Director?" Cheung asked, in his black, oily voice.

"I have not counted them recently."

"Ah. And of course the birth certificates are on file."

"Of course." She was certainly lying, Cedric thought, but the papers could soon be forged if she ever wanted them.

"And the nose?" Grundy inquired. "Cedric had one just like that. Must we presume that, in a moment of trivial sibling dissension, they reacted with the identical reflexes of their monozygotic inception and simultaneously punched each other on the snoot?"

Neither Cheung nor Gran paid any attention, and for a moment there was thoughtful silence. Of course Grundy and Cheung must know that Cedric was Hastings's clone. He had been

brought along as a threat, perhaps, or as a confusion, to throw
them off balance. They would be wondering how he had escaped
the Nile tragedy and how many more clones might there be. He
himself had never considered that there might be more of him
around somewhere, but of course there could be. That thought
made him feel even more insecure and worthless than before; he
shivered.

"You will speak for Hastings, then, Director?" Grundy inquired.

"I think I do have some influence with him." She seemed
quite impervious to the cold, or the godless hour of night, or the
threat of hundreds of armed men and women waiting menacingly
on the distant sidelines. She was as calm as if she were back in
her office with its big pentagonal table and expensive holo walls.

"Then we can dispose of this lean young man?" That was
Cheung's deep organ tone. He might be a very fine bass singer.

Agnes glanced up at Cedric thoughtfully. "No, he may yet be
useful. Do you recognize this man, Ce—Morris?"

"Dr. Cheung. I've seen him on the news often."

"You haven't seen his face anywhere else?"

"No, Gran, I—*Oh, God!*"

"Well?"

"Gavin!" It was not really true that all Chinese faces looked
alike. Cedric had just never noticed the resemblance.

"Gavin?" his grandmother echoed.

"Wong Gavin—at Meadowdale! His father's president of—"
Nonsense! Chipper, cheeky little Gavin was another clone. The
lump that suddenly filled Cedric's throat was so real that for a
moment he thought he would choke. He forced a deep breath
somehow. How old was Gavin—ten, maybe? So another eight
years or so would see him fully grown—fewer if there were an
emergency need, for a heart, say. "Harvesting" his grandmother
had called it.

Cheung had not changed expression at all. "Let us to our
business," he said deeply. "All those gun-toting apes are making
me nervous. What are you asking, ma'am?"

"Me?" Hubbard seemed astonished. "I am asking nothing.
Your presence here makes you the petitioners. Ask."

"No, you ask," Grundy said. "For mercy."

Again the other two paid him no attention, but Cedric inspected him with growing distaste and a vague feeling that he
ought to know him also. He had recognized Gavin's resemblance
to Cheung because Cheung's face was smoothly round and flat

and almost babyish. Grundy's features were much bonier, and his baldness did not help. His long skull seemed to have grown out through his hair, and his chin was long and pointed. His eyes were baggy, his brow marred by spots.

"China has declared," Cheung said. "Withdrawn its recognition of the U.N. It will hold elections for Chamber representation." He moved a hand in a small gesture that seemed to convey many things. He had thick hands with short, powerful fingers, but they were quite hairless. "We heard the news on the way here. Both Japans have followed. Others will do so as the day progresses."

"My congratulations." Hubbard Agnes sniffed, as though disapproving of the metallic, oily scent of the hangar. "Why should that concern me?"

Cheung studied her impassively for a moment. His massive stillness conveyed to Cedric a sinister sense of power that was missing from Grundy's sneering restlessness.

"Today marks the end of the General Assembly," the deep voice said. "The end of the U.N., and of Hastings."

"And of you," Grundy interjected, with a leer at Gran.

She shrugged. "Maybe. You lack the financial resources of the U.N., of course." She gazed inquiringly at Cheung, and for a moment the two locked eyes. Cedric remembered Jathro explaining how Stellar Power financed the U.N. officially, and Hastings's graft unofficially.

Grundy made another of his shrewish remarks, but Cedric did not hear it. Grundy had clenched his fists. His hands were all bones, wrapped in mottled parchment, and his wrists were thin and hairy. Somehow those fists had the same tantalizing familiarity as his face. Cedric was working his way through every child in Meadowdale. It had to be Meadowdale—his whole life had been Meadowdale. The half memory was like a maddening, unreachable itch. Who?

Still his grandmother seemed unworried. Her curt, precise tone had not changed. "Of course your joy at the China news can hardly be undiluted, Dr. Cheung."

"Why do you think so, ma'am?"

"Because the present China delegates are so-called 'temporaries,' appointed by you. Under your own rules, as I understand them, they are now discredited. Also the Japanese, and all those others you mentioned."

"They will be replaced by officially elected representatives very shortly."

"But that will take time, won't it?" She waited for him to comment, but when he didn't she said, "And meanwhile the old ones cannot vote. By your own rules, I repeat."

"What's she getting at, Ollie?" Grundy barked. His voice grated, rough and uncultured compared to Cheung's.

For the first time the mask shifted, the butter seeming to shift and become less bland—Cheung was favoring Hubbard Agnes with a small frown. "That is so. It is true, then, that Hastings has actually been encouraging some of the fence-sitters to come down on our side?"

A wisp of satisfaction thinned Gran's pale lips. "I did suggest that he should recognize the difficulties certain parties were having in remaining loyal." She considered, then added, "And that he ought not hold them too harshly to a course that may have become untenable for them. The Japans, for example."

"This is surrender!" Grundy crowed.

"Not quite, I think." Cheung was still studying Agnes.

"Why? You mean she's got some trick up her sleeve?" Grundy waved a fist.

That did it—*Dwayne!* Kroeger Dwayne! He had been about three years older than Cedric. Kroeger Dwayne and McClachlanne Greg had liked to take younger boys behind the barn for puberty experiments. They had tried to do some on Cedric himself once.

He shivered, but whether it was memory or the temperature in the vast hangar, he could not be sure. He had hated and feared Kroeger Dwayne, but the guy had not deserved *that* . . .

"Tell us, ma'am," Cheung said.

"You have lost your majority," Gran said simply. "By Friday or so, Huu Ngo will be the new speaker of the Chamber."

Cheung leaned back and gazed up at the high sweep of the dome. "I don't count it that way."

"Try again. We have forty-two from Neururb, over eighty from Nauc. What remains of the Mediterranean is solid for us. You must withdraw voting rights from most of India, China, Japan . . ." The litany droned on. There was no triumph in her voice, only clinical authority and the usual impatience.

The Grundy man was an older version of Kroeger Dwayne. He looked just as mean. He had his long fangs bared again, as he waited for Cheung and Gran to complete their calculations.

The big man sighed and straightened.

"You may be right. It will certainly be close. But not all those you have bought will stay bought, and a quick adjournment—"

"No adjournment," Agnes said firmly.

"Then dissolution and a general elec—"

"No dissolution."

For a long moment Cheung studied her with a face as unreadable as pulped newspaper. When he spoke, his voice had sunk even lower, an unbelievable bass. "Your coalition is unstable, ma'am. It will not hold together for long. And even if I have to go into hiding for a month or so, until the new representatives take their seats—"

"Fool!" Grundy shouted. "Dolt! Huu will control those elections! You thought you were only up against that senile old coot, Hastings. I warned you he would call for help from this—this pestilent witch!"

Dwayne had enjoyed blaming others, too.

Cheung continued to ignore his companion. He and Hubbard Agnes studied each other once more, as though each were waiting for the other to make the first move. If so, then she won, and for the first time the big man showed traces of anger.

"I would be naive to say you fight unfairly, Dr. Hubbard, but you have introduced a whole new factor into the game now. You have been wielding a new threat—but I am not at all sure you can sustain that particular blackmail for very long. You fight with children! Where are they? What have you done with them?"

Cedric tore his eyes off Grundy, an unpleasant reflection of the odious Dwayne. What was that about children?

Gran's cold glare had become colder yet. "I did not start that, Dr. Cheung. Besides, are they children? Technically they are referred to as COC's."

Cedric broke her rules to ask, "What's that stand for?"

She flashed him a glare of warning. "Cultured Organ Complex."

Cheung sighed very deeply. "You will not believe this, for of course I have no evidence." He glanced at Cedric, including him in the negotiations for the first time. "I admit I have a clone which goes . . . who goes . . . by the name of Wong Gavin. He was a rash decision on my part, one I now regret. I have long since vowed that I shall not molest him. When he reaches adulthood I shall give him his liberty and let him find his own way in the world."

"You think so?" Grundy jeered. "You think so now! Wait until the chest pains start, or the jaundice. Every drowning man breathes water in the end."

"You may be right." Cheung turned back to Gran. "The point

is that I now no longer have the choice, do I? Certain unwritten rules have been breached, and the consequences are incalculable. What will you do with them, Director? Dump them in a refugee camp, or sell them back to their owners? Put them out of their misery? You can't go public with them, because you have used them to buy votes, haven't you? Will you kill them all?"

"I bought votes with them, but return of goods was never included, only confidentiality."

"Hah!" Grundy shouted. He jabbed a finger to emphasize his words, and that had been a Dwayne trick, too. "She's been threatening to expose, but she can't expose some without blowing the whole organage business! Then her big stick is broken—call her bluff, Ollie!"

"At the moment I am more concerned with finding out why the rules were changed."

"I repeat—I did not start that, Dr. Cheung."

"That's utterly irrelevant—" Grundy began.

Cheung's dark voice cut him off. "Explain, please?"

Gran indicated Cedric with a casual wave of her hand. "Cedr—Morris—my grandson was raised in Meadowdale. On Tuesday I sent him credit for a ticket and told him to come to HQ, in Nauc. I deliberately gave him a day in hand and more credit than he needed. Of course he set off to explore—but he headed straight to the Norristown sector—and BEST."

Cedric was about to tell them how Cheaver Ben had suggested Norristown to him. He didn't, because they all seemed to be waiting for something—waiting, he saw at last, for Dr. Grundy to call it a coincidence. But Grundy did not speak, either.

"Three BEST agents tailed him," Gran said.

"And how many 4-I agents?" Grundy growled.

"I had set a bodyguard to watch over him, naturally. I knew he would break cover at the first possible moment, so I had a bull standing by. What's your excuse?"

Grundy's eyes held a look that Cedric had sometimes seen in Kroeger Dwayne's. It had usually meant pain coming to someone. "If there were any BEST employees in the area, Director, then I'm sure their purposes were quite innocent. As you murdered them, we can't ask them what they were doing, can we?"

"My agent was outnumbered, and perhaps a little overzealous."

"As in the President Lincoln Hotel?"

Hubbard Agnes made a faint impatient noise, as though that remark was too ridiculous to answer.

"Tell me about the President Lincoln Hotel, too," Cheung said in cellar tones.

"The boy took a room there. My agent went to guard him, and BEST's goons opened an unprovoked military campaign. At least twenty noncombatants were killed or part-fried."

"Overzealous?" Grundy suggested. He yawned and stretched, glancing around the hangar at the little clumps of guards still watching from the distance, in hair-trigger silence.

Gran turned a glance of deadly contempt on him but spoke to Cheung. "His dogs certainly overreacted. The main reason, I think, was that they had lost their quarry. They'd been watching the exits—the lev stations and airfields and so on. They hadn't realized that Cedric didn't even know his danger. They were tired, and frightened by the likely results of their own incompetence. BEST has a bad reputation for trimming its pension obligations."

"I thought this one was Morris?" Grundy sneered.

"How did they get on to him again, then?" Cheung asked.

Cedric found his grandmother's eyes throwing the question to him, with an amused sort of disdain.

The hangar was very, very cold. "I called Meadowdale?"

She nodded. "And Cheaver reported your call to his employers. They back-trailed it." She turned to Cheung. "So I was not the one to breach sanctuary."

"I heard about the affair at the President Lincoln. I did not know the details."

"Of course, that was all a farrago of lies," Grundy said, "but before I denounce it, I have a question—a hypothetical question. When your bull broke into the kid's room, the first thing he did was deactivate the snoopers, all of them."

"Standard practice?" Cheung murmured, deep as a sleepy organ.

"But what did he get up to then, mmm? My men—if this were true, of course—my men had a long wait. Man and boy in a bedroom for three hours? Did you have fun, lad?"

Cedric felt sick. Just the voice was enough—the tone, the baiting—and the gloating smile. He could almost smell that barn again, and remember his terror when they hauled his pants off. He had butted Greg in the face and jammed a lucky elbow in Dwayne's groin, and then run screaming all the way back to Madge's kitchen, much more frightened of the UV on his bare little ass than of whatever Greg and Dwayne had wanted to do.

He must have been about twelve, maybe. And a couple of years later how glad he had been when those two had left Meadowdale! Oh, God!

Cheung dismissed the matter with a faint shrug and turned to Gran. "One of the representatives from Greater Levant, the Honorable Levi Mohammed—he has put forward some interesting proposals."

Cedric sensed a sudden tension and forgot Grundy and Dwayne and the President Lincoln.

"I am aware of their main points, I think," Gran said.

"And what might they be?" Grundy snarled, but quietly.

Cheung waited, letting Gran fill the gap.

"The Chamber replaces the Assembly, with a two-year phase-in," she said. "The Institute's charter is ratified by the Chamber and its present structure continued. Stellar Power begins remitting taxes to the Chamber, gradually, as it assumes responsibility for U.N. programs. All U.N. personnel receive job continuation or a generous settlement. It would be a peaceable transfer of power."

Cedric might have been an ignoramus in politics, but even he could grasp the significance of that! Important meeting? This was historic, epochal! No more United Nations?

Color had drained from Grundy's horsey face, leaving the brown blotches like patches of decay. "And your lover, Hastings? When do we got him in the dock?"

"He's old," Gran said sadly. "And frightened. He no longer has any stomach for the game. I've promised him sanctuary here. As long as Cainsville stands, he will be safe."

"That should be about a week!" Grundy snapped, rather shrilly.

Gran chuckled, sharing a joke with Cheung. "I offered Will the position of deputy director for Media Relations, which has just come open. He said he'd consider it."

He could hardly do worse than the previous incumbent, Cedric thought. But that little chuckle had been a signal. Peace had broken out.

Cheung's round face relaxed into a smile almost as wide as Gavin's. "With fewer great powers, the world ought to become more stable. Too often we have had you threatening to pull the plug, and Julian, here, threatening to hit the bricks. Hastings and I have twisted the political ropes too long, and the media play us off against each other. Please tell Will I bear him no grudge.

Whatever sins he has committed in the past, I expect I shall match in future."

"Representative Huu is planning a speech on Thursday, supporting Levi's initiatives," Gran remarked. She straightened and rubbed her back, as if she were weary and anxious to be gone.

"I am willing to make one on those lines this afternoon, when I welcome the Chinese declaration," Cheung said quietly.

"Will and I will applaud."

Those quiet words marked agreement, Cedric thought. History had just been made. The U.N. was gone—but the Institute would remain.

"Well, well!" Grundy was pallid with fury, and it made him look much more like Dwayne, his younger clone—his dead clone, of course. Cedric wondered if Gran knew about that one and if he should mention it, but then he remembered what had happened to Eccles Pandora. Better not!

"The Treaty of Cainsville, is it?" Grundy sprang to his feet. "So you, Hubbard, betray Hastings. And Cheung—you betray me? What happens to our agreement, the brave words we shared yesterday?"

"Sit down!" Cheung snapped. "Or the goons will start burning things."

Grundy sat down reluctantly, fangs still bared.

"I'll tell you what happens, I think," Gran said softly. Something about the tone sent shivers through Cedric. "We have the matter of the President Lincoln Hotel. We also have the matter of a clone, reared and harvested."

"What has that to do with you?" Grundy was blotchier than ever, leaning forward on his chair, almost hissing his words. "Are you a self-appointed avenging angel, running around handing out retribution for dead clones?"

Gran, having paid him very little attention since she arrived, gave him a cold and contemptuous appraisal. "No, I do not run around looking for such people, but if one ever gets in my way, then I give that person no more consideration than the clone received. I value such a person's life as that person values life."

Cedric shivered again. *If I wanted to kill one of them during his visit . . .* He had thought she was bragging to the bull. It was impossible, surely? All four of them had been searched for every possible concealed weapon known to man. There were hundreds of armed guards standing in a great circle, all watching. They could be there in seconds. The result might be a shootout that would kill everyone. She was bluffing—obviously.

"A clone," she murmured. "Did you know him, Cedric?"

Cedric could only nod. His throat felt as though an unseen hand was strangling him.

Gran glanced at Cheung. "Mostly still in storage, I understand. Only some teeth have been used so far. And the genitals, of course."

Cheung seemed to ponder for a moment. Then he nodded faintly and curled his lip in a sign of distaste—but it might also have been a sign of agreement, of acquiescence. A new partnership had been forged, and must be tested.

Grundy's eyes flashed a look of fury at him and went back to glaring at Gran. "You murdered Eccles Pandora," he said. "Show me the moral high ground in that?"

Gran's face was as inscrutable as Cheung's, her voice flat. "Eccles Pandora is doubtless alive and reasonably well, and Devlin Grant likewise. They deserve each other. That brings us to another matter. While we have never met with success at retrieving broken strings in the past, we shall certainly try to contact Nile again on the thirteenth. It is not impossible that we may succeed, and bring back the unfortunate castaways."

Grundy looked startled. He glanced at Cedric, who suddenly knew why he was there—to prove that the broken string had been a fake.

"Including the genuine Cedric?" Grundy demanded. "Or is he Morris? Including that ranger? Our System came up with a very curious identification of the ranger."

"Only Devlin concerns me now," Gran said. "I suspect that he would be willing to testify against his accomplice in the murder case—in return for some mitigation of his sentence."

"Testify?"

She sighed. "No, I suppose I am just an overage idealist. I keep remembering the formal courtroom justice of my youth. And we don't need Devlin's evidence anyway—do we?"

She was asking Cheung, who was frowning. Grundy seemed on the verge of losing control; even his clenched fists were trembling. And Cedric did not think his grandmother was as calm as she was trying to seem. Was she trying to provoke an attack? Was that her plan? She had told Cedric he was to be there as a bodyguard, and he had not believed her. If Grundy sprang at her, then she expected Cedric to intervene. He did not think he was in Cheung's weight class, but surely he could handle that Grundy

one for a few minutes, unless his bulls opened fire. Then other
bulls would retaliate. Sweat prickled on his skin, in spite of the
cold.

"Explain, please," Cheung requested in his sepulchral bass.

"It was not the first case," she said, watching Grundy closely.
"He has killed others before with his meddling. He duped Devlin
completely. If BEST could unionize the Institute, then Devlin
was to be appointed director, or so Devlin was led to believe. It
was Devlin who slipped the cuthionamine aboard the skiv."

"Where did he put it?" Cedric was surprised to realize that the
eagerly querying voice was his own.

Apparently Gran did not mind. "It was in a tiny spring-loaded
capsule, something like a clamshell. Devlin hid it in among
Chollak's spare clothes. The day Chollak reached for that pair of
socks, it flew open."

Grundy laughed unconvincingly. "And what was Devlin's
purpose? What could he possibly gain from murdering three people, two of them his own subordinates? And so exotically, too?"

"Nothing," she said. "That was why he panicked when he
realized what had happened. What he had expected we don't
know—just van Schoening, probably. Chollak was a powerful
man. Had he been the only one affected, most likely he would
have killed van Schoening. One insanity, leading to one murder
and one rape—Devlin did not expect three deaths. It was a
sloppy plan, but maybe that was part of its strength. Had it failed,
there was no loss."

"And?" Cedric asked, fascinated and terrified at the same
time.

"The Moscow faculty is officially open shop. van Schoening
was a secret member of BEST. The plan was Grundy's."

"He wanted a casus belli?" Cheung asked.

Before Cedric could ask, his grandmother nodded. "Yes, an
excuse to declare war, to provoke a showdown. With one of
BEST's members dead, he would have claimed foul play, or that
Institute's safety procedures were inadequate. Nile is a fungoid,
high-pressure world. He might have tried to show that the cuthionamine was a contamination—certainly he would have demanded access to Cainsville to investigate. Ultimately he was
going to call a worldwide technical strike to force unionization of
the Institute."

Grundy spat out an obscenity. "Absurd," he added.

"No. We have seen the proclamations you had already prepared. You provided the poison. Unlike Devlin, you must have known that there was enough there to contaminate the whole skiv. You wanted to create the maximum possible scandal. You'd promised Devlin the directorship, of course—and you'd already double-crossed him, because three deaths made his hopes very shaky. He was deputy for Operations, and therefore responsible for safety. He knew that!"

Silence fell.

Everyone looked at Cheung.

"What evidence can you provide?" he asked softly.

Again Gran rubbed her back, but Cedric saw that her shift of position masked a quick glance around the dome. Was she checking out the guards? Was she seriously expecting violence?

They would all die in the crossfire.

"In the matter of the Nile murders, I have very little evidence against Grundy himself," she said, "unless we recall Devlin. In the matter of the clone, I have ample. In the matter of the President Lincoln Hotel—the final orders may not have been Grundy's, but he must have launched the program in the first place, knowing that it might lead to violence; indeed, planning violence upon my grandson. And there are other matters—like Italy, for example."

There was a long pause then, while Cheung made his decision. Then he nodded. "The Italian affair was disgraceful. What do you propose?"

Again Grundy sprang to his feet. His fists were clenched, eyes staring. "So!" he shouted, and he was slavering. "The brave new alliance is to be sealed in blood, is it? My blood? Well, I won't stand for it. You'll have no mikes for your precious speech, Cheung. You, bitch, will find that the power you pump into the space grid has nowhere to go, because there will be no one to accept it. It is time for Brain Power! It is time that the people who make the world run were allowed to run it. It is time—"

Cedric heard himself moan.

"Grundy Julian Wagner," Gran said, pointing a bony finger up at him. *"Krishna kamikaze Kamehameha!"*

Screaming in fury, Cedric leaped from his chair. He landed bent-kneed, already starting to pivot before his right foot came down, his arm swinging like a scythe. Grundy's reflexes were hopeless. He never registered that he was within Cedric's long reach; his eyes never saw that stiff-fingered hand coming at him like a sword blade. His watching guards saw it, but even their fine-honed reactions were not fast enough for them to finish drawing their guns before the edge of that hand struck exactly on target with all of Cedric's weight and strength and leverage behind it, and Grundy's scrawny neck snapped with an audible crack.

24

THINGS BECAME VERY confusing in Hangar Four. They were supposed to—Bagshaw Barney had planned them that way. For what had felt like several days, he had been leaning back against a huge black tire, relaxed, yawning and scratching, making lewd comments to the mistrustful gold uniform on one side of him and the suspicious green on the other. But his eyes, like their eyes and six hundred other eyes, had stayed locked on that epochal meeting, that little group of four in the middle of the metal emptiness.

Then Grundy had risen, and Mother Hubbard had pointed. As Cedric leaped, Barney had reacted a split-second before the protectors in his helmet slammed down on his ears and the lights went out. His hand had been ready by the preset dose pack on his belt. He pressed the button and felt the needle slip through the fabric of his pants and pump a double shot of KRp into his hip.

He thought he had already launched himself from the wall and was running before the dome was even dark, which was not exactly likely. But certainly he was moving when the shock grenades went off, and probably no one else was. He could put on a fair turn of speed in spite of his bulk, and the tiny glowworm of the inertial compass in his gun butt gave him direction. Of course, he was expecting the grenades, but even so, the sheer brutality of the noise threw him off his stride. *Nine . . . ten . . .*

His head felt as if it had cracked open. Hopefully BEST's troops would be much more stunned, and the Chamber's, also. Cheung would need time to call off his dogs, and no one could guess which way the golds would jump: throw down their weapons, or go for suicidal vengeance. System's last signal, before it had signed off, had been to predict that they would split almost fifty-fifty.

Eighteen . . . nineteen . . .

Running at full speed into pitch-dark was unnerving, something he had not done since basic training. His numbed ears could not detect the crackle of the gas bombs, but already he caught a whiff of riot smoke, pungent and bitter. His head was starting to throb. He could also feel the KRp burning through his veins. The visiting bulls would be equipped with that also—it was one of the standard antidotes—but they would not have been all ready to use it, like him. When the lights had gone out they would have needed a few seconds to fumble, and more seconds for the KRp to work—even the good guys were cutting it as fine as he had dared allow—so there should be a few minutes while the enemy were at least groggy and possibly even immobile. *Twenty-eight . . .* And some of them would fudge the shots, or go for night-vision enhancer before they realized—G9 or Isophot. A KRp headache was bad enough without mixing that junk into the bloodstream, too. A few might even be stupid enough to snap on their darkseers, which would waste time and . . . *Thirty . . .* He closed his eyes.

Light blazed pale pink through his eyelids; he felt it warm on his face, and then it faded to an olive afterglow. There went any darkseers presently in use, and who could say that darkseers might not be useful later? And any idiot who had shot himself full of G9 would not be seeing anything at all for days. The night was young.

That had been one of Adele's sayings: "The night is young and so are we." She would never return, but she was avenged. The kid had done both of them for him—first Devlin, now Grundy. All that was left to do was rescue the kid. *Forty.* If events forced Barney to choose between the kid and his old witch of a grandmother, he thought he might even go for the kid. The boy had earned it.

Riot smoke was potent stuff for a woman of her age at the best of times, and Barney was planning concentrations damned close to lethal. It might kill her before they got KRp into her, but she had understood the risk and been willing to take it. His own head was pounding as if it were about to burst.

He registered the third flash. Normal lighting would follow. He opened his eyes on a heaving, unworldly landscape of writhing white hills. Even in the troughs the smoke was deep enough to reach his neck, as if he were running through a ghostly giant surf. Briefly he saw other reds sprinting in from all around, but no greens or golds, and then the wave of smoke swallowed him —then cleared. He changed direction marginally, orienting on ceiling fixtures, and again was buried in whiteness. He held his breath as much as he could, still running. *Fifty-two . . . fifty-three* . . . A long, gasping breath, and he did not even stumble, so the KRp was working. The hammering in the middle of his forehead was fairly diagnostic, too. His ears still rang from the grenades. He snapped the ear protectors up, out of the way. He was holding his gun before him like a club.

The smoke was almost as bad as darkness, but not quite. Visibility was about a meter. That would allow a little evasive action as they all converged on—

Sixty! He should be there.

He almost fell over a chair. Gasping for breath, he fumbled around for a moment in the mist. Another figure loomed up, but he was red, also. Where the hell was everyone? The three survivors would have all run outward, of course, so he had come too far. Damned headache was making him woozy already, and the ringing in his ears . . .

"Jamming has ended," System told him.

His earpatch had been turned on again—he was glad to have System back. He had felt lonely without it, but with luck the wide-spectrum jamming had wrecked the enemies' cryotronics.

Then he almost trod on a crouching figure . . . red. . . .

"Give me a hand," she yelled, and he could barely hear her over the bells in his ears, but he recognized Smith Lucy. And the flagpole she was trying to lift could only be—

"He's had a shot?" Bagshaw asked, slinging his torch on his shoulder and bending to take a grip on Cedric. But it was a stupid question; Lucy knew her job. He hoped she had not heard. "I'll take him," he shouted. How much smoke had the kid breathed? He might be out for hours. The fight was on now—he could hear screams all around, and sometimes the *phsst!* of a torch, if it was close.

Lucy helped arrange the kid over Barney's free shoulder—and he weighed a sight more than he looked as though he should. He had also peed his pants, so he was out very deep. Lucy had spun around and started to jog. Barney staggered after, just barely keeping her in sight. Thinks I'm Samson...

"Friend at two o'clock. Friend at nine o'clock." System had radar.

The redcoat at two o'clock emerged momentarily from the mist and then vanished; the one to the left did not show at all. Oh, this *god*damned headache! If only they had dared take the KRp earlier—but of course each force had done spot-check medicals on the other two, and that stuff would have shown up like red flags.

"Visitor at twelve o'clock."

Lucy had received the same message. She veered, but not soon enough. A golden figure loomed, size exaggerated by the fog. *Phsst!* Her torch blazed in a fuzzy red blur and the guy screamed as if she had murdered him. He could not have caught more than a blister through his uniform, but he reeled out of the way without returning fire. Riot smoke dissipated lasers, even at that range.

"Veer thirty left," System directed.

Bagshaw obeyed. He had lost Lucy, which was hardly surprising, for the fog was as thick as concrete, dark gray now. He heard more *phsst*! sounds and more screams. His burden stirred and groaned. The kid was definitely getting heavier. Hanging upside down was not going to help his head—nothing would help his head. Bagshaw's own head thundered with every step as if it were about to explode, and he had taken the KRp before the smoke. Taken afterward, that stuff was pure hell.

He almost ran into a solid blackness, as big as a truck, a Boeing undercarriage. He sent off a silent curse to System for not warning him. He staggered around behind it, too winded to run farther, and found a gap like a narrow cave between two wheels. It would do. He lowered Cedric, who moaned and began to struggle. Bagshaw sat him on the floor, leaning back against the giant wall of the tire. Then he knelt beside him, puffing obscenely. He was not young anymore.

His ears were calming down, but his forehead was bursting in all directions. Hard to think with an exploding brain.

He threw his gun down. "You alive, Sprout?"

Cedric mumbled and twitched—and suddenly blurted out a loud obscenity. "... my head," he finished, clutching it with both hands. "No."

"Yeah. It's the antidote. It'll hurt for an hour or so."

"Hurt? You call this hurt? Sonof*abitch!*"

"Just relax. You're safe." Maybe. Bagshaw wanted to snap on his wrist mike and call for reinforcements, but the baddies would have monitoring equipment in their aircraft. Had Cheung called off the greens yet?

"You did my nose again!" It sounded like "Doodiddydoada-dain." Cedric lifted his head in both hands. "Wha' happened?"

"A little fracas. I got you. Others got your grandma, and Cheung." I hope they did, he thought. I hope they wore red.

Cedric groaned and mumbled something.

There was sudden silence. Here it comes, Bagshaw thought.

The kid's face came up, a white puddle, peering at Bagshaw through the murk. "I killed him! I broke his neck! Oh, *God!*"

"You didn't, kid."

"I did! I rabbit-punched him! Oh hell—hand—" He peered groggily at his right hand, which did not look good, even from Barney's position.

"Your grandmother did it. She pulled the trigger. You were just the gun."

The kid made a strangling noise and threw up loudly. KRp did not usually do that. Maybe it was the pain—or just the memory. Or he had swallowed blood from his nose. Cedric straightened back against the wheel and wiped his mouth with the back of his good hand. He moaned again.

"I killed him. I heard his neck break!"

"No. You couldn't help it. Your grandmother did it. Or I did."

"Huh?"

"You didn't learn that karate chop in an organage. Not you, Sprout, me!"

"You?"

"Me. I did it, if you like. Not you. No one can blame you!"

Sounds seemed deadened by the fog, but the fighting was certainly going on—screams and the *phsst!* of lasers in the smoke; and a lot of shouting, as if people were starting to get organized, and those could only be the baddies. Why was System not sending help?

Then Bagshaw heard an amplified voice booming, but between the racket and the echoes and his own pounding head he could not tell—he hoped it was Cheung, calling off his greenies. If BEST's golds were not disarmed before they knew for sure that they had lost their client, then the gods themselves would never guess what they might do. Some bulls let themselves be imprinted with a code of honor like samurai fanatics—imprinted as

Cedric had been, except that Cedric had been tricked. Those bastards had looked at the wires voluntarily—and that was selling one's soul.

"Why'd I do that?" Cedric mumbled. His voice was even more slurred than before. He was going deeper into shock.

"You didn't. You couldn't help yourself."

"Tell me, damn you!" he screamed.

Boom! Barney felt the floor shudder, and a red-hot pain jarred his head. His gut twisted—what the hell had that been? There was no loud stuff on the program. Someone was using it, though. Oh, hell! Things were coming unstuck. The BEST guys might be going to take the whole parade with them. *Boom!* There was a sound of falling debris and tearing metal, as if all the cook pots in Creation had just hit a concrete floor.

"Up, Sprout! We'd better get the hell out of here."

The kid made no move, just sat there with his long legs straight out and his face a blur. "Tell me why I did that thing!"

"I'll explain later."

"Now! Now! Now!"

Barney toyed with the idea of giving him a needle, but knew he dared not. Shock was tricky, and the kid had a ton of guilt to carry.

"I checked your retinas, remember?" And I couldn't believe my luck when you agreed to it. Dumb, dumb kid, green off the farm!

"And they didn't when I got to HQ," Cedric mumbled.

"Right. We don't use retina scanners anymore. Just in old holodramas. Real world—they're too dangerous. Strobe hypnosis."

"Huh?"

"Look, we've gotta go!" The fog swirled, and Barney felt cold air. That last crash must have been the doors. The smoke would lift . . .

"I imprinted you, kid. As soon as you focused on the crosswires in that scanner, you were gone. I put you way down in a deep trance, and I planted a code in your head. When your gran gave the signal, you attacked."

Cedric muttered something that sounded uncomplimentary.

Barney did not want to hear. He deserved every syllable. It was good to know that Adele was avenged, but he had never felt like a genuine, hundred-percent, unarguable shit before. Not only Cedric had guilt. "I made you into a walking gun, Sprout. No one can resist a strober—no one!" But I know one who came damned close.

"Turd! You're a—"

"Yes, I am. And I'm trying to help now. We gotta go before BEST's goons get you. Your princess is waiting. Come *on*!" He hauled at the kid's arm, and he stayed limp.

"In the hotel," Cedric mumbled. "That was why it took three hours?"

"Yes. Now come!"

But it should not have taken three hours. It should not have taken five minutes, there in that grubby hotel room. Barney had called in System to help, and even with System calling the shots he had needed all that time to break the kid's will. They had taken him deeper and deeper, and he had screamed and refused and yelled and fought back. Tough! That was what his DNA had predicted, and even System had found no record of anyone ever resisting a strobe that long, but they had finally exhausted him— worn him out and hammered down into his subconscious till he had no will left and had almost stopped breathing, and finally the compulsion had taken.

That was the only bright thought—that a man as tough as this human cable should be able to handle the guilt.

And he was still refusing to cooperate. Barney dragged him almost out of the undercarriage cave, and he just slid along the floor on his seat.

"Sprout! Cedric! Come on, lad! I'll take you to Alya. You can go to Tiber. She's waiting!"

Cedric muttered something inaudible, but clearly a refusal.

Icy wind swirled. The light was growing brighter—Barney looked up and saw the spots shining blearily from the roof. There were two or even three megaphones blaring, drowning each other.

He bent to lift the lad—and stopped a punch in the mouth that almost knocked him over. He felt a tooth crack. He straightened angrily, tasting blood on his lips—suckered by an amateur with his butt on the floor and not even properly conscious!

"If BEST's men find you, they'll skin you alive, kid! Let's go!"

"Go to hell. Leave me." Cedric rolled over, facedown on the floor. He was in shock. The dope from the smoke, the antidote, and the guilt of being a killer—he wasn't capable of thinking.

"Coward!" Barney said, rubbing his mouth. The fog was very thin now.

"Huh?"

"Some ranger you'd have been! And that little flat-faced brown broad you've been humping—"

Cedric rolled over with an oath, pulled up his knees, and lurched upright in one leap—a very unwise procedure with a headache like his. He screamed, stumbled, and fell into Barney's waiting arms.

"Hold it right there!" another voice said.

Barney twisted his head around and peered behind him—into the lenses of six torchguns. The men holding them were wearing blue.

Cedric tried to move, and his knees buckled. Barney hugged him more tightly while he gaped at the twisted, crumpled hangar doors and the cargo plane beyond, lit by the cruel light of a snowy dawn. Troops in dark blue were still pouring off and running into the dome. Bodies lay all over the floor—red, blue, green, and gold. He looked for anyone who was upright and not wearing blue, and the few he could make out had their hands up.

Cold, deadly despair washed over him as the extent of his failure penetrated—disaster! And to be crapped by those small-time hoods. . . . Those were not even uniforms they were wearing, just old jeans and patched denims, all dyed dark blue. Even their helmets were that cruddy Nepalese junk.

Then someone stepped up behind Bagshaw Barney and rammed a zomber into the small of his back.

25

Cainsville, April 11

THERE WAS LITTLE except pain in Cedric's universe. The agony in his head was a great, red, pulsating sun. Other people, other things—they only rotated around the edges, and he caught glimpses of them now and then. He knew when Bagshaw collapsed, because he fell on top of the bull and hit his broken hand on the floor. The sudden jarring made the red sun angry; it exploded terribly, blinding him completely for a while. He lay still and tried not to think about *crack*!

Crack! was the sound a neck made when it broke—a thick and juicy, breaking-tearing *crack*.

Then two men hauled him to his feet, and the red sun in his brain blazed worse than ever, pumping surges of nausea up from his belly. A voice shouted at him, wanting to know his name, and he peered around that great red pain, trying to find the man's face.

He wanted to say his name, but his mouth was not moving very well. Everything else about him was moving—he was starting to shake. Hands and feet and elbows and chin—he was quivering all over, in all directions, and that was shameful. Cold, cold . . .

"Zomb this one, too?" someone asked.

"Maybe a little . . . Naw, don't. It'd kill him, state he's in."

"Jeez, he looks dangerous, sir!"

They all laughed, and the noise hurt.

Why blue? Not U.N. blue. His grandfather's troops wore pale blue, sky blue, and this was darker, sort of royal blue, or navy blue. They wore a silver logo, but he couldn't see it properly. He couldn't see much ... Someone had asked him a question, and he wasn't sure of the words, so he just drooled.

Then the man—he was a very short, tubby man—slapped Cedric's face. The red sun exploded, the waves of nausea broke, and instantly Cedric puked, even more violently than before. The little man jumped back, screaming oaths, and there was some stifled laughter. Cold; the world was ice. Hands and feet were all ice. He shivered.

"What've you got here?" The voice was new. Another man had arrived, a big brusque one, leading a large platoon.

"It's the old bag's grandson, sir. The one who did the killing."

"Doesn't look capable of stomping beetles, does he? Bring him along. One more hostage to put on trial later."

Dimly, while Cedric was trying to understand all those words, he saw Bagshaw being ordered to stand up and then told to go where a dark blue arm was pointing; and Bagshaw obediently slouched off in that direction without a murmur—and without his gun. That was not in character. That was scary enough to seep in around the blazing red pain. That meant *zombie*. Bagshaw would be a mindless husk for days—or forever, depending on the dose they had given him.

The shoulder patches looked like a number: O1.

Then Cedric was being hustled toward a massed plantation of golfies. Every step hurt. He wanted to die. He kept on remembering that *crack* noise. He was a killer! Maybe these people would take him away and hang him for murder. He thought he would rather be hanged than shut up somewhere for the rest of his life. Why O1?

He would never see Alya again. But he would not be able to face her, anyway. What would a princess want with a murderer?

Then he was being ordered into a golfie. It was good to sit down. He felt a cold click at his wrist. He peered, trying to make his eyes focus. His good hand had been cuffed to the rail. A man in dark blue climbed in on his left and said, "Whew! You stink!"

"I barfed," Cedric mumbled carefully.

"I know that!"

"And I think I peed my pants, too."

"At least." The man did not sound very old. Cedric scrunched up his eyes, although they hurt, and somehow he squeezed out a less blurred picture. His companion was young and slight—but sitting next to someone in Cedric's condition would be a job assigned to a junior. The golfie lurched forward, and the red pain burned again as Cedric's head jerked, threatening to blow up and splatter burning brains everywhere. *Crack?*

No, his neck had not broken. He rather wished it had. In fast convoy the golfie shot out the big door and raced along the dim corridor. It cornered, and Cedric's two-ton head swayed again, with more of the terrible internal consequences. He swallowed horribly.

"System?" Cedric mumbled. "It's helping you?"

The skinny guy chuckled. "Sure is."

Why would System be running all these golfies, working for the enemy? Who were the enemy? Again Cedric squinted down at the shoulder beside him. Not O1, he saw, but a round globe symbol and a big numeral 1.

Oh, hell.

The mist lifted a little. The kid was wearing jeans and a blue sweater, both patched, and a shiny helmet with the visor up.

"Who are you guys?" Cedric asked.

"We're the Earth First Society," the guard said, with a curiously juvenile pride.

Another agony-filled corner, and then the convoy was racing along a brighter tunnel, a big one with loading docks along both sides.

"What're you doing?" Cedric muttered. He tried to hold himself as still as possible, but the golfie was swaying, and of course he was too tall to lean his head back against the headrest. Also, his knees were cramped and his left wrist was chained, which restricted his choices. He could not even raise that arm to speak into his wrist mike; but then he remembered that the bulls had taken that away. He reached around carefully with his free hand—which was a pain center all its own. Probably he had cracked a bone or two in there, but he managed to rip off the tape they had stuck over his earpatch. It made no difference—no one was trying to call him.

"We're going to stop you bastards before you pollute the world!"

"Pollute? Stellar power doesn't pollute."

"Infect, then. None of this planet stuff. We'll keep the power, but no more exploring other worlds. That's out!" He was almost shouting—a fanatic. Bagshaw, Cedric recalled, had not thought much of Earthfirsters.

Cedric was going to ask how they had gotten in, but the answer was obvious, even to his bursting, aching head. There had been a traitor, probably Devlin. Grundy must have wormed or blackmailed some of System's overrides out of Devlin, and he had brought the Earthfirsters along as a private backup in case Gran pulled some trick to outsmart him at the meeting, which of course she had done, and so Grundy's last card had been played posthumously, or had played itself, and things were in one hell of a mess. Cedric had killed Grundy, and Bagshaw was a zombie, and where was Gran, anyway?

Another sharp corner; another choked-back scream. But maybe the pain was not quite so bad, or maybe a guy could get used to anything, or maybe he had just remembered Alya and Tiber.

"What're you going to do?" Cedric asked.

The youth crowed. "Take over completely. Blow up all the domes except Prometheus. Put the criminals on trial and then hang them. Shut down 4-I before it looses something worse on the world than it has already." He was wild-eyed, flying high on something.

"Such as?"

"Such as Mexican Sweats, or Blue Rash."

That was *bunk*! Those diseases had nothing to do with the Institute. They were a result of too many unhealthy, undernourished people crammed into unsanitary camps, which meant too many bugs, and then some bug tried a new mutation and there was a worthwhile stock of people to spread it and support it until it got itself perfected. To blame that on Cainsville was crazy. Cedric had seen a special where Eccles—

Oh, no! Think about Alya instead.

Alya! Cedric felt panic. Had she gone yet? If she hadn't, then he must warn her about these lunatics loose in Cainsville. Witless, childish jelly, sitting here whimpering because he had a headache! Bagshaw had been right—he would not have made much of a ranger.

Control! He set his teeth.

His left wrist was chained. The guard was on that side.

A wrist mike was not necessary in a golfie, for it had its own comset.

Cedric took a deep breath. "*Code Arabian*," he said.

System's familiar twang sounded in his ear. "Acknowledged."

But absolutely nothing happened except that the guard yelled and twisted around to slap his hand over Cedric's mouth. "You young bastard!" he shrilled, although he could not possibly be any older. "What're you doing? What did that mean?"

"Mmmph!" Cedric said, meaning that he could not breathe through his nose.

"Institute shithead!" The kid was frightened. "I'll shut you up!" He grabbed Cedric's hair in his right hand, removed his left hand from Cedric's mouth, and used it to punch him in the gut.

It was a slow and clumsy move, and Cedric had time to knot up his muscles. The blow hurt, but it probably hurt him less than it hurt his assailant's hand, for he yelped and fell back on the bench again. But the effect on Cedric's headache was diabolic, which made him lose his temper.

The guard has not thought to lower his visor. He was bent over, sucking his knuckles. Cedric rammed his left arm back. Had the chain not interfered, he might have broken his own elbow. As it was, the guard recoiled with a scream, and there were two bleeding noses on that cart.

At that moment the golfie entered a wider corridor. Suddenly it had room to overtake, so it made a dramatic swing out of line and began racing toward the head of the column—hurtling past cart after cart of the enemy, who yelled in surprise at being passed, and then in anger when they saw the fight in progress. They began unslinging guns.

Cedric had never fought no-hands-against-two before, but he was fairly sure that his best strategy would be to deliver everything he had as soon as he could. He jumped up and twisted around to lean on the front rail, held by his left hand underneath him, his broken right hand waving uselessly. He brought up his right foot and stamped the kid's face just as he was straightening up from the last blow. Cedric swayed, steadied himself by planting that foot on his victim's belly, and raised the other for another face shot. He found the guy's chin and heaved. The golfie swayed. Cedric thought he would tip out. His left arm was taking all the strain. The guard was being bent backward over the headrest, scrabbling uselessly at Cedric's legs, unable to reach high enough to do significant damage.

Then he remembered his gun and reached for it. Oh, hell! Cedric closed his eyes and straightened his knee. *Crack!* He did not hear it—not really—but he knew he had done it again.

With his right wrist and what was left of the strength of his left arm, Cedric hauled himself back into the golfie beside the slumped body. He thought he was going to pass out—his head, his hand, and blood all over him from his inevitable nose.

He had done it again! And this time he had not been forced into it by hypnotic compulsion. He had just been trying to save himself from a beating.

He was a killer.

It was habit-forming.

The golfie flashed by the head of the line with its motor screaming. When he had set up his emergency codes, he had thrown in everything he could think of, including maximum overrides. *Code Arabian* meant, "Take me to Princess Alya as fast as you can." He had picked the word because the stud stallion at Meadowdale had been a Arabian. At the time, he had thought that funny.

So Alya could not have left yet!

The cart came to a corner and went around it in a hair-raising four-wheel drift. The dead body began to slip; Cedric grabbed at it instinctively, but he was too late, tangled by his manacle. It vanished over the side, and he hooked a foot just in time to stop the torchgun from sliding out, also.

He caught a blurred glimpse of the wall hurtling by, flashing and smoking, and then it was gone also, before he had realized what it meant—the Earthfirsters had been firing at him. He ducked quickly, then raised his head to see. None of the following carts had reached the corner yet, but there was a long straight stretch ahead.

The back of the golfie was smoking already. If they fired the tires, then almost certainly System's emergency routines would override the override, and the cart would stop. The Earthfirsters would have seen the body. In a few seconds they would be coming round that corner, howling for blood.

The 2048 Pacurb Firearm Association Junior Skeet Lasering Champion would have to show his stuff.

Full combat gear was reflective, almost completely torchproof, but nobody was wearing full combat gear, not that he had seen. Grunting and cursing, he managed to pick up the gun with a right hand that was swelling like a balloon on a water tap.

The trouble was that lasering needed steady hands. It was all steady hands, Ben had said often enough. No wind correction to make, no recoil, but a laser was never powerful enough to do serious damage in less than a second or two—except in an eye shot, of course—and that meant it had to be held on target when the target reacted. Cedric knew which way a gopher jumped when it felt itself go on fire, or a magpie, and once he had even drilled a coyote, mostly by luck. Standard practice skeets had to be held in the sights for a second and half before they detonated.

Of course, he could not hope to do much one-handed, twisted around almost inside out, and firing backward from a leaping, careering, screaming golfie. He was not even sure his right hand was capable of squeezing the trigger.

The torch was a Winchester Thor Four, and he had never seen one before, let alone fired one. Still . . .

He twisted around, almost inside out, keeping down as much as he could, his chained left arm stretched out uselessly behind him, right arm resting on the headrest, aiming back along the corridor. He flicked off the safety, wincing at the pain in his hand. He took a long, deep breath and held it.

The first golfie hurtled into view, canted on two wheels and looking as though it, also, had been booted up to some highest override velocity. As it came out of the curve, both men jumped to their feet and aimed.

They had left their visors up! He saw their eyes in the scope, and the chance was irresistible—a single fast pass, burning the right eye of the one on the right and looping over to catch the left eye of the other. A couple of milliseconds was enough on an eye shot. He had done it before he knew he had started. Both men screamed and reeled and fell out. Their golfie jammed on its brakes.

Then the second cart appeared also, with one man already on his feet and aiming. He had his visor down, but Cedric saw a tiny spot of bare flesh below it and fired. That was tricky—the visor could have reflected his own beam back at him, but his aim held true, and he kept the crosshairs dead on target as the man obligingly toppled straight back, his gullet starting to blacken and smoke. That would give him another hole to whistle through. Then his cart swerved to avoid the bodies, and he also fell free.

Not bad at all, champ!

The third cart gave him a tricky eye shot, and after that the range was too great; but the corridor was jammed with stalled golfies and writhing bodies; the air full of shouts and the screech of tires. No wonder Bagshaw had not thought much of Earth-firsters.

Cedric's cart cornered again, and he lost sight of the pursuit. He would draw ahead anyway, probably, because there was only one of him in the golfie, and the enemy would have to clear the road. Having a good day, aren't we? Two dead, three blinded, one wounded . . . His insides heaved, and he told them sternly to behave.

Of course, the chase was far from over, for now there was blood on the scoreboard. At least some of the intruders would certainly tell System to take them to Cedric, just as he had ordered that he be taken to Alya. Or they might just follow his trail, for the back of his golfie was still smoking, and there was much worse smoke streaming out from the motor vents, also. The engine was screaming like a maniac. Maybe he should not be leading the danger to Alya like this.

Or maybe he could interfere? *"By what authority are you obeying the visitors' orders?"*

The golfie skittered around another corner, almost tipping him out and reminding him that he had a historically significant headache. "Data confidential," it said smugly.

"Override."

"Data confidential."

So much for that idea—the real deputy directors had higher authority than Cedric's Grade One. But obviously the traitor had been of high grade, and therefore Devlin.

Then Cedric yelped as the cart dived through a still-opening door and went clattering down a flight of stairs. He whimpered as his headache came thundering back, blindingly. Then, mercifully, he was on the flat again, and his wits began to seep back.

He wondered how literally his instructions would be obeyed. Suppose Alya were in a bathtub?

"Call to Dr. Fish."

"Dr. Fish is not presently accepting calls."

"Does he know about the Earthfirster invasion?"

"Data confidential."

"I must report an emergency!"

"Emergency calls are not being accepted at this time."

"Why not?"

"Because of an emergency."

"Arrrggh!"

"Message not understood."

Then he yelped again and hung on tight as the cart made a series of fast bends, zipping through circular openings where great armored doors stood open. Cedric peered back incredulously. Surely that had been a decon chamber? He had not recognized it, but there must be dozens of them, several for each dome.

Then the golfie balked like a spooked pony, almost throwing him. Another of the massive armored ports was swinging open. *He had no bubble suit on!* He could not believe that his authority would overrule standard quarantine regulations—he would be surprised if even Gran could do that.

With smoke still streaming from its motor, the golfie lurched forward again, into the gloomy vastness of a transmensor dome. It snapped on headlights—for others' benefit, surely—and purred decorously down the slope, angling around to the right. Cedric heard the door thump shut behind him. Of course the transmensor was not in use. There were no cranes or gantries in evidence, so most likely he was in Bering Dome. He knew all the others, either firsthand or on holo.

Then he registered the people, lots of people, hundreds of them. The center was packed with bedding and canvas fences.

His lights had attracted attention. People were scrambling to their feet in dozens and scores, many of them leaping and jumping like kids. In fact, many of them were kids. A group ran forward to meet him; the golfie slowed and beeped angrily at them. That attracted more attention. Voices were shouting. Some of them seemed to be pointing out that his cart was on fire. Alya must be somewhere in the crowd.

"Mister, you're on fire!" The cry echoed back and forth as he rolled on through a gathering crowd of spectators. The golfie slowed even more and made angrier noises at them. Then it shuddered, gasped, and jerked to a stop. It hissed and crackled for a moment, turned out its lights and died. Smoke continued to curl upward.

"System, acknowledge!"

Silence.

A wizened old man in a white bed sheet and a turban stepped forward and said something urgent, pointing at the smoke.

"Yes, I know," Cedric said. "Do you have a bucket of water handy?" He held up his left wrist and rattled his chain, to show why he was not dismounting. The spectators muttered among themselves, rubbing sleep-blurred eyes. They were crowded tightly in a dense wall, staying warily back from the burning cart. Its power supply would be flywheels running in hydrogen, and if those got loose, they could create mayhem all across the dome. He coughed as the smoke billowed back at him. Alya? He needed Alya.

"Cedric!" A youngster squeezed through the throng of adults and ran forward. He was chubby and oriental, and his grin was as wide as a sunrise. "You're on fire, you know? *Phew!* What did you fall into?"

"Gavin! Wong Gavin!" Cedric gaped at the boy. That certainly was Gavin's grin. *Gavin!* Cheung's clone! Cedric looked around at the crowd and then back to Gavin. "How'd you get here?"

"You're on fire, Cedric—did you know that?"

"Yes. I'm also tethered."

Gavin frowned, then stepped closer. "I can fix that!" he said, and began unscrewing one of the knurled knobs that held the ends of the handrail.

"Oh!" Cedric said, feeling extremely foolish. "Tell me how you got here. Are the others here?" His head still hurt.

Gavin tried to reply, but he was drowned out as more voices began shouting "Cedric!"

Lew and Jackie and Tim and Bev—they all came popping out of the crowd like gophers out of burrows, some even wriggling through between adult legs. They shouted and laughed at seeing him, they jumped up and down, and they all wanted to hug him until they got close, and then they all told him he didn't smell good; but by then Gavin had unfastened the rail and Cedric was free. He left the smoking golfie, taking the Winchester with him. He shouted at everyone to stand farther back; he reached out to ruffle hair on small heads, touch hands with adolescents. The crowd of brown-faced adults in bed sheets was being pushed back, muttering, by the influx of children. Cedric had a lump in his throat, and the smoke had made his eyes prickle. Meadow-dale—looted! The kids were not going to be butchered after all.

"Is Ben here? Or Madge?" he demanded.

A chorus of voices said no, they weren't—all the kids and none of the adults. He was glad. Apparently the older ones were in charge—Sheila and Sue and Roger—and then Sue herself appeared with a howling baby on each arm, and she was obviously very, very relieved to see Cedric.

"The day after you left!" she shouted over the racket. "We were raided—rounded up!"

"Who by?" It hurt to shout.

"Men in red. 4-I men."

Gran! That must be what Cheung had meant when . . .

Crowds were no obstacle for Cedric. Over heads he saw a swirl approaching and recognized high-piled black hair. He plunged forward to greet her, spectators retreating rapidly out of his way.

"Alya!"

"Darling!"

"Hold it!" he said, raising a warning hand. "I'm not very sanitary."

"So what!" She looked just as happy to see him as he was to see her. "I stink of baby!" She leaned over the particular baby she was clutching and they kissed briefly; but he noticed that she wrinkled her nose and backed away a couple of steps afterward. "There are dozens of these little tykes here . . ." She stared up at Cedric blankly. "You look awful! You're white as death. What's wrong?"

"Lots," he said, knowing suddenly how beat he was. He was reeling. "But all the Meadowdale kids are here!"

Obviously Alya felt as he did—her smile would have melted granite. "And not only Meadowdale! At least a dozen others. Two lots at least are from Neururb, and a lot of brown faces—I haven't placed them all yet. We should have guessed—your grandmother couldn't just threaten exposure, or all the—" She stopped, conscious of the large audience of big-eared children. "Or she might have provoked what she wanted to prevent?"

He nodded—early harvest, kill the evidence.

"So she just sent her army and picked them up!" Alya added triumphantly.

Maybe Gran was not quite so bad, then. He would have to think about that when he got his head glued together. Meanwhile he desperately wanted to take Alya in his arms, but the open space around him was evidence of how little he inspired intimacy. He would have liked to lie down, too; even more, sleep for a month . . .

"So by the time she was lampooning you at the press conference," Alya said, "her troops were already moving in—all over the place. She must have been planning this for years!"

"And—the others?" He gestured at the characters in white.

"Refugees. From Banzarak, and Zaire, I think. And Bangladesh."

But Cedric was staring at the two kids who had pushed in beside her. One was adolescent, maybe sixteen, the other a couple of years younger. They both had shaggy ochre hair and freckles, and they were skinny—and both obviously tall for their ages. They were glaring back at him with very resentful expressions.

Alya noticed his gaze and bit her lip. "This is Oswald," she said. "And this is Alfred. The one strangling the guitar over there somewhere is Harold—he's about seventeen." She smiled again, much less certainly, and indicated the baby. "And this one is Bert. I think that's short for Egbert, but I'll stick to Bert. He looks like he's another of you, darling. Guys—this one's Cedric."

It was too much. For moments that seemed like hours, Cedric's brain could do nothing except register overload. Clones! How many clones had Hastings wanted? But as he stared at them—at his own younger selves—he saw that they didn't really look like Hastings Willoughby at all. The old man had great flappy ears, and neither he nor these youngsters had. He remembered Bagshaw saying something about ears.

"There may be others," Alya said. "I haven't had time to—"

A skinny blond boy of around eight had emerged from somewhere to stare up at Alfred with a very puzzled expression.

"Why?" Cedric whispered. "What's been going on? Who am I?"

Suddenly the whole dome began to brighten. Then he saw heads turning, and he swung around to see what they had seen. The door he had entered by had opened again, and golfie headlights were pouring through it, but it was overhead spots coming on that were making the place lighter. The Earthfirsters had taken control of the dome.

Between Gavin and Alya and all his own clones, he had forgotten the pursuit. He wailed. "Quick! Your mike! Give me your mike!"

"I haven't got one," Alya said, frowning. "I've been trapped in here for over an hour."

He wanted to ball his fists in fury, but the right one hurt too much. "I need a com! Any com!"

"Cedric, dear? Who are all these men? Bulls? Blue?"

Golfies were still streaming into the dome, the whole line heading straight for Cedric—but that might have been accidental. The ceiling spots were up to full, merciless brilliance.

"They're Earthfirsters. They've invaded—killed off the Institute's bulls and a lot of others. And at the moment they're after me!"

"What? Why?"

"I killed one of them. And wounded four others. And I also killed the president of BEST. And I want a mike!"

Alya gave him a strange look. "Do you think anyone would refuse you after that?" she asked. "Nobody here has a wrist mike. There are coms by most of the doors, but they aren't working. No response. I was expecting Baker to come for me, but he hasn't."

Cedric sank to his knees to be less conspicuous. He did not want to die yet.

"Use the mike on your golfie?" Alya said, puzzled.

"I can't. It's dead."

"Oh." She adjusted the baby and gazed over toward the army of golfies. "Lots of mikes there."

"They'll shoot me on sight!" Cedric yelled. "How come you're not worried?"

Alya gasped. "I hadn't—oh, Cedric! You're in danger?"

"Danger? All those hundreds of men after me, wanting my blood, and you ask if I'm in danger?"

She shook her head, puzzled. "I was worried sick until a few minutes before you arrived—then I felt better. Oh, darling! I thought you were important!"

Glaring up from his knees, smelling so bad that he sickened himself, and hurting in numerous places, Cedric did not feel very dignified. "I'm important to me!"

"I didn't mean that! I mean, why aren't I worried about you?" She looked idiotically happy.

"Are you worried about anything right now?"

She shook her head, astounded at the realization. "No! I should be, shouldn't I?"

Nothing but her damned intuition would ever worry Alya, and it obviously was not bothering her at the moment.

The crowd had begun to move, shimmying around him, people backing up. With a stupendous effort, Cedric rose to a crouch, feeling the dome sway around him. He looked cautiously between heads. The golfies had spread out abreast in line to herd the crowd before them. The occupants were standing up, peering around, and they had their guns ready. If shooting started, then all sorts of kids and women were going to get hurt. He ought to give himself up and prevent further bloodshed.

"Alya!" The voice was familiar. "What's going on?"

Cedric looked around and it was like seeing a mirror—himself in a blue poncho with a guitar round his neck. The newcomer gaped back at him.

"This is Cedric," Alya said. "Dear, this is Harold."

"Get your head down!" Cedric shouted.

Eyes still wide, Harold drooped into a crouch to match his.

Cedric turned back to study the Earthfirsters. They were still coming slowly, herding the crowd back against the central rail-

ing. There was no doubt he was trapped. And all he needed was a
mike, and the only mikes around were on those golfies. But before he could get within shouting distance, he would be burned
down . . .

The crowd was backing faster, knocking over fences and
trampling bedding. Children were weeping, women wailing, men
yelling in nervous anger.

"Darling?" Alya said, sounding worried at last. "What can we
do?"

"If I only had a mike! I've got codes set up!"

"Tell me!" she shouted, adjusting her grip on Bert, who was
starting to squirm. "I can get close enough!"

"No good! Wouldn't work for you." Why had he been so
stupid as to make the codes voice specific? And what code would
save him now? He had prepared one to turn off lights—but the
Earthfirsters could make light with their torches, and people
would get trampled in the panic. He had a code to call Frazer
Franklin—God knows why he had thought he might need that
one. He had one to call Fish, but Fish wasn't accepting calls.
And one to—

He grabbed Alya's arm, almost causing her to drop Egbert.
"Tiber!" he shouted. "Is the window still open?"

"I think so."

"Is it Class One?"

"Yes! Yes!"

But that didn't solve the problem.

"If I had a mike, I could get us there!" Maybe—it was a hell
of a long shot.

"Tell me, then!" she repeated angrily.

"No good—it has to be my voice!"

"Your voice?" Alya swung around to the about-sixteen-year-
old version of Cedric. "Oswald! You'll do it, won't you?"

"Do what, Alya?" the kid asked nervously.

"That's it!" Cedric shouted, so loud he made his own head
rattle.

The crowd had stopped moving, and the Earthfirster leader
was bellowing, trying to make himself heard over the racket.

"Go forward, close as you can to a golfie. Then just yell,
'Code jumper!' Got it? System'll think you're me!"

The kid nodded and grinned Cedric's grin back at him.
"'Code jumper'?" He squeezed off into the crowd. He was
younger and shorter and dressed differently—he would be safe
enough.

"Me, too?" Harold demanded nervously. "Should I try?"

"No, you're too tall!" Cedric realized that he had almost straightened up. He stopped again apprehensively.

"How about me?" Alfred squeaked, in treble.

Cedric and Alya said "No!" together.

A firearm cracked loudly, and a nasty sound of ricochet whined off into sudden silence. The crowd seemed to hold its breath.

"Hubbard!" the Earthfirster leader roared. "Come out, Hubbard!"

Silence. Cedric glanced guiltily around him. He was a pied piper, surrounded by youngsters. What sort of a coward would hide among children?

"Hubbard! We know you're in there. Come out or we start firing."

And somewhere a voice exactly like Cedric's yelled, "*Code jumper*!"

Nothing happened. System did not acknowledge. Cedric sank to his knees. It was all over, then—he had played his last card. *Code jumper* meant, "Get me to Tiber as fast as possible." But he had never seriously believed that his authority was high enough to mess with the transmensor. Maybe the window had closed by then anyway. Maybe it was open at another dome and people were using it.

Which would mean a small delay while System closed the window at that dome and opened it here, in Bering . . .

And then System did just that. Air pressure equalized with a clap of thunder that battered every eardrum in the dome. Daylight blazed up from the pit and a shower of golden leaves and butterflies swirled high in the blast. The tops of trees swayed within the central railing.

For a moment there was panic. The whole crowd spun around to see, and Hubbard Cedric lurched to his feet and ran, crouching to disguise his height, shoving and elbowing his way through, throwing people aside in his haste. He fell against the rail, and right below him was a placid forest stream. The water looked deep, and it was only two or three meters down.

Cedric vaulted over—and landed in Tiber with a resounding splash.

26

THEY HAD NAMED the city Rome. It would be the capital of the world for at least as long as the string lasted, and the string was showing no signs of ending—each window was longer than the one before. Unless some evil-minded star came blundering by, the string might well survive long enough to make Tiber the Institute's greatest success.

Meanwhile Rome was a hopeless sprawl of Quonset huts and tents along the bare floor of the valley, stripped of the virgin woods that had once adorned it. Streets were either dust, or mud, or both, many still full of tree roots. A ditcher was laying waterlines and sewers. Away from the river, the shacks soon dwindled to animal sheds and lumber piles, until on its outskirts the town faded off into barns and airplane runways, barbed-wire fences and supply dumps. Already, with only three windows gone by, the supply dumps were huge. One flat patch of churned mud had been set aside for the window, whenever it was open. Someday, Abel thought, there would be a monument on that spot.

Meanwhile the sun was setting, an exhausted peace settling over Rome. The last wraiths of dust drifted away on a rumor of a breeze, and the smoke of cooking fires rose in sleepy coils amid the tents. Twenty-eight-hour days were just like twenty-four-hour days with four more hours' labor added. The overworked inhabitants had already developed a tradition of going to bed at dusk.

Noticing the fading light, Abel had pushed himself away from his desk and gone outside to watch the sunset and catch some fresh air. His home and office were located in a solitary outlying Quonset hut, close to the window site. Some irreverent wag had painted the words "Presidental Palace" on one side and "El Supremolar" on the other. Everyone thought that it had been done by Abel himself, and of course they were right.

He was pooped. His eyeballs were raw, his throat worse. He made a thousand decisions a day, spoke to a hundred people, ate on the run. Emily kept telling him that he had never been happier in his life, but he had not yet had time to consider the matter. His bad leg ached, which usually meant dry weather ahead.

Near the front door a clump of three and a half trees had survived humanity's onslaught. They had, in turn, preserved a minute triangle of pseudograss. The National Forest . . . He sat down there and leaned back against a glossy gray trunk. He wondered where he could squeeze some patio furniture into the priority schedule.

He watched a crimson and lavender butterfly float by, returning to its hive. The shadows were long, the sky a medley of colors beyond reproach. Tiber was a glorious planet, which had so far sprung no worse surprise than humanity's normal reaction to unfamiliar surroundings, a universal attack of the trots.

Twenty-three years old and king of the world? No, he had never been happier. Absolute power was certainly fun. It would not last long enough to spoil him . . . unfortunately.

The peace was too good to last, too—a long finger of shadow needled across the presidential lawn.

"Hi," Hubbard Cedric said.

"Hi, yourself," Abel said. "Take a chair."

Cedric dropped to his knees and offered a large and horny hand. He was wearing shorts and boots and a gun. He also wore a splendid tan and a patchy stubble of definitely reddish hue. He was not wearing much of a smile, Abel noticed, but his nose was almost back to normal, and he no longer had a bone-mender on his hand.

Abel had seen Cedric around, but they had not really had a chance to chat since the trip to Nile. "How's the world treating you?" he asked. "This world, that is."

"Fine."

Abel would have liked more enthusiasm. "The princess okay?"

"Oh! Oh, yes, she's fine." A very stupid grin slid over Cedric's face. Abel had seen much the same look on Emily sometimes, when her eye caught his, and maybe he wore it himself also, at those times. He had seen something similar on Alya when she talked of Cedric. Or Gill Adele when Bagshaw Barnwell K. came in sight. Strange creatures, humans.

"No one's taken any more potshots at you?"

Cedric pouted and shook his head. He had a burn on his cheek where someone had drawn a beam on him, the second day. The assailant had not been caught, but it must have been one of the Earthfirsters. Beyond doubt, the attack would have succeeded had Alya not rammed bodily into Cedric and knocked him down, about a thousandth of a second before the fire.

The moody silence needed lubricating, obviously. "Would you like a beer?" Abel offered.

"Yes, please!"

Abel sighed deeply. "So would I."

Cedric shot him an exasperated look, then settled himself more comfortably, crossing his meter-long legs. "What're you going to do with the Earthfirsters?"

"Put 'em on Devil's Island. We already have—most of 'em—only we told them it was called Paradise Island."

Cedric grinned briefly. "Which is it?"

"Oh, it's okay," Abel said. "Good as this—water and pseudo-grass. It's bigger than Ireland, so they shouldn't be bothering us much for a century or three." He yawned. "And we've promised to deliver their families, and supplies—they'll do a lot better than they deserve."

"Yeah."

Abel frowned at him. "Don't go blaming yourself, buddy. You did great. I just wish you'd fried more of them." Seeing that Cedric continued to stare glumly at the ground, he added, "We lost a lot more guys than they did. Served them right, what you did to them. You're a hero back in Cainsville."

"What's the word on Barney?"

"Oh, he's going to be fine," Abel said. "Good as new." That was a lie, but the kid did not notice.

Suddenly Cedric smirked under his stubble. "I guess I did do a job on those Earthfirsters. I wish I could have seen their faces when they realized I'd opened a window on them and they couldn't go home!"

It had not been Cedric who had opened the window—it had been Abel himself, and Fish Lyle. They had closed de Soto and

opened Bering, but they would never have managed to corral all
the invaders inside one dome had not Cedric knocked out the
leaders and then unwittingly turned himself into a human fox and
drawn the mob of hounds after him. Fish had accepted the lucky
break like the champ he was, overriding the overrides, diverting
the two golfies that contained Mother Hubbard and Cheung, and
sending the rest on after Cedric. Yet there could be no harm in
letting the kid believe that System had obeyed his commands.

But Cedric had gone back to poking grass with a twig.

"What's on your mind?" Abel asked innocently.

"Alya and I—we'd like to—we thought it might be a good
idea to explore the pass through the mountains. The one on the
satellite photos." He waved at the distant peaks, all salmon and
peach in the evening sun, and then looked anxiously at Abel. "If
you think so?"

The idea had come from Alya, of course, who had gotten it
from Abel himself in the first place.

"I dunno . . ." Abel rubbed his chin. His stubble was gratify-
ingly much more widespread than Cedric's. "She's a wonder at
translating. We should have called this dump Babel instead of
Rome, and it's going to get worse. Sikhs and Brazilians coming
next—can we spare her?"

Cedric looked up, worried. "We'd be a good scouting team—
she can sense danger, and she knows so much—all that science
stuff! And I can manage the ponies."

"You're also the best shot in the world."

Cedric shrugged, indifferent. "That's just a knack, though."

The hell it was! With a laser, marksmanship was pure iron
nerve. The kid was as tough as steel bars and steady as a range of
mountains, although he didn't know it. He was also important to
Alya's intuition, for she had known to save him from the bush-
whacker. She claimed that that sort of secondhand warning had
never happened before, so he must be critical to her future, and
that might mean critical to the colony's. Cedric was also the best
all-round outdoorsman they had. Like it or not, and in spite of his
low ambition rating on the GFPP, he was going to start collecting
followers. In a few years he would rise to whatever heights the
new world then offered: statesman, tribal headman, or senior
horse thief.

Abel leaned back to inspect the sunset again, enjoying the
balmy evening air and pretending to consider the request. "You'd
be gone—what? Three weeks, maybe? Alya's all right. Don't
know if we can spare you, though, Cedric."

"Me? What use am I?"

"Might run short of tent poles."

"How would you like a broken jaw?"

"Very much—then I wouldn't have to talk so much!" Abel laughed and thumped his companion on the shoulder. "Look—it sounds like a great idea. We're going to have to move half an army through to the other coast before winter, and I'd prefer to make them walk, if I can—good psychology! Exodus, you know? The Long March? Sure! You go scout the best route. Radio back and we'll pick you up by air, and then you can lead the migration."

The Banzarakis would willingly follow their princess, and that would shift Jar Jathro's political power base well away from the supply depot. Baker Abel's own power base lay in that cache of supplies and the Institute that was feeding it, and when the string came to an end, then the fast footwork would start. Whoever controlled the equipment would run the world. Having inherited some potent political genes from both his parents, Baker Abel was hoping to give all the Jar Jathro types a few pointers.

Cedric was scowling, probably at the thought of leading a mass migration. Abel tried to imagine him with a long beard and a staff, and decided that he would make a very good prophet figure. More important, though, a couple of weeks away from camp would do him a world of good. He would stop brooding over the killings and over all the Cedric clones he must keep running into—there were six of them—and it would give Abel a chance to round up the last of the Earthfirsters and ship them off to Devil's Island. Besides, the guy had earned a honeymoon. Any newly paired couple needed to go off alone and nuzzle undisturbed. It was basic human instinct.

Seven Cedrics! Of course they would start banding together fairly soon, like identical twins. And this one would be the leader. He was a hero already.

"When'll you leave?"

Cedric beamed. "Tomorrow, first light."

"Mmm," Abel said noncommittally. "Window's due around noon."

Cedric grunted and turned his face away to study the sunset. "Talked to one of the rangers," he remarked. "One who'd been out west. He said the ocean there is really something. Jellyfish with sails as big as yachts, he said. And things like seals that lie on the rocks and sing."

"While vigorously combing their long blond hair, I suppose? She keeps asking for you."

"Let her ask." Cedric rose and stretched, making Abel feel about knee high.

"What's so hellish hard about saying goodbye to her?" Abel demanded, craning his neck to peer up at the giant. "Is it Devlin and Eccles that bother you? I know the old woman plays hardball—if she didn't, you wouldn't be here, bud!"

"Sure. That must be it. We'll call you when we get to the sea." Cedric began to move.

"Wait, dammit! Sit down again."

"No. Gotta go. Lady waiting."

Abel sighed and scrambled to his feet also, but he hated having to argue with a man's collarbones. "Then please, as a favor to me, will you wait around tomorrow and say goodbye to Hubbard Agnes when the window opens?"

"No."

In the baffled silence that followed, Cedric just stood with his arms folded, staring placidly over Abel's head at the lights spread across the valley, among the tents. Finally he remarked, "See that glow in the west? Alya says it's the galactic center. She thinks it'll be a helluva show in the winter sky, when it's higher."

"It's the clone thing, isn't it?" Abel asked, wondering how it felt to greet oneself six times every morning.

Cedric looked down coldly at him, his eyes glinting. "Can I go now, please, sir?"

"No."

The big guy growled low in his throat. "All right. Yes, it's the clone thing. Who or what am I? Can you imagine what it's like not to have parents? I thought I was a Hastings clone, but I guess I'm not even that. Not a person! Not human! How the hell do I know what I am?"

Huh? This was not what Abel had expected.

"You could ask her."

"I wouldn't believe her if she told me the sky was blue."

"It's damned near black right now. No, you're not a Hastings clone—"

"Then why did System say I was?" Cedric's voice almost cracked.

Ah! "It did? What exactly did you ask it?"

Cedric scratched his chin loudly. "Don't remember my exact words—but I asked it to compare my DNA and his."

"How? Sequence the nucleotides? Just the active sites, I

hope?" Surely the kid could not have been dumb enough to ask for chemical analysis?

"Don't recall."

Abel chuckled. "You may not have asked the right question. If you told it to compare your DNA and a chimpanzee's, it would tell you a better-than-ninety-nine percent fit, you know."

Cedric balled a gigantic fist.

"Me, too!" Abel said quickly. "Me, too! Human and chimpanzee DNA is that similar, honest! Of course, only about one percent of your DNA is genetically active anyway. Didn't you know all this?"

Cedric relaxed somewhat, still suspicious. "I don't know anything."

"You're learning. But obviously any two human beings are going to be more alike than a man and a chimp, so most of your DNA would match Hastings Willoughby's—almost all of it, for that matter. If you'd asked System to estimate the relationship between the two of you, it would have compared the common alleles and reported twenty-five percent. You really are his grandson, Cedric."

For a moment Cedric was silent. "How can I trust you?" he asked finally.

"If you're calling me a liar, then I think I'm going to take you down, sonny, big as you are. Now, which is it to be?"

For an icy moment Abel wondered if he'd been rash. Then Cedric growled, "Sorry."

"Okay. And furthermore, you're the original, the real Hubbard Cedric Dickson."

A long sigh escaped from Cedric's bony chest. "I am?"

"Yes, you are. You have six clones, and they're all here on Tiber now, but you are the genuine article. Cedric—I swear this!"

"Umph!" Cedric said, then quietly added, "Thanks."

Abel poked him with a finger. "And because you're wondering, yes, I do know what I'm talking about. Because for the last three years I've been her backup with the organages. That was why all the Cedric clones, see? She's been working on this for twenty years. The clones gave her access. Whenever she handed over a clone to be reared, then she became one of the gang; she was trusted. You see?"

Cedric nodded reluctantly.

Choosing his words with care, Abel said, "You're not unlike

Willoughby, you see. At three or four weeks old, you're a quite believable baby Secretary General."

"Too believable for comfort! The organages all thought she was fronting for Hastings?"

"Of course. And of course she had help. There were others in this with her—have you seen the Iskander girls? Four of them? There's a couple of other sets around. Anyway, she's old, so she appointed me deputy in case anything happened to her. I've been keeping an eye on you all. I liked what I saw."

"Damned spy!"

"Yes," Abel said, unruffled. Of course, it would take the kid time to adjust. "I was glad to hear you were coming along on this jaunt. Or might be coming along. She had some uses for you first—"

Cedric grunted angrily. "Even if ends justify means, the means don't have to like it!"

"Maybe not." Abel shrugged. He had done about all he could.

"And if she planned that, then why did she tell Alya that I wasn't coming?"

"Dunno. Maybe she didn't want emotion messing up intuition? I know she was mad as spit at Alya for turning up in public at HQ. But she's truly your grandmother and you're truly what she said—the son of Hubbard John Hastings and Dickson Rita Vossler. The one and only. The real McCoy. *Bona* very *fide*. Conceived in utero. All others are imitations."

Cedric made an odd noise that seemed to express both satisfaction and surrender. "Awright! Thanks, Abe. Thanks for telling me. And just for that, I will wait around and say goodbye to the old bag. She can thank me for saving Cainsville, if that's what she wants. I may even thank her for breaking up the organage racket. But I won't say I love her, because that wouldn't be true. Or that I forgive her for the way she used me."

"I don't think she'd believe you if you did."

"Likely not. But I'll talk with her. Besides, there's something else I want to ask her about. G'night." Cedric turned and started walking away into the dusk.

Oops!

"And what might that be?"

Cedric stopped. He rubbed his chin. "Well . . . Now I can see roughly what she was up to. She paraded me like a purple poodle at that press conference—but Alya says she was passing different messages to different people. She made me look like a retarded hayseed, and herself not much better—senile old woman doting

on idiot grandson. That was one feint, and she maddened the
media. That was another. At the same time, she was using me as
a red flag over the organages, hinting at clones and going public
and so on—threatening hundreds of important people. Thirdly—
or ninthly? I've lost count . . . Lastly, then, she was planning to
go fishing for the murderers. The poison time capsule was the
bait, I was the bent pin, and when they bit, she was waiting to
haul in the string."

"So?" Abel inquired cautiously, surprised at how well Alya
had worked it all out.

"And the worse mess I made of things the better, from her
point of view, right?"

"I suppose."

"Devlin would never have gone to Nile without me along.
And you, because he knew you were important to the Tiber mission."

Devlin had known more than that. "Thanks," Abel said.

"But I'm still wondering," Cedric concluded quietly, "why she
gave me Grade One rating on System? I mean, it came in damned
handy at the end, against the Earthfirsters, but even Gran
couldn't have foreseen that!"

"Um."

"It just seems out of character somehow." Cedric's voice
trailed off uncertainly. "Well—I'll ask her. Night, Your Majesty."

And it was out of character for Cedric to have thought of the
problem in the first place. Obviously it was Alya's thinking—
which made no difference. "Wait!" Abel said. It could not matter
now, anyway. When all else fails, be honest. "I would really be
much happier if you didn't bring up that subject with your grandmother, Cedric. Please?"

"Why not?" Cedric demanded, bristling. His assertiveness and
confidence were growing day by day. Pairing with a girl like Alya
would do exhilarating things to a man's self-esteem, of course.

"Because Mother H. knows nothing about it." Abel sighed.
"She assigned you straight nines—personal grade and work
grade both."

"Then who—"

"In confidence? No one else knows this."

"Sure. I may tell Alya, of course."

"I'm sure you will. It was me."

"What? Why? How?" After a spluttering sound, Cedric
added, "When?"

"When? Just as you were flying in with Bagshaw. How? It

was easy enough. I grew up around Cainsville and Nauc HQ. Nobody else—nobody!—knows this, but I broke System's master code when I was thirteen."

"Bullshit," Cedric said calmly.

"No."

"It's impossible—how?"

"I hid under a bed and overheard some very high-rank passwords being used."

Cedric's answer was a grunt that stopped just short of expressing more disbelief.

Abel chuckled. "I can't make it do everything I want—like I couldn't find you anywhere that night when she took you off to meet Cheung and Grundy—but most things I can get by." He grinned at the memories. All through adolescence he had used System as his personal genie for voyeurism, practical japing, cheating—Lord, it had been fun! "I could see you in bed with Alya that morning. You were lying on your belly and you pulled the sheet over your head."

"Bastard!"

"You don't sound very grateful."

"Well . . . Then she didn't know . . ." Cedric started to laugh, then stopped suddenly. "Why d'you do it? You go around giving Grade One to all your friends?"

"Ahh!" Abel stretched and yawned while he considered the question. It was a tough one. Why exactly had he thrown virtual control of Cainsville to that elongated hay-in-his-hair innocent? As a practical joke it had been going too far, even for him. Partly he had done it in a fit of anger. Baker Abel had lost his temper only twice before in his life, but that night he had been eavesdropping on the scene in the President Lincoln Hotel bedroom—spying on what Hubbard and Fish were spying on—and he had been sickened. The strobe hypnosis itself, the ruthless ferocity with which it had been applied, and the beating that Bagshaw had then administered—apparently strong emotion right afterward was supposed to lock in the mind control, but it had still been a beating—all of those things had roused Abel to fury. The way the kid had resisted the treatment without buckling had won his heartfelt admiration.

Even so, Grade One rating had been going a bit far.

Abel's yawn ended. "Dunno. As you say, you made good use of it in the end. Guess I just had a hunch, that's all."

Cedric snorted disbelievingly. "And I didn't know you grew up in Cainsville!" He sounded hurt, cheated.

"Given the choice, I'd have taken Meadowdale. Any kid would."

"Organage?" Cedric sneered. "That's for clones, not real people."

"Goddammit it, man! Forget that! There's nothing wrong with being a clone."

It must have been his tone, or else Alya's brains were infectious—Cedric drew in his breath with a hiss. "Tell me!"

"Sit down."

"No. Tell me."

Abel sighed and leaned back against the tree to ease his leg. "Okay. Your grandmother's a strange woman, lad. She doesn't like failing, not at anything. And she failed at being a mother. She and John fought twenty-five hours a day, eight days a week. She dominated; he rebelled. He skipped when he was in his teens, and they didn't speak for years. She finally located him when he won the world calf-roping championship."

"Ah!" Cedric said, as though in sudden divine revelation. "He picked the sort of work she'd hate most?"

"Very likely. She tried to make up. She offered him a whole new planet—for him and his bride."

"Oak?"

"Oak. And it killed him."

A soft breath of wind brought a sudden odor of cooking wafting over the grassland. Sounds of children and distant singing or prayer came drifting up from the valley.

"And?" Cedric asked softly.

"She doesn't like failure—I told you."

"She tried again?"

"She tried again. She had a tissue sample on file. She had him cloned."

The dim blur that was Cedric's face nodded in the gloom. "So that was why Devlin insisted you go on the Nile trip? He wanted you along as insurance?"

"I guess so."

"Then . . . then Hastings Willoughby's your biological father? What did he say?"

"He doesn't know. She never told him what she'd done. I found out from System, but of course I couldn't tell anyone, even him, or they'd have wanted to know how I knew. When she did tell me—not very long ago—I decided not to bug him. He was too old to be interesting. He was a worse father than she was a mother, anyway."

"That's crazy! He must have seen you in the holo. The Mari-gold expedition? Or Buzzard. I knew you! Everyone knows your face!"

Abel sighed. "He's old. He has no interest in other worlds. And he hardly knew his son—John, the first version. They seem to have met about twice after John grew up. I told you—he wasn't much of a father. You're not the only orphan in the family."

"She wasn't much of a grandmother to me," Cedric said rue-fully. "Even at a distance. I can't imagine her rearing a son."

"Oh, I fought, too! But not as bad, maybe. She'd learned a few things about mothering. I think my gawdawful sense of humor was my defense—it really used to rile her."

More silence, then Cedric said, "But . . ."

"But what?"

"But if Oak killed John, how'd she ever let you be party leader for this Tiber planting?"

Jeez! *This kid was a leopard in drag!* "When you're as old as I am, son," Abel said, as calmly as he could manage, "you'll learn that women are never predictable."

"Mmph?" Cedric muttered, his voice oily with suspicion. "It wouldn't have been because System was doing the evaluations, would it? That maybe none of the other candidates measured up—according to System? That you were the only possible choice—according to System?"

"Oh, I doubt that."

Cedric chuckled dryly. "I think I know now who was really pulling the strings, though. Well . . ." He held out a hand. "Good night, er, Dad?"

"'Night, son," Abel said. "See you in the morning."

"Yeah."

"Give Alya my love."

"Not findangle likely! She's got all of mine, and that's as much as any woman can handle." Hubbard Cedric stalked off into the dark, humming contentedly, and no doubt wearing that stupid grin again.

Postscript

YES, VIRGINIA, THERE is a superstring theory. In fact there are several, and they disagree on how many dimensions there really are—I wish the physicists would get their facts straight so I could know what I'm twisting. Nevertheless, if you want to buy a transmensor, I suggest you check with your local hyperdrive dealer.

There are string theories in cosmology, too, but they're different. That's one type of string I didn't manage to weave into the story.

The environmental stuff, unfortunately, is a lot more probable. I began this book in 1987, which turned out to be the warmest year on record, and moved the problem of atmospheric degradation out of the SF ghetto into the popular press. I'm writing these final lines near the end of 1988, which is going to be either the warmest or second warmest. By the time you read this, we'll know about 1989. I'm very glad I'll not be around to know 2050.

And without a transmensor, there's no way out.

About the Author

DAVE DUNCAN was born in Scotland in 1933 and educated at Dundee High School and the University of St. Andrews. He moved to Canada in 1955 and has lived in Calgary ever since. He is married and has three grown-up children.

Unlike most writers, he did not experiment beforehand with a wide variety of careers. Apart from a brief entrepreneurial digression into founding—and then quickly selling—a computerized data-sorting business, he spent thirty years as a petroleum geologist. His recreational interests, however, have included at one time or another astronomy, acting, statistics, history, painting, hiking, model ship building, photography, parakeet breeding, carpentry, tropical plants, classical music, computer programming, chess, genealogy, and stock market speculation.

An attempt to add writing to this list backfired—he met with enough encouragement that he took up writing full-time. Now his hobby is geology.

DAVE DUNCAN

Fantasy Novels:

The Seventh Sword